About t

The author of more than ninety books for children and adults, **Janice Kay Johnson** writes about love and family – about the way generations connect and the power our earliest experiences have on us throughout life. An eight-time finalist for the Romance Writers of America *RITA* award, she won a *RITA* in 2008 for her Mills & Boon novel *Snowbound*. A former librarian, Janice raised two daughters in a small town north of Seattle, Washington.

Lynne Graham lives in Northern Ireland and has been a keen romance reader since her teens. Happily married, Lynne has five children. Her eldest is her only natural child. Her other children, who are every bit as dear to her heart, are adopted. The family has a variety of pets, and Lynne loves gardening, cooking, collecting all sorts and is crazy about every aspect of Christmas.

From as far back as she can remember **Michelle Conder** dreamed of being a writer. She penned the first chapter of a romance novel just out of high school, but it took much study, many (varied) jobs, one ultra-understanding husband and three gorgeous children before she finally sat down to turn that dream into a reality. Michelle lives in Australia, and when she isn't busy plotting, she loves to read, ride horses, travel and practise yoga. Visit Michelle: michelleconder.com

A Dark Romance Series

June 2025
Veil of Deception

July 2025
Thorns of Revenge

August 2025
Surrendered to Him

September 2025
Bound by Vows

SURRENDERED TO HIM:

A Dark Romance Series

JANICE KAY JOHNSON

LYNNE GRAHAM

MICHELLE CONDER

MILLS & BOON

First Published in Great Britain 2025
by Mills & Boon, an imprint of HarperCollins*Publishers* Ltd
1 London Bridge Street, London, SE1 9GF

www.harpercollins.co.uk

HarperCollins*Publishers*
Macken House, 39/40 Mayor Street Upper,
Dublin 1, D01 C9W8, Ireland

ISBN: 978-0-263-41753-1

FSC www.fsc.org
MIX
Paper | Supporting responsible forestry
FSC™ C007454

This book contains FSC™ certified paper and other controlled sources to ensure responsible forest management.

For more information visit: www.harpercollins.co.uk/green

Printed and Bound in the UK using 100% Renewable Electricity
at CPI Group (UK) Ltd, Croydon, CR0 4YY

THE LAST RESORT

JANICE KAY JOHNSON

For Barb, a great editor and even better friend,
and for her faithful sidekick, Panda.

Chapter One

Leah Keaton eased up on the gas pedal too late to prevent her right front tire from dropping into an epic pothole with a distinct *clunk*. She winced.

Along with a gradual rise in elevation, the road was getting narrower, the dense northwest forest reclaiming it. The roots from vast Douglas fir, spruce and cedar trees created a corrugated effect as they crumbled the pavement. Long, feathery limbs occasionally brushed the sides of her modest sedan. Pale lichen draped from branches. Thick clumps of ferns and wiry branches of what might be berries overhung the edges of the pavement.

Her mother could have been right, that this was a wasted and even unwise journey.

All of which was assuming, Leah thought ruefully, that she hadn't taken a wrong turn. In her distant memory, a carved and painted wood sign had marked the turnoff to her great-uncle's rustic resort in the north Cascade Mountains, not that far from the Canadian border. She reminded herself this was rain forest, which by definition meant wood rotted quickly. Once the sign fell, moss and forest undergrowth would have hidden it in a matter of weeks.

Forcing herself to loosen her grip on the steering

wheel, Leah caught a glimpse of Mount Baker above the treetops. At not quite eleven thousand feet in elevation, Baker wasn't the largest of the string of volcanoes that stretched from California to the Canadian border, but it was plenty imposing anyway with year-round snow and ice cloaking the mountain flanks. Leah remembered from when she was a kid seeing puffs of steam escaping vents at the summit, a reminder that Mount Baker still had the potential to erupt.

Weirdly, the memory relaxed her. This road felt familiar. If she was right, it would soon climb more sharply yet above a river carrying seasonal snowmelt that ultimately joined the larger North Fork Nooksack River. As a child, she'd hated the drive home from the resort because the edge was so close to the road, the drop-off so precipitous. She hadn't trusted the rusting guardrail at all.

What if a tumultuous spring had undercut the cliff and the road no longer went all the way to the resort?

The tires of her car crunched onto gravel as the pavement ended. She had to go slower yet, because potholes and ruts made the way even more perilous.

Although he'd closed the resort something like fifteen years ago, Uncle Edward had continued living here until his death last fall. Had he really not minded navigating this road when he had to stock up on groceries? According to Leah's mother, he'd declared flatly, "This is home," and remained undaunted by the perils of living in such an isolated location as an old man.

"Stubborn as that old coot Harry Truman, who wouldn't evacuate when Mount St. Helens blew," Mom had grumbled, mentioning the name of a rugged individual who'd refused to leave the mountainside before the volcano erupted in 1980. "He'll end the same way. You just wait and see."

Leah's dad had gently pointed out that, despite being in his nineties, Uncle Edward hadn't displayed even a hint of dementia and therefore was fully capable of making his own decisions. Dad had shaken his head. "He's lived up there most of his life. Imagine what it would be like for him to move to a senior apartment with busybody neighbors all around and traffic going by night and day."

"But we could find him a nice—" Mom had broken off, knowing she'd lost the argument. She just didn't understand her uncle, who'd spent his entire life in the north Cascade Mountains.

She did understand why he'd left the resort to Leah, the only one of his nieces and nephews who had genuinely loved vacations spent at the remote resort. Leah would have been happy to spend every summer there—at least until teenage hormones struck and hanging out with friends at home became a priority—but her mother refused to let her stay beyond their annual two-week family vacations spent in one of the lakeside cabins.

The road started to seriously climb, blue sky ahead. A minute later she saw the small river to the left, water tumbling over boulders and pausing in deep pools. This was July, the height of the melt-off on the mountain above. By fall, the water level would lower until barely a creek ran between rocky banks.

She stayed close to the steep bank on the right. After sneaking a few peeks at the guardrail in places it had crumpled or even disappeared, she decided she just might do the same thing coming down. It wasn't as if she was likely to meet any oncoming traffic, for heaven's sake. She could drive on whatever side of the road she wanted. And, while she'd brought a suitcase, sleeping bag and enough food to hold her for a night or two, she knew the old resort buildings might be so decrepit she'd have no choice but to turn right around and head back down the mountain. Uncle Edward had been ninety-three when he died. He wasn't likely to have done any significant maintenance in many years.

Still…the location was great, the view of Mount Baker across a shallow lake and an alpine meadow spectacular. There'd even been a glimpse of the more distant Mount Shuksan, too. Backed by national forest, the land alone had to be worth something, didn't it? She hoped Uncle Edward hadn't envisioned her building up the resort again and running it; despite good memories of the stays here, she'd grown up in Portland, Oregon, gone to college in southern California. Wilderness girl, she wasn't.

Learning about the inheritance had given her hope. She'd been dreaming of going back to school to become a veterinarian. The cost was one factor in her hesitation. Animal doctors didn't make the kind of income people doctors did, but finished four years of graduate school with the same load of debt.

Never having dreamed Uncle Edward would leave the resort to her, she couldn't help feeling as if he'd somehow known what it would mean to her.

To her relief, the road curved away from the river and plunged back into the forest. Leah's anticipation rose as she peered ahead through the tunnel formed by the enormous old evergreen trees.

It was another ten minutes before her car popped out into the grassy meadow, spangled with wildflowers, and there was the resort.

Except…there were already people here. Her foot went to the brake. Half a dozen—no, more than that—SUVs were parked in front of the lodge and cabins. Not a single car, she noted in a corner of her mind. These all looked like the kind of vehicles designed to drive on icy pavement and even off-road.

This was weird, but…she'd come this far. Surely, there was a legitimate reason for people to be here.

After a moment she continued forward, coasting to a stop in front of the lodge. Head turning, she saw that some of the cabins had been repaired in the recent past. Several new roofs and the raw wood of new porches and window frames were unmistakable.

A woman on one of those porches looked startled at the sight of her and slipped back inside the cabin, maybe to tell someone else about the arrival of a stranger.

Two men appeared around the corner of the lodge, probably having heard her car engine.

Who *were* these people? Had Mom been wrong, and Uncle Edward had kept the resort open? But still, he'd died eight months ago. Could he have sold it, with no one knowing?

She'd braked and put the gear in Park, but unease stilled her hand before she turned the key.

What if—? But she'd hesitated too long. The men had reached her car, their expressions merely inquiring. There had to be a reasonable explanation. She should be glad the resort buildings hadn't begun to tumble down.

In the sudden silence after she shut off the engine, the car keys bit into her hand. Taking a deep breath, Leah unbuckled her seat belt, opened the door and got out.

One of the men, gray-haired but as fit as a younger man, smiled. "You must be lost."

The muscular guy behind him had full-sleeve tattoos bared below a muscle-hugging tan T-shirt. And…could that be a holstered pistol at his waist?

Dear God, yes.

Say yes. Claim you were heading anywhere else. Let them give you directions and then drive away.

She could go to the nearest small town—Glacier, population 211—and ask about the group staying here. There was only one highway in and out of this area. These people had driven here. They'd have been noticed.

But the older of the two men looked friendly, not hostile at all. There'd be a logical explanation.

"No, actually," she said. "Um… I own this resort."

His smile fell away. "You're the *owner*?"

"That's right. I inherited the place from my great-uncle, Edward Preston."

Outwardly, the man relaxed. "Oh, we've been wondering what was going to happen to the place. The old man let us mostly take over the resort these past few summers in exchange for working on it. We had no idea he'd died until we got here in late June and found it empty."

"Didn't you ask in Glacier or Maple Falls? Surely, people there knew he'd died."

"Some bed-and-breakfast owner I talked to said she hadn't heard anything." He nodded toward the lodge. "Why don't you come on in and we can talk? I don't know about you, but I could use a cup of coffee."

Conscious of the other man's eyes boring into her, she hesitated again, but what else could she do but say, "Sure. Thanks. I'd forgotten what a long drive it is to get up here."

The pair flanked her as they started toward the lodge, which sounded deceptively grand. The old log building only had six guest rooms, all upstairs, a large kitchen and living space and the owner's small apartment at the back. Mostly, Uncle Edward had rented out the ten cabins. What guests he'd allowed to stay in the lodge understood they had to bring their own food and cook for themselves. "Not like I'm going to wait on them hand and foot," he'd snorted.

Leah became nervously aware that several other men had stepped out of cabins, their gazes on her. Most wore camo cargo pants, as did the so-far silent man walking to her right. None of them called out. Their appraisal felt…cold.

She was imagining things. They were curious, that was all.

Only…why weren't there other women? Children?

The porch steps were solid, having obviously been replaced. The older man opened the front door and they ushered her in. *Herded me in*, that uneasy voice inside her head whispered.

She did smell coffee. In fact, a couple of empty cups sat on the long plank table where guests had eaten or sat around in the evening to play board games or poker.

"Let me get that coffee," the gray-haired man said. "You want sugar? I have milk but no cream."

"Milk's fine. Just a dash, and a teaspoon of sugar."

"Coming right up. Have a seat." He nodded toward the benches to each side of the table.

Knowing she'd feel trapped once she was sitting with her feet under the table, she strolled instead toward the enormous river-rock fireplace where she had once upon a time roasted marshmallows for s'mores.

None of the men she'd seen thus far looked as if they'd do anything that frivolous. Chew sixteen-gauge steel nails, maybe. Graham crackers, gooey charred marshmallows and melted chocolate? Hard to picture.

The silent guy remained standing, a shoulder against the log wall right beside the door out to the porch. He watched her steadily.

Maybe he'd be friendly if she was. But before she

could think of anything to say that wasn't too inane, the older man returned from the kitchen with a cup of coffee in each hand.

He glanced toward the second man but didn't offer to fetch him a cup, too.

Leah didn't feel as if she had any choice but to go back to the table and sit down.

He took a sip before asking, "Mind telling me your plans?"

"Um… I wanted to see what condition the buildings were in. And, well, probably I'll sell the place."

"Sell it, huh? You have a price in mind?"

"I have no idea what land is worth up here." If it was worth anything. She had to be honest with herself. "Are you interested?"

"Could be. We'd hate having to relocate."

Feeling and sounding timid, she asked, "Do you mind telling me what you're doing up here? I'm assuming you're not all vacationing here three months a year."

The flicker of amusement in his eyes wasn't at all reassuring. He thought she was funny. Naive.

"No," he said thoughtfully. "No, this is a business."

More unnerved by the minute, she gripped the handle of the mug. She could buy herself time by throwing hot coffee in one of the men's faces if she had to run for it.

Just then, the front door opened and two more men walked in. Cool gazes assessed her. One of them raised dark eyebrows as he looked at the man acting as host. Leah had no trouble hearing the unspoken question.

Who the hell is she and what does she want?

One of the newcomers was short and stocky with sandy hair. Sort of Dennis the Menace, with the emphasis on *menace.*

The other was formidable enough to scare her more.

Eyes a crystalline gray could have been chips of ice. Tanned and dark-haired, he had the kind of shoulders that suggested he did some serious weight lifting.

And, dear God, both men wore holstered handguns at their waists.

Paramilitary was the word that came to mind. What had she walked into?

Be up front, she decided.

"I'm starting to feel a little uncomfortable," she said, focusing on the older man who almost had to be the leader of this bunch. "Why don't I head back to Glacier and find a room for the night? I'll talk to a real estate agent, and if you'd like you can come down tomorrow, meet me for lunch, maybe. We can talk."

Still appearing relaxed, he said slowly, "That might work. Ah…in answer to your earlier question, what we do is run paintball camps. It's mostly men who come up here. They immerse themselves in the wilderness and harmless war games, have a hell of a good time. We've built up a serious seasonal business. Like I said, finding another location anywhere near as perfect as this one would be next to impossible."

Because this land was so remote. Leah had to wonder whether it was true Uncle Edward had let them use his place for several summers in a row, or whether they'd somehow heard he had died and moved in under the assumption no one would be interested enough in a falling-down resort in the middle of nowhere to bother checking on it.

She stole another look at the three men on their feet, now ranged around the room. "Those…look like real guns."

Boss Man across from her shrugged. "Sure, we have a shooting range set up. A bunch of us have been out there all morning. Gotta keep sharp, even if we're mostly using paintball guns."

Nobody else's expression changed.

"Well," she said, starting to push herself up.

The sound of the back door opening was as loud as a shot. Bounced off the wall, she diagnosed, in a small, calm part of her mind surrounded by near hysteria.

All of the men turned their heads.

Grinning, a man emerged from the kitchen. Over his shoulder, he carried a *huge* gun, painted army green. Even as he said, "Hot damn!" before seeing her, Leah's blood chilled.

She'd seen pictures, taken in places like the Ukraine and Afghanistan. That wasn't a gun—it was a rocket launcher.

Son of a bitch.

Spencer Wyatt restrained himself from so much as twitching a muscle only from long practice. His mind worked furiously, though. Could this juxtaposition be any more disastrous? An unsuspecting woman wandering in here like a dumb cow to slaughter, coupled with that cocky, careless jackass Joe Osenbrock striding in with an effing *rocket launcher* over his shoulder? *Yee haw.*

Especially a young, pretty woman. Did she have any idea what trouble she was in?

Flicking a glance at her, he thought, yeah, she had a suspicion.

In fact, she said, in a voice that sounded a little too cheerful to be real, "Is that one of the paintball guns? I've never seen one before."

Good try.

Ed Higgs didn't buy it. "You know better than that. Damn. I wish I could let you go, but I can't."

She flung her full coffee cup at his face, leaped off the bench and tore for the front door, still standing ajar. Smart move, trying to get out of here. She actually brushed Spencer. He managed to look surprised and stagger back to give her a chance. No surprise, the little creep Larson was on her before she so much as touched the door.

She screamed and struggled. Her nails raked down Larson's cheek. Teeth set, he slammed her against the wall, flattening his body on hers. Spencer wanted to rip the little pissant off and throw *him* into the wall. Went without saying that he stayed right where he was. There was no way for him to help now that wouldn't derail his mission.

He had more lives than hers to consider.

Ed snapped, "Get her car keys. Wyatt, go over the car. When you're done, bring in her purse and whatever else she brought with her. Make sure you don't miss anything. Hear me?"

"Sure thing." He knew that once he had the keys, he'd have to hand them over to Higgs, who kept all the vehicle keys hidden away. No one had access to an SUV without Higgs knowing.

Arne Larson burrowed a hand into the woman's jeans pocket. When he groped with exaggerated pleasure, his captive struck quick as a snake, sinking her teeth into his shoulder. Arne yanked out the set of keys and backhanded her across the face. Her head snapped back, hitting the log wall with an audible *thunk*.

Spencer jerked but once again pulled hard on the leash. If she would only cooperate, she might have a chance to get out of this alive.

Arne tossed the keys at him and Spencer caught them. Without a word, he walked out, taking with him a last glimpse of her face, fine-boned and very pale except for the furious red staining her right jaw and cheek where the blow had fallen.

She hadn't locked the car, which didn't appear to be a rental. He used the keys to unlock the trunk and pull out a small wheeled suitcase, sized to be an airline carry-on, as well as a rolled-up sleeping bag and a cardboard box filled with basic food. Then he searched the trunk, removing the jack and spare tire, going through a bag of tools and an inadequate first-aid kit.

He couldn't believe even Higgs, with his paranoid worldview, would think the woman in there was an undercover FBI or ATF agent.

She hadn't packed like one, he discovered, after opening the suitcase on the trunk lid once he closed it. Toiletries—she liked handmade soap, this bar smelling like citrus and some spice—jeans, T-shirts, socks and sandals. Two books, one a romance, one nonfiction about the Lipizzaner horses during World War II. He fanned the pages. Nothing fell out. A hooded sweatshirt. Lingerie, practical but pretty, too, lacking lace but skimpy enough to heat a man's blood and in brighter colors than he'd have expected from her.

Not liking the direction his thoughts had taken him, he dropped the mint-green bra back on top of the mess he'd made of the suitcase's contents.

There was nothing but food in the carton, including basics like boxes of macaroni and cheese, a jar of instant coffee, a loaf of whole-grain bread and packets of oatmeal with raisins. The sleeping bag, unrolled, unzipped and shaken, hid no secrets.

A small ice chest sat on the floor in front. No surprises there, either, only milk, several bars of dark chocolate, a tub of margarine and several cans of soda.

He took her purse from the passenger seat and dumped

the contents out on the hood of the car. A couple of items rolled off. Plastic bottle of ibuprofen and a lip gloss. Otherwise, she carried an electronic reader, phone, a wallet, hairbrush, checkbook, wad of paper napkins, two tampons and some crumpled receipts for gas and meals. Her purse was a lot neater than most he'd seen.

Opening the wallet, he took out her driver's license first. Issued by the state of Oregon, it said her name was Leah E. Keaton. She was described as blond, which he'd dispute, but he didn't suppose strawberry blond would fit on the license. Weight, one hundred and twenty pounds, height, five feet six inches. Eyes, hazel. Age, thirty-one. Birthday, September 23.

She'd smiled for the photo. For a moment Spencer's eyes lingered. DMV photos were uniformly bad, no better than mug shots, but he saw hope and dignity in that smile. She reminded him of a time when his purpose wasn't so dark.

Did Leah E. Keaton know it wasn't looking good for her to make it to that next birthday, no matter what he did?

Chapter Two

Leah watched out the small window in an upstairs guest room with fury and fear as one of those brutes dug through her purse. He'd already searched her suitcase; it still lay open on the trunk of the car, the scant amount of clothing she'd brought left in a disheveled heap.

Everything that had been in her purse sat atop the hood. She felt stripped bare, increasing her shock. They would now know her name, her weight, that she used tampons. Her credit cards and checkbook were in their possession, along with her keys and phone.

That wasn't all. They had her, too.

Wyatt, if that was really his name, stood for a moment with his head bent, staring at the stuff he'd dumped out of her bag, before he began scooping it up and dropping it unceremoniously back in. Then he systematically examined the car interior, under the seats, the glove compartment, the cubbies designed to hold CDs, maps or drinks.

Following orders, of course.

Still gripped by fear, she saw him lie down on his back and push himself beneath the undercarriage. Looking for a bomb? Or a tracking device? Leah had no idea.

Her heart cramped when he shifted toward the rear of the car. How could he miss seeing the magnetic box holding a spare key?

From this angle, there was no way to tell if he pocketed it.

Eventually, if her parents didn't hear from her, they'd sound the alarm and a county deputy might drive up here looking for her, but that wouldn't happen for days. Maybe as much as a week. She'd been vague about how long she intended to stay, and they knew she was unlikely to have phone service once she reached the rugged country tucked in the Cascade Mountain foothills.

Would these men kill a lone deputy who walked into the same trap she had?

When the man below climbed to his feet and closed her suitcase, she took a step back from the small-paned window. He didn't so much as glance upward as he carried the suitcase and her purse toward the lodge, disappearing beneath the porch roof. The groceries, ice chest and sleeping bag sat abandoned beside her car.

A rocket launcher. Or was it even a missile launcher? Was there a difference? The image flashed into her mind again. Leah tried to absorb the horror. Her knees gave out and she sagged to sit on the bed, fixing her unseeing gaze on the log walls with crumbled chinking. She wasn't naive enough not to be aware that, with enough money and the right connections, anybody could acquire military-grade and banned weapons. But…what did these people intend to *do* with this one? And what other weapons did they have?

Her cheekbone throbbed. When she lifted her hand to it, she winced. The swelling was obvious at even a light touch. By tomorrow, a dark bruise would discolor half her face and probably crawl under her eye, too. Her head ached.

Leah wished she could hold on to hope that, whatever the group's political objective, the men might follow some standards of honor where women were concerned. After the stocky blond guy who'd slammed her against the wall had leered and tried to grope her while his hand was in her pocket, that was a no-go. Not one of the other men present had shown the slightest reaction.

But she was sure she'd seen a woman on the porch of one of the cabins. If women belonged to the group, would they shrug at seeing another woman raped? Somehow, she had trouble picturing this particular group of men seeing any woman as an equal, though. Armed to the teeth, buff, tattooed and cold-eyed, they made her think of some of the far-right militia who appeared occasionally on the news. Every gathering she'd ever seen of white supremacists seemed to be all male. If they had women here, they might be no more willing than she was.

But maybe…this group had a completely different objective. Could they be police or, well, members of some kind of super-secret military unit?

That thought didn't seem to offer an awful lot of hope.

Nausea welling, Leah pressed a hand to her stomach and moaned. She'd driven right into their midst, offering herself up like…like a virgin sacrifice. Except for not being a virgin. Somehow, she didn't think they'd care about that part, not if their leader decided to let them have her.

No one would be coming for her. She had to escape. Would they leave her in this room, the exit guarded? Feed her? Talk to her? Give her back any of her things?

Not her keys, that was for sure. She'd have to take the chance that Wyatt had missed the spare key. If not, she'd rather be lost and alone in the dense northwest rain forest miles from any other habitation than captive here. It would get cold at night, but this was July. She wouldn't freeze to death. At least she had sturdy athletic shoes on her feet instead of the sandals she'd also brought. Thank goodness she'd thrown on a sweatshirt over her tee.

The idea of driving at breakneck speed down the steep gravel road running high above the river scared her almost as much as those men did, but given a chance, she'd do it. If she got any kind of head start, she might be able to reach the paved stretch. Along there, she could look for a place to pull the car off the road and hide.

The hand still flattened on her stomach trembled. Great plan. If, if, if. Starting with, *if* she could get out of this room. *If* she could escape the lodge. *If...*

No, at least she knew she could escape the room. For what good that would do, given that she'd still have to pop out in the hall where a guard would presumably be stationed.

Footsteps followed by voices came from right outside her door. Her head shot up.

AT WAR WITH HIMSELF, Spencer sat at the long table with a cup of coffee. Other men came and went, buzzing with excitement. They liked the idea of a captive, particularly a female. They were eager to see her. Only four of the guys had brought women with them, and they weren't sharing. Wasn't like the single guys could go into town one evening and pick up a woman at a bar. For one thing, Spencer hadn't noticed any bars or taverns any closer than Bellingham. The only exception, in Maple Falls, had obviously gone out of business. Higgs didn't let them leave the "base" anyway.

Their great leader had gone upstairs a minute ago. If he didn't reappear soon, Spencer would follow him. He thought Higgs intended to bring Leah Keaton downstairs. Let her have a bite to eat, try to soothe her into staying passive. The way she'd sunk her teeth into Larson's flesh, Spencer wasn't optimistic that passive was in her nature, but maybe she'd be smart enough to pretend. He was screwed if she didn't—unless he kept his eye on the goal and accepted that there were frequently collateral losses—and this time, she'd be one of them. Except, he wasn't sure he could accept that.

Footsteps.

He took a long swallow of coffee and looked as if idly toward the woman Higgs led into the big open space.

She'd come along under her own power, without Higgs having to drag or shove her. If she had any brains, she was scared to death, but her face didn't show that. Instead, it was set, pale…and viciously bruised.

Spencer's temper stirred, but he stamped down on it.

"Have a seat." Higgs sounded almost genial.

Leah Keaton's gaze latched longingly on to her purse, sitting at one end of the table. Wouldn't make a difference for her to grab it; Higgs had taken the keys and probably her phone, which wouldn't do her any good anyway, not here.

"Dinner close to ready?" Higgs asked.

The wives and girlfriends were required to do the cooking and KP. Spencer had heard a couple of them come in the back door a while ago. Soon after, good smells had reached him.

Tim Fuller leaned against the wall right outside the kitchen to keep an eye on his wife, who was the best cook of the lot. Now he wordlessly stepped into the kitchen and came out to say, "Ten minutes. Spaghetti tonight."

Higgs smiled. "Sounds good. That'll give us all a chance to settle down, talk this over."

Leah sat with her back straight, her head bent so she could gaze down at her hands, clasped in front of her on the plank tabletop. Her expression didn't change an iota. Higgs's eyes lingered on her face, but he didn't comment.

Spencer continued to sip his coffee and hold his silence.

Eventually, Shelley Galt, thirty-two though she looked a decade older, brought out silverware and plates, then pitchers of beer and glasses. She kept her gaze down and her shoulders hunched as though she expected a blow at any moment. Spencer wanted to tell Shelley to steal her husband's car keys and run for it the next chance she had, but he knew better than to waste his breath even if that wouldn't have been stepping unacceptably out of his role. Shelley had married TJ Galt when she was seventeen. She probably didn't know any different or better.

Spencer had read and memorized her background, just as he had that of every single person expected to join them up here. He wasn't a trusting man.

The food came out on big platters, some carried by Jennifer Fuller, and the remaining members of the group filtered in, the men almost without exception eyeing Leah lasciviously. The four women were careful not to make eye contact with her.

Leah shook her head at the beer but took a can of soda—one, he suspected, from her own ice chest—and allowed Ed Higgs to dish up for her.

You can lead a horse to water, Spencer thought… but this one was smart enough to drink. And eat. She understood that starving herself wouldn't accomplish a damn thing.

Higgs tried to start a few conversations, earning him startled looks from his crew. He didn't do any better with Leah, who didn't react to any comments directed her way. What did he think she'd say to gems like, "Spectacular country here. Your uncle was smart to hold on to the land."

She blinked at that one but didn't look up.

Only when they were done and he said, "I need to talk to Ms. Keaton," did Spencer see her shoulders get even stiffer. "Wyatt," Higgs said, "you stay. You, too, Metz."

Rick Metz was an automaton, following orders without question, whatever they were. He carried the anger they all shared, but kept a lid on it. He rarely reacted even to jibes from the other guys. Spencer didn't see him raping a woman just because he could, which allowed him to relax infinitesimally.

Grumbles carried to Spencer, but none were made until the men stepped out onto the porch. If Higgs heard them, he offered no indication. Among this bunch, rebellion brewed constantly. Metz might be the only one who wanted to be given orders to carry out. The others accepted them, maybe seeing dimly that Ed Higgs, a former US Air Force colonel, was smarter than they were, his leadership essential to their accomplishing their hair-raising intentions. He reminded them constantly of his military service, happiest when the men called him Colonel. Compliance didn't mean they didn't seethe at the necessity and bitterly resent the inner knowledge that they were lesser in some way than Higgs. Spencer took advantage of that ever-brewing resentment when he could, giving a nudge here and there, inciting outbursts that had helped him climb to second-or third-in-command.

Once the other men were gone, Higgs said into the silence, "No reason for you to be afraid."

Leah did raise her head at that, not hiding her disbelief.

"We only need a couple more months. You'll have to

stay with us that long. Once we're ready to move, you can go on your way."

A couple more months? Did Higgs really think he'd have this bunch whipped into shape that soon? Although maybe it didn't matter to him; he wanted to make a statement, truly believing that somehow an ugly display of domestic terrorism and some serious bloodshed would inspire a revolution. The men who shared his exclusionary, racist, misogynistic views were supposed to join the fight to restore America to some imaginary time when white men ruled, women bowed to their lords and masters, and people of color—if there were any left—served their betters. How a man of his education had come by his beliefs, Spencer hadn't figured out.

"What is it you intend?" she asked, voice clear and strong. She hadn't yet so much as glanced at Spencer or Metz, who stood to one side like soldiers at attention on the parade ground. Pretending they weren't there at all?

"For you?" Higgs asked.

"I mean, your plans. Once you *move*."

If there was irony in her voice, Higgs either didn't acknowledge it or didn't hear it at all.

He launched with enthusiasm into what Spencer hoped would be a short version of his rabid passion.

"What made this country great has been lost since we started paying too much attention to the elites, who believe in opening the floodgates to immigration—and it doesn't matter to them if plenty of those immigrants are the scum of society, criminals who sneaked into the US. What happened to the days when people whose ancestors built this great country decided what direction it would go? Now we have people running for office with such thick accents you can hardly understand them! People that don't look American."

Leah blinked a few times, parted her lips…and then firmly closed them. Definitely not dumb. Then she spoke after all. "That doesn't explain what you plan to do to get attention."

He smiled at her as if she was an acolyte crawling before him. Not that he'd accept her into the fold, her being a member of the weaker sex and all.

"You don't need to worry about the details. Just know it's going to be big. We're going to shake this whole, misguided country and raise an army while we're at it." More prosaically, he added, "You can see why we need to keep our plans quiet until we're ready to launch our op. I'm asking for your cooperation. I don't think I'm being unreasonable. After all, this isn't the worst place to spend the rest of the summer." His sweeping gesture was presumably meant to take in the vast forests, mountains, lakes and wildflowers. "Got to be one of the most beautiful places in the world."

"I don't suppose you're going to let me go hiking or fishing like I did when I was a kid up here."

"Once you've settled in, why not?" Higgs said expansively. "I think you might learn something while you're here, come around to my way of thinking." He paused, a few lines forming on his brow. A thought had clearly struck him. "What do you do for a living, young lady?"

Please, God, don't let her be an attorney or an activist working with migrant workers or... Spencer sweated, running through the multitude of dangerous possibilities.

"I'm a veterinary technician."

When Higgs looked blank, she elaborated, "I treat injured or sick animals under the direction of a veterinarian. I assist him in surgery, give vaccinations, talk to pet owners."

His eyes narrowed. "So you have some medical knowledge."

"I know quite a bit about health issues affecting dogs and cats, and even horses. Not people."

"Never stitched up a wound?"

She hesitated.

"You might be able to help us. In the meantime—" the colonel pushed back from the table, the bench scraping on the worn wood floor "—I'll have one of these fellows carry your suitcase upstairs for you, and wait while you use the bathroom." He nodded at Spencer.

Was he to guard her overnight? If so, could he let her club him over the head and flee into the night? He'd have to make it look good.

For the first time since she'd come downstairs, Leah looked at him. Her dignity might be intact, but the raw fear in her eyes told him she knew what she faced. He hated knowing she was afraid of *him*.

Earlier, her eyes had been so dilated he hadn't been sure of the color. Had he ever seen eyes of such a clear green? And, damn—the courage she'd shown hit him like a two-by-four. With her fine bones and the redhead's skin that wouldn't stand up to any serious exposure to the sun, not to mention the purple bruising on her puffy cheekbone and beneath her eye, Leah Keaton couldn't hide her vulnerability. It moved and enraged him at the same time.

She was a complication he couldn't afford, but knew he couldn't shrug off, either. Spencer couldn't pretend to understand men like Arne Larson and Ed Higgs who didn't feel even a fraction of the same powerful wave of protectiveness that he did at the sight of her, damaged but using her head and holding herself straight and tall.

He picked up her suitcase and nodded toward the staircase. She rose stiffly and stalked ahead of him as if he was less than nothing to her. He admired her stubborn spirit, but knew it would backfire big time if she tried it on some of the other men. He still couldn't risk offering her a word of advice.

If he had to step forward to save her, it would be only as a last resort.

EVERY NERVE IN Leah's body prickled as she climbed the stairs ahead of Wyatt. She'd felt his gaze resting on her throughout dinner and also while the apparent leader spoke to her afterward, yet his thoughts had remained hidden. It was all she'd been able to do not to shudder when some of the men looked at her. This one almost scared her more because he didn't seem to have a single giveaway. All she knew was that he might be the sexiest man she'd ever seen—and that he had the coldest eyes. Her skin crawled at the idea that he was sizing up her body from his current vantage point. Or was he wishing he didn't have to waste time on the woman who'd stumbled on their training grounds and in doing so became a potentially dangerous problem? One *he* might be assigned to solve?

At the top of the stairs, she hesitated, hoping he'd forget how well she knew the resort.

He said only, "Isn't your room at the end of the hall?"

Her room. Sure.

"We can put the suitcase down and you can get out your toothbrush and toothpaste."

Without looking at him again, she continued down the short hall and went back into the very rustic room that had been designated her cell.

He followed, setting down the small suitcase on the

bed, unzipping it and then stepping back. Of course, the contents were in a mess. Thanks to *him*.

Resisting the urge to hide the bra that lay on top, she poked through the tangle of clothing, feeling for her toiletry bag and evaluating what was missing. Unfortunately, the closest thing to a weapon she'd packed was her fingernail clippers. Useless, but if they were still in the toiletry bag, she'd pocket them.

"Your name is Wyatt?" Appalled, she couldn't believe she'd blurted that out.

His hesitation lasted long enough to suggest he was deciding whether even that much information would be dangerous in her hands. "Spencer Wyatt." His voice was deep, expressionless and tinged with a hint of the South.

Finding the toiletry bag, she asked, "Are you supposed to go into the bathroom with me?"

Something passed through his icy eyes so fast, she couldn't identify it. "I'll wait in the hall."

He let her pass him leaving the room, clearly assuming she knew where the bathroom was. She took pleasure in closing that door in his face.

Honestly, there was enough space in here, he could have come in, too. There were two wood-framed toilet stalls, two shower stalls and two sinks. This bathroom had served for all six guest rooms. It was lucky they'd rarely if ever all been in use at the same time.

The fingernail clippers were there. She hurriedly stuck them in her jeans pocket, brushed her teeth, then used the toilet. Not exactly eager to face him again, Leah thought about dawdling, but couldn't see what that would gain her. Presumably, once he'd escorted her to the bedroom, she'd be left alone anyway. So she walked back out to find Spencer Wyatt lounging against the wall across from the bathroom door.

He looked her over, his icy eyes noting the bag still in her hand, and jerked his head toward the bedroom.

Head high, she obeyed the wordless command, walked into her room and shut the door. Her fingers hovered over the lock, which could probably be picked, and she made the decision not to turn it. Why annoy them?

They'd be annoyed enough in the morning when they discovered she wasn't where they'd left her.

Chapter Three

Lying on the bed in the dark, Leah waited for hours, even though eventually she had to struggle not to fall asleep. Twice she heard men's voices outside her room. The first time Spencer Wyatt's was one of them, the other unfamiliar. She tensed when one of the two walked away. Which man remained? Whoever he was, he didn't even look in.

Sometime later a muffled sound of voices had her hurrying to the door and pressing her ear to the crack in hopes of hearing what they were saying.

"…saving her for himself," growled one man.

The second man said something about orders.

She jumped when a thump came, followed by a scraping sound. Had they brought a chair upstairs so they could guard her comfortably? This had to be a change of shift, she decided.

Damn, she'd counted on one man being stuck on guard all night. He'd get sleepy, nod off, sure he'd wake up if her door opened. But if he stayed alert…

Or, oh, God, was the new guard the one complaining that someone was saving her for themselves? Who was he talking about? The gray-haired leader? Or Spencer Wyatt? What if grumbled defiance led to this latest guard deciding he could walk right into her room, and who was awake to stop him?

Rigid, she wished she'd locked the door after all. At least that would have slowed him down.

Receding footsteps were followed by silence out in the hall.

She needed to get out of here. In one way it might be smarter to pretend to be docile for a few days, until they lowered their guard. But the blatant sexual appraisal from so many of the men scared her more than any thought of being killed. Would she really be safe from rape if she played dumb and stayed?

Leah didn't believe it. At the very least, she could hide temporarily. She wished desperately that she knew what time it was. In her fear, she might have exaggerated the passing of time, until only a couple of hours felt like half the night. She had to go with her instincts.

After slipping out of bed, she put on her athletic shoes and tied the laces while straining to hear the slightest sound. Then she used most of the clothes in her suitcase to create a mound beneath the covers that might fool someone who glanced in to be sure she was really there. Finally, she tiptoed to the closet.

Earlier, she'd pulled the folding doors open. If Wyatt checked on her, she reasoned, he'd assume she was exploring, looking hopelessly for some out. Now, once inside the closet, she gently pulled first one door and then the other closed behind her. Kneeling on the floor facing the right side of the closet, she felt for the crack that betrayed the presence of a removable panel.

Uncle Edward had showed her and her brother the spaces between closets upstairs. She'd have been sunk if they'd locked her in either of the first bedrooms at the top of the stairs. But rooms two and three on each side of the hall had closets with removable panels that *connected* one closet to another. He guessed the builder had intended the few feet to be storage. Guests staying all summer could stow a suitcase away, for example. By the time Uncle Edward bought the resort, though, either the spaces—the passages—had been forgotten, or nobody had thought to tell him about them.

Apparently, all of the interior walls were what he called board and batten, which in the old lodge meant horizontal boards had been nailed up in rows. In the rooms and hall, they'd been covered by either plaster or wallpaper. Nobody had bothered in the closets. If you looked closely, you could see into cracks between the old boards, which might have shrunk over time. The whole subject had come up because her brother Jerry had cackled at the idea of spying on guests in the next room.

After issuing a stern warning against trying any such thing, Uncle Edward had smiled down at his great-niece and great-nephew. "Took me a few years here to notice the outline." He'd looked at the dark, dusty opening with satisfaction. "If we were down South, I'd think these were built to hide runaway slaves. 'Course, this place wasn't built until just over a hundred years ago, long after abolition."

He'd had to explain what abolition was for Jerry's sake. Leah remembered from school.

Now she held her breath, lifted the panel away and leaned it where she'd be able to reach it once she was inside. There hadn't been so much as a creak. If the next bedroom was occupied…she'd have to retreat.

Hesitating, she wished she'd brought a flashlight, instead of intending to rely on her phone. Although, that, too, would have been confiscated. Well, the spooky dark wasn't nearly as frightening as the men holding her captive. And yes, as she started to crawl through the opening and cobwebs brushed her face, she shuddered but kept moving. She could do this. She could deal with a few spiders.

Awkwardly turning around, she closed her fingers around the crude panel and tried to pull it into place. A quiet *clunk* had her freezing in place, but it wasn't followed by anyone swinging open the bedroom door and turning on the overhead light.

Dizzy, probably because her pulse raced, Leah used the short file from her fingernail clippers to pull the panel back toward her until it slotted into place—at least, as well as she could. Sliding her fingers over the edges, she thought it was snug. Her next challenge was to open the panel on the other side while preventing it from falling to the floor. *That* would make enough noise to bring the guard to investigate.

She scooted forward until her head brushed the rough wood that was the back of the panel leading into the next room.

Somehow, this wasn't nearly as fun as it had been when, as children, she and Jerry used these passages to perplex their parents.

She lifted her hand, feeling for the crack at the top... and something crawled over her hand. Suppressing a shriek she shook off the bug—a spider?—and made herself start again. Finally, she applied a little pressure, then more—and when the panel gave way, she grabbed the top of it.

And then she froze. She reminded herself that one of the men might be *sleeping* in this room. Surely, the group was using at least some of these upstairs guest rooms.

Breathing as slowly and steadily as she could, she told herself she'd made the assumption about empty rooms for a good reason. She hadn't seen anyone go up or come down the staircase, unless it was with her. When the leader had dismissed the group, nobody had headed for the stairs.

Which was reassuring, but hardly conclusive since it had still been early evening when she was escorted to bed.

Would she have heard someone come upstairs, a door opening and closing? Surely, her guard and another man would have exchanged a few words.

Her pulse continued to race and her teeth wanted to chatter. Could she have chosen worse timing for a panic attack? She took a deep breath. She wouldn't hesitate now.

Gradually, a surface level of calm and resolve suppressed the fear.

If she was quiet enough, she could grope around the closet and find out if someone was using it. She could peek into the room without waking a sleeper. If there was one, well, then she'd have a decision to make.

She eased the panel out and leaned it against the back of the closet. Creeping forward, she patted her way along, cursing the complete darkness. She waved her hands over her head, not feeling any hanging clothes.

Would men like this bother hanging up a shirt, or would they just stuff clean laundry into a duffel bag? No shoes, either. But feeling confident the closet was empty didn't mean the room wasn't occupied. Somehow, she suspected these guys hadn't packed big wardrobes for their training session.

If someone really was sleeping in this room, he'd probably set his handgun aside. If she was quiet enough, she could take it. She might actually have a chance then.

If, if, if.

AFTER METZ TOOK his place outside Leah Keaton's door, Spencer had made a point of hanging around downstairs for a while. Higgs wanted to talk through the problem she presented. He rambled, Spencer mostly keeping his mouth shut.

"Would have been better if you'd been able to let her go in the first place," he couldn't resist saying.

The colonel grunted. "That idiot Osenbrock."

Knowing the variety of weapons of mass destruction the group had acquired, Spencer's blood still ran cold. Spencer refrained from saying the whole damn bunch were idiots, including and especially Air Force Colonel Edward Higgs, retired. Spencer could almost wish to be present to see Higgs's face when he learned that he had a snake in his cozy hideaway.

Yeah, not really, Spencer thought, even as he nodded and made supportive noises.

Eventually, he'd had no choice but to announce he was heading for bed. He'd rinsed out his cup and set it on the dish drainer, gone out the front door after a last good-night and headed straight for his cabin. He had no doubt there were eyes on him. At least three of this crowd resented him bitterly. So far, they hadn't risked laying it on the table and thereby earning Higgs's displeasure. Sooner or later, someone would find a good enough excuse to throw down the gauntlet. The longer he could put that challenge off, the more likely he'd get out of here alive.

Although the likelihood of that had plummeted with the arrival of a gutsy woman who didn't deserve to become a victim.

Grimacing, he clumped up on the small front porch of the cabin he'd claimed, unobtrusively drew his weapon and went in for the usual search before he could relax at all.

And before he slipped out again, this time staying unseen, to maintain a long-distance watch over Leah.

THE ROOM PROVED to be vacant, and likely had been for a decade or more. A broken bed frame left the mattress tipping. A front on one of the dresser drawers had split in half.

Light from the hall showed beneath the door.

When Leah tiptoed over to the sash window, she felt a draft. Standing to one side, she felt the cold glass until she found the corner that had broken out.

Taking a chance, she stood right in front of the window, turned the window latch and tried to heave the lower sash upward. Absolutely nothing happened. The warped, painted-too-many-times frame didn't so much as groan. For an instant she thought she saw something—some-*one*—move out at the edge of the treeline, but then decided her eyes had tricked her.

She could break out the rest of the glass—but that would alert the guard. If she could swing out, dangle and drop, she might make it to the ground uninjured… but they'd be on her right away. And what if she sprained or broke an ankle? She might not be able to drive, even if the hideout key was still there, and she sure as heck couldn't run away.

If only she knew what time it was. If the door to the hall would crack open without a squeak of rusting hinges.

She stopped herself from creating a list of dire consequences for every decision she made. She'd come this far. She had to peek into the hall and see if there was the slightest chance at all of making it unseen to the stairs. Maybe even whether there were any lights on downstairs, or whether she'd be able to descend into blessed darkness.

No floorboards creaked underfoot as she crossed the room. Prayed the door and frame had been as solidly built. Holding her breath, she very gently turned the knob, then drew the door toward herself a fraction of an inch at a time. It was quiet, so quiet.

Until she heard a muffled sound. A curse?

She had the door open wide enough to allow her to poke her head out into the hall. When she did, she saw a tattooed, muscular guy who hadn't stood out to her if she'd seen him at all. Chair pushed aside, he sat on the floor, leaning back against the door to her original room, legs stretched out. His head sagged to one side, and another snort came from him.

He was snoring. Asleep.

If she'd opened that door, he'd have awakened instantly. As it was…she slipped out into the hall and tiptoed toward the stairs. There was a light on down there somewhere—the kitchen?—but not in the main room.

First step, second, third. She hesitated. One of the stairs had squeaked on her way up. The next—she thought. Gripping the handrail, she stretched to reach the step below, then kept going. Once she was far enough down, she turned her head, searching for movement. For a second guard. For a Rottweiler. For anything, but all remained still.

Within moments she was at the front door.

SPENCER KEPT STARING at the window into the middle bedroom upstairs in the lodge. He'd seen someone; he'd swear he had. Durand, who was currently on guard? Maybe he'd heard something outside, was doing some rounds? But he was an exceptionally big guy, and the figure Spencer had seen had been slight. But how in hell could that woman have gotten past Durand and into a different guest room? He shook his head. Maybe it had been a damn ghost.

He waited. Waited.

Something happened in the deep shadows of the front porch. A person, moving tentatively, emerged into the moonlight and started down the half dozen steps.

Careful, Spencer urged silently. She reached the ground, apparently unheard and unseen except by him, and ran for her car. She went straight for the back fender, crouched out of sight and then stood and rushed around to the driver's side.

A light came on in one of the cabins. For an instant, the woman froze, looking in the same direction.

It was probably just somebody out of bed to take a leak, but you never knew. Spencer had crossed paths with some other night owls from time to time. Paranoia had that effect on a man.

She opened the car door, still unlocked, and jumped in. She was smart enough not to turn on headlights, but seconds later the engine purred to life. Given the silence out here in the forest, it sounded more like a roar.

Lights in other cabins came on.

The car didn't move.

Goddamn. Somebody must have taken the precaution of screwing with her car. Disabled the transmission, maybe, or the CV joint.

Why hadn't Higgs mentioned that to him? Spencer wondered.

Men were running toward her. She flung open her door, fell out and scrambled back to her feet, then took off for the trees.

He couldn't intervene. Even feeling a crack tear open in his iron control, Spencer knew there was too much to lose, and she wasn't going to make it anyway.

It killed him to stay back in the darkness and watch her be tackled by the fastest pursuer. Even down, she screamed and fought furiously. Finally breaking, he started toward them, but too late.

A second guy reached her, and the two of them wrenched her to her feet, still struggling but in an uncoordinated way, as if her limbs no longer worked right.

It was TJ Galt who'd reached her first. Curt Baldwin second. They'd pay for the unnecessary brutality, Spencer swore.

By the time they dragged her to the foot of the lodge steps and dropped her on the ground, the porch light had come on and lights shone in all the cabins. They'd all been awakened and closed in on her. Spencer circled until he could join them in a way that would appear natural.

"What the hell happened ?" Spencer asked, just as Higgs pushed his way to the center of the group.

The colonel swore viciously before turning his head. "Where's Durand?"

"Here."

Everyone else drew back from the man who'd failed at his appointed task. Higgs didn't accept failure.

"How did she get by you?"

"She couldn't have." Seeming dazed, Don Durand gazed down at the woman lying in the dirt at his feet. "That bedroom door never opened. Maybe…the window."

All but Spencer looked up at the obviously closed windows.

Was she conscious? It was a minute before he could reassure himself that at least she was breathing. He should have run to her first, pretended to smack her around to avoid this. He gritted his teeth, wishing she'd made it into the woods.

"Get her up!" Higgs snapped.

Galt pulled her up in one vicious motion. One of her

eyes was swollen completely shut. The other was open, but dazed. How aware was she?

"Who has a gun?" Higgs demanded.

After a heartbeat, Durand handed over his. Higgs grabbed a handful of her hair and yanked hard while grinding the barrel into her temple.

"How'd you get out?"

It was a long time before she spoke. Then her voice was a mere thread, so faint Spencer found himself leaning forward to hear.

"Way to get from one bedroom closet to another."

Spencer stirred. When he was a kid, his still-intact family had vacationed at a rustic resort on one of Georgia's barrier islands. He remembered discovering that a panel could be removed in the back of the closet to expose an additional space.

Higgs swore some more. "Why shouldn't I kill you?"

Half the men clustered around her wore avid expressions Spencer had seen too often before, the kind you'd see on faces in the audience at an MMA fight when blood spattered, or in the crowd at a car race after a collision that might leave fatalities. These men were excited, wanted the shock of seeing blood and a young woman go down right in front of them. If Higgs's finger tightened even a fraction…

Spencer pushed forward. "That'd be an awful waste."

"What?" Higgs's head jerked around.

"You heard me." Spencer smiled slightly and leaned on his Southern accent. "She's a real pretty woman."

A chorus of agreement broke out. "Hell, yeah. We can keep her too busy to get in trouble."

Spencer looked into Higgs's eyes. "Give her to me, and I'll guarantee no more trouble from her."

The two men stared at each other; Higgs's eyes narrowed. Spencer didn't dare relax enough even to see how she had reacted, or if she had. Arguments broke out around them. They wanted to share her, or a few of the men thought they were entitled to have her, sure as hell more than that Southern bastard who'd joined the group late. This was a gamble that Higgs would acknowledge him as second in charge by giving him what he wanted.

Higgs's hand holding the gun dropped away, and he used his grip on her hair to twist her toward Spencer. Then he gave her a hard shove, sending her flying into Spencer, who pulled her tight against him.

"She's all yours," Higgs said in a hard voice. "You screw up, on your head be it."

Spencer nodded at their fair leader, then half carried Leah through the crowd, ignoring the chorus of protests and the glares. Every hair on the back of his neck stood up as he broke free and steered her toward the refuge of his cabin.

How the hell *was* he going to control her?

Chapter Four

Supporting most of Leah's weight, Spencer propelled her up the steps to his porch and into his cabin. He laid her down on the futon that would have once served a dual purpose when a family rented this cabin. The damn thing was uncomfortable, but he didn't suppose she'd notice right now. Aware that they'd been watched all the way, he was glad to be able to close and lock the door.

The damage to her face was severe enough this time; he wondered whether her cheekbone might be broken. He worried even more that her brain had been traumatized. Knowing there wasn't a thing he could do if that was so, Spencer gritted his teeth and went to the corner of the room that served as a kitchen. She hadn't moved when he returned with an ice pack and a T-shirt he'd left lying over the back of a chair.

He sat beside her on the futon, wrapped the ice pack in the thin cotton T-shirt and gently laid it over her cheekbone, eye and brow.

She jerked and flailed.

"Hey," he said quietly. "I know this doesn't feel good, but it's only ice. You've got some major swelling going on."

Her eye—the one that wasn't swollen shut—opened, looking glassy and uncomprehending.

"That SOB clobbered you," Spencer continued, working to keep his voice reassuring instead of enraged. "I'll give you something for the pain once the ice has had a chance to help." And once she demonstrated some coherence. If she didn't…well, that was a bridge he'd cross when he had no other choice.

Her eye closed and a small sigh escaped her.

His hand was cold, but he didn't move it, just kept looking down at her, taking in every detail of her face, from the old and new damage to her lashes and eyebrows, both auburn instead of brown. Just long enough to tuck behind her ears, her hair was ruffled but obviously straight. A high forehead gave her some of that look of innocence and youth he'd first noticed. She had a pretty mouth, now that it wasn't pressed into a tight line.

With a grimace, he corrected himself. What he'd really meant was, *Now that it was lax because she was semiconscious*.

"Leah?"

His anxiety ratcheted up a notch when she didn't respond.

He tried again. "Can you hear me? I need to know how you're doing."

Her lashes fluttered and the single eyelid rose. She tried to focus a still-dazed eye on him. "Why—" she licked her lips "—would you care?"

He'd bent his head closer to hear a question that was more a prolonged breath than words. There were any number of possible responses, but he went with, "You didn't deserve this."

"Tried…run away."

"I know."

"You…missed car key."

Okay, she was with him, if still feeling like crap. He smiled. "I didn't miss the key. I left it for you."

"Car wouldn't drive."

"I didn't do that. Didn't know anyone else had, either."

Tiny lines formed on her forehead above the ice pack. "Why would you want me to get away?"

The side of him that was utterly focused on his mission hadn't. A police response would have majorly screwed up this operation. He'd invested too much in it to want it ended prematurely. But he hadn't been able to stand back and watch her be raped or killed, either.

"I don't hurt women," he finally said.

Was that a snort? He wasn't sure, and she'd closed her eye again.

"If you can hold this in place—" he lifted her hand and laid it over the ice pack "—I'll get you some painkillers."

"'Kay," she murmured.

He kept a sharp eye on her for the short time it took him to dig in his leather duffel bag in the bedroom and return to the main room with a bottle of over-the-counter meds. He had some better stuff tucked away, too, but he'd hold off on that for now.

Bringing a glass of water, too, he helped her half sit up and swallow the pills, then gently laid her back again.

"Have you gotten any sleep tonight?" he asked.

Her nose wrinkled. "Maybe…hour or two?"

That was what he'd thought. "Once the pain lets up a little, I'm hoping you'll be able to get a few hours."

She didn't comment. Spencer had to wonder if her busy little brain wasn't already plotting how to escape. As in, waiting until he had fallen asleep. And, damn it, he did need some sleep. He didn't like his best option here, and she'd like it even less, but he didn't see a workable alternative. Now that he had her safe, he wouldn't let her risk herself unnecessarily…and he was back to focusing first on what he needed to do.

She paid enough attention to him to lift her arms when he asked, and tell him where else she hurt. He manipulated her right shoulder and decided it, too, was inflamed and deeply bruised from when she hit the ground with TJ's weight atop her.

He cracked open another ice pack and applied it to her shoulder. When she started shivering, he grabbed his fleece jacket and spread it over her.

Leah peered suspiciously at him from her one good eye.

Finally, he said, "Okay, tell you what. I'm going to move you to the bed so you can really get some sleep. We'll ice any swelling in the morning." Which wasn't very far away.

She didn't move. Spencer took away the ice packs and tossed them in the small sink. Returning to her, he slid an arm behind her back and said, "Upsy daisy."

"I want to stay here."

"Not happening," he said flatly.

"Why not?"

"You didn't get away. There won't be a second chance."

She twisted out of his grip. "I won't!"

"I didn't ask you." This time he lifted her using both arms.

Her pliancy vanished. She fought like a featherweight champ, landing blows with her small fists. He averted his face and endured as he walked to the bedroom, but when she managed to clip his jaw, he snapped, "That's it," and dropped her on the bed.

Of course she rolled for the other side and thudded off onto her knees, then scrambled to her feet. "If you think I'm getting in that bed with you—"

"I'm not giving you a choice," he said grimly, and pulled a set of handcuffs from his back pocket.

ALREADY SCARED, LEAH completely lost it then. Gripped by a suffocating terror, she knew only that once he clicked those cuffs on her, she'd be utterly helpless.

He was already shifting toward the foot of the bed, expecting her to come around. She threw herself across the bed instead, her shoulder hitting his hard belly when he moved to intercept her. Fighting mindlessly, Leah used every weapon she had, including her teeth and nails. He let out a stream of invectives when she raked her fingernails over his cheek and sank her teeth into his biceps. Sobbing for breath, she kept fighting even as he subdued her with insulting ease, throwing her again onto the bed and, this time, coming down on top of her.

Even that didn't stop her. She bucked and kicked and screamed until he covered her mouth and half her face with a big hand, somehow managing to capture both her wrists with his other hand and plant them above her head.

Now she couldn't breathe at all. With that powerful body, he was crushing her. She wrenched her head side to side until she was able to bite the fleshy part of his hand below his thumb.

"Enough!" he snarled, and before she knew it he'd pushed her to her side and clicked the handcuffs around one wrist. Her face was wet with tears and probably snot as she continued to fight uselessly against his greater strength.

He snapped the other side of the cuffs onto the old iron bedstead and rolled off both her and the bed to land on his feet where he glared down at her, his teeth bared, his hands half curled into fists.

Leah went still, hurting everywhere, terrified in an

all new way. She had no doubt at all that he intended to rape her.

I don't hurt women.

Sure. Right. Her shoulder screamed and her head throbbed. One hip hurt, too, and she tasted blood. Her gaze flicked to his powerful biceps where she saw the bite mark. It was *his* blood in her mouth.

"Damn," he said suddenly, and scrubbed one of his hands over his face. When he looked back at her, his expression had changed. Instead of triumph, she thought she saw regret. No, probably pity. But even that was good news, wasn't it? If he felt sorry for her, would a man still rape a woman?

"Let me get a wet cloth to wipe your face," he said unexpectedly, and left the bedroom.

She tugged at the cuffs, just to be sure they really had clicked shut. The metal bit into her wrist. Leah turned her face away from the door.

A moment later she heard his footfall.

"If I sit down, will you attack me again?" he asked in that deep voice tinged with a softening accent.

Did he wear a pistol? She couldn't remember noticing. If she could get her hand on it…

She had to roll her head to see.

No gun.

He held a wet washcloth.

"No," she whispered.

Watching her, those oddly pale eyes unblinking, he sat beside her, much as he had out on the ancient couch. When he'd tried to take care of her, Leah couldn't help remembering.

That didn't mean she was safe from him, though. Why would he have claimed her if he didn't want sex from her?

But she only closed her own eyes when he laid the

warm washcloth over her face and very carefully wiped away her tears and probably some blood and, yes, snot. The heat and rough texture felt so good, she heard herself make a tiny sound that might have been a whimper.

"Better?" he asked quietly.

She bobbed her head. Pain stabbed both shoulders, now that her arm on the uninjured side was stretched above her head, but everything was relative.

"Then we need to talk." He paused. "I want you to look at me."

Leah rolled her head enough to be able to see him out of her right eye. The other one had to be swollen completely shut despite the ice this man had applied to it. Why would he have bothered unless…

"You're not going to escape at this point," Spencer said, his gaze steady, his tone rock hard. "You're alive, and not in the hands of one of those animals, because I took responsibility for you. Everyone here will respect that unless they see me as failing. Say, if you make any kind of serious attempt at taking off. It'll be a free-for-all then, and you could end up in anyone's cabin. Or shared between them. Do you understand that?"

After a moment she nodded. She did see that; she just didn't know what kind of threat *he* represented.

"You have to cooperate. For both our sakes, I wish you could stay holed up in this cabin, but that's not an option. I have to participate in training exercises and planning sessions. That would leave you alone. What you need to do is join the other women and imitate them." He paused. "You saw them at dinner."

This time her nod was uncertain. She hadn't paid that much attention. Mostly, she'd hoped for…she didn't know, maybe a signal from one of them? Any hint that one or all of the women would help if they could?

"They're abused women." His expression was grim. "They each try not to meet the eyes of any man but their own husband or boyfriend, and that rarely. They tend to keep their heads down, shoulders hunched. They scuttle across open ground."

Could she act that well? Leah thought so. Fear was a great motivator.

He continued relentlessly. "The women are expected to do all the cooking and cleaning. They don't complain, because they know their role in life. They talk among themselves only when they're working together in the kitchen, and then it's quietly, and about their work. One of the men—the husbands and boyfriends—always keeps an eye on them while they're together. The message is that they can't be trusted."

Feeling growing horror, she whispered, "You'll do that, too?"

"Damn straight I will, as often as I can."

He startled her by planting a hand on each side of her torso and leaning over her. Dominating her, so she couldn't look away from him if she tried. The triple scratches she'd inflicted showed vividly on his angular cheek above dark stubble. A small bump on the bridge of his nose wasn't her fault.

"*I* am your only protection," he continued relentlessly. "You can't forget that. Right now they're all afraid to cross me."

"Even the boss?"

"Colonel Higgs?"

The irony in his voice had her blinking. "That's what he's called?"

"He is a retired US Air Force colonel. He doesn't let anyone forget it."

"That's scary."

His eyebrows twitched. Leah couldn't tell if he agreed or was pleased to have a leader with a legitimate military background.

"I wouldn't say he's afraid of me," Spencer continued. "Wary, maybe. Preferring to keep my loyalty. Apparently, he has no interest in taking you on himself."

She shuddered.

"You might have been safer with him," the big man with the icy eyes told her. "Nobody would have thought to argue with him. I'm…not popular with a few of the men. We may run into trouble if someone works up the guts to challenge me."

We? This bizarre conversation had her bewildered. *Us against them.* Did he imagine she'd be *happy* to be one of those stoop-shouldered, timid, obedient women?

Or… Leah replayed everything he'd said. His expressions, subtle though they were. His actions, if it was true he'd left the hideout key to the car deliberately to give her a chance to get away. His care with her injuries, the flickers of rage she'd seen. Even when she fought, when she hurt him, he'd still been careful not to hurt *her.*

Very slowly, she said, "You're not one of them, are you?"

SPENCER QUIT BREATHING as he stared at her. Only long practice allowed him to keep his face impassive despite his shock. After a moment he said, "That's not a smart thing to suggest. Not to me, and especially not to anyone else."

Her eyes searched his. The impulse to confide in her took him by surprise. Part of it, he understood. Seeing her so terrified of him that she'd fought with crazed ferocity had hit him hard. If she hadn't calmed down, he might have had no choice. As it was…he shouldn't even *think* about trusting her to that extent. One careless word, a reaction that seemed off to one of the men, and he and she both would be dead. She *had* to be seen to be scared of him, unwillingly bowing to necessity, or somebody might get curious. No cover was good enough if someone was willing to dig deep.

No.

Bending even more closely over her, he said softly, “Do you hear me?”

She shrank from him. “Yes.”

“Good.” He straightened so that he was no longer caging her body with his.

“You can’t tell me—” she began.

Spencer almost groaned. She was either very, very perceptive, or just naturally rebellious. Neither quality served them well right now.

“I’ve got to get some sleep,” he said abruptly, bending to pull off his boots and socks. “I don’t think you have a concussion—your eyes seem pretty focused to me—but I’ll keep a watch for any problems. You can try to sleep.”

Her eyes widened.

Ignoring her, he pulled his belt from the loops, then unbuttoned and unzipped his cargo pants.

Wearing only the T-shirt and knit boxers, he went out to the living room to check locks again, pick up his Sig Sauer and turn off lights. Returning to the bedroom, he briefly thought about switching the cuff from the bed frame to his wrist but decided against it. She couldn’t go anywhere, and if she attacked him again, he’d wake up in the blink of an eye and deal with her. He might have slept on the futon so that she could relax a little—but he couldn’t afford for someone to look in the uncurtained window above the sink and see that he was pandering to Leah. Besides—even rocky ground would be an improvement over the futon.

He adjusted the bedroom curtains to block anyone trying to steal a look, turned off the light and tugged the covers out from beneath her so that he could pull them over both of them. Then he claimed one of the two nearly flat pillows, doubled it over and stretched out beside her.

Leah lay rigid, as close to the far edge of the bed as she could. Given that the bed was only a full size—his feet hung over at the bottom—that wasn't very far away. Besides…the mattress was as old as the futon and the stained kitchen sink. Once she nodded off, she'd roll to meet him in the middle.

A rueful smile tugged at his mouth as he pictured how happy she'd be waking up plastered against his body.

Chapter Five

She dreamed about being stretched on a medieval rack. At the same time she was weirdly comfortable, the cozy warmth feeling as if it came from a heated blanket, but more…solid. Comforting.

Leah surfaced slowly, realizing that she lay on her side with her head resting on her upper arm. That arm was stretched above her, and ached fiercely. Not stretched, she thought on a sudden memory; pulled.

And somebody spooned her, his hips pressed to her butt, thighs to the backs of hers. A heavy arm lay over her, his hand tucked—Leah quit breathing. If his hand wasn't so relaxed, it would have enclosed her breast.

His chest felt like a wall. Was it possible she could feel his slow, steady heartbeats?

He. Spencer. The man who'd claimed her and now expected complete obedience as payback. How had she let him wrap her in such an all-encompassing embrace?

When he climbed into bed with her as if that was routine, she'd resolved to stay awake. Obviously, that hadn't gone so well, and no wonder, considering how desperately tired she'd been by then. Not just from lack of sleep. Shock and pain and fear had taken a toll.

Lying completely still, as if she could fend off the reality that she shared the bed with a very large, muscular man who might well have squeezed her breast in his hand while she slept, Leah understood how poorly prepared she'd been for any of this. She'd grown up in a middle-class home with loving parents, had a good relationship with her sometimes irritating little brother, enjoyed college and even her job, although she did want more. Her only major stumble had been being so blind where Stuart was concerned, and compared to her current predicament, that was…normal. Her letting love, or some facsimile thereof, blind her. And to think of the agonies she'd suffered over that jerk. If only she'd known.

Now she had to face the fact that there was a really good chance she'd be gang-raped or—no, make that *and*—killed in the next few days. It would seem her only chance at survival was to obey the stranger who shared this bed.

His pelvis wasn't all that was pressing into her butt, she became gradually aware. That hard bar hadn't been there when she first woke up. His breathing had changed, too.

"I have to use the bathroom," she said loudly.

His chuckle ruffled the tiny hairs on the back of her neck. "Gotcha."

He gently squeezed her breast, gave a regretful sigh, and he rolled away from her. The mattress rebounded without his weight.

"Now, what did I do with that key?" he said.

She growled; he laughed.

A moment later he'd unfastened the cuff on the bed frame. Leah scrambled to get out of bed. She hadn't thought about her bladder until she'd told him that, but now she *really* needed to go.

Amusement on his face, Spencer stepped out of her

way. She rushed for the small bathroom. The warped door didn't quite latch, but stayed closed. Relief.

The mirror was spotted, but she inspected her face. It wasn't pretty. She could see out of both eyes, although the one side was still really puffy, the discoloration gaining new glory. The last time she'd had a black eye, a scared Labrador mix had head-butted her in an attempt to escape. This one would be way more spectacular before it was done.

She surveyed the bathroom before she went back out, but didn't see anything useful. A good, old-fashioned straight razor, or even a disposable kind of razor, might have come in handy. But no; a rechargeable shaver lay on the pedestal sink.

Arming herself might be stupid at this point anyway. A razor blade would look wimpy to men all carrying semiautomatic pistols. And really, given her inexperience, even a gun in her hands might get her in more trouble than it would solve.

Whatever else she could say about the man who'd stepped forward on her behalf—an optimistic way of phrasing it—he exuded danger. So much so, none of the other men had been prepared to challenge him, as he put it. That made him the best weapon she could have acquired…assuming he didn't have an end game that had nothing to do with her welfare.

She ran through a plus list. A) he hadn't raped her when he could easily have done so; B) he had done his best not to add to her injuries, even when she was attacking him; and C) he had actually seemed to care that she was hurt and had tried to make sure she was comfortable.

Plenty of negatives came to mind readily, too, starting with the fact that he was a member of a frighteningly well-armed white supremacist militia with big, scary plans. Moving on to B, if she tried something, he could handle her without breaking a sweat; and C, she had no idea how much of what she'd seen was facade and how much real.

She didn't know him, and one of the greatest threats right now was an unreasoning belief that he wasn't a member of the group at all, that he despised them and was really an honorable, good man. Oh, yeah—and she would have been sexually attracted to him in any other circumstances at all.

Maybe even *these* circumstances, which meant…she didn't know. Was this a primitive response to the fact that he claimed to be standing between her and the world?

Not happening, she told herself firmly. She'd do as he asked, for now. What choice did she have? But she'd watch for an opportunity to escape, and she couldn't afford to soften toward Spencer Wyatt—or to entirely trust him.

SPENCER FELT ANTSY from the minute he left Leah in the large kitchen at the lodge and headed out to the shooting range with the others. The women were washing up from breakfast, Lisa Dempsey planning lunch while Jennifer Fuller handed out cleaning assignments. Spencer wasn't sure he could have made himself walk away if TJ Galt had been the one "supervising," but Dirk Ritchie was staying behind this morning. He'd brought the fourth woman along, Helen Slocum.

Helen didn't seem so much terrorized as mentally slow, Spencer had come to think. Dirk could be unexpectedly patient with her, even showing flashes of genuine caring. In fact, he seemed like a decent guy in many ways, which left him the low man on the totem pole in this crowd. Decency registered as weakness here. Spencer made a point of supporting the guy. Dirk's background suggested a reading disability, a lousy school district and a father who was disappointed in his only son's spinelessness. As with Shelley, Spencer wanted to quietly tell Dirk to take Helen and drive away—and not go home to daddy.

He'd as soon not feel sorry for any of this crowd, but couldn't entirely shut down that side of himself.

Obviously, or he'd be able to keep his mind on business. As it was, he should have taken this shot two minutes ago.

He lay prone in the dirt looking through a scope at a target that he'd calculated was five hundred and seventy-five yards out, give or take a little. It was crystal clear. He breathed in, out, in, out…and gently pulled the trigger.

Higgs squatted beside him, peering through military-grade binoculars. "Hell of a shot."

As had been every one he'd taken today.

Higgs was in love with the Barrett M82 rifle, not because of accuracy, although it was fine. What he liked—and why he'd acquired several of these rifles—was that they fired the exact same .50 BMG cartridge used in the heavy machine gun. The heavy-duty round excelled at destroying just about everything up to armored vehicles. Higgs wasn't interested in subtlety. He wanted a big boom.

One of the downsides of this particular rifle was the lack of accuracy for truly long-range shots. In fact, anything over nine hundred yards. Personally, Spencer had preferred the M40A5, one of many descendants of the Remington 700 rifle commonly owned by hunters. He had comfortably made shots at twelve hundred yards and farther, although there were military snipers who could make longer ones. So far, Higgs hadn't asked for anything remotely difficult for a man with Spencer's experience, which meant a simple assassination wasn't on Higgs's agenda.

Now Spencer peeled off his ear protection and rose to his knees still cradling the rifle. "That's it for me. You know I had sniper training at Fort Bennett. I've spent enough time on a range to stay sharp. Let's focus on some of the guys who need the work."

Happy with what he'd seen, Higgs stood, too, letting the binoculars fall to his chest. "I agree. We'll be lucky if any of the men become reliable at even a hundred yards out. We could use another real sharpshooter, but unless you have a former army buddy you can recruit, we'll have to get by with what we have."

Temptation flickered at the opportunity to bring in another agent, but Spencer was inclined to think the risk was too great. Aside from backup, how much could a newcomer achieve anyway? He was well enough established to be in a good position to be included the next time Colonel Higgs met with his arms dealer. Nailing down who was stealing and selling contraband US Army weaponry to the group was one of his highest priorities, along with finding out the final details of the spectacular attack that Higgs was so convinced would not only deal a major blow to the government, but also fire-start a civil war.

The crack of shots interspersed their few words. Spencer didn't need binoculars to see how badly Tim Fuller, stationed closest to him, was shooting.

Another week or two, he told himself, but he'd thought the same before. Ed Higgs was being cagey even with Spencer, who wanted some serious time alone with Higgs's laptop. As it was, he had to hold out for that upcoming exchange of cash for arms.

He'd had better luck tracing the source of the funding, and managed to share that much with his superior the last time he'd been part of a supply run to Bellingham and had had a minute to get away to make a call. Some names weren't all, though. A lot of the money was coming from someone who remained cloaked in shadows. Even the one chance to share what he'd learned had been a few weeks ago, but now instead of hoping he'd have the chance again, his gut told him bad things would happen if he left Leah for an entire day.

In fact, when he looked around he didn't see Joe Osenbrock.

"Where's Joe?" he asked sharply.

The older man's gray head turned. "Don't know. Taking a leak?"

The AK-47 Osenbrock had been using lay in the dirt where he'd apparently left it. Spencer had spent time drilling these idiots in how important it was to treat their weapons with care, but nothing he said had sunk in. They thought they were ready, their impatience building almost as fast as their confidence, until they had begun looking at their great leader with doubt. What use was more target shooting? Hand-to-hand combat? Why did they need any of this, when they had the weaponry to shoot planes out of the sky? Spencer had heard the whispers.

Just the other night, for example. Thinking he was alone with Shawn Wycoff walking at the edge of the trees, TJ had said, "I'm starting to think he's all talk." Hidden in the darkness, Spencer hadn't been ten feet away. He didn't miss so much as a mumble. It never occurred to them anybody could be near, far less breathing down their necks.

That arrogance was good. It would bring these fools down.

Unfortunately, it also explained Higgs's continuing hesitation as well as his unwillingness to trust anyone.

Speaking of trust, Spencer said, "I need to go check on Leah. Make sure she's behaving herself and that Joe hasn't forgotten who she belongs to."

Leah's face had looked better this morning, but that wasn't saying much. He still feared she'd suffered a concussion. He'd checked on her a few times in the night and not seen anything too worrisome, but he wanted to be vigilant.

Higgs's eyebrows rose, but he nodded. "I don't need you out here. Let's talk after lunch, though."

Yes. Why don't we talk about who's footing the bills, he thought. *Better yet, some details about your endgame.*

But Spencer only nodded and, carrying his rifle, walked toward the lodge. He was careful to keep his pace unhurried until he was out of sight of the range set up in what had been a beautiful high alpine meadow. They'd undoubtedly destroyed much of the fragile ecosystem.

Then he broke into a run.

LEAH WAS ON her hands and knees scrubbing the floor in the downstairs bathroom when she heard someone stop in the hall. She stiffened, sneaking a look. Without lifting her head, all she knew was that a man stood there, and he wasn't Spencer or Dirk.

Feet in heavy black boots were planted apart, meaning he filled the doorway. Camo cargo pants didn't hide powerful legs.

"May I help you?" she asked timidly.

"You sure can," he said.

Oh, God. She'd heard his name at breakfast. Joe Osenbrock. He hadn't been one of the two who'd tackled her during her escape attempt, but his perpetual sneer didn't make him likeable. Plus, she'd seen hunger in his eyes when he looked at her. Almost as tall as Spencer, he was broad and strong.

Swallowing, she stayed on her knees and kept her head bent.

"See, Wyatt's got no reason to keep you to himself. What he don't know won't hurt him, now, will it?"

She bit her lip so hard she tasted blood. Where was Dirk Ritchie? Had he seen Osenbrock come in?

"You think he won't know?" she asked, still diffident.

"If he finds out, so what? Not like I'd be spoiling the goods." His voice changed, hardened. "On your feet, woman."

Her mind scrambled for any way to get away from this would-be rapist. She couldn't just let this happen. Finally, she straightened her back, lifted her head and met his eyes, holding his gaze. "If you touch me, he'll kill you."

"Nothin' to say I won't kill him, you know."

A dark shape materialized behind him. "*I* say you won't," Spencer said, voice as cold as his eyes.

Joe whirled to face the threat he hadn't anticipated. "What're you talking about?"

Spencer spoke softly, but with a sharp edge. "I'll also tell you right now that if you bother her again, if you lay a finger on her, she's right. I *will* kill you."

"I was just teasing her a little. That's all. Ain't that so, Leah?"

She kept her mouth closed, even though agreeing might lessen the tension that made the air hard to breathe.

Spencer leaned toward the other man until he was right in his face. "Do you hear me?"

"I hear you!" Joe yelled, and stormed forward. His shoulder bashed Spencer's, but he kept going. A slam seconds later was the front door of the lodge.

Spencer took Joe's place in the doorway. "Where's Dirk?"

"I don't know." She used the hem of her T-shirt to wipe her forehead. "He might still be in the kitchen. Why?"

"I expect him to watch out for you when I can't be here."

"I thought he's here to make sure none of us make a run for it."

The grim set of Spencer's mouth didn't ease. "Well, that, too."

"Will you expect TJ Galt to watch out for me? Or Jennifer's husband? Or… Is Lisa married?"

"Not married. She lives with Del Schmidt. And no, I wouldn't ask any of the other men to protect you. Which leaves me with a problem."

How reassuring. "Leaves *you* with a problem? That sounds like *my* problem."

He shot a glance over his shoulder. "Keep your voice down."

Leah opened her mouth again but had the sense to close it. She hadn't sounded meek or deferential at all, which would set any of the others wondering about him, too.

"I'm sorry," she whispered.

As usual, his expression remained unemotional, even as his gaze never left her face. "Did you have a choice of jobs?" he asked after a minute.

Leah shook her head. "I wouldn't expect to when I'm the newcomer. They don't know me."

"No." He rubbed a hand over his face in what she'd decided was the closest to betraying frustration or indecision that he came. "Finish up here. I'll decide what we're going to do after lunch."

She nodded, hesitated…and went back on her hands and knees to resume scrubbing. Not that this ancient linoleum would ever look clean again.

"I'LL TAKE OVER here this afternoon," Spencer said during a break in conversations around the table while they ate.

Heads turned, the silence prolonged. When Higgs said, "I'll stick around, too," the atmosphere changed.

Many of them had the same interpretation: their leader intended to discuss plans with Spencer, the chosen, while everyone else, the mere grunts, continued physical training.

And yeah, Spencer thought with some irony, he'd been guilty of plenty of apple polishing to achieve just this outcome. What he earned today were some hateful glances directed his way only when the colonel wouldn't see them.

Only Rick Metz kept chewing with no visible reaction. It wouldn't have crossed his mind that he could have a planning role. The question was why Dirk looked relieved. The same man was never allowed to hang around the lodge all day. Spencer wondered if Dirk knew the other women weren't safe from TJ or Tim Fuller.

By God, maybe he should slip Leah a knife so she could protect herself.

Nice thought, but even if she could bring herself to stick it into her attacker, the ultimate outcome wouldn't be good.

Fear of him was her only real protection. He had to say a few quiet words to men besides Joe Osenbrock.

As he and Higgs waited while the other men left the lodge and the women cleared the long table, Spencer tried hard to focus on what might be an important step in closing this damn investigation, instead of on the woman who had become his Achilles' heel.

LEAH WISHED SHE could hear what the two men were talking about at the table, but she couldn't make out a word. She had a feeling it was important, but she couldn't think of an excuse to sidle close enough to eavesdrop. Jennifer Fuller was in the pantry making sure she had everything for tonight's dinner, which was to be lasagna. Leah had noticed that she poked her head out pretty regularly to survey her worker bees. As intimidated as she was around the men, she seemed to relish lording it over the other women.

Helen was well aware of when they were alone. Now, as she handed over a rinsed pot for Leah to dry, she whispered, "Spencer said something to Dirk that shook him up real bad. Do you know what happened?"

Just as quietly, Leah said, "Joe Osenbrock got me alone when I was cleaning the bathroom and threatened to…you know."

Helen blushed and ducked her head.

"Spencer heard him and was really mad. I guess he thought Dirk should have kept Joe away from me."

"Dirk didn't know nothing about Joe being back here in the lodge. He wouldn't have let anyone hurt you if he'd known!"

Leah hadn't known a whisper could sound indignant. She smiled at the small, anxious woman. "I believe you. He seems nice."

She didn't actually know any such thing, but at least he didn't look at her the way most of the other men did, and she hadn't been able to help noticing that Helen didn't seem afraid of Dirk.

"Spencer was mostly mad at Joe," she confided.

"I bet." Elbow deep in sudsy water, Helen wielded a scrubbing pad with vigor on the pot that had held the baked beans that were part of the lunch menu. They'd been really good, considering the limited resources anyone cooking had to draw on. Plus, the commercial stove and oven had been installed at least thirty years ago. The miracle was that they mostly still worked.

Possibly that was because Uncle Edward had hardly ever used them himself. Most of the time, he'd insisted the hot plate in his apartment was all he needed. Why make baked beans from scratch when you could open a can? Leah remembered her mother's rolled eyes. Mom had bought him a microwave their last summer here, which had intrigued him. It was safe to say that, as her great-uncle got older and crankier, he would have been even less likely to be inclined to bake a cake or cook anything from scratch.

Too bad he hadn't lingered as a ghost. If he could know, he'd be horrified by the consequences of his gift to her. If he'd actually rented the resort to this group in previous summers—and she increasingly doubted that story—he couldn't have known what those men believed, and especially not what they intended. He'd been courtly, old-fashioned in some ways, but also accepting of people's vagaries. Not for a minute would he have condoned hate-mongering or a threat to the country he loved. Having served as a paratrooper in World War II, Uncle Edward had spent time in a Nazi prisoner-of-war camp. Maybe those experiences explained why, upon returning, he'd chosen a solitary life in the midst of one of American's wildest places.

Handing Leah the next pan, Helen whispered again. "Dirk says you *own* this place."

"My great-uncle left it to me in his—"

Helen jabbed her hard in the side. "Sshh!"

"What…?" Oh. Spencer had settled himself in the doorway between the main room and the kitchen, his posture relaxed, his gaze shifting between the two women. Leah almost whispered that Helen didn't need to worry about Spencer—but if his reputation as the baddest man here was to survive, she needed to keep her mouth shut. If Helen told Dirk what she'd said, he could tell anyone.

She was supposed to be afraid of him, and she needed to act the part. In fact, she immediately imitated Helen's fearful posture. But her forehead crinkled as her hand stopped in the act of wiping out the pot. *Wait*, she thought in alarm. *I* am *afraid of him.*

Wasn't she?

Chapter Six

"How would you feel about going for a walk?" Spencer asked once they left the lodge, post Leah's KP duty after dinner. He felt restless, but didn't dare take a run and leave her behind. The sky was still bright, with night not falling at this time of year until close to ten o'clock. Then he took another look at her. She moved without any noticeable pain, but she'd been brought down to the ground hard yesterday. "Scratch that. You're probably beat."

Flashing him a surprised look, Leah said, "Beat? Why...oh. The cleaning. You do know I don't sit behind a desk all day back home, don't you?"

He hadn't thought about it, but of course she wouldn't.

"I'm on my feet all day long. I see patients, package bloodwork to send out or run screens myself. Medicate and give fluids. Assist in surgery. Like just about everyone else, I help clean kennels and runs. And I subdue everything from snarling Dobermans to raging bulls while one of the vets does an exam or procedure. Oh, and then there's the wildlife. We do the care for a local refuge, which means holding down an eagle with a broken wing or a cougar dented by a car bumper. A little house cleaning is nothing."

Spencer would have laughed if he hadn't felt sure they

were being watched. He appreciated this woman. Leah's bravado was welcome in place of self-pity.

"Of course," she continued, her tone musing, "on the job I wouldn't be worrying whenever a man walked into the room whether he had in mind raping or murdering me. That does take a toll."

"Yeah," he said, a little hoarsely. "It would do that."

"A walk sounds good. After all," she added wryly, "as Colonel Higgs said, I couldn't be held captive in a more beautiful place on earth."

Spencer turned his head, for a rare moment letting himself take in the extraordinary panorama. It had been many years since he'd spent time in the Pacific Northwest, a fact he suddenly regretted.

White-capped Mount Baker dominated the sky to the southeast, while more jagged, and farther distant, Shuksan would have been impressive enough. Other mountains were visible almost everywhere he looked. This was rugged country, and yet not far from the Puget Sound and Strait of Georgia to the west. They were surrounded by forests that had never been logged, an arc of vivid blue above, thin grasses and a dazzling array of flowers. Once they passed the last cabin, he found himself picking his way more carefully than usual because of the wildflowers.

"This is one of the prettiest times of the year here, with so much in bloom," Leah remarked.

Grimly focused on his task, he'd hardly noticed the flowers until five minutes ago. After a moment he said, "I know a few of these. Who hasn't seen a foxglove or a tiger lily?"

For some reason the idea of him gardening in some distant future crossed his mind. Not like he wanted to spend another decade living this way. Once this was over...what if he bought an actual house? Even thought about a wife, having children. What would it be like, coming home at five most days?

His picture of that kind of life was vague, not quite in focus, but he discovered it did include a bed of flowers and a lawn. He hadn't mowed a lawn since he was a boy.

As if she'd followed his thoughts, Leah looked around almost in bemusement. "My mother is a gardener. I always figured someday I'd have a house and yard, too." She went quiet for a minute, likely reflecting on the very distinct possibility she'd never have that chance. But she forged on. "I remember Uncle Edward telling me about the wildflowers. There." She pointed. "That's an easy one, a red columbine. And yarrow, and bleeding heart, and monkshood."

"Isn't monkshood poisonous?"

"I think so. I don't remember if it's the leaves or the flowers or what." She looked pensive, then shook her head. "Oh, and that's goat's beard and..."

He let the recitation roll over him. He wouldn't remember which flower was which, but he liked that she knew and was willing to talk to him.

"When's the last time you were up here?" he asked at one point.

"I think I was twelve, so it's been forever." A pained expression crossed her face. "I'm thirty-one. I don't know why I never thought to get up here to see Uncle Edward. I loved our visits when I was a kid."

"We tend not to look back." He was ashamed to realize how many friends he'd let go over the years. He couldn't even claim to have a close relationship with his own brother or parents anymore. Disappearing for months at a time wasn't conducive to maintaining ties with other people.

Leah stopped walking feet away from the bank of the lake that filled a bowl probably scoured by a long-ago glacier. That was not where she was looking, though. Instead, she turned a gaze on him that was so penetrating, it was all he could do not to twitch.

Instead, he raised an eyebrow. “See anything interesting?”

“Yes. Is there a single other man up here even remotely interested in the names of wildflowers?”

“It’s not the kind of thing we talk about,” he admitted, although he knew the answer. No. “Anyway, who said I am?”

She frowned. “Do you have any hobbies?”

He ought to shut her down right now, but she’d taken him by surprise, as she often did.

“I target shoot. That’s relaxing.” More reluctantly, he said, “When I can, I play in a basketball league.” Baseball, too.

“All militant white supremacists?”

“Ah…we don’t talk politics.” For good reason.

“Why didn’t you assault me last night?”

Spencer was offended enough, he was afraid it showed.

“I told you, I don’t hurt women,” he said shortly. “It doesn’t turn me on at all.” Except that she had to have felt his morning erection, so she knew that she did turn him on. For all she knew, though, he woke up with one every morning.

She nodded slowly, the green of her eyes enriched by the many shades of green surrounding them. His fingers curled into his palms as he resisted the desire to cup her good cheek, trace her lips with his thumb.

Damn, his heartbeat had picked up.

But she wasn’t thinking about him kissing her, because what she said was, "I don't believe you'd blow up innocent people to make a point."

This time he felt more than alarm. "Who says we intend to kill anyone who's innocent?"

"How can you not?" she said simply. "Unless you plan to blow up Congress..."

That idea was enough to make him break out in a cold sweat. He was beginning to fear that Higgs's plans really were that grandiose.

But she shook her head. "I refuse to believe there aren't good politicians."

Having met some decent men and women who had run for office because they believed in service, he conceded her point. "What are you saying?"

"I think you're an undercover federal agent."

He should laugh. Jeer, tell her to take the rose-colored glasses off. He should slap her, which would fit with the role he played.

Instead, he growled, "I told you how dangerous it is to suggest that."

"We're all by ourselves."

She'd made mistakes today. Carried herself with too much pride, looked people in the eye when she shouldn't. Would she be more careful, or less, if she knew the truth?

"If I tell you why I'm here, you have to become an Oscar-worthy actress," he said harshly. "I can't afford for you to get mouthy with anyone, or say something to me when we can be overheard. Do you understand?"

Her expression altered. "Yes. That little episode today with Joe was a good reminder that not only am I in danger every minute, but you are, too."

"I would be either way." He shrugged. "Me demanding an exclusive on you came on top of what some of the men see as Higgs's favoritism. I wasn't popular anyway. Now it's fair to say jealousy and dislike have become hate."

"Isn't hate their reason for existence?" Leah pointed out.

"For the men." Whether the women took the same world view, he had no idea. And it wasn't all of the men. He wished he could figure out how to get Dirk out of the hole he'd dug, but nothing had come to him. There were a couple of others he'd wondered about, but it wasn't his job to separate the deadly fanatics from the ones who were willing to go along. As Leah put it, to blow up innocents.

She didn't say anything else, just waited.

While undercover, Spencer had never, not once, told anyone his true identity or purpose. He'd also never let himself get tangled up with a nice woman who depended on him for her very survival, and who was handling a terrifying experience with dignity and determination.

He sighed, half turning away from her. "You're right. I'm FBI. I've been under with this group for five months now, although we only moved up here for intensive training four weeks ago. Higgs has been on our radar for a long time. Even before he retired, he'd expressed some really marginal ideas. In fact, his obvious contempt for his boss at the time, a two-star general who happened to be black, led to a behind-the-scenes push to early retirement. Unfortunately, it appears that enraged him, helping motivate him to turn militant."

Out of the corner of his eye, he saw that she hadn't done much but blink during this recitation. She'd seen right through him, all right, which made him question how convincing *his* act was.

"I have plenty of evidence to bring down everyone here. We can't let them get to the point of launching their attack. But there's more I need to know. Like when that main event is scheduled for, and what the target is."

"Does that matter if, well, you prevent it from ever happening?"

"Yeah. What if there's another cell training for the same attack? I've seen no indication Higgs is working with anyone else, but we don't have phone service up here. A few times he's made a trip down to Bellingham. Nobody knows what he does while they're shopping for supplies. He could be meeting someone. If he's emailing, it could be from a computer at the library." Frustration added extra grit to his voice. "He has added new posts to a couple of extremist sites, but they're so cryptic we suspect they might really be messages." He gave his head a shake. "We need to keep walking."

"Oh!" She cast a nervous glance back toward the lodge. "Yes, of course."

Circling the lake, he walked fast enough she had to ask him to slow down. He kept talking, telling her his larger goals: making sure they knew who was backing the group, and who was supplying the arms. Moneyed, powerful men were his real target.

"That really is a…a rocket launcher?"

His jaw tightened. "US Military issue. We have two of 'em."

Leah breathed what was probably really a prayer. He agreed with the sentiment wholeheartedly.

Well before they neared the tree line, he said, "I shouldn't have told you this much, but I don't see that it matters. Just remember, even the smallest hint of any of it is a death sentence for me."

She wasn't looking at him. "And me."

"Unless you get the idea you can bargain with Higgs."

Her shoulders stiffened and her chin came up. "I wouldn't!"

"No." He let his tone soften. "I don't think you would."

She sniffed indignantly.

The color of the sky was deepening, the purple tint making it harder for the eye to see outlines.

"This is the end of our discussion," he told her. "I can't be a hundred percent sure the cabin isn't bugged. From here on out, your job is to avoid notice as much as you can."

"What if…if I was able to get a look at Colonel Higgs's room when I'm cleaning?"

"Don't even think about it," he said flatly. "You are not a federal agent. You're a vet tech."

"My life depends on you learning what you have to so we can leave, you know. I'm not going to sit and wait if I can help."

"If you found names or numbers, you wouldn't recognize their meaning. I would. I repeat. The answer is no."

Her chin went back up but she didn't argue again. Spencer wasn't entirely reassured. This was why he shouldn't have told her so much. That said, people talked within earshot of the women as if they were pieces of furniture, much as servants might have been treated in a big house in eighteenth-century England. They could get lucky—but he didn't mention that possibility, because she was too gutsy for her own good. If she got caught where she shouldn't be, *trying* to eavesdrop—she was dead.

They were dead, since he couldn't stand back and let her die, whatever his priorities ought to be.

As they approached the line of cabins, she whispered, "Is Spencer your real name? Or Wyatt?"

Damn her insatiable curiosity.

"It doesn't matter," he snapped.

A faint squeak came to his ears. In response to his irritation, Leah's step hitched and she hunched a little, probably not realizing that she was looking cowed. As little as he liked having that effect on her, her timing was impeccable. That little creep Arne Larson had just stepped out on the porch of his cabin, the one at the end.

"Got her trained, I see," Arne remarked.

Spencer gave her an indifferent glance. "She's smarter than Osenbrock. She knows what's good for her."

Arne laughed, acid in the sound. "Yeah, I heard you told Joe what's what. He didn't like it, you know."

Spencer shrugged. "He's not thinking about what counts. I watched you shooting today and saw a big improvement."

Arne might not like him, but he preened. Spencer's sniper creds inspired some awe among this bunch.

Then he and Leah were past Arne's cabin and the one beyond it, finally reaching his. She trailed him up the porch steps like the obedient little woman she wasn't. She stayed right inside next to the door, too, while he did his usual walk-through with his Sig Sauer in his hand.

THE SHOWER AFFORDED only a tepid stream of water, but it was adequate for Leah to wash her hair. The shampoo dripping down her face stung, though, and had her mumbling, "Ow, ow, ow."

Somebody had absconded with her hair dryer before Spencer grabbed her suitcase. He had even reclaimed her purse, minus everything important.

"I have your wallet," he told her, not offering to return it. "Phone and keys are in our great leader's possession."

She'd heard him use that phrase before, equally laden with sarcasm. Never in anyone else's hearing, of course.

She couldn't wrap her mind around everything he'd

told her. He'd confirmed her suspicion and more, but… could he have lied to ensure her cooperation? Of course he could have—but she didn't believe he had. The very fact that he'd gone out on such a limb in the first place for her sake was a strong argument for his honesty and, yes, possession of what some people would call the old-fashioned quality of honor. Personally, Leah was big on honor right now. Where would she be without it?

She towel-dried her hair as well as she could, brushed it and left the bathroom.

Spencer looked up from where he lounged on what she'd realized was a futon in the living area. Every time she saw him, she was hit afresh with awareness of how sexy he was. Partly it was a matter of bone structure and the contrast between icy, pale eyes and deeply tanned skin, but that wasn't all. He had a brooding quality that got to her. And he'd tried to protect her.

He hadn't even taken off his boots, and his gun lay within easy reach. He was prepared for anything at a moment's notice. The tension really wore on her, but he seemed to take it for granted.

"What are you reading?" She nodded at the book.

"Huh?" He seemed to turn his eyes from her. "Oh. It's Calvin Coolidge's autobiography."

"Really? Is he that interesting?"

"You might say he's become relevant again." If there was dryness in his tone, Leah doubted anyone else would have noticed it. "Coolidge endorsed a law in 1924 that cut immigration by half, with national origin quotas. He considered southern and eastern Europeans to be genetically inferior. The law led to something like forty years of reduced immigration. Higgs thought I'd like to read this. I'm not sure he paid any attention to Coolidge's other policies."

"Is it interesting?"

"His prose isn't riveting." With a grimace, Spencer stuck a torn strip of paper between pages as a bookmark. "You ready for bed?"

"I guess."

He ushered her into the bedroom, then returned to the main room to make his rounds of the windows and check locks. For what good they'd do, she couldn't help thinking. There were new, shiny dead bolts on the front and back doors, but two of the windows had cracked panes, and the frames would splinter under one blow. Of course, that would alert him instantly, and she'd already seen how fast he could move.

When he returned, she still stood beside the bed.

He raised his eyebrows.

"You aren't going to put handcuffs on me again, are you?"

"That depends. Can I trust you not to try anything?"

Somebody could be listening, she reminded herself. "I won't." She went for very, very humble. "I know you'll take care of me."

He cracked a smile that made her mouth go dry, so drastically did it alter his face. Not soften it, exactly, but a hint of warmth along with wicked sensuality shifted her perception of him. Sexy when somber, angry or expressionless, he might be irresistible if he just kept smiling at her.

Of course he didn't. Dear Lord, he wouldn't dare get in the habit! Imagine what the others would think if they saw him.

His eyes burned into hers. Had he read her mind? Well, thinking he was sexy, and okay, feeling a yearning ache deep inside didn't mean she was having sex with him.

She managed a glare that resulted in the corners of his mouth curving again, but once she climbed into bed, he did turn off the light before he stripped and slid in beside her.

Even his whisper held a little grit coming out of the darkness. “I’d complain about the mattress, but I like knowing what’ll happen the minute you fall asleep.”

The trouble was, so did she.

Chapter Seven

Leah had zero chance to get anywhere near her great-uncle's apartment, appropriated by Colonel Higgs. Jennifer Fuller had the privilege of cleaning it, although only when he was there. Otherwise, another of those shiny new dead bolts kept the nosy out.

However tempting an opportunity would be, Leah wouldn't have seized it. Spencer was right; she'd have no idea what she should be looking for. Anyway, she had no desire to find herself in another spot like she had when Joe Osenbrock cornered her. If Spencer hadn't shown up, she wanted to think she could have fought back effectively or that Dirk would have intervened, but she wasn't stupid enough to buy into comforting lies. Joe was muscular, mean and lacking in a conscience. Dirk had an athletic body, but his muscles didn't bulge quite as much, and he struck her as a little quieter and less aggressive than most of the others. Even if he'd tried to step in to protect her—albeit for Spencer's sake, not hers—he'd have had the shit beaten out of him. Then Joe would have been mad.

Today, in between breakfast and lunch, Leah volunteered hastily for cleaning jobs that would keep her in the main spaces and working with at least one of the other women. There were four of them here, instead of five; TJ said Shelley wasn't feeling well.

Lifting benches around the table while Lisa Dempsey swept under them, Leah tried to start a conversation. If she made friends, she might learn something, right? Well, it wouldn't be with Lisa, who completely ignored her, responding only when Leah said something relevant, like, "I see something under there you missed."

She never looked Leah in the eye, either, which was a good reminder to her that she was supposed to imitate the other women, not befriend them.

Jennifer cracked briefly when Leah said, "That lasagna you made was amazing. You must have worked in a restaurant."

"Thank you," she said grudgingly. "I learned from my mother, that's all."

"Oh, well, I hope you have a daughter who'll learn from you."

Jennifer turned her back and walked away.

A few minutes later Helen whispered, "You shouldn't've said that to her. She's had miscarriages. I think—"

A footstep presaging the appearance of Del Schmidt silenced her.

Chagrined, Leah scraped frost out of the old chest freezer. Could Jennifer's body just not hold on to a fetus? One of the veterinarians Leah worked with had had two miscarriages. She and her husband had been devastated.

In this case, though, Leah couldn't help wondering whether abuse from her husband had ended each pregnancy. Maybe that was unjust, but she didn't like the way Tim talked to his wife, or how he'd shoved her hard up against a wall when he thought she was giving him some lip. It was all Leah could do to pretend she hadn't seen what happened.

Spencer was one of the last to show up for lunch, shredded beef tacos and Spanish rice today. He glanced at Leah when she was the last to sidle up to the table and take a seat, but he was immediately distracted by something the man beside him was saying. Shawn somebody. Or was that Brian… Thompson? Townsend? These guys looked an awful lot alike, all Caucasian although tanned, hair shaved or cut very short, big muscles, tattoos on their arms or peeking above their collars. Arne Larson's looked a lot like one arm of a Nazi swastika, which she thought was more than a little ironic, given how the Scandinavian countries had resisted the Nazi invasion. Obviously, he identified with the invaders and maybe even their genocide.

Leah had a sickening thought. What if her mother had married a black or Latino man? Things would have been different if she, a woman with dark skin, had driven up to announce that she owned the resort. Would Spencer have had any chance at all to save her?

No. How could he have? Higgs wouldn't have bothered giving her his impassioned speech about inciting a civil war to restore this great country to the *true* Americans, because she wouldn't have been one in his eyes.

Her appetite scant, she picked at her food and kept her head down by inclination as well as orders, not even looking toward Spencer.

Toward the end of the meal, though, she heard Tim Fuller say into a lull, "We're running low on food. Jennifer made a list."

Higgs mulled that over for a minute before saying, "Wyatt, you take Lisa tomorrow." He scanned the men around the table. "Schmidt, you go, too."

Leah didn't dare look at Spencer to see if he'd betrayed any emotion at all. She hoped she'd succeeded in hiding how she felt, but she was quite sure she wouldn't be able to take another bite, not when she couldn't swallow it. Fear squeezed her throat as if a powerful hand had closed around it.

HIGGS TURNED A cold stare on Spencer, who had stopped in front of him with crossed arms. The two men were on their way toward the obstacle course built their first week up here, taking in part of the meadow and forest. "I don't want to hear it."

Spencer said what he was thinking anyway. "You didn't like me taking Leah out of your control."

Frosting over, the colonel said, "*Nobody* here is out of my control. Did you forget that?"

He had, misjudging how Ed Higgs would see him stepping in to remove Leah from the chessboard. Damn, Spencer thought incredulously, he was going to have to take her and run, tonight while they still had a chance.

"Are you planning to have her yourself?" he asked.

Higgs's eyes narrowed. "I don't rape women."

"You just encourage your followers to do it."

"Is that what you think?"

Jaw jutting out, Spencer couldn't back down. "I think that's what you're threatening. Take me out of the picture, show me how I rate."

"I've developed a lot of respect for you. I thought I could trust you. Since you set eyes on her, I'm having to wonder."

What was it he'd said to Leah? *You have to become an Oscar-worthy actor.* That was it.

He scoffed, "You seriously think I'd let a sexy piece of tail divert me from our plans? I took her because I don't like doing without, and I figured I was entitled. If you want her—" *I'll have to kill you. Nope, shrug as if she's nothing to you.*

Higg's relaxation was subtle. "I don't."

"Then what's the problem?"

"The problem is you getting in my face because I chose you to run an errand and you don't want to do it because you're afraid someone will put a move on her in your absence."

"No," Spencer said coolly. "I'm afraid someone will think they can get away with taking what's mine, and then I'll have to kill him. You don't want to lose a soldier in our war, do you?"

"You said yourself, she doesn't matter worth shit," the colonel said impatiently. "What's your problem?"

"My problem is that I laid my reputation on the line. *That* matters to me. If you expect me to exert any authority over this bunch, it should matter to you, too. If someone hurts her and smirks at me when I get back tomorrow, what's it going to look like if I back down from what I promised?" He let that settle for a minute before shaking his head and raising an eyebrow. "I'm not willing to do that. I'll do your errands tomorrow, but if I find out anyone touched a hair on her head, there'll be violence. I'm just telling you, that's all. Don't be surprised."

Higgs muttered an obscenity. "Fine. I get it. I'll reinforce your message tomorrow. If that'll satisfy you, General?"

Spencer snapped a salute. "It's Captain, as you know quite well."

"I never could verify your service." This was an old complaint.

"The army can be secretive, even with an air force

lieutenant colonel. More so when it comes to the records of spec-ops soldiers."

"Especially snipers," Higgs grumbled. "I got nothing out of them at Fort Bennett."

"Well, it's not as if that's something I could fake," Spencer pointed out. "You want to get me a different rifle, I can make a kill shot from over a thousand feet out."

"Why not the rifle you're using?"

Spencer had said this before, but he didn't mind repeating himself. "The M82 loses accuracy over nine hundred yards. It's a mallet, not a stiletto."

"A mallet's what we want, and you're right. You've proved your abilities and more. I'd take one of you over ten of the rest of these grunts."

"They have their uses."

Higgs smiled. "Indeed they do."

Repelled by that smile, Spencer stifled his need to hear Higgs promise that they had a deal. Demanding any such thing would undo all the good he'd just accomplished.

If he had to kill someone tomorrow, he was prepared, but that would do shit for Leah.

His self-control was rarely strained, but as he held back a growl, he was freshly reminded that she'd put more than a few cracks in it.

SCUTTLING ALONG AT Spencer's shoulder in the morning, Leah asked, "Won't Higgs be outside most of the day, like usual?" Spencer hadn't wanted to talk about it last night. In fact, his mood had been foul.

"Probably." His long stride ate up the ground. "He promised to reinforce my message where you're concerned. He knows what will happen if anyone bothers you."

"Well, that's reassuring," she mumbled. Nothing like

knowing he'd take revenge for her, even if by then she was a bloody, bruised piece of pulp.

"Stick with the other women and you should be all right," he ordered before they reached the lodge and there was no more chance to talk.

Should was not the most reassuring word in this context.

Since she'd been designated cook for the first time this morning, she had to shove her worries to the back of her mind. With only a little advice on the quantities needed to feed nineteen men and five—no, four—women, she competently turned out pancakes and two platters piled with nice crisp bacon. Nobody said, "Hey, good job," but as they served the food she felt part of the quartet in a way she hadn't before.

Of course they'd pretend not to see if someone like Joe Osenbrock assaulted her in the middle of the kitchen.

During the meal Spencer ate mechanically, never so much as glancing at her. The table was barely cleared when he, Lisa and Del Schmidt went out the door. Feeling hollow, Leah pretended not to notice.

While the other men headed out for whatever training scheduled for today, Tim Fuller took up a position in the kitchen, his irritation plain.

Did he hate this detail? His wife seemed more self-effacing than usual, which made Leah suspect either he'd been posted out of rotation or was missing something especially fun—say, they were going to find out today what happened when they fired a rocket into a big pile of boulders.

Had they tried out their rocket launchers yet? They surely wouldn't dare shoot one upward. Wouldn't that be picked up on air force or civilian airport radars?

As she was setting the table for lunch, two men walked

in. Joe Osenbrock and Carson somebody, another look-alike. Joe's expression turned ugly as he looked at her.

"Coffee," he snapped.

She set down the pile of silverware on napkins and wordlessly returned to the kitchen.

"Joe and Carson want coffee," she said.

"I'll pour it," Helen offered.

Leah smiled weakly. "Thanks."

A minute later she set the mugs down in front of the two men, careful to follow Spencer's instructions. Head bowed, shoulders rounded, avoid meeting their eyes. She hoped they couldn't tell that her pulse was racing so fast she felt light-headed.

Neither thanked her, of course. Joe flicked a glance past her, as if checking to see whether anyone was watching.

Knowing she had no choice, she continued setting the table. She finished and headed for the kitchen just as she heard the front door open again, followed by a burst of voices. She hadn't realized Tim had come out to the dining room until she almost bumped into him.

He stopped her with one hand on her arm. "You're a lucky bitch," he murmured. "Don't count on that lasting."

Leah shuddered. The minute he released her, she hurried into the kitchen. Had he been assigned to watch out for her? Was that why he'd followed her from the kitchen...and why Joe had kept his distance?

Maybe...but she knew a threat when she heard one.

GETTING AWAY FROM Schmidt long enough to make a phone call wasn't easy, but Spencer managed. He'd ordered Schmidt to stay with Lisa while he used the john. Then he helped himself to a phone he had spotted at a momentarily empty cashier's station and took it down the hall toward the public restrooms, an office and what appeared to be an employee break room. It was likely password protected, of course, and he had a phone he could use, but he couldn't be a hundred percent sure that it was still secure. Even if it had been found, he doubted anyone in the group was sophisticated enough to know how to record his conversation or trace numbers he called, but better safe than sorry. If he could get away with borrowing—

Yes. He'd gotten lucky.

Thank God Ron answered. "Special Agent Ron Abram."

"This is Wyatt." No, that wasn't his name, but he didn't use his own name even in theoretically safe moments. He had to *think* of himself as Spencer Wyatt. "I've only got a minute."

"I'm glad you called. I've been worrying."

A woman emerged from the restroom, head bent over her own phone as she passed.

"I have problems," Spencer said. He summarized the events of the past few days, from Leah Keaton's arrival to the "deal" he'd made with Ed Higgs to ensure her safety. "Even though I don't want to quit until I have all the info we need, part of me wants to throw her in my SUV and take off. Trouble is, I'm not even betting we'd get away with that. Del Schmidt drove today. I'm wondering if I won't find the starter or alternator have kicked the bucket. Or worse, it runs for five minutes and then dies. As it is, Higgs keeps the keys when we're not using the vehicles."

"You're not driving today?"

"No. I wasn't given the option, which is one reason I suspect sabotage. By standing up for Leah, I awakened suspicion. Higgs has called me on it. I think I talked him around, but I can't be sure."

"If you have to cut and run, we'd have no choice but to raid the resort and pull the plug on the operation."

"Exactly." He watched two teenage boys laughing and bumping shoulders as they headed for the men's room. "Leah's smart. I think she can play her part for a few days. Higgs wants me with him for a meeting Saturday." The day after tomorrow. "I think it'll be a meet to acquire some new arms."

"That's worth holding out for," Abram said.

"I hate keeping a civilian in the mix," Spencer said.

Abram was quiet for a minute. "Damn. I wish you had a panic button."

"You and me both. I can't promise when I'll be able to call again." He saw a woman wearing a checker's nameplate at the cashier station where he'd swiped the phone. "Gotta go."

He quickly deleted a record of his call, shoved the phone in a pocket and strolled that way. Just as he reached it, he said, "Hey! Somebody lost a phone," and bent over, rising with it in his hand.

"Oh, thank goodness!" she exclaimed. "You'd think I'd have heard it drop."

"It's not damaged, is it?"

"Well, there's no crack anyway." She beamed. "Thank you."

"No problem."

When he rejoined Lisa and Del, now heaping packages of meat into one of the two carts, he asked, "We get any desserts? My sweet tooth has been aching."

Lisa almost forgot herself so much as to smile. "I'm supposed to pick up some flats of strawberries and blueberries for pies, and rhubarb for a cake."

"What about some apple pies? Let's get plenty of ice cream."

Nodding in agreement, Del said, "We need to load up on chips, too."

"I'm supposed to keep to a budget," she said nervously.

"If it looks like we're going to run over, I'll pick up the extra," Spencer said. "Remember, we're feeding another mouth, too." Even if Leah hadn't eaten enough to keep a bird alive, as far as he could see. He'd have to get on her about that.

"Thanks," Lisa said shyly. "I don't want to make anyone mad."

"I'll be mad if I don't get an apple pie," Spencer joked.

The mood stayed good as they shopped and then packed huge quantities of food in the rear and on one backseat of the big SUV. Spencer made sure neither of the others saw even a trace of his growing tension as they made the drive heading northeast on increasingly poor roads.

If he found Leah hurt, he wasn't sure he wouldn't grab the closest fully automatic weapon and start spraying bullets.

When at last they pulled up in front of the lodge, he hopped out, waited for the rear hatch to rise and grabbed bags of potatoes and a couple of flats of canned goods, then took the steps to the porch. He had to shift the load a little to reach the knob, shouldered the door open and walked in. The first person he saw was Joe Osenbrock, sitting beside Tim Fuller at the long table. Spencer clenched his teeth until his back molars hurt.

He passed the two without a word, without pausing long enough to read expressions, and went into the kitchen.

One of the other women was off to his right. He didn't even know which one. All he saw was Leah, turning from the sink, her hands encased in plastic gloves, a scrub brush held in one of them. The relief and something more that suffused her face did a number on him.

"Leah," he said hoarsely.

Can't drop my load and take her into my arms.

He couldn't even ask if she was all right. He hated that.

Her eyes widened at whatever she saw on his face. What she did was flush, draw a deep breath and say, "Oh, good. I was hoping potatoes were on the list. I'm not sure we have enough..." She bit her lip and ducked her head. "I'm sorry."

Sorry for? But he knew. Some men here would have backhanded her for that artless chatter, especially given the implication that he might have screwed up by not buying everything that was needed.

He tore his eyes from her, saw Jennifer watching them. "Where do you want this stuff?" he asked.

"Oh, in the pantry." Maybe reading his expression, she added hastily, "Or...anywhere is good. We can put everything away."

Footsteps behind him heralded Del's arrival with more food. On his heels, Lisa carried more than she should have to.

"Wherever is best," he said shortly, and went to the pantry.

As he made three more trips back and forth from the SUV, he couldn't help wondering what Jennifer thought she'd seen, and whether she talked to her husband. Or whether he listened to her if she did.

After depositing the last load, he said, "I hope dinner isn't far off. I'm starved."

It was Jennifer who answered, the tiniest edge in her voice. "No, not if Leah gets on with that potato salad."

"I'm hurrying," Leah said, sounding chastened.

Turning to stalk out of the kitchen, Spencer knew he'd be happy never to hear her sounding so diminished again.

But if they were going to hold out long enough for him to make this mission a success, that was one wish he wouldn't get.

Chapter Eight

They didn't talk during the walk back to the cabin. With the sun still high in the sky, it might have been midafternoon. Days were noticeably longer here than even in Portland, Oregon, she'd noticed.

Inside, Spencer did his usual walk-through, then said, "Waste of a goddamn day."

"We…we really were running out of food."

He made a rough sound. "Higgs should have sent Ritchie or Jack Jones."

Leah only vaguely knew who the second man was. Would Spencer dare talk like this if there was any chance at all of a listening device?

Maybe. This barely muted contempt went with the arrogance he projected so well. Deliberately, she thought. Higgs would expect it from him.

"I want apple pie tomorrow," he said. "See to it there is some."

Seeing her bristle, he winked.

In her best "I'm nobody important" tone, Leah said, "Jennifer makes up the menu. She doesn't like it when any of the rest of us make a suggestion."

"Tell her it's from me." He flat-out grinned now. "Lisa knows what I want."

Leah rolled her eyes.

Smile gone, he growled, "Did any of the men bother you today?"

"I… No."

His gaze bored into hers. "You're mine. If anyone so much as laid a hand on you…"

"No. I think they're all scared of you."

"They should be."

Neither of them had sat down. It was too early to go to bed. Leah felt restless and could tell he did, too, but they couldn't go for a walk every evening.

Eyes heavy lidded, he took a step toward her, his fingers flexing. The hunger on his face ignited her own. Leah swallowed. Sex was something they could do. In fact, if the cabin was being bugged, they definitely *should* be having sex. And if that wasn't an excuse, she'd never heard one before.

But he seemed to pull down a shutter, turning away from her and saying gruffly, "You have some books in your suitcase. Why don't you get one? I want to read before we go to bed."

Would anybody buy that? But she knew; he didn't really believe there was a bug, he was just being cautious. She should be grateful he wasn't the kind of man who would use "we need to convince any listener" as an excuse to get her naked.

So she only nodded, went to the bedroom and grabbed one of the books at random. She didn't want to read; she wanted to hear whether he'd had a chance to call his office today and, if so, what he'd learned. She wanted to tell him about the threat issued by Tim, and about the inimical way he and Joe Osenbrock had stared at her. She wanted to know what his lips would feel like on hers.

And she wanted desperately to know when he thought

they could leave—if there was any way they could without getting killed.

But he'd finally lowered himself to one side of the futon, stacked his booted feet on the scarred coffee table and opened his book. He appeared to immediately immerse himself.

Leah sat at the other end of the futon, which really meant she could have stretched out an arm and touched him, and opened her own book. She read a few pages, realized she hadn't taken in a thing, and turned back to start over. She thought the one side of his mouth she could see curled up. So he wasn't any deeper in the biography than she was in the romance she'd picked up.

The next hour dragged. She read, reread and finally plunked the book down without bothering to save her place. She was going crazy here, and Spencer continued to read as if unaware of her. She felt quite sure that wasn't true.

Her mind wandered.

He hadn't answered her question about his name. She *liked* the name Spencer Wyatt. What if his real name was something like…she entertained herself by coming up with a list of not-so-sexy possibilities. Elmer. Homer. Barney. Cornelius. Wilbur.

All names, she realized, that would have been her grandparents' or even great-grandparents' generation. If she'd been born then and *her* name was Dolly or Kitty or…or Winnie, she'd probably have been fine with Barney.

The name Barney wouldn't reduce the man beside her in any way, she admitted to herself in dismay. She couldn't think of much that would.

I can't fall in love with him, she thought in shock. What a ridiculous idea. This gooey mess of emotions in her were completely natural, considering he'd dedicated himself to saving her life and virtue. And *that* was a silly way to think of a vicious crime like rape.

She sighed. She couldn't exactly whine that she was bored.

Only, she didn't want to know when they'd get there; she wanted to know when they could *leave*.

"Why don't you go take a shower?" he said irritably.

"Fine." Leaving her book where it lay, Leah stomped into the bedroom, grabbed clean clothes and went straight to the bathroom without so much as looking in his direction.

The fixtures were all chipped and stained, but they worked. At least she'd be bored *and* clean.

Or scared for her life and clean.

She was sitting on the toilet to take off her shoes and socks and tug her shirt over her head when the bathroom door opened again, almost bumping her knees in the tight space. Startled, she looked up at Spencer.

He crowded her even more to allow him to shut the door behind himself. Then he squeezed past her and turned on the shower.

"What…?" she whispered.

He crouched in front of her. For a second she fixated on the power of his forearms before being distracted by the long muscles in his thighs outlined with the camouflage fabric pulled tight. Then she lifted her gaze to meet his eyes.

"I thought we should talk," he said in a low voice. "I worried about you all day."

"I really am fine. There was only one weird moment." She told him about Joe and Carson coming in, the glance Joe exchanged with Tim and then what Tim had said.

"That son of a bitch threatened you."

"It wasn't that overt. I mean, he didn't say, 'I'll hurt you.' It was more like, 'Next time I won't stop Joe.'"

"I still want to shove his teeth down his throat." Spencer rolled his shoulders. "Damn. Saturday I'll be gone part of the day again."

A greasy ball lodged in her stomach. "Why?"

"Don't know for sure. Higgs asked me to accompany him for a 'meet.'"

"To buy weapons?"

"That's what I think."

The pale silver of his eyes was almost like glass, except not so transparent. Quartz crystal. Shimmering, clear, but still hiding the secrets inside.

"That was one of your goals, wasn't it?"

"Yeah." He cleared his throat. "But I'm asking a lot of you."

What if she said, *Too much?* Could she persuade him to take her and leave? Leah didn't know for sure, but thought he might choose her if she begged.

It took her only a moment to steady herself. "What you're doing is important. If all goes well, you'll prevent a cataclysmic attack on this country." If her voice shook a little, well, who could blame her? "It's my country, too. What's more, anybody stealing weapons bought with my and every other American's tax dollars needs to be locked up for good."

She'd swear that was pride in his eyes. He lifted a hand to her face, gently cupped the injured cheek and said, "You're an amazing woman, Leah Keaton."

Her tremulous smile probably didn't enhance the kick-butt speech, but it *was* a smile. "And don't I know it."

Now he grinned openly. "Pretty bra, too."

"What?" She looked down at herself and felt her face

heat. The vivid green satin probably made her skin look pasty, but she liked the color.

If she wasn't mistaken, his gaze lingered on the swell of her breasts above the fabric, not the bra. He was so close, his hand still holding her jaw, his face nearly level with hers. If she scooted forward…

His pale eyes speared hers. "I won't do that to you." Low, his voice was even grittier than usual.

"Even if I want you to?"

"Even if. You know the balance of power thing. It's swinging heavily in my favor right now."

Leah couldn't deny that was true. But… "I know what I want."

He rose to his feet, letting her see his arousal, but his gaze never left hers. "I want, too," he said quietly. "But we can wait."

She managed a nod, and he left the bathroom.

Did they *have* enough future to allow for some distant, ideal day? she asked herself. But…he was right. Of course he was. What if they triumphed and made it out of here and then she realized she didn't really like him that well? Mightn't she question whether she'd used her body as bribery so he'd keep her at the top of his priority list?

And no, she didn't think he was that man, or she was that woman.

Maybe what she needed to do was believe in him and herself. Believe they'd make it.

She could do that…but she was more aroused than she could ever remember being just from a touch, an exchange of looks.

NOW THAT SPENCER knew Leah was willing, he didn't know if he could survive many more nights with full-body contact but him blocked from being able to make a single move. He seriously considered sleeping on the futon, but that would be as torturous in a different way. He still had the original issues, too: he didn't want to be seen sleeping separately from her, and he didn't like the idea of her alone, a room away from him.

Her cheeks were pink when they met in the bedroom, but she wore a long T-shirt over panties that did a number on his libido, slipped into bed and turned her back on him without saying anything.

Spencer swore silently, set his gun within easy reach and stripped down to his own boxers and T-shirt. He turned his back on her, too.

It was not a good night. Far as he could tell, Leah slept better than he did. He couldn't get comfortable, couldn't control his body's reaction to having hers pressed against him, and when he wasn't brooding about why he hadn't taken her up on her offer, he worried about Saturday.

If Tim's suggestion to her meant what Spencer thought it might, she could be in big trouble. Individually, they were all afraid of him, and rightly so. But what if, when he returned, he wouldn't be facing a single man, but several? Would Higgs intervene, or let them tear him up? If he did step in, would the simmer of resentment boil over?

Did Higgs know a couple of the guys were cocky enough to think they could take his place?

Spencer knew he had allies, guys that were glad he could hold the vicious ones in check. Joe Osenbrock, Tim Fuller, TJ Galt and Arne Larson weren't popular with the rank and file. The question was, how many of the others would have the will and guts to stand up with him?

Who should he talk to before he left Saturday with Higgs? Or was there someplace he could stash her before he left? She probably knew this mountainside better than any of them did. She might have an idea.

But then, could he afford the fallout from her temporary disappearance?

Spencer groaned and rolled over again.

One day, a lot of decisions to make—and another night tucked into bed beside Leah.

THE FOLLOWING EVENING, as they left the lodge after dinner, he said curtly, "We're taking a walk." Well aware several men were within earshot, Spencer ignored them. Beside him, Leah ducked her head and nodded.

He strolled down the line of cabins, Leah keeping up. A single sidelong glance let him see her bewilderment.

"What will they think about us doing this?"

He used an obscenity to tell her how little he cared. He *should* care; he and Leah had been so careful to fly under the radar. Somehow, today, he'd met his breaking point.

Leah looked alarmed but was smart enough to say nothing.

When they reached the meadow of wildflowers, he pointed at one with deep pink, almost bell-shaped flowers. "You know that one?"

"Um...a penstemon, I think. There are clumps of hybrid penstemons in my mother's garden."

Last time they were here, he hadn't noticed the faint trace of a path. Left from the days when the resort would have been filled with guests? He followed it toward the lake.

"What did you want to tell me?" Leah asked.

He appreciated her directness.

"I want to talk about tomorrow, but I needed to get away," he admitted.

"Oh. Me, too."

"Everything okay today?"

"Sure. It was a relief having Dirk there again."

"You're getting Del tomorrow. I don't think he'll bother you."

She didn't say anything, but Spencer knew what she was thinking. Would Del stand up to any of the dangerous men on her behalf? Why would he?

Spencer asked himself again if he was doing the right thing. He didn't know any of the potential victims of the planned attack. He knew, liked, admired, wanted Leah. She was the first woman in years who'd gotten to him like this, and he'd only known her for a matter of days. Maybe it was her spirit, relentless in the face of adversity. Or her courage, facing up to dangerous men while suppressing her fears. She'd sure as hell complicated his life. If they had the chance, he could see being happy to have her go right on doing just that.

"Once you sell this place, what'll you do with the money?" he asked, going for the positive. The question was out of the blue, but he was hungry for a few minutes of normalcy. At least, what he vaguely remembered as normalcy.

Obviously surprised, Leah stayed quiet for a minute. Then she said, "I want to go back to school to become a veterinarian. I'd have done that instead of training as a vet tech, except the idea of graduating with such a massive load of debt is really daunting. I'm pretty sure I have the grades and now the experience to be accepted. The money…would make a difference."

"Your parents can't help?"

"I don't want to ask. Mom's a teacher and Dad works for our local utility district. They make a decent living, but they're not rich. They put me through college, and now they should be saving for retirement."

"You intend to specialize as a veterinarian?"

"I don't know. Surgery fascinates me, and I think I'd

get bored if I had to do spays and neuters all day, even if they're important." She shrugged. "One step at a time."

Unfortunately, her next step wouldn't be talking to a real estate agent or filling out graduate school applications.

He said gruffly, "I never asked whether you have a boyfriend."

Leah shook her head. "It's been a while. What about you? I suppose it's hard, given your job."

He fixed his gaze on the mountain, gleaming white, somehow pure. "Next to impossible."

"I don't believe that," she said stoutly. When he didn't say more, she asked, "Was becoming an FBI agent always your dream?"

Dream? Spencer wasn't sure he'd ever had one, the way she meant. Given his lousy mood, that struck him as sad.

He didn't love talking about himself, but he owed her. No, he corrected himself immediately; if he had any thought of pursuing these unexpected feelings for her, he had to open up, at least partway.

"My goal was to get away from home." He hoped she couldn't hear the sadness. "My father and I butted heads for as long as I can remember. I think he loved me—loves me—but his way of showing it was by being a harsh disciplinarian. I joined the army two days after my high school graduation. Barely looked back."

They'd reached the lake now, the surface of the water utterly still, mirroring the rich blue of the sky. Some plants that probably thrived in wetter conditions grew on the shores, but he didn't ask about them.

"I spent ten years in the army." Too much of it killing people. "Got my college degree along the way. A friend who'd left earlier suggested I apply to the FBI, too. I was feeling less sure that the US military was accomplishing anything. I thought I might do more coming at problems from a different direction."

"Isn't one of their biggest divisions counterterrorism?"

"Yeah, I'm in domestic counterterrorism. Unfortunately, we never have the chance to get bored."

"You said you've done this before."

"Gone undercover? Oh, yeah. I'm good at it." His struggles this time all had to do with her.

"I can't imagine living under that kind of stress."

"Right now you are," he pointed out.

She made a face. "That's why I know I wouldn't like it long-term."

"This may be my last time," he heard himself say. "I've almost forgotten who I am."

Ignoring her role, Leah reached for his hand and squeezed.

He turned his body to block anybody watching through binoculars from seeing the physical contact. When she started to withdraw her hand, he held on.

Her cheeks turned pink, but she didn't look away from him. "To me, you're a hero. That's a good place to start."

Spencer shook his head. "Undercover, you get your hands dirty. It's too easy to forget the moral standards you began with. That's one reason—" He broke off. "If I'm ever going to have a life outside the bureau, I figure I ought to get on with it. I'm thirty-seven."

They had reached the edge of the forest on the far side of the lake. His gaze strayed to shadowy coves between tall fir and cedar trees. It wouldn't be such a sin to draw her out of sight and kiss her, would it? If things went south tomorrow… But he refused to think like that. No reason to believe anyone would be stupid enough to attack Leah. He'd made himself clear enough. And what he'd told her last night would hold true until they got free of this bunch. What if she kissed him back mostly because right now she needed him desperately?

Shoring up the walls of his reserve, he released her hand but moved to face her. "Let's talk about tomorrow," he said. "I'd rather you follow your usual routine, but do you know anyplace you could hide if necessary?"

"Now I wish I hadn't given away the hidey-holes between the closets."

He wished she hadn't, either. "No other secret passages in the lodge?"

Leah shook her head. "If I could get as far as the tree line..."

"That would work only if you had a serious head start. Otherwise, they'd be on you like a pack of wolves."

Seeing her already creamy white skin blanch, he was sorry he'd been so blunt, but she needed to know what she faced.

He'd ruled out giving her his backup gun. It would be a disaster if anyone noticed her carrying. He'd also had to consider whether, in a struggle, she could bring herself to pull the trigger quick enough, or at all. However courageous, Leah was at heart a gentle woman, if he was reading her right. Even if she did manage to shoot and kill or at least disable her assailant, then what would happen? He didn't have a suppressor fitted to either of his handguns. The sound of a shot in the vicinity of the lodge versus at the range would bring everyone running.

"Chances are good I'll only be gone for a few hours. Nobody has said anything, so I don't think the rest know Higgs and I are going anywhere tomorrow. I'd try to get you the key to my SUV, but I can't think how to check it out for sabotage without drawing notice."

She was shaking her head even as he spoke. "Even if

I could take off...what would happen to you when you get back?"

"That doesn't matter."

Her expression turned mutinous. "I'm not going to just run away and desert you."

"Leah." Unable to help himself, he took her hand again. "If you ever see an opportunity—a good one—take it. Let me worry about myself. You got that?"

She searched his eyes in that way she did, undoubtedly seeing more than he wanted her to. Finally, she said, "I'll think about it."

Always stubborn.

"You do that," he murmured, and turned away to resume their walk.

Chapter Nine

"Turn in here." Higgs leaned forward, the action pulling against his seat belt. "Go around behind the building."

The long, ramshackle log structure along the old highway might once have been a restaurant or tavern. "What's this place?" Spencer asked as he braked and turned into a weedy gravel lot.

"Somebody told me it was a visitor's center back in the fifties or sixties. Then a restaurant and gift shop." The older man shrugged. "Not sure what else. Not a lot of traffic up this way anymore."

The reason this meeting had been set for here.

Given how little traffic he'd seen in miles, he was surprised the highway was maintained this well. About all he'd seen in ten miles or more was beautiful forest, a waterfall plunging off a cliff only feet from the road and moss and ferns everywhere. Pale, lacy lichen draped like tinsel over branches. When they first set off, mist had clung in dips of the road, blurring the outlines of the evergreens. Half an hour ago they'd risen above it.

Spencer tensed as he drove around the building and saw a pickup already here, parked facing out. It was a dually built for especially heavy loads; black plastic tarps crisscrossed with cord hid whatever was being hauled in the full bed.

"Park so we can load easily," the colonel suggested.

As he backed in, two men climbed out of the pickup, slamming their doors. Even before he saw faces, he noted both men were armed. Of course Spencer was, too, and he felt sure Higgs was, as well.

Turning off the engine and setting the emergency brake, he was slower getting out than Higgs was. He and the older of the two men were already shaking hands when Spencer walked forward.

He knew that face. It set off alarms in him, even if a name to go with it didn't come to him immediately. He just needed to figure out the context where he'd seen the guy before—or his photograph.

Photograph, he decided. In his line of work, he studied thousands. Soon, he'd have a name to go with that face.

The high and tight haircut on the younger man looked military. His scrutiny suggested he, too, was trying to fit Spencer's face into a context. The older guy's was more buzz-cut, graying like Higgs's hair. Same generation, sure as hell their paths had crossed during their military careers. Both, maybe, getting more and more dissatisfied with the direction their country was going as gay marriage became approved, a black man was elected president of the United States and now women wearing hijabs had been elected to congress.

They'd believe passionately that the violent mission they'd chosen was patriotic. Spencer didn't see any hint of deference between them. They saw themselves as equals, he decided. The younger guy was just muscle. Hey, maybe that was all Higgs considered Spencer to be, too.

Spencer exchanged nods with both. The closest to an introduction came when Higgs said, "My second-in-command." Two pairs of eyes raked him appraisingly. He lifted his eyebrows but didn't otherwise react.

"Let's get this done," Higgs's buddy said.

Spencer unlocked and opened the rear doors on the Suburban. Evaluating the load, he thought it would fit. Then he joined the younger guy in pulling the cord off so the tarps could be removed.

This was just like Christmas Day, he thought sardonically. What would be inside the wrapping?

THAT MORNING LEAH and the other women hadn't even started clearing the table before Colonel Higgs swung his legs over the bench and said, "I'll be running an errand."

Everyone around the table looked startled, except for Spencer, of course. He nodded. "Shall I drive?"

Higgs took a set of keys from his pocket and tossed them to Spencer. "We'll take my Suburban. It has more hauling capacity."

Spencer gave a clipped nod, took a last swallow of coffee and rose to leave with Higgs. His gaze passed over Leah without pausing on her, but she made a determined effort to hold on to this last sight of his face as if she'd taken a snapshot.

None of the men moved until they heard the engine start outside. Tim Fuller looked at her.

"Where are they going?"

"I don't know," she said softly. "He doesn't tell me anything."

Every man in the room was staring at her. The effect was unnerving, making it easier to act scared. She stood up and began gathering dirty dishes.

"We're running low on some of the ammunition," one of the men she didn't really know commented.

"He's been promising a new rifle the army is supposed

to be testing. I wouldn't mind getting my hands on that." Brian Townsend.

They threw out wilder and wilder ideas. But when somebody said "bomb," a deafening silence ensued. Apparently, there were some things they weren't supposed to talk about in front of the women.

Leah had been pushing through the swinging kitchen door and hoped they all thought she'd already gone back into the kitchen. Carrying a teetering load of dirty plates, Helen was right on her heels. Leah set down her pile, then took some of Helen's.

Jennifer clapped her hands. "Let's hurry! Along with lunch, we should do some baking."

By all means. Bake goodies while the men planned to build bombs.

Not waiting to be assigned a task, Leah filled the sink with hot, soapy water and began washing while the others brought in the remaining dirty dishes and Lisa carried a coffeepot out to top off mugs.

Leah let most of the talk about the menu go over her head, but when the women turned to discussing what to bake, she decided to volunteer. Staying in the kitchen, in company with other women, would be smart today.

"I make a really good apple-raisin cake." She suggested they think about picking huckleberries, too, currently ripe. "They're as good or better than blueberries, and they'd stretch our supplies."

Picking huckleberries would give her a reason to be well away from the lodge, too. She might be able to give herself a significant—no *serious*—head start. Wasn't that how Spencer had put it? She couldn't help remembering the rest of what he'd said, too.

If you ever see an opportunity—a good one—take it.

Let me worry about myself. The ache in her chest told her it wouldn't be that easy.

"I'll ask Tim," Jennifer said briskly.

Leah only nodded. She wasn't sure she'd ever been truly timid a day in her life, and she could only hope all this deference didn't get to be a habit.

Finished with the dishes, she joined the other women in the baking, putting together a double recipe of her apple-raisin cake while they worked on blueberry pies.

After lunch Jennifer reported that Tim said they could maybe pick berries tomorrow, but not today.

Damn.

She assigned Leah to mop the floor in the main room. She was to do beneath the table by hand, Jennifer said firmly.

The scarred fir planks really needed a new finish. After this many years, the original varnish had been almost entirely worn away. Soap and water weren't really good for the wood, she couldn't help thinking, in one of those absurd moments. Because, gee, did it really matter if the floor rotted and collapsed? As things stood—no.

At least the task shouldn't leave her isolated. Helen had to clean the downstairs bathroom today, Lisa to sweep the front and back porches and clean the mudroom. Jennifer intended to reorganize the pantry and continue baking.

The benches pulled out, Leah was underneath the table on her hands and knees when she saw Del go into the kitchen and let the door swing shut behind him. On a sudden chill, she stopped scrubbing. From here, she couldn't hear voices in the kitchen. He'd probably gone out the back to check on Lisa, she realized. He might stay there for a few minutes talking to her. Helen, here in the lodge, wasn't that far away, but more sweet than a lioness at heart.

Leah made herself get back to work. Any minute Del would return as part of his appointed rounds. Anyway, the men were all too scared of Spencer to mess with him. She'd *seen* Joe back down. Still, she listened hard for any sound at all.

Like the sound of the lodge door opening. She froze. Del might have circled around. That would make sense—

Booted footsteps approached. From her low vantage point, Leah peered out. This wasn't Del, who wore the ubiquitous desert camo today with desert tan boots. This man had on black boots with heavy cleats and forest-green camouflage cargo pants.

Joe Osenbrock.

Staying as utterly still as a mouse that had seen a hawk's shadow nearing, she even held her breath. Did he see her beneath the table?

Who was she kidding? How could he miss her bucket filled with soapy water and probably her lower legs? In fact, he walked right to her.

"Alone at last," he gloated.

Go with ignorance. "Who's there?" She dropped the sponge in the bucket and turned to sit on her butt facing the threat. "Joe? Do you want a cup of coffee?"

"You know what I want."

Maybe she ought to hold to her timid—now terrified—persona, but she couldn't make herself. Still unable to see his face, she said, "Have you forgotten what Spencer said?"

"He's not going to mess with our team. What we're planning is more important than any piece of ass," he scoffed. "He told Higgs that himself." He crouched to look straight at her. "Don't kid yourself that he gives a damn about you."

"I don't." Scared as she was, Leah knew her chin jutted out at a defiant angle. "But I know he *does* care about his reputation. You'd be a fool to challenge him."

Seeing the fury on his face, she knew she'd just made a big mistake. *She'd* issued a challenge. To save face, now he almost had to rape her and face down Spencer. What she'd forgotten was that Spencer wasn't the only one to value his tough-as-nails reputation.

Lightning quick, Joe grabbed her ankles and wrenched her toward him. Leah screamed and grabbed for purchase, not finding anything. Her butt slid on the wood floor. No, there was the bucket. Even as he was still dragging her forward, she snatched it up and flung the water, followed by the bucket, too, in his face.

Joe bellowed and momentarily let her go. Maybe the soap stung his eyes. Leah seized the chance to scramble backward, desperate to come out the other side of the table within reach of the kitchen.

Water dripping from his hair and face, he ducked to grab her again. His head clunked against the edge of the table. By now he was yelling a string of invectives.

At that moment the swinging door slapped open and she heard the thud of running footsteps. Whimpering, Leah crawled out from the shelter of the heavy table right beside Del.

He didn't even look at her. His hand rested on the butt of his pistol, though. Beyond him, Jennifer hovered in the doorway, watching.

Joe snarled as he rose to his feet. "Get out of here."

Leah hardly dared take her eyes off Joe, but she turned her head anyway to see Del. What if he shrugged and walked back into the kitchen?

But his hard gaze stayed on Joe and he said, "No. She's Spencer's girl. You got no right."

"He had no right to snatch her away right out from under our noses."

Del's expression didn't change. "You could have done something then. You didn't."

Joe's eyes narrowed to mean slits. "You calling me a coward?" And—oh, God—his hand slid toward the butt of *his* gun.

"That's not what I said."

Preparing to drop to the floor at any sudden movement, Leah hoped Jennifer was smart enough to fade back into the kitchen. Couldn't they feel the tension?

As the two men held a staring contest, she prayed for Spencer to appear. He hadn't expected to be gone long, and it had already been at least four hours.

Joe said in a low growl, "Butt out of this, Schmidt. She's not your business."

"My job today is to watch out for the women. All I'm saying is, you need to take this up with Spencer, not sneak behind his back."

"You and who else will stop me?"

That should have sounded childish, but didn't. The threat of violence had a weight; it raised prickles on the back of her neck. These men wouldn't take a few swings at each other. They'd pull semiautomatic weapons and start shooting. Killing.

Over her.

Would either of them notice if she eased back until she could dart for the kitchen? And would that do any good if Del lost this confrontation?

A man's voice came from the kitchen. Then heavy footsteps. Two men walked in. Jennifer was no longer visible.

Shawn Wycoff, tall, lean and blond, was accompanied by another of the men who'd so far remained anonymous to Leah. He didn't say much around the table, and like too many of the others, was distinguished by a shaved head, a powerful build and full-sleeve tattoos.

When the men took up positions to each side of Del, Leah did edge backward.

The guy she didn't know was the one to say, "What's this about?"

"None of your goddamn business!" Joe snapped. "Get lost."

"He wants Leah," Del said, not taking his eyes off Joe. "I told him to take it up with Spencer, face-to-face, not stab him in the back."

"What's he done to you anyway?" Shawn asked.

"He's suddenly giving us orders? Where was he six months ago? Where'd he come from? Does anybody even *know*?" Joe asked.

No-name said with surprising calm, "I'm betting Colonel Higgs does, or he wouldn't be here. And the only orders he's given are during training. The guy can shoot like no one else I've ever seen, and I had two deployments. I hear while he served he was spec ops. You don't think you can learn from him?"

Joe made a disgusted noise. "He's so sold on himself, I wouldn't be surprised if he didn't make up that shit."

"You think the army would keep a guy who can make his shot from a thousand yards plus as a regular grunt?"

Joe let them know, obscenely, that none of that mattered. Spencer had overstepped himself when he claimed exclusive rights over the only decent-looking woman any of them had seen in six weeks or more.

"Del doesn't have to do without." He was trying for persuasive, which scared Leah enough to have her inching back again.

Should have gone sooner. Should have run for it.

"What say the three of us have a good time? I mean, come on. What's Spencer going to do? Take us all on?" He grinned. "I've seen you looking, Wycoff. You can't tell me you haven't." He tipped his chin at the other man. "You, too, Zeigler."

Zeigler shook his head. "Not me."

"Looking ain't the same thing as taking," Shawn Wycoff told him. His lip curled. "*I* can get women without raping them."

By goading such an unstable man and appearing to enjoy doing so, Shawn might as well have lit the fuse on a stick of dynamite.

Joe's face turned ugly again with a snarl. "You saying I can't?"

"I'm not saying nothing, 'cept Del's right. Take it up with Wyatt. We're teammates. We gotta trust each other. That's the right thing to do."

Hear, hear! Except the idea of Joe Osenbrock "taking it up" with Spencer scared her. He hated Spencer and would kill him in a second, if he could.

Before, he hadn't had the guts to face off with him. After this standoff, with not one but three of the other men looking at him with doubt, he'd think he had no choice.

And, oh, dear God, did she hear a vehicle outside?

FOLLOWING ORDERS, SPENCER drove around behind the lodge to the sturdy outbuilding that served as their armory. It was a natural. Constructed of logs, too, it appeared to have been added some years after the lodge and cabins had been built, which meant it was solid. Even the shake roof was in good shape. Mostly empty when they first opened it up, it had held only a few chainsaws, a heavy-duty weed whacker, assorted hand tools and an old Jeep with a custom-mounted snowplow. A quiet guy named Jason Shedd had given the Jeep a lube job and oil change, replaced a few belts and gotten the thing running. It was too small to be of much use, but Spencer figured you never knew. He'd been thinking a lot about that Jeep in recent days. The key hung on a string from a nail just inside the rusting steel garage-style door.

The trick was that a heavy hasp and padlock on the door ensured it could only be opened by Higgs, a fact that pissed off some of the men. The ones who'd begun to question his leadership.

Spencer really wanted to get his hands on that key.

Now he backed the Suburban up to the outbuilding door, set the emergency brake and turned off the ignition.

"I'll look inside and see if anyone's there to help us unload," he said, careful to betray none of the edginess he felt.

"Do that." Higgs reached for the door handle.

Spencer crossed the twenty-five yards to the back door into the lodge with long strides. His nerves had been buzzing since they left this morning. Pretending he was unconcerned had taken everything he had. There wouldn't be any relief for him until he saw Leah unhurt, safe.

The unlocked door opened into a mudroom and then the kitchen. Lisa and Jennifer hovered just outside the entry into the pantry, their anxiety palpable.

His heart lurched. Ignoring them, he walked quietly to the swinging door that stood open.

Before he reached it, voices came to him.

"I'll wait." Joe Osenbrock. His voice turned vicious. "But sweetheart, I'll win. I know better than him how to treat a woman."

"Gee, that might be why you're so desperate," Leah said flippantly.

Spencer hoped no one else heard the slight tremor in her voice.

One part of his tension abated. She was still on her feet swinging, which meant she had to be all right.

The ugly epithet from Joe sent Spencer into another state of being, one all too familiar. He felt…very little. Combat ready, he walked into the dining room just as something big crashed.

On the far side of the table, Joe must have just picked up and thrown one of the long benches. He stood above it with his teeth showing, breathing hard, face flushed with rage.

Only a few feet from Spencer, her back to him, Leah faced Joe…as did three men, all in battle stance, hands hovering over their guns.

Voice arctic, Spencer announced his presence. "Seems I missed some excitement."

Chapter Ten

Leah and two of the three men spun to face him. Del Schmidt had the presence of mind to keep his attention on the armed idiot throwing a temper tantrum.

Both gladness and fear shone from Leah. He wanted her to fly into his arms, but at the same time he hoped she'd know better than to do that. They needed to maintain their cover—and he needed to keep his mind on what was coming.

The two men looked relieved at the sight of him. From the sweat and dirt coating them, it appeared Garrett Zeigler and Shawn Wycoff had just come from running the obstacle course.

Harder to tell with Joe. He was either sweat-soaked or had dunked his head under running water.

Spencer nodded at the two backing up Del. He didn't like owing any of this bunch, but this was different. "Thank you."

Garrett Zeigler's lip curled as he glanced over his shoulder. "He thinks he can take you," he said quietly enough not to be heard by Joe.

"He can try." Would he really have to kill Osenbrock? Yeah. Probably. "Higgs and I need help unloading."

Quick as a rattlesnake striking, Joe started to pull his weapon. In the blink of an eye, Spencer had his own in his hand. "I wouldn't mind blowing your head off, and you know I don't miss."

Joe's face went slack with momentary fear, but he blustered, "Hand to hand. Winner takes Leah." His eyes slid to Leah, who looked strong in spirit but physically fragile as she stood with head high and expression defiant.

Not seeing a way out, Spencer inclined his head, even as he held his Sig Sauer in a two-handed stance aimed at Joe Osenbrock's heart. "Tomorrow morning. In the meantime, put that gun down. You've shown us all you're not trustworthy." Seeing such hate in another man's eyes disturbed Spencer, even as he stayed cold inside.

When Joe didn't move, Spencer said, "Del?"

The other man walked around the table. "He's right, Joe. Give it to me. You can have it back later."

That burning stare turned briefly to Del. "I won't forget this."

"Let me have it."

Spencer took a step closer, making sure even Osenbrock couldn't miss his deadly intent.

With a jerky, furious motion, Joe yanked the handgun the rest of the way from the holster and slapped it on Del's outstretched hand. Then he wheeled around and stormed out of the lodge.

There was immediately relaxation in his wake, although Spencer didn't share it. Joe probably had half a dozen more weapons stockpiled in his cabin. Whether he'd go get one and commit cold-blooded murder in front of his fellow "soldiers" was another matter. This was all about ego, and if he really wanted respect, he had to make the fight seem aboveboard.

Spencer straightened and reholstered his own gun. "Higgs must be wondering where I am. Let's go unload," he said as if nothing had happened.

Leah stood ten feet away, her face parchment-pale, her eyes dilated. Her hands were clenched in small fists. He wanted to know everything that had happened, how it was that not only Del had stepped in, but the other two men, as well. But that had to wait. Right now appearances were everything.

"Don't you have a job to do?" he asked.

Some emotion flew across her face, too fast to read, which was just as well considering they weren't alone. She nodded, but also stole a look toward the front door.

"Del," Spencer said. "Can you stay?"

"That's the plan."

"I need to refill the bucket," she said tightly.

"Throwing it at him was smart," Del said unexpectedly, addressing Spencer rather than her. Still, he'd gained some respect for her, which might or might not be good.

So the bucket hadn't spilled because someone tripped over it. A pail full of soapy water explained Joe's dripping wet hair, and some of his temper, too.

Ignoring all the men, Leah circled around the table and picked up the bucket, then trailed Spencer, Zeigler and Wycoff into the kitchen. As she went to the sink, the other two women stared at the men.

Walking out the back door and across the bare yard to the Suburban with Zeigler and Wycoff, Spencer asked, "How'd you two get mixed up in that?"

"Del sent Lisa to get help. We were, ah, heading up to the lodge to take a break."

Shawn grinned. "What he means is, the women did some baking this morning. Blueberry pie and an apple-raisin cake. Decided we needed seconds."

"I'll look forward to dessert tonight."

Higgs had the garage door lifted and the back of the Suburban open. "What took so long?" he grumbled.

"Osenbrock was up to the same crap," Spencer said as if unconcerned. "These guys and Schmidt told him he had to take it up with me."

Higgs's attention sharpened. "He attacked Leah?"

"Appears so. She fought back. Del came running. He sent Lisa to get these two."

The colonel flicked a glance at the other two men, then leveled a steady look at Spencer. "Can you handle him?"

"We agreed to hand to hand in the morning." He nodded at the packed rear of the SUV. "Let's get this done. Be careful. Some of the boxes are heavier than they look."

He wasn't sure what was in all the boxes, except the one crate he'd watched Higgs inspect. It held at least a dozen rifles. Markings on some of the boxes indicated they were the property of the US Government. A lot of those contained ammunition to replace what they'd used. Then there was the something mysterious that had had Higgs and his confederate talking quietly for quite a while.

Given half a chance, Spencer intended to find out what other weapon had just been handed to a bunch of alt-right nutjobs.

The men worked in silence, Higgs directing where he wanted each box put.

"Getting crowded in here," Wycoff remarked at one point.

Higgs frowned at the Jeep. "We can move it out of here if we have to."

Spencer liked the idea but didn't want to go on record saying so. Even if the key stayed on the nail inside the armory, he was confident he could hot-wire a vehicle as old as this one. The Jeep was a standard CJ-5, probably dating to the sixties or seventies.

Five minutes later Spencer turned with deliberate incaution and bumped into Zeigler, who bashed a hip into a sharp corner of the old Jeep. Cursing, he barely held on to the box he carried.

"Oh, hell," Spencer said. "I'm sorry."

"Let's get the damn thing out of there." Higgs took care of moving it himself, parking it to one side of the armory. "We can throw a tarp over it if it looks like rain."

"I wonder if you could sell it to some classic car buff?" Wycoff suggested.

Spencer laughed. "I doubt you could give it away. You know how common these were?"

"Yeah." Wycoff studied the rusting metal and tattered remnants of a canvas cover that had snapped on. "It's no beauty, I'll give you that."

They continued to work. Once the Suburban was empty, Spencer moved it to its usual parking spot out front of the lodge and handed the keys to Higgs.

The two men were now alone.

"Osenbrock is becoming a problem," Higgs remarked.

"Becoming? He's an arrogant hothead."

The boss grunted. "I'd boot his ass out, except that would mean turning him loose. Resentment and a big mouth make for a dangerous mix."

"He's a fighter," Spencer said more mildly than he felt. "He believes in our goals."

Higgs's brows climbed. "You plan to leave him alive?"

"Depends how it goes."

"Whatever you have to do." Higgs nodded and walked away.

Spencer followed him only as far as the dining area, where Leah seemed to be finishing up. Sweaty and disheveled, she looked worse than the men who'd come to her rescue—but she was still on her feet, doing what she had to do.

She was also beautiful, even now. In the intervening days, the discoloration and swelling on her face had diminished significantly, making more obvious the delicacy of her features. The pale, strawberry blond hair was sleek enough to fall back in place whatever she put it through.

"Can I get some coffee?" he asked.

He especially liked the glare that should have incinerated him.

She grabbed the bucket and rose to her feet. "Anything else?"

He barely refrained from grinning. "How about a piece of that cake?"

Leah stomped into the kitchen.

It was Helen who delivered the cup of coffee and a generous square of a rich, dark cake. He could see the apples and raisins in it.

"Leah made this," Helen said softly.

"Did she?"

She backed away. "If you need anything else…"

"I'll be fine." He nodded, watching as she hurried away and out of sight. It was unlikely any of the women would go to prison, but he wondered what would happen to her without Dirk.

Shaking the worry off, he took a bite of the cake. The taste lit up all his synapses, as rich as it looked. Sweet, but with enough spice to offer complexity. Damn, Leah could cook, too.

She appeared ten minutes later, hesitating when she saw him but then advancing. "Do you want a refill?" She nodded at his cup.

"Sure. That's fabulous cake. Helen says you made it."

"My grandmother taught me. It's my go-to recipe when I have to contribute to potlucks."

He nodded and lowered his voice. "You're really all right?"

"Yes. He…was dragging me out from beneath the table when Del came running. He tried to talk Shawn and—"

At her hesitation, Spencer supplied the name. "Garrett."

"Garrett into having some fun with him. He suggested you wouldn't take on all three of them."

Enraged, Spencer ground his molars. "They didn't consider going for it?" If they had…

But she shook her head. "Joe said he'd seen Shawn looking. I had the feeling Shawn doesn't like him."

She was right. With very few exceptions, these were aggressive men, angry at the world. Small as the group was, it had broken into cliques, the alliances shifting.

Leah continued, "He sort of sneered and said *he* could get women without raping them. It was like he wanted Joe to blow."

"Joe's got friends here, but not those three." His voice still sounded guttural. If Joe had had Arne and Chris Binder and TJ Galt backing him, Leah would have been gang-raped. TJ wouldn't have let a marriage certificate stop him.

Slammed by how he'd have felt if he'd gotten back to find Leah huddled in a small, battered ball, forever damaged by that kind of assault, all the violence in his nature rose in outrage. That was a mistake none of them would have survived to regret.

"Are you all right?" Leah still hesitated several feet away.

"Yeah." It was all he could do to clear his throat. "Coffee?"

She took his cup, reappearing a minute later. As she carefully set it down, she asked, "Is anyone else here?"

"No, I think we're alone except for the women."

"Are you really going to have to fight him?"

"Yes."

"He wants to kill you. Did you see the way he looked at you?" She shivered.

"I saw." He reached out and squeezed her hand quickly before releasing it. "He can't take me down."

"You won't underestimate him?"

"No." Hearing the front door open followed by voices, he said, "You'd better get back to work."

Without another word, she fled. Thinking about his last glimpse of her face, Spencer had a bad feeling he'd failed to reassure her. And the truth was, he'd spent most of his time in the military belly down, with an eye to a scope and his finger resting gently on the trigger of a rifle. He'd wrestled and boxed, sure, but had never tried out any martial arts.

He didn't picture Joe Osenbrock embracing martial arts, either, though. They required discipline he lacked. He was a brute force kind of guy. Joe lost it when he got angry enough or things weren't going his way.

Spencer had to count on cold determination defeating blind fury.

LEAH KEPT SNEAKING peeks down the table during dinner. Spencer acted as if nothing at all was wrong. He ignored Joe, but not so obviously that he was doing it as an insult. More as if… Joe just didn't impinge on his awareness at all.

Joe ate, but she doubted he knew what he was putting in his mouth. He barely took his burning stare from Spencer. Everyone else noticed, which made for awkward conversation and uncomfortable silences.

Shelley Galt had reappeared for the first time in days

to help with dinner and join them at the table. Leah could see immediately that she hadn't been sick at all. She'd been beaten. She still moved stiffly, her left wrist was wrapped in an ACE bandage, and while the long-sleeve tee probably hid bruises, the foundation she'd plastered on her face wasn't thick enough to disguise the purple, yellow and black that enveloped her cheek, temple and part of her forehead, wrapping around an eye that wasn't yet quite all the way open.

Leah knew exactly how that felt. Just looking at the other woman made her shake with fury. Once she saw Spencer's gaze rest on Shelley's face. His expression never changed, but she knew what he thought behind the mask.

After dinner the group broke up more slowly than some times. As usual the women took turns refilling coffee cups or bringing second servings of one of the desserts. Helen was the first to be able to leave. Dirk took her hand and led her out the back door. That he didn't mind people seeing him touch Helen, or his tenderness toward her, said a lot about him. Too bad he was part of a group planning some kind of major attack meant to shake the foundations of Americans' faith in their government.

Shelley left alone. TJ had told her to go, she said. No kindness there. Twenty minutes later most of the rest departed en masse, leaving Leah by herself in the kitchen. She peeked out to see Spencer and Colonel Higgs sitting across from each other at the table, engaged in a conversation that even an outsider could see was intense. What were they talking about? The morning fight? Or the attack that was to be the climax of all this planning and training?

She sat on a stool in the kitchen and tried to think about something, anything, except Joe and Spencer slamming their fists into each other, twisting and tangling in combat. Would the other men surround them and cheer on their favorite, like middle-school boys excited by a fight? She shuddered, imagining the rise of bloodlust, and wondered if Joe's death—or Spencer's—would satisfy the audience.

She knew, *knew*, that Spencer would never concede, not with her life at stake. As terrified as she was of being left to Joe Osenbrock's mercy, that wouldn't be the worst part. How could she ever accept Spencer's death?

She couldn't. Wouldn't.

As a woman who cried when an animal hit by a car didn't make it onto the vet's operating table, she wasn't used to wanting to hurt anyone. But there was no doubt in her mind.

If Joe somehow won, she'd make him pay. No matter what it took.

THEY WERE BARELY inside the door of the cabin when Spencer groaned and snatched Leah into his arms. Leaning back against the closed door, he held her tightly, his cheek pressed to the top of her head. This had been one of the most hellish days he could remember.

He should have taken her and fled already, to hell with his job. Yeah, he'd had two breakthroughs today, but the price was too high. He'd been so cocky, too sure he could protect Leah. He still believed he'd come out the winner tomorrow...but what if he didn't? Or what if he won but was injured badly enough that he was unable to keep protecting her? Joe wasn't the only threat.

She burrowed against him. His resistance to making love with her had hit a low. He needed that closeness, that relief, and thought she did, too.

"Leah," he muttered.

She lifted her head from his shoulder, letting him see the tears in her eyes. "I don't want you to do this."

Desperately, he said, "Let's forget it all, just for a while. Can we do that?"

Even with her eyes shimmering wet, he'd swear she saw deep inside him. He made himself wait until she whispered, "Yes. Oh, yes, please."

He tried to start off gently. They'd never kissed before. His good intentions lasted maybe thirty seconds before one of his hands was on her ass, the other gripping her nape. His tongue was in her mouth, her arms locked around his neck, and she seemed to be trying to climb him. He ached to have her cradle his erection. Her taste, her softness, her acceptance and eagerness, her vulnerability and strength, combined to blast his good intentions to smithereens. He wanted to strip her, lift her up against the door and take her without any finesse. He actually started to turn her and gripped the hem of her T-shirt to strip her when he remembered that damn uncovered window.

He couldn't do it like this. A monumental shudder racked his body. The effort of persuading his fingers to release her shirt tore another groan from his chest. Wrenching his mouth from hers, he said rawly, "Bedroom."

Her green eyes were so dazed, he doubted she understood.

Too frantic for her to wait, he bent to slide an arm beneath her knees and swing her off the floor. Since he started kissing her again, he blundered more than walked across the small living room.

As he turned to fit her through the opening into the bedroom, some part of her body thudded into the door frame and she cried, "Ouch." The next second she pressed her lips back to his and the kiss became deep and hungry again.

Once he laid her on the bed and came down on top of her, they slid into the dip at the middle of the mattress. Spencer didn't care. All he could think about was getting her clothes off. As he tugged her shirt over her head and groped for the fastening for her bra, he wished he'd thought to turn on the light so he could see her. Much as he wanted that, he couldn't make himself leave her.

He had to rise to his knees to untie her athletic shoes and peel her jeans and panties down her legs. While he was there, he took care of his own clothes. He barely had the sanity to remove a condom from his wallet. She was trying to touch him but wouldn't have been able to see well enough to put the damn thing on. He felt clumsy, and realized the dark wasn't responsible. His hands were shaking.

Too much tumult, fierce need and the knowledge that they could fall any minute off the knife-edge that constituted their only safety, all combined to rob him of any patience. The incoherent, needy sounds she was making—moans, whimpers, he didn't know—told him she was as ready as he was.

Sliding inside her was one of the best feelings of his life. Tight, slick, she welcomed him by planting her feet on the mattress and pushing her hips up to meet every thrust. He set an urgent, hard pace that couldn't last. Her spasms, the way she cried out his name, pulled him with her. His throbbing release seemed to last forever. He collapsed, unable to find the immediate strength to roll off her slender body.

For all the joy and satisfaction he felt, Spencer hated that she hadn't cried out his real name. That she didn't even know it. She'd just made love to a man playing a role, not him.

Whoever I am, came the bleak thought.

Chapter Eleven

Leah woke up to find herself alone in bed. She didn't hear a sound. Not the shower or a whistling teakettle or the creak of a floorboard. Where was Spencer?

They'd made love a second time, slower and more tenderly, his voice deep and almost velvety in the darkness, the Southern accent strong as he told her how beautiful she was, how soft. He called her strong, defiant, smart. He hadn't said how he felt about her, but that would have been expecting too much. Really, how could either of them know so quickly?

Just for a minute she pushed back at the sense of dread that would swallow her if she let it, and instead remembered the feel of Spencer's callused fingers, the raw hunger in his kisses, the way he filled her until she felt complete. She wished…she wished so much, but her chest suddenly felt as if a band squeezed, tightening until she couldn't draw a breath.

He wouldn't have left her behind when he went to meet with Joe, would he?

Horrified, she threw back the covers, struggled out of bed and only grabbed a dirty T-shirt of Spencer's to throw on before she rushed out of the bedroom.

Spencer sat on the futon, feet on the coffee table, appearing his usual composed self. He held a coffee cup in one hand and gazed at her in mild surprise.

She lurched to a stop, her heart hammering. “I thought…”

“I might be gone?” His voice was low and tender despite his impenetrable expression. “I wouldn’t do that to you.”

“What…what time is it?”

He glanced at the steel watch he wore. “We have twenty minutes.”

“I didn’t know you’d set a time.”

“Higgs did. He wants us to get the fight out of the way before breakfast.”

“Oh, God.” Her sense of impending disaster wasn’t alleviated. “I need to take a shower.”

She should have done laundry yesterday at the lodge, she thought in that part of her mind still capable of mundane thoughts. Rooting through her suitcase, she found a pair of jeans that she’d only worn one day and a clean T-shirt. Her last pair of clean panties.

Right now she couldn’t care less if she was filthy. Even the shower was only a way to put off facing what was coming.

Clutching the small pile of clothes, she went to the bathroom without looking again at Spencer.

What if…? But she couldn’t let herself think that.

She stayed under the thin stream of water only long enough to get clean before drying herself with the pitiful towel and hurrying to dress. She combed her wet hair, then looked down at herself. Her battle armor didn’t seem adequate.

Taking a deep breath, she went back out, set on not letting Spencer see how scared she was. What he needed from her was trust and confidence. She should have felt both wholeheartedly, but the dread remained.

As soon as she appeared, his gaze landed on her. "I've been in fights before," he said calmly.

Some of her fears had to be leaking out, like too-bright light between the slats of blinds. "Don't hold back," she begged him. "He'll do anything to win."

He still looked unfazed. "Cheat, you mean?"

"Yes!"

"Let's go out on the porch."

He rose effortlessly to his feet. Bemused, she followed him. He closed the door behind them and leaned against the porch railing. Leah desperately wanted the chance to soak in the comfort of his strong arms around her, but they could be seen.

Not heard, though, she realized, at least not from a bug inside the cabin.

Confirming her guess, he spoke very quietly. "There's something you need to know. You're imagining that I always take the high road. I don't. I've long since lost count of the number of men I've killed. I told you I was military, but not that I was a sniper. I saw those dying men's faces." Gravel roughened his voice even as he kept it low. "Some of them will haunt me for the rest of my life, but I kept doing what I thought I had to do. If I have to kill Joe Osenbrock today, I won't hesitate. Do you understand?"

"Yes," she whispered. "Maybe I shouldn't be glad, but I am. It's not just for my sake that you need to win, you know."

The bones in his face seemed more prominent than she remembered. "I do know."

She nodded.

"We need to get going."

He touched the back of her hand lightly as they descended the steps. She studied him, bothered by that seemingly unbreakable calm. Today he wore black cargo pants and a gray T-shirt that showed his powerful pecs and biceps, as well as flexible black boots that would allow him to move fast. He wouldn't be able to kick or stomp the way Joe would, but speed was surely more important. At Spencer's belt, he wore his usual black leather holster holding a steel-gray and black handgun. The men here seemed to go armed all the time as a matter of course. Maybe as a law-enforcement officer, Spencer always did. Leah hoped not, that he could sometimes set that part of his nature aside.

The minute they started down the porch steps, she saw the crowd gathered in front of the lodge. Were they excited about the entertainment? Or were some worried about the outcome?

"If you get out of here and I don't," he said in that same low voice, "the attack's set for November 11, Veterans Day. The president is set to speak, although the location hasn't yet been identified. And they have the components to make a dirty bomb. Remember that."

She opened her mouth in an instinctive protest but closed it. Nodded. "Will you tell me your real name?"

He cut a glance at her sidelong. His hesitation was infinitesimal but real, replaced by a flicker of amusement. "Alex Barr. Alex, most of the time. But stick to Spencer."

"Thank you."

That was the last thing she had a chance to say. They'd reached the crowd, now re-forming into a circle. She followed in his wake until she was close enough to the front to be able to see.

Joe Osenbrock already waited in the center. Not patiently; he was pacing, rolling his shoulders, acting like

Leah vaguely thought heavyweights did in the ring before the bell.

Spencer stopped to unclip his holster and hand it and the gun to Garrett Zeigler. Then he walked into the clear space within the ring of bodies and stopped, still seemingly relaxed. Despite appearances, he had to be poised to explode into action.

The mood was more subdued than she'd expected. Even low-voiced conversation stopped when the lodge door opened and Colonel Higgs appeared. He walked forward, took in the scene with one sweeping glance, then asked, "Are they both disarmed?"

"Yes." Del Schmidt held up one weapon. Zeigler raised Spencer's.

"Good. Let's not waste too much time with this." Higgs studied the two men in the ring, his thoughts hidden. Then he said, "Go."

It all happened so fast, Leah wasn't sure which man moved first, only that within seconds they were toe-to-toe, fists swinging. Grunts of exertion and pain rang out. Blood splattered.

Spencer swiped blood from his face with his forearm, then stepped back to let Joe charge past him. When their bodies collided again, they fell hard to the ground. Spencer got a headlock on Joe, but only briefly. They rolled, pummeling each other, grappling for any advantage, punishing each other brutally with fists and holds that contorted their bodies in ways that had her whimpering.

They fought their way back to their feet.

A few men called out. Occasionally a warning, sometimes a "Good one!" But mostly they were silent, so intent on the battle in front of them, she could have plucked a gun from one of their holsters and started spraying bullets.

Except…she couldn't tear her eyes from the savage fight, either.

Twice she had to step back along with the entire side of the circle when the two men flung themselves in that direction. Mostly, she knew she was begging, or even praying.

Please, please, please.

After a strike against his neck, Joe roared with rage and seemed to redouble his attacks. Spencer countered them, once tripping Joe, who crashed to the ground, somersaulted and came back up.

Spencer spat out some blood and jeered at his opponent. "Getting tired?"

With another roar, Joe charged forward like a three-hundred-and-fifty pound linebacker ready to drop the quarterback. But Spencer was not only fast, he was as big a man if not quite so muscle-bound. A quick side step and an elbow to the gut sent Joe to the ground again. He seemed slower to get up, pausing with one knee still down, even his head slightly bent. Was he done?

Spencer came at him with a kick that sent Joe sprawling again, but he latched on to Spencer's leg and brought him down, too. And suddenly, something metal flashed.

"Gun!" somebody yelled, but it wasn't. It was a knife, and he slashed at Spencer. Blood didn't just spatter, it spurted.

Ready to leap forward herself, she saw Spencer grab Joe's wrist and wrench his arm back. Spencer's teeth showed in a snarl; Joe fought that powerful grip in silent agony.

A couple of the men did surge forward, but before they reached the two combatants, Spencer flipped Joe, slammed his hand on the ground to force him to release the knife, and slugged him in the face so hard Joe's head bounced.

The next second he'd gone limp.

Spencer rolled off him and lay on his back, his chest heaving, his clothes blood-soaked.

Above the tumult of other voices, she heard Higgs's. He'd descended into the crowd and now raised his voice. "Wyatt's the winner. Tim, Brian, haul that cheating scum up to one of the bedrooms." He jerked his head to indicate the lodge behind him. "Shawn, Rick, you're responsible for getting Spencer back to his cabin." Higgs looked around, spotting her. "You've had practice sewing up wounds. Make yourself useful."

Oh, God, oh, God. Her teeth wanted to chatter. Somehow, she managed to say, "Do you have a first-aid kit?"

"Townsend, you know where it is."

It took three men to lift Joe and carry him up the porch steps and into the lodge. Leah only peripherally saw them go, Joe's arms flopping. On her knees beside Spencer, she snapped, "I need something to stop the bleeding."

Spencer watched her, one eyelid at half-mast. The socket holding his other eye was grotesquely swollen, purple. His teeth were clenched, and she'd swear what skin she could see was gray beneath the tan. Or maybe it only looked gray as an accent to the shockingly vivid color of the blood.

She bent her head close to his. "You'll be all right. You won."

One side of his mouth lifted as if he was trying to smile but couldn't quite make it work.

Two bare-chested men thrust cotton T-shirts at her. Neither looked very clean, but they were the best she had. She wadded one and pressed it hard against Spencer's thigh, looked around until she saw Del Schmidt and said, "Can you hold this?"

He dropped to his knees and complied. She pulled up Spencer's shirt, used the second T-shirt in her hand to wipe at the blood until she saw a narrow slit over his rib cage, and pressed it down. Panic scratched at her. If there were more wounds, they'd have to wait, but what if one she hadn't found was fatal? The slit frightened her the most. That one was a stab instead of a slice. She hadn't seen it happen. What organs lay beneath?

Out of the corner of her eye she saw someone pick up the huge knife lying in the dirt. Blood dripped from the double-edged blade.

A man ran up carrying a metal box big enough to look as if it held fishing tackle. "Do you want it here?"

"Take it to the cabin," she decided. Three men prepared to lift him, Leah ordering Del to keep the pressure on his thigh while she did the same on his muscular torso.

They moved slowly, awkwardly, with five of them bumping into each other, but finally made it up the two steps onto the porch.

"Not locked," Spencer growled.

The man with an arm under his shoulders—Rick Metz, built like a boulder—fumbled for the knob with one hand and got the door open. Once inside, she said, "Can we pull out the futon?"

Del did it while she used her free hand to maintain pressure on Spencer's thigh, too. The mattress looked grungy enough she wished desperately for a clean sheet to lay over it, but hadn't seen one. Pain tightened Spencer's face until it was all bones and skin stretched taut between them. He groaned when they laid him down.

To her distant surprise, the men continued to follow her orders. One put on water to boil on the single working burner here, while another ran for the lodge to boil more. A third went for any clean bedding and towels he could find.

Spencer never looked away from her.

HE COULDN'T DIE.

Through the pain, that was all Spencer could think. Leah needed him. *Don't give in. Don't lose consciousness.*

A couple of times she whispered, "Stay with me," and once he even managed a nod. He didn't know if she meant stay in the sense that he had to remain conscious, or that he couldn't abandon her by dying. Either way, he hung on. At least he was done with Joe, who was as good as a dead man.

The guys around him seemed to be doing their best for him. He wasn't even sure who *was* here. He'd have had to look away from Leah to be sure, and he couldn't do that.

He managed to tell her he had pills in his duffel. At least, he thought he'd told her.

Don't give in. God, that hurts. He wanted to curl up to protect his belly, sensing that wound was the most dangerous. If the knife had sliced into his guts, all the resolve in the world wouldn't save him. Half-digested food would be spilling into the abdominal cavity, introducing bacteria where it didn't belong.

But Leah looked focused and determined in a way he didn't remember seeing her before. She was fighting for him, and he could do his part.

Don't give in. Trust her.

He floated in a sea of pain as she worked. There had to be broken bones.

Paper ripped. Somehow, she'd come to have a wicked-looking pair of scissors in her hand and was cutting most of his clothes off him. Wet washcloths, hot enough to have him jerking involuntarily, ran over his legs.

"I'll need to stitch that one up," he heard her say to someone else.

All he felt was pressure on his thigh again.

Once, they rolled him. His back hurt like hell, but in a generalized way.

"Man, he's going to be one solid bruise," a familiar voice said. Del.

It went on like that. He hazily understood that they were searching his body for knife wounds.

"Think the blade hit a rib," Leah said. "If it went very deep…"

He lost the thread of what she was saying.

Eventually, something cold was sprayed on his thigh. Her face appeared above his. "This should numb you enough to help," she said.

Still gritting his teeth, he nodded.

He felt the needle pricking in and out of his flesh. Pricking, hell; stabbing. The spray hadn't numbed anything, but he fought to hold still.

Then on his torso, almost on his side. He couldn't stop a raw sound from escaping.

They produced ice and what he vaguely saw were bags of frozen vegetables to lay on his face and half a dozen other places on his body. The worst bruising? He didn't know, only that the cold burned.

Time passed. He wasn't always sure he *was* conscious. Leah was his anchor, distressing him when she moved out of his line of sight a few times. Dripping ice packs and frozen veggies were removed and replaced at least once.

Rick—yes, that was Rick Metz—was the first to leave and not reappear. Given his lack of emotional content, Rick was a strange one to tend him with care.

When Spencer was able to roll his head slightly, he saw Shawn Wycoff and Del Schmidt. They were more logical as nursemaids. He also became aware that when Leah asked for something, they jumped. Funny that Higgs had appointed her medical director early on. The first day? He didn't remember. Spencer hadn't guessed *he* would be the one to need whatever trauma-care expertise she possessed.

He had to get her to safety so that she could go to veterinary school, the way she deserved. Since the slightest move brought stabbing pains—yeah, that was a pun—he couldn't figure out how he'd protect her, but he'd do it. Somehow.

He surfaced to hear her thanking the two men, sounding almost tearful. Del shrugged. "Let us know what you need."

Say, *I need to go home. Help me get away.*

Of course she didn't. "I will."

The door closed quietly behind them. The mattress shifted enough that he knew Leah had sat down beside him. Her fingertips stroking his forehead was the first good thing he'd felt.

No, he could wriggle his toes with no pain. In fact, thanks to his boots, his feet seemed unscathed. That was good news. If they had to walk out of here, that was what they'd do, he decided.

"You with me?" she asked softly, her eyes so vividly green he would have been happy never to look away.

"Yah," he mumbled.

Her smile lit the room like the sun coming out from behind a cloud. She sobered faster than he liked.

"Thank heavens you didn't lose consciousness! Even so, I'd give a lot to be able to send you for X-rays, or even a CT scan. I think your left wrist might be broken, although I can't be sure. It's wrapped tight enough to immobilize it."

He arrowed in on his wrist. Yeah, that felt like a break. Ribs, too, he guessed, although those might be only cracks or even just bruising.

He could hope.

"It's really lucky you had that oxycodone. Aspirin wouldn't have helped much." She gave an exaggerated shudder.

He shared that gratitude. So he had told her. He hadn't quite realized what those pills he'd swallowed were.

"What will they do with Joe?" she asked, worry carving lines in her forehead. "Should I go volunteer to look at him?"

"No." That sounded almost normal. "Don't shink—" he tried harder "—*think* he'll survive."

"Why? Did you—" Comprehension changed her face. "You mean…"

He managed a tiny nod. Best not to say it out loud.

"Oh, dear God," Leah whispered.

He somehow lifted a hand enough to lay it on her arm. She looked down, then up to meet his eyes, and understood. *Careful.*

"Later I'll have Del and Shawn or somebody else move you to the bedroom. I know the futon must be horribly uncomfortable. But if we were going to ruin one or the other with blood, I decided it should be the futon."

He absolutely agreed. After last night, he'd developed fond feelings for that bed.

"*Could* somebody take you to an ER?"

She meant, would it be allowed. "No," he said. Steeled himself and added, "Okay."

That earned him a wrinkled nose. "You're a long way

from *okay*. But I suppose you must have been injured during your years in the military."

Another slight inclination of his head, although even that set off fireworks. He had to close his eyes momentarily.

Yes, he'd been hospitalized several times. Strange to think that he might have come closer to dying today than he had from bullet wounds or shrapnel from an IED. If that knife blade had plunged deeper, or struck higher or lower, it could easily have been curtains for him, given that the best medical care available was from a veterinary technician with access only to a basic first-aid kit. He'd been damned lucky, and he wouldn't waste that luck.

He really was done with undercover gigs. No hostage rescue for him, either. He'd transfer as soon as he could—once he'd taken down Colonel Higgs and his hatefully misguided army.

And Leah. If she wanted him, he'd do what he had to do to have her in his life, too. He could transfer to the Seattle office, or the office closest to wherever she would be attending grad school.

All good plans. Unfortunately, right this minute a soon-to-be-needed trip to the bathroom reared ahead like Kilimanjaro. Only positive was, he knew he was thinking more clearly.

These injuries would buy him a day or two off from a role that he hadn't been able to set down in months. That said, would Leah still be expected to cook and clean rather than care for him? That would leave her vulnerable...although he thought Higgs had been pissed off enough about Joe's behavior to lay down the law where she was concerned.

Maybe.

Spencer grunted. What he needed was to get back on

his feet as quickly as possible. For starters, he wouldn't have a chance to pocket the key to start the Jeep unless he rejoined activities, even if only as a spectator.

A good place to start was with that short journey to the bathroom. The hell he was going to piss in a jar and make Leah dump it out.

Despite the explosion of pain, he started to shift his body toward the edge of the futon amid her cries of, "What are you *doing*? Stop!"

Chapter Twelve

The stubborn man insisted she lay a sheet over the dirty, blood-stained futon mattress and bring him some pillows so he could spend the day out there. Leah would have argued more vehemently, except he was right that he could get up and down more easily from the futon than the sagging mattress in the bedroom that fought every attempt to escape it. She'd had to stick her head outside and ask the first person she saw—someone named Jack, she thought—to bring bedding and towels from the lodge. Actually, she said meekly, "Spencer wants some bedding for the futon, and, um, our towels are all bloody. I'm afraid to leave him yet. Do you think…?"

The guy complied.

Spencer refused to let her fetch help for him to go to the bathroom. Pain aged his face a decade or more as he pushed himself to his feet, leaning heavily on her. Two hours ago she'd never have considered that he could shuffle even this short distance on his own.

Needless to say, despite the fact that he was swaying in front of the toilet, he evicted her until he was done and flushed.

Around midday she did leave him alone long enough to walk to the lodge for food. She slipped in the back door, where all the women surrounded her and, whispering, demanded to know what had happened. Leah gave them the CliffsNotes version, then filled a bag with a few dishes, a saucepan and some silverware as well as sandwich makings, cans of soup and desserts. She didn't see a single one of the men as she hurried back to the cabin.

During her absence Spencer had gotten to a sitting position again on the edge of the futon. Stress on his face eased the minute he saw her.

"What took you so long?" he asked. With his lips grotesquely swollen, words were hard to make out, but Leah found she got the gist.

"I wasn't gone very long." She set down the two bags on the short stretch of counter next to the tiny sink. "Jennifer and everyone wanted to know about the fight. They were all ordered to stay in the kitchen and missed the whole thing."

"You get an update on Joe?" A note in his voice she didn't recognize had her turning to look at him.

"No. They served breakfast like usual, and when Lisa asked if she should take a plate up to Joe, Higgs snapped at her. Said he isn't in any shape to eat."

"He wouldn't be," Spencer agreed slowly.

Was he wondering if he *had* killed Joe? Or disturbed by the possibility of his death, however it came about? Yes, she decided, that was it. She wondered if, instead of becoming numb and inured to tragedy after all the death he'd seen, Spencer still had the capacity to grieve. There'd been nothing about Joe Osenbrock she could sympathize with, and yet… Who knew what his childhood had been like? What had made him so violently inclined and insecure enough to need so desperately to win?

And if Spencer's suspicion turned out to be true, she really hated the idea that one of those men she'd gotten to know was willing to steal upstairs in the lodge—perhaps to the very room where she'd been held captive—to break Joe's neck or slit his throat or… Leah didn't even want to think.

It bothered her even more to picture one of the men who'd protected her or helped Spencer today as the one willing to commit cold-blooded murder. Del? Shawn or Garrett? Chilled, Leah thought, *surely not Dirk Ritchie.* And yet…all of them intended to commit mass murder in the near future. Why balk at killing a single man?

"Will you eat something? I thought you might be able to drink soup from a cup."

"Not hungry."

She turned in alarm. What if the knife had reached his intestines or…maybe his liver or kidney? The pain relievers could have masked the effect that was only now catching up with him.

She evaluated him, deciding that his color was much better than it had been when they first carried him to the cabin. His eyes—well, eye—looked clear. If she made him open his mouth so she could look at his gums the way she would an injured dog's, would they be a healthy color or worrisomely pale?

"Will you try?"

He grunted and very carefully rested against the extra pillows Jack had included in the pile he brought from the lodge earlier. Spencer lifted each leg individually, using his good hand to guide it into place so he could stretch out. Only then did he say, "Yah."

She warmed cream of tomato, thinking it would go down easily and that milk would be good for him. When she took him a mugful and sat beside him to help prop him up, he did slowly drink it all.

Relieved, she had a bowlful herself.

She checked his watch, sitting on the old coffee table

that had been pushed aside. "It's almost time for another painkiller. You won't try to be a tough guy and do without, will you?"

On a face that had suffered that much damage, it was hard to be sure, but she *thought* his expression was sardonic.

"No. Not tough."

When she gave him the pill half an hour later, he swallowed it, and after a period of staring broodingly up at the wood-paneled ceiling, dozed off. Leah tried to read but couldn't concentrate. Fictional adventures—or the very real ones during World War II—couldn't keep her attention when her current situation was so perilous.

Spencer was fighting his infirmities with a willpower that awed her. If the damage had been limited to the punches and bruising, however massive, she thought he'd be up and around in only another day or two. As it was, he'd lost a lot of blood, and she couldn't help fearing what harm that knife blade thrust between ribs might have done.

Had Spencer been ready for them to attempt an escape? He'd obviously learned a lot of what he'd been sent to find out. Now...how could they get away?

Was it possible for someone to get to any of the car keys?

Helen was the only one of the women Leah could imagine being willing to try to help her, but she wouldn't betray Dirk by helping Leah steal his truck, even if that was possible.

She and Spencer couldn't possibly set out on foot. Certainly not for days.

Her worries went round and round, but even when he was awake, she didn't vocalize them. Didn't need to. He was surely running the same scenarios and coming up with the same dead ends.

We should be okay for a few days, she told herself, but didn't quite believe her own assurance.

SPENCER HAD A hell of a time sleeping. No position was comfortable. Once Leah dropped off, she couldn't prevent herself from rolling into his aching body, or her arm would flop across his torso, and it was all he could do to stifle a bellow. Her head on his shoulder awakened sharp pain.

He didn't think he'd ever been battered from head to... not toe, calves before.

Come morning Spencer woke feeling as if he'd just regained consciousness after being run over by a semitruck with lots of huge tires. He tried not to move a muscle. Even breathing hurt. When he assessed his body, he found several places that felt like burning coals against the more generalized pain. Wrist, left cheekbone, the site of the stab wound, a searing strip down his thigh and his rib cage on the left.

All those could be managed, he convinced himself, and he knew from other times he'd taken a beating that the day after was the worst. Then the body would start healing itself.

Okay. One more day before he seriously considered an escape plan.

Leah stirred beside him and he had to grit his teeth. "Are you awake?" she whispered.

"Yah." His mouth was still swollen, making it difficult to shape words. But he got out the two that were most important. "Pain pills."

"What?"

He had to repeat himself before she said, "Oh, no! I

should have woken you up earlier to take those. I'll get them right now."

She had to separate herself from him, the mattress rocking as she clambered out of bed. Teeth clenched, he held back the groans.

She hurried back. Sitting up enough to swallow the pills was agonizing. He needed the bathroom, but his bladder had to wait.

He caught glimpses as she got dressed, but as much as he normally enjoyed being tantalized by the fleeting sight of her curves, he didn't dare lift or even roll his head.

Wait.

It was a full half hour before the rigidity in his body eased enough, he was able to get up, shuffle to the bathroom and then lie down on the futon. As uncomfortable as the thing was, he needed to be out here where he could keep an eye on Leah and any possible entrances. He was able to half sit against the pile of pillows, so if something happened he could easily reach for his handgun.

Leah poached eggs for him and poured him a glass of orange juice. He was swallowing it when there was a polite knock on the door.

He called, "Who is it?" before Leah could reach the door.

"Del."

Spencer nodded at her and she let Del and Dirk in.

Del's gaze flicked to the gun then back to Spencer. "I'd say you look better, except..."

Spencer might have grimaced if that wouldn't have hurt. "Colorful?" he got out.

"Pretty as a rainbow," the other man confirmed. "You on your feet yet?"

"Sure." Spencer gave what was probably a death's head grin. "Hurt like hell today, though."

"Yeah, ain't that the way."

Dirk looked at Leah. "Anything you need?"

She succeeded in looking shy and even submissive. "I think we're okay. I went over to the lodge yesterday for some food and dishes. You know."

"Helen said you'd been by."

Spencer couldn't help asking. "Joe?"

Del answered, voice expressionless. "Died during the night."

Leah pressed her fingers to her lips to stifle a gasp. Both men glanced at her before returning their gazes to him. Dirk wasn't hiding his perturbation as well as Del was. He didn't like knowing Higgs had ordered—or even committed—the murder.

"Whatever I said about killing him, I didn't mean him to die," Spencer managed to get out.

Del obviously made out what he'd said because he nodded. "Figured. Ah…the colonel says he'll stop by later."

"Good. It'll be tomorrow before I can walk as far as the lodge." And, damn, he wished that wasn't true.

Leah saw the two men out, closed the door and waited through the thud of them descending the few steps before she turned around, distress on her face. "You were right."

"About Joe?" He was careful to sound…indifferent. "He wasn't in good shape when they hauled him away yesterday."

"Neither were you," she said tartly.

He let himself smile, although it couldn't look good. "I had the services of the only medic on site."

She opened her mouth, no doubt to remind him that she'd volunteered to look at Joe, too, but was again smart enough to let that remain unsaid.

"You were restless last night. Why don't you try to get some sleep?" she suggested.

He might do that. She'd wake him up soon enough when Higgs came calling. "You'll be here?"

"Won't go anywhere." She sketched a cross over her heart.

That made his misshapen mouth twitch.

He drifted in and out of sleep for much of the afternoon, helped along by the pain meds. Leah made sure he ate a little for lunch, and did wake him up midafternoon when Higgs came knocking.

He didn't have a lot to say, probably thanks to Leah's presence. "Shame about Joe," he remarked, his tone holding not a smidgen of regret.

Spencer met his eyes. "Sure is."

"We picked out a place to bury him. Can't let authorities get involved."

No shit. Couldn't let the body stay in the lodge long enough to start decomposing, either, Spencer reflected.

He stiffened when Higgs looked at Leah. "We're missing you in the kitchen. I suppose Spencer needs you today, but he should be on the mend by tomorrow. I'm hoping you'll make that cake again."

Her eyes glittered with dislike. Her acting had some limitations, it appeared. But she said, "I'll be glad to make it again."

Spencer spoke up. "I liked it, too."

To Higgs, she said, "Did Jennifer talk to you about picking huckleberries? We could make some great cobblers and pies with them, and stretch supplies, too."

He looked surprised. "No. I noticed some ripe berries. Wasn't sure whether they were edible."

"They're delicious. The mainstay for birds and bears and probably some other animals."

"I'll set it up," he said, glanced at Spencer and added, "Hope there's a big improvement by tomorrow."

Was that an order? Irritated, Spencer didn't show how he felt. "You and me both. I'm not built to sit on the sidelines."

A monster cloaked in an average body and mild manner, Colonel Higgs left. Spencer ground his teeth a few times to keep from verbally venting his anger.

Leah didn't like it, but he started doing some stretches and getting up to walk for a few minutes every half hour or so. They could not afford for him to stay down.

THE NEXT MORNING they took the short walk to the lodge slowly. Leah stayed close to him, but Spencer didn't reach for her. His face was so blank, she knew he was intent on hiding how much pain he was still in. Somehow, he walked evenly, betraying no need to favor one side or the other. He had allowed her to rewrap his wrist, and of course his face was at its worst: still swollen and vividly colored. The black eye was barely slitted, his mouth distorted.

Something like halfway, he said out of the blue, "Know how to hot-wire a car?"

"Hot-wire…?" She sounded startled. "Unfortunately, no. To tell you the truth, I'm completely ignorant where cars are concerned. Beyond how to start and drive them, of course."

He grunted.

"What are you thinking?"

"The Jeep." He'd mentioned it. "Want to get my hands on the key, but if I can't…" He frowned. "I can hot-wire it myself. Old vehicles like that are easy. Plus, the Jeep is back behind the lodge. We'd have a chance of getting a real head-start. I was thinking just in case."

Just in case he was dead or captive and she had to run

by herself. Sick to her stomach, she said, "The Jeep is out if I'm on my own."

He nodded, almost matter-of-factly. "We'll make sure it doesn't come to that."

Oh, good. She was completely reassured. She didn't have a chance to comment, though, because Arne Larson emerged from his cabin and fell into step with them.

"Good fight," he said admiringly.

So much for what had appeared to be a friendship with Joe. This was a guy who wouldn't have felt at all squeamish watching one gladiator troop mop up the other in the Colosseum. Spencer put on a front of being unemotional about what he'd had to do in the army and now, with the FBI, but she didn't believe in it. He still had a human reaction to events and people. He must; she couldn't be falling for him if he didn't. He wouldn't be so ready to sacrifice himself for her.

As for Arne…she'd swear she saw a trace of envy and dislike in his eyes.

Spencer didn't comment, probably saving his energy for mounting the lodge steps.

HE FELT ON edge all day, starting with finding out that Leah had been sent with two of the other women—Shelley and Lisa—to pick huckleberries.

"Galt will make sure no bears get 'em," Higgs told him, smirking.

"What's he going to do if a bear charges them?" Spencer asked.

"Shoot it, what else? What are you worrying about? Black bears are supposed to be afraid of people."

"Not all. And they're big enough to be dangerous, you know. Bullets from a handgun wouldn't even slow one down. And then there are the grizzlies. No matter what, you wouldn't want to get between any bear and her cub."

"Grizzlies? What are you talking about?"

Spencer looked at this idiot. "Grizzlies were reintroduced to the north Cascade Mountains years ago. They're around. I've seen plenty of pictures of them browsing through thickets of berries."

Not sure his slurred speech had gotten through, he was satisfied to see Higgs alarmed and studying the tree line covertly. Spencer instead looked around at the empty range. "I thought the others would be here."

"I had them stop to pick up the new rifles and ammunition."

He'd have to find a way to involve himself in returning the weaponry to the armory at lunchtime.

"You're pulling my leg, aren't you?" Higgs said suddenly.

"Pulling your leg?" Ah. "Nope. We'd have seen any bears around if we'd been careless enough to leave out food."

Colonel Higgs scowled at him. "Why didn't you say something?"

Spencer pulled off surprised. He hoped, given the state of his face. "You'd already chosen this site. I assumed you'd done your research." He shrugged. "I've heard guys talking about bears. Anyone from the northwest would know."

"You're not from around here."

"No, but I've climbed mountains here and in Alaska." He let the silence draw out a little before adding, "You're right that bears are mostly shy. If you stumble on 'em, they can be a problem, but we make enough racket to warn them off."

But the women picking berries wouldn't be, unless

they maintained a conversation, something that was unlikely with TJ Galt standing over them with his sneer and his Beretta M9A3 semiautomatic, a shade of brown that went with his favorite desert camo T-shirts and cargo pants. Spencer found his sartorial taste especially ironic since TJ was one of the few men here who had never served in the military.

"You up to trying out the new rifle?" Higgs asked. "I'd like your take on it."

"Tomorrow," Spencer said. "I'm one solid bruise right now. Getting up and down is a chore, and any recoil wouldn't help me heal."

Higgs accepted his answer, which made Spencer grateful that some of his injuries were so visible.

He did take one of the rifles that were supposedly being tried out by army rangers. The balance was okay. The optics were as good as anything he'd used before, but not an improvement. He only said, "Interesting," staying noncommittal as he handed it back to Ken Vogel. Then he glanced around.

"Where's Fuller?" He frowned, realizing a couple of other men were missing, too.

"More supplies. Fuller took his wife along with Jones."

Damn it. What did they need so soon after the last shopping expedition? Only food? This group did eat like hungry locusts. Still… Spencer tried to remember what day he, Lisa and Del had gone down to Bellingham. They'd seriously stocked up. Wednesday, he decided after counting back. Only five days ago.

Mine is not to reason why, he thought flippantly, before remembering the rest of the quote. *Mine is but to do and die.*

That seemed to sum up his current situation all too neatly.

Chapter Thirteen

After giving the other women instructions on how to tell which berries were ripe, Leah kept a sharp eye out for bears while they picked. For what good advanced warning would do. Either a black or grizzly bear could outrun any human over a short distance, should it feel inclined.

She ignored TJ, even when he wandered by her.

Otherwise, as she plucked berries and dropped them into a plastic bowl, she pondered the others, starting with him and Shelley.

If he wasn't such an unpleasant man, TJ would have been attractive: tall, broad-shouldered, fit. He walked like an athlete, had medium brown hair and hazel eyes. His nose had clearly been broken at some point, which didn't detract from a handsome face…except she couldn't help thinking he'd probably deserved to be slugged. She was ashamed to find she actually hoped that was what had happened, rather than a collision on a soccer field or a baseball pitch delivered too high.

She had only enough abstract knowledge about the dynamics in abusive relationships to understand why Shelley stayed with him. Real understanding eluded her. The dullness in that poor woman's eyes, her body language, the way she cringed whenever TJ came close… Leah would be willing to bet Shelley had grown up abused as a child, too, or at least watching her mother being hit by her father, or even by a succession of men. If somehow she escaped TJ, the odds were good she'd find another abusive man.

Jennifer was deferential around Tim, but not scared in the same way. Helen lit up when she saw Dirk. Lisa Dempsey… Leah was less sure about her. She wouldn't think of challenging Del or any man, but Leah had heard Lisa talking comfortably to him a few times, and his low voice as he actually talked to her, too.

It felt weird to imagine them all under arrest, diminished by convict uniforms and handcuffs, the women seeing their men only through glass if they stuck by them at all.

Shelley would, Leah knew, and Helen, too. The others…she was less sure.

How on earth had all these men gotten sucked into an objective so horrifying? She wanted to be able to hate them all, but discovered it wasn't that simple. Colonel Ed Higgs, she could hate. *He'd* dreamed up this evil, a betrayal of the nation that he had supposedly served. *He'd* recruited all these guys, who were fearful of a changing America but not necessarily fanatical until then. *He* could coolly and with a secret smile say, *Shame about Joe*, when he had ordered him to be executed.

Rick Metz…lacked personality. Did he need to be told what to believe? Maybe he'd been at loose ends until Colonel Higgs gave him a clear objective and whatever nonsense justifications he used.

She sifted through the names of the men she knew best, finding it harder than it should be to label them evil, or even bad. Del Schmidt pretty much ignored her, and Lisa sometimes shrank from him. Beyond that, he mostly seemed decent. He'd been courageous defending her. Same for Garrett Zeigler and Shawn Wycoff.

Except…she wondered if any of the three had been thinking about *her.* Maybe all they'd been doing was currying favor with Spencer while Shawn at least could enjoy poking a stick at Joe.

Dirk Ritchie seemed downright nice.

Arne Larson wasn't nice; Leah remembered him slamming her against the wall and groping her while leering. And she hadn't forgotten how brutally TJ Galt had tackled her when she tried to escape, slugging her before hauling her back to face Higgs, their unlikely alpha wolf, without a semblance of gentleness.

Gee, could that be why she hoped someone had, once upon a time, slugged *him* hard enough to permanently dent his nose?

There were others she definitely didn't like, and a whole bunch who treated the women as if they were barely useful. Did they really feel that way? Or were they just blending in, the way school children were sometimes cruel because they didn't have the courage to stand up and say no?

Spencer must know them all a whole lot better than she did. Did he regret what would happen to some of these men? Or had he become inured from previous undercover investigations? Nobody was all bad or all good; she did believe that. Even though Spencer must use people he was investigating to achieve his objectives, he'd have to stay focused on the crime they'd been willing to commit—or *were* willing to commit, in this case.

"Leah!" A heavy hand gripped her shoulder and spun her around.

Wide-eyed, righting her bowl before the berries spilled, she realized it was TJ.

"What were you doing, spacing out?"

She knew what she had to do. Bow her head, hope her hair fell forward to partly veil her expression and grovel. "I'm sorry," she mumbled. "I… I was worrying about bears."

The other women stole surreptitious glances at their surroundings.

"Their bowls are full. Yours is, too," he said impatiently. "Time to get back. This is a waste of my time."

Except she knew perfectly well that all he'd do once they got back was lean against the wall in the kitchen and watch them with both contempt and suspicion.

She bobbed her head and hurried toward the lodge, Lisa and Shelley keeping pace with her, TJ silently following. So much for using a berry-picking expedition to make a run for it. That scheme had been downright delusional.

FROM PARTWAY DOWN the table during dinner, a low voice carried to Spencer.

"…get down where I can have internet access…"

He didn't turn his head, making himself depend on peripheral vision. For once Higgs hadn't taken a seat near him. Instead, he'd grabbed a place beside Tim Fuller, and they'd had their heads together ever since. Damn. Had Fuller and the others gone to Bellingham at all?

"Don't like losing you for two days…" Higgs's voice got drowned out. Surfaced again. "…think it's important enough."

Fuller's fervor made the hair rise on the back of Spencer's neck. Probably whatever nugget of information he so eagerly sought had nothing to do with Spencer or Leah—but there was a lesser chance that it did.

Higgs seemed unconcerned, though. Even talking quietly, his enthusiasm could be heard. "…more like the SAKO TRG 42…big jump forward from the…"

Spencer couldn't hear the rest, but didn't need to. The SAKO TRG 42 was a Finnish rifle, much admired among the sniper community. He knew guys who'd sworn by it. Except for the unusual stock design, which did indeed remind him of the SAKO, he couldn't say anything special had jumped out at him about this latest weapon sent to army spec ops for experimentation. Arms makers did that often. Most of those rifles didn't prove themselves any better than what snipers were currently using or regular infantry carried.

When Higgs called down the table, "You handled that baby, Spencer. Tell Fuller what you thought."

Spencer dredged up a few admiring comments that got all the men excited, even though most of them lacked the skills to take advantage of a cutting-edge weapon.

What worried him more was the disappearance this afternoon of two of the men along with Higgs. Spencer had seen them coming out of the makeshift armory, expressions satisfied. He knew from background checks that Ken Vogel had spent a decade on a police bomb squad, while Steve Baldwin had been expelled from Stanford's physics program for reasons no one had wanted to talk about. Another Ph.D candidate had hinted that he'd been caught walking out with materials too dangerous to let out of the secure labs.

Spencer knew how most of these men had hooked up with Higgs: the internet. As fast as one fringe site that urged violence and revolution was shut down, another popped up. Like recognized like. He'd also done enough research to know that quite a few members of the group had been at a crossroads in their lives when they saw an opportunity that gave them a sense of purpose.

Baldwin was one example. No other grad program would take him. He must already have been working out what he could do with his knowledge, education and possibly some stashed-away dangerous material. Vogel had just gone through a divorce during which his wife claimed he abused her and the children. His visitation with those kids was to be supervised. He'd have seen that as an unforgivable insult; not only an attempt to humiliate him but also to steal *his* children.

Higgs, of course, had been forced out of the military for his views. Likewise, Arne Larson, given a dishonorable discharge that would limit his job opportunities.

And so it went. TJ Galt had had an unapologetic, vile presence on alt-right websites for several years.

Spencer had to make guesses about a few of them. Leaving the military to find themselves qualified only for poorly paid, low-end jobs, maybe. Don Durand's wife had left him, too. Dirk Ritchie's father had disowned his "embarrassment" of a son.

Yeah, most of these guys had been desperate to latch on to something that would salvage their self-esteem, make them feel important. Not hard to understand.

They wouldn't like prison, he thought grimly.

Even if he was knocked out of the equation, the investigation had been going on long enough, and these men, the pawns, would go down. It would be a shame to see them taking the fall for the scum financing Higgs's great dream, or stealing munitions from the United States.

Dinner was ending, people drifting away as the women cleared the table. Spencer took his time finishing a sizeable piece of Leah's cake and his third cup of coffee. When Higgs, bringing his own coffee cup, slid down the bench to join him, Spencer said, "Did you see Durand today at the target range? He's showing a real knack." Which was, unfortunately, true. "I may try him out at two hundred yards tomorrow. Get him working on positional shooting. It's never safe to assume you can settle in prone and not have to move. Plus bullet trajectory, zeroing in and understanding his range finder." He paused. "Is there any reason to focus on night observation devices?"

"Shouldn't think so." Higgs mulled that over. "If we have time, it probably wouldn't hurt."

Apparently, the plans were still in flux. Or else Higgs knew his small army might find themselves pinned down into the night.

Spencer nodded.

Looking frustrated, Higgs asked, "Is Durand the only one with sniper potential?"

Spencer waggled a hand. "Jason Shedd is getting there. He wasn't a hunter and didn't have comparable experience to the others with a rifle coming in, but he does have patience, an understanding of things like bullet trajectory, and a soft touch. He just had further to go."

"Given his experience as a mechanic, some of that makes sense."

"You don't mind me cutting the two of them out of the herd for more intensive training?"

"No, I'm lucky to have you. Originally, I thought I had two other former snipers on board, but one of them…" He shook his head. "Art Scholler. He was too glib. I got a bad feeling."

"You think he wanted in undercover?"

"Yeah."

Art Scholler *was* FBI, although of course that wasn't

his real name. Spencer had been brought in when Art got cut off cold.

"The other guy?"

"Didn't think he'd take orders. The guy had serious issues."

Spencer grunted. "After enough deployments, a lot of men bring home a cargo plane full of issues."

The colonel grimaced. "True enough. The anger is useful. The rest of it gets in the way."

From a man who'd been a member of the "Chair Force," Higgs's know-it-all attitude rubbed Spencer the wrong way. He knew plenty of airmen who'd been in war zones, but Higgs didn't impress him as one who'd gotten his hands, let alone his boots, dirty. As usual, he stayed agreeable and emphasized how invested he was as they discussed problems concerning a couple of other men on the team, including TJ Galt.

"He makes me think of a pit bull trained for fighting. Keeping him on a leash takes some effort," Higgs observed.

The guy did have a gift for reading people, which wasn't uncommon in predators. Talk about useful skills. In this case… Galt made no effort to hide his anger. If he had PTSD, it likely dated to his childhood. Spencer hadn't uncovered any adult trauma that would explain it.

They parted amicably, which didn't entirely settle the uneasiness Spencer felt, awakened by the half heard conversation. All he could do was pack it away with all his other worries. The weight of them, he thought, was like the kind of hundred-pound pack he'd once thought nothing of hefting. The cargo plane…well, he had other issues, too.

THE NEXT DAY passed in what Leah thought of as deceptive peace. Tim Fuller took off on some errand of his own, which surprised her. This was the first time since she'd been here that any of the men had left alone. Had he been sent to make phone calls for Higgs? Or might he have something personal he had to take care of? She had the uncharitable thought that he could have a meeting with his parole officer.

Along with the other women, she baked, cooked, cleaned and waited on the men. Her real life had come to be out of focus enough to seem hazy. She told herself she was better off that way. She was surprised when she counted back to realize she'd been here nine days. It seemed longer. Well, she couldn't afford to dwell on resentment or have an outbreak of rebellion.

Spencer couldn't afford for her to blow it, either. She suspected he was hurting a lot more than he let on, especially once he joined the other men. His eyes met hers briefly before a large group left for the shooting range. She read reassurance in that instant, but who knew?

In a few minutes the quiet would be shattered by the nonstop barrage. Were these guys really getting a lot more accurate, or were they just wasting ammunition and scaring wildlife for a mile or so around? It spoke to the isolation of the resort that nobody at all had heard the gunfire and reported it to the county sheriff's department or a ranger.

At lunchtime the men inhaled cheeseburgers, baked beans and apple pie *à la mode*. During the afternoon they seemed to break up into smaller groups for—who knew?—hand-to-hand combat training, lessons on stealth?

Or were some of them building a bomb?

That made her shiver.

Dinner was Jennifer's lasagna, loaves and loaves of garlic bread, and a grated carrot and raisin salad Leah made. It was sweet and substantial enough to appeal to men who wouldn't touch a green salad or plain broccoli, but still mostly qualified as a vegetable.

As if she cared about their nutritional intake. But everything she could do to blend in, to make herself valued, was good.

She was first setting out serving bowls when Tim Fuller walked in. Higgs didn't notice at first; Tim ended up sitting at the far end close to the women. The colonel glanced that way but didn't comment.

In her intense dislike, Leah thought, too bad the mythical parole officer hadn't found cause to lock up Tim and throw away the key. She must have smiled, because she discovered he was looking at her with an ugly expression. He and TJ Galt were two of a kind. With Joe Osenbrock, they'd made a vicious triumvirate.

With dinner over, Spencer stayed at the table with his usual refill of coffee, tonight talking to two men she hadn't had much to do with. Jason something and… She couldn't remember the other man's name at all.

The swelling in Spencer's face was going down, she noted, but the bruises had turned a multitude of colors. As she poured coffee from the carafe into Jason's cup, Spencer was saying something about wind, his speech much clearer than it had been even that morning.

The three of them weren't alone; a bunch of the men lingered, happy to hang out with friends, she gathered. During her last trip around the table to refill coffee cups, she shivered at the way several of the men watched her. She wasn't *afraid* of them, exactly—certainly not with Spencer present—but she could tell what they were thinking, and it gave her the creeps.

If there was another demand for more coffee, one of the other women could handle it. Clearly, Spencer wouldn't be ready to go for a while yet, so once she put leftovers away in the commercial refrigerator, she borrowed a sweatshirt hanging on a hook and slipped outside. She'd stay close to the door so she could hear Spencer calling for her. She knew eventually someone would notice she was out here. Sometimes, the other women took breaks like this, only to be chased inside when one of the men came to check on them.

The crisp evening air felt good, and when she tipped her head back, she saw the first stars appearing against a deep purple sky.

It had to be a lot later than usual, to be already getting dark. Fine by her; her new domestic tasks didn't exhaust her, but she'd barely sat down today except for perching on the bench to gobble each meal. Besides…she'd seen a glint in Spencer's eyes when his gaze strayed her way while she was wiping down the table. If he was feeling better enough…

Uncle Edward had built a couple of crude benches back here, wide boards laid over cut-off tree stumps. She chose one and sat, knowing she was almost hidden in the shadow of a cedar that would soon have to be cut down if the lodge was to survive. The roots probably already burrowed beneath the foundation.

Male voices drifted to her, abruptly becoming louder. Leah stiffened, ready to hustle back in the kitchen door if they came any closer.

One of them was Ed Higgs's, she realized.

"You're *sure*?" It was a demand; he didn't want to believe whatever he'd been told.

"Positive. It took some serious searching, but I found a picture. He was coming out of a courthouse, wearing the typical FBI getup."

She quit breathing. *Oh no, oh no.*

Tim Fuller was ebullient, really glad to be able to bring down a man he'd deeply resented. "You know," he continued, "black suit, white shirt, shiny black wingtips, blue tie. He was identified as Special Agent Alex Barr. Chicago office then. Now, I don't know."

"God damn." Anger threaded Higgs's weariness. "I can't believe it."

"Believe it," Tim said. "I printed the picture. Left it in my cabin."

Leah rose to her feet and began feeling her way toward the two steps up to the kitchen door. She stopped just short. No—the minute she opened it, light would spill out. Slip all the way around the lodge, she decided. Spencer might have only minutes.

The last few words she heard before going around the corner of the old log building were "no choice."

Chapter Fourteen

Spencer had stood to go looking for Leah when the front door opened. He turned automatically to see who'd come in. It was her, and the flat-out terror he saw on her face had even the hair on his arms rising. An instant later she'd mostly blanked that out, and he hoped the two men with him hadn't seen her naked emotion.

"I'm ready to head back to the cabin," he said easily. "See you two in the morning. We'll do some more work on setting up shots from different vantage points."

Both appeared eager. Neither had let ego get in the way of learning all they could from him. Amidst the "good-nights," he walked toward Leah.

"Ready to go?"

"Yes." The tremor in her voice would have had him on full alert even if he hadn't already shot straight to maximum readiness. He took her arm as they went out the door and descended the stairs. Then, seeing no one, he bent his head and asked softly, "What's wrong?"

"They know." It tumbled out of her. "Even your real name. Tim told Higgs he'd found a photo of you coming out of a courthouse somewhere."

"Where were they?"

"Out back."

The wheels in his head spun. "We don't dare go back to the cabin." He started hustling her in the opposite direction, to the nearest tree line. Thinking aloud, he said, "The Jeep."

"But…it's dark. And don't you need some tools to hot-wire it?"

"Got the key today," he said, more grateful than he could remember being for anything, except maybe seeing an unconscious Joe Osenbrock being carried away. He still didn't like their only option. The minute anyone heard the sound of the engine being fired up in back, the hunt would be on.

Their best hope, he concluded, was that neither Higgs nor Fuller had had a chance to spread the word. The other guys would wonder, maybe think someone was using the Jeep to drive out to the range to collect something that had been forgotten earlier.

The longer the hesitation, the more chance he and Leah would have to make a clean getaway.

The bigger, more powerful vehicles wouldn't have much, if any, advantage over the Jeep during the first mile or two. The rutted, winding gravel road on the edge of that steep plunge to the river had to be taken with care no matter how hot the driver was to catch someone ahead of him. Unfortunately, he'd have to drive cautiously, too.

Once past that stretch, they'd be overtaken quickly unless they got a big enough head start.

A plan forming in his head, he said, "We have to go for the Jeep. Pray nobody noticed the missing key."

Leah didn't say anything, just jogged at his side. He was glad to see that she'd put on a sweatshirt over her T-shirt; borrowed, he thought. He didn't have any equivalent, which meant he'd be damn cold at night, but the temperature hadn't dropped below freezing anytime this past week, so they should be all right.

He didn't want to even think about how long it would take for them to walk out to the closest neighbor or tiny town where someone might have a working telephone. Shit, why hadn't he kept his own with him, even if it was useless up here? He might have had coverage before they got as far as Glacier or Maple Falls.

Or…what would happen if they headed north for the border? He tried to envision a map, but had a bad feeling that was even rougher country. And it wasn't as if they'd know when they reached the border, or that the entire thing was patrolled 24/7. No towns or highways within remotely easy reach of where they'd emerge, either.

At least heading for the Mount Baker highway, they'd be going downhill. Given his condition, that was a real positive if they had to eventually go on foot.

He stopped Leah as close to the armory as they could get without stepping out in the open. As they stood in silence, he searched the ground between them and the lodge. The only movement was the dart of bats. A faint "whoo" came to his ears from somewhere behind them.

"Okay," he murmured, "I want you to turn around and go back to the head of the road leading out of here." The moon had risen enough to let her see where he was pointing. "When I get there, I'll stop for you to jump in."

"Why don't I just get in the Jeep with you now?" she asked.

He shook his head and talked fast. "There's a chance they'll be waiting for me. If so, you need to take off on your own. You can't follow the road—they'll find you. Traveling in the dark is hard, but try to get a ways before you hide. Got that? I know you can do it. You know this area, wildlife. Better than they do."

"Do you really think we can outrun them?" she whispered.

"No, but I have a plan for that, too."

She pressed her lips together, but nodded instead of arguing as he felt sure she wanted to. Her resistance to the idea of abandoning him to save herself was a part of why he'd fallen for her so fast.

Right now all he did was give her a quick, hard kiss and a push. "Go."

She went, slipping away and disappearing more quickly in the thick darkness beneath the big trees than he'd expected.

He had no choice but to cross the thirty yards or so of open ground to reach the back of the armory. Hating to be so exposed, he did it at a trot. Reaching the back wall, he flattened himself against it, pulled his Sig Sauer and took a moment to slow his breathing.

Then he slid like a shadow around the side, instinct throwing him back to when he'd been a soldier, letting him place his feet soundlessly.

There were no voices. The only light came from lodge windows and, more diffused, the first cabins. The Jeep sat where it had been since Higgs moved it out of the building.

Spencer stepped from the cover of the building, just as another man appeared from where he'd hidden behind the low branches of one of the old cedars. Spencer froze, weapon trained on the man.

"Is what Fuller says true?" asked Dirk Ritchie.

Finger tightening on the trigger, Spencer sweated over

what to do. If he fired, men would pour out of the lodge. And, damn, he didn't want to kill Dirk.

"How did you know I'd be out here?"

"I saw you take the key," Dirk said simply. His hands remained at his sides, even though he was carrying, too.

"Did you?" Spencer said tensely. "You and Helen need to take off, too. Use the confusion after I'm gone."

Dirk stayed quiet.

Spencer pitched his voice low, yet filled it with intensity. "Do you really want to be party to slaughtering what might be hundreds of people who are just thinking about going to their kids' parent-teacher meetings, or the guy they just met, or a sick parent? Remember the Oklahoma City bombing that killed *fifteen* preschooler children?"

Somebody else would come out any minute. He had to *go*.

He took the last steps to the Jeep. "Stop me, or don't."

Only a few strides separated the two men now. Shooting Dirk would feel like murder, but if he didn't—

Dirk stepped back. "Get out of here."

"Thank you."

The other man turned and walked toward the lodge, not hurrying. Switching his attention to the Jeep, Spencer had a sickening thought. What if Dirk had told Higgs he'd seen Spencer pocket the key? What if the Jeep had already been disabled?

He couldn't hesitate. Didn't have time to think of a Plan B. What were the chances he'd make it to the tree line? Gripping the overhead bar above the seats, Spencer swung himself in behind the wheel, grimacing as the quick movement tugged at his stitches and ignited pain in his ribs. No need to open or close a door. He pulled the key from his pocket, inserted it, held his breath and turned it.

The engine roared to life.

The porchlight above the back door into the kitchen came on. A voice called out.

He put the Jeep in gear and slammed his foot down on the gas pedal.

LEAH HADN'T QUITE reached the meeting place when she heard the engine start. Spencer had gotten that far. Thank God. Thank God.

Running, she crossed the weedy gravel to reach the other side and turned to see the Jeep racing toward her. The headlights switched on just before he came even with her. He braked, she grabbed for the door handle and yanked. Metal squealed, but the door refused to give way.

"Jump in."

What she did was fall in, but it worked. The Jeep was rocketing forward long before she untangled herself enough to sit up. If there was a seat belt, her groping fingers didn't find it. Instead, she gripped the edge of the seat with one hand and flattened the other on the dashboard.

The feeble, yellow beams cast by the headlights didn't illuminate the road ahead more than ten or fifteen feet.

"I hope you know this road," she heard herself gasp.

"I do."

He'd been aware from the beginning that there was the possibility he'd have to run for it, she supposed, which meant being ultra-observant about little details like the only outlet from the resort. Spencer sounded awfully tense, though.

"Do you hear—?"

He didn't have to finish. Yes, deep-throated engines had been started. Aside from her own car, every vehicle she'd seen up here dwarfed this old Jeep. The giant SUVs and pickups could almost run right over the top of it.

She craned her neck to see behind her. Bright lights appeared.

Spencer mumbled a few obscenities.

"You have a plan." How did she sound even semi-calm? The cold wind whipped her hair and made her eyes water. Gravel crunched beneath the tires. She dreaded the moment when they reached the stretch above the river.

She ought to be thankful it was dark, and she wouldn't be able to see the valley floor.

"I'm going to take a few curves," he said tersely, "brake long enough for you to leap out and run for the woods, then try to set up a skid so that the Jeep goes over the edge and down into the river. They'll think we screwed up."

"What if you can't jump out?" she said numbly.

"I don't have time to try to find a heavy enough rock to brace the accelerator."

"There's something behind the seat." She'd caught a glimpse when she was facedown after her tumble into the Jeep. She didn't know what she'd seen, but now she got on her knees and felt down in the cavity. "I think it's a car battery. They're heavy, aren't they?"

"Yes. Damn. That should work. Can you pick it up?"

"I think so." Her position was completely unsafe, crouched instead of sitting while trying to heft a heavy object between the seat backs. If he started that skid too soon… Laughter almost bubbled up. Unsafe. *Right.*

She tugged and rocked it until she got her fingers beneath the rusty metal, and then twisted, plunked onto her butt and lowered the battery to her lap.

She sensed Spencer's quick glance.

"We're coming up on a good place to let you out. Just

beyond, there's a gap where the guardrail has rusted and broken. That's what I'll aim for."

Leah's head bobbed as if she was just fine with any of this. "You'll find me?"

"Yes." He braked, skidded enough to have him swearing again and stopped. She scrambled over the door, leaving the battery on the seat. He accelerated again before she started running.

THIS WOULD ALL be for nothing if the Jeep hung up on a stubbornly intact stretch of guardrail, but he had no time to waste to scout ahead to be sure he knew where the break was. All Spencer could do was judge distances from his memory.

Here.

He braked, cranked the wheel hard, then lifted the battery over the gearshift. Got out.

The sound of approaching engines was too loud. No time.

He slipped the gearshift into Neutral and shoved the battery down on the accelerator at almost the same moment. The Jeep leaped forward, the open door whacked him and he tumbled free.

Without looking to see if he'd succeeded, he ran full out for the bank on the uphill side of the road and scrambled up it. There, he paused only momentarily, turning. The Jeep had disappeared, the sound of its engine drowned out by approaching vehicles. Had the steering somehow corrected itself?

Then he heard metal tearing, screaming in agony… followed by an unholy explosion.

Just as the first set of headlights illuminated that stretch of road he faded back into the forest.

Deep in the trees, Spencer couldn't see any better than he would have in a cavern a mile below the ground. He should have set up some kind of plan for him and Leah to find each other when separated. If she didn't stick pretty close to the road, it would take sheer luck for them to stumble onto each other.

Swearing silently as the receding shouts faded behind him, he made his way uphill, trying to stay twenty feet or so from the road. If the sound of pursuit reached him, he wouldn't be able to keep doing that. At least he could be assured he *would* hear anyone chasing him on foot; it was impossible to pass through the tangle of vegetation without making some noise.

Something swiped him in the face. He shook his head and spun. A swag of lichen, pale even in the limited light, still swayed.

He had a memory of telling Leah *not* to follow the road if she had to take off on her own. Surely to God she'd use common sense and realize they didn't have a prayer of finding each other if she didn't.

He kept moving, pausing every ten feet or so to listen.

Uphill, he heard a muffled cry. Animal? Bird?

Some thrashing followed.

Moving as quietly as he could, he headed that direction. What if she'd hurt herself? he thought suddenly but pushed the fear aside.

Quiet closed around him. Maintaining any orientation took determination, and Spencer wouldn't swear he wasn't veering off a straight line toward a sound that could have been a porcupine waddling through the forest, or a bear crashing on its way.

Guessing himself to be close, he finally said, "Leah?" All he could do was hope he wasn't too close to the road—and that Higgs hadn't been smart enough to have men walking it, listening and watching for any indication that someone was in there and not dead on the rocky bank of the low-running river.

"Spencer?"

"Hold still."

She didn't answer. He stepped forward carefully. He felt renewed irritation at himself; if he'd had his phone, he'd have also had a flashlight—although he wouldn't have dared use it now.

He put out a foot and found only space, teetering before he drew back.

A woeful whisper came from the darkness. "I fell in."

Spencer crouched. His eyes had adjusted well enough for him to see fern fronds waving wildly. Presumably, they disguised a hollow. Maybe a giant tree stump had rotted into nothingness; who knew?

"I'm here," he murmured. "Are you hurt?"

"I don't think so."

"Okay." Relief flooded him. He held out a hand. "Can you see me?"

"Yes." More stirring among what he thought was mostly lush clumps of sword ferns. A slim hand seized his, and he exerted steady pressure until she scrambled out of the hollow and fell against him.

Her arms wrapped his torso even as he held her tight, ignoring the pain in his wrist.

Against his chest, she mumbled, "I was so scared! And afraid I couldn't find you, and—"

Exhilarated because they *had* found each other, he chuckled. Her hair stirred against his cheek.

"I was getting a little worried myself," he admitted.

Her head came up. "What *happened*?"

"The Jeep sailed over the cliff and exploded when it hit the rocks at the bottom. Last I knew, the SUVs coming up behind us stopped there. I heard voices. Whether they bought it entirely… I don't know. I'm betting they don't find a way to get to the Jeep until daylight, though. Whether they're taking into account the possibility we weren't in the Jeep, I don't know."

After a moment she nodded. "Now what?" she asked, sounding as if she was running through options in her head.

That was an excellent question. From where they stood, downhill would take them southeast. They'd almost have to hit the highway. Even so, he'd give a lot for a topographical map. And, hey, food, warmer clothes, possibly a sleeping bag, the flashlight and phone, the absence of which he'd already regretted, and probably a lot of other things that hadn't yet occurred to him but would as soon as he or Leah needed them.

He winced. Like the bottle of pain meds. Except, he'd stuck two of them in his pocket, meaning to take them with dinner but decided not to show his vulnerability so publicly. He'd hold out as long as he could before taking them one at a time.

Preferably after they came on at least a trickle of water.

Right now…

"Two choices. Keep going, away from the road. Or hunker down for the night. If we're going to do that, you found us a great place to hide."

He kind of thought she made a face before saying, "I agree. What's your preference? You okay?" She glanced at his still-bandaged wrist.

Reluctantly, he said, "I'm fine. I think we move on. We're too close to the road here. By morning, if not sooner, they'll be looking for us. I haven't had the impression that any of them are real outdoorsmen. A few say they've hunted, so maybe I'm wrong. Still, most outdoor experience doesn't prepare you for a temperate rain forest."

"Have *you* ever spent any time in the north Cascades?"

"Yeah, did some climbing here years ago." Over the course of several leaves, a buddy, Aaron, and he had ascended seven mountains altogether, from the Rockies to the Teton Mountains and here in the Cascades. Spencer hadn't gone climbing since Aaron had been killed in a firefight.

"What about bears? I know what they can do, remember."

He decided not to remind her about porcupines, also nocturnal. "They're rarely aggressive with humans, as you know."

After a minute Leah straightened away from him. "I'm ready."

Conscious of his many aches and the sharp pain in his side and thigh and wrist, he'd have liked to sleep for a few hours. But he wouldn't feel any better tomorrow morning, the next day, or the next. Even a little distance covered tonight would give them a head start tomorrow.

He nodded and led the way, hoping like hell he was going approximately in the right direction—and that they wouldn't stumble out on the winding road where someone might be waiting for them.

The parable about the blind leading the blind crossed his mind. Aesop? Just as well he couldn't remember how that story ended.

Chapter Fifteen

Because of his recent wounds and undoubted pain, Leah insisted they take regular breaks to rest. He didn't argue, but gave away his tension by regularly pushing a button on his watch to check the time. She didn't bother asking how long they'd been on their way, and he didn't offer the information. The day's stresses had caught up with her ages ago—and if she found out that was really only half an hour ago, she might scream—but really she was grateful to be so tired; she couldn't do any concentrated worrying. She just followed in Spencer's wake, knowing at least that she wouldn't tumble into another hole unless he did first.

The ground was soft and uneven, though. Squishy in places, more from the depth of the moss and decomposing organic matter. They clambered over and walked around fallen trees, some that might have come down last winter, others already rotting and serving as nurse logs for saplings. In some of those places faint rays of moonlight found them, and she glimpsed tiny distant stars. Much of the time enormous trees reared above them, blocking out the sky. She had a vague memory of Uncle Edward talking about some true old-growth forest close by and wondered if that was what this was.

It might be, because at some point the walking became easier since they weren't having to fight the ferns and salmonberries and who-knew-what that scratched and tripped them. The darkness was almost absolute, the boles of standing trees enormous. Not that the ground didn't remain uneven, the extreme dark hiding obstacles that would cause Spencer to growl under his breath before he helped her around or over them.

She walked right into him when he stopped.

"I'm beat," he said. "I suggest we get on the other side of this log and try to sleep a little."

Since she was very close to sleepwalking, Leah thought she could do that. And she knew Spencer must be dead on his feet to actually admit to needing a rest.

They had to go around this time. Taking her hand, he guided her. The trunk must have been six or eight feet in diameter. Even decomposing, it reared above her head. On the back side, he advanced slowly before stopping, seeming to feel his way. "This looks as good as anyplace."

Looks? *She* couldn't see a thing, but she wasn't about to quibble, either.

Once she'd squatted and then plunked down, she tried very hard not to think about what insects inhabited a rotting log. Would there be snakes around? Not poisonous ones, she was pretty sure. Her hand bumped something that sort of...crumbled. Recoiling, she made out a lighter shape against the dark backdrop of loam and moss. Mushrooms. Now, *those* could be poisonous, but she didn't plan to eat one.

She heard a groan as Spencer carefully lowered himself beside her. Oh, heavens—she should have helped him. Given the possibly broken wrist, he wouldn't lean any weight on that arm, and the gash in his thigh had to hinder him.

Too late.

"God, this feels good," he said after a minute.

"Uh-huh." Except she felt herself listing sideways until she came up against his big, solid body. "Can we lie down?" She was slurring.

"We can."

They shifted, she squirmed, he wrapped her in his arms and they ended up prone. He spooned her body from behind. His arm made a perfect pillow. Her eyelids sank closed, she mumbled something that was supposed to be "good night" and fell asleep.

CRADLING THIS WOMAN he suspected he loved, Spencer wasn't as quick to drop off to sleep.

When things went to shit, it happened fast.

If not for the damn fight, he'd be in a lot better physical shape and thus more confident that he and Leah would make it safely out of this densely wooded, uninhabited forest. If he'd had even ten or fifteen minutes' warning, he could have filled a pack with food, first-aid supplies, flashlight and more. As it was, they were screwed if either of them so much as developed blisters on their feet. His boots protected his ankles, while Leah's athletic shoes were fine for walking, but wouldn't keep her from turning an ankle.

They just about had to move during the daytime rather than at night even though they might be spotted. Especially given their physical condition, they had to be able to see where they were stepping. In fact, they were lucky no disaster had already occurred with them blundering around in the dark.

He cast his mind back to that brief encounter with Dirk. Spencer had had no idea he'd been seen pocketing the key. If it had been anybody but Dirk…if Dirk had told

Higgs, or when he saw Spencer at the Jeep had opened his mouth and yelled… No point in going there now.

He hoped Dirk *had* kept his mouth shut and did find a way to take off.

His thoughts jumped again.

How the hell had that idiot Fuller stumbled on the photo?

He actively tried not to be photographed. With the press sticking their noses in everywhere, he'd been unable to completely evade them given that he had to testify in court. Most outlets were good about not publishing those pictures, but he knew of a couple that had made it into newspapers or TV news stories. There were undoubtedly more online. In fact, the one Tim Fuller had described in Leah's hearing had to be one of those.

His ascendancy in Higgs's estimation had rubbed Tim, in particular, wrong for months. But had he made mistakes that gave away his law-enforcement background? Spencer shook his head slightly. He had no idea, and at this point that was irrelevant. Permanently irrelevant, if he declined to go undercover again.

Tim had to have sensed/heard/seen something to make him do that kind of online prowling. Or, hell, had he contacted a friend who was more of a computer wizard? Maybe, Spencer concluded.

For all that things had gone to shit, he and Leah had made their getaway and, right now, were fine. They wouldn't starve to death in the next two or three days.

The tricky moment would be when they had to approach a road.

He nuzzled Leah's silky hair and let sleep claim him.

HIS BODY'S DEMAND awakened him before Leah had so much as moved. In fact, it didn't appear either of them had made any of the restless shifts in position normal to sleepers. Her head still rested on his biceps; he still spooned her.

He'd have enjoyed the moment if he didn't need to empty his bladder, and if his body wasn't reporting multiple other complaints. His shoulder ached, his arm was stiff, his wrist felt broken, his thigh throbbed and his whole left side was on fire. In a general way, he felt like crap. What if he was coming down with a cold or the flu?

Stuffing a groan back down where it came from, he gently shook Leah. "Time to rise and shine."

She whimpered, stirred and whimpered again. "I'm stiff. Although I don't know why I'm whining. You're the one who is injured."

He didn't say so, but he dreaded getting up.

Leah did get to her hands and knees, then to her feet. She suddenly said, "I need—" and bolted for a nearby tree.

Since he'd rather she not see him dealing with his infirmities, he got up, too, in slow increments. Water or no water, he was taking one of those damn pills. Just as she reappeared around the tree, he shuffled toward a different one.

There, he used the facilities, then did some stretches before returning to Leah.

"Turns out GrubHub can't find us to deliver that Denny's breakfast," he said. "Guess we'll have to do without."

Her smile rewarded him. "There are berries ripe, if we can find a clearing."

"Stumble on one, you mean."

"At least we can *see*."

That was an improvement, he'd concede.

He started out. He got the pill down, but was left with a foul taste in his mouth. Walking loosened muscles, and the pill did some good, too, but he felt as if someone was stabbing his thigh with a red-hot poker. All he could do was block out what he couldn't change and go on.

By the time sunlight made it to the forest floor, it was diffuse, soft, even tinted green-gold. He still had to watch carefully for the best places to set down his feet, which made for slow going. Common sense did battle with a sense of urgency; what if finding out they were being dogged by the FBI inspired Higgs to launch an early attack?

Helplessness didn't sit well with Spencer, but practically, there wasn't a damn thing he could do to prevent any immediate action Higgs took. He doubted a bomb had actually been built, but the debacle during the Boston Marathon had demonstrated how much damage could be done by really primitive bombs. He was afraid Ken Vogel, with his bomb squad experience, could put together any number of lethal explosive devices even without input from a budding physicist with an interest in nuclear fission.

Until he got his hands on a phone, he had no way to alert his office that the operation had blown up on him.

Then focus on the moment. Except for my aching body. Best not to think about that.

Deciding it was time for a short break, he spotted a moss-covered rock more or less the right height to let them sit.

Once they did so, Leah looked at him with worry in her eyes. "What do you think they're doing?"

"Right now?" He checked his watch. "Struggling upriver to the wreck. That'll take them at least a couple of hours from the best place to leave vehicles."

"And then?"

Trust her to echo his concerns.

"I think there are two logical options for Higgs. One is to pack up and leave, probably have the others disperse until he can line up an alternate place for them to train. The other is to go for an immediate attack."

"Immediate?"

"Once he realizes we're on foot, he may decide to have the men hunt us for a day or two. Catching us would solve their problem with timing." He didn't have to say, *executing us*. "Otherwise, he could pull together a plan for an attack that might not be quite as spectacular as he intended, but those rocket launchers alone give him the firepower to threaten a gathering of politicians or even the president himself."

"You know him. Which is more likely?"

He didn't hesitate. "Dispersing. He likes the pieces to fit together. He'll want the big bang, so to speak. To accomplish that, the attack was to take place on a lot of levels. Bomb or bombs, rocket launchers, snipers picking off counterattackers or survivors trying to get away. Maybe even sending in a squad of men who don't have the range to be snipers to mow people down."

Leah looked more horrified by the minute. "That's why he wanted you."

"He needed a sniper to train others. That's what I was doing."

The urgency tapped on his shoulder, and he rose to his feet. "I'll stiffen up if we stop for long. Let's get going."

They continued in silence, Spencer straining to hear any sounds unnatural for the forest. Every now and again, a bird would flit by, most unidentifiable, a few common enough he recognized them, like the crow and later a jay, although that had unfamiliar coloration. They weren't plagued by a lot in the way of insects. Mosquitoes and even flies would prefer moist areas, butterflies open meadows with flowers. The rotting logs were no doubt rife with crawly things, centipedes, sow bugs and the like. Nothing that stung, as far as he knew.

And, on a glass half-full note, it wasn't raining. He knew from experience that rain wasn't uncommon here even in July and August. Some water to drink would be welcome; in fact, thirst was increasingly making itself known. But getting wet and having to keep going, pants chafing their legs, even socks soaked, that could be miserable.

"I hear something," she whispered.

He stopped and cocked his head. Speak of the devil. That had to be running water.

He turned, held a finger to his lips and progressed with even greater care. The small stream they found took enough of a tumble over rocks to have caused the delicate rippling sound. A deer that had been drinking saw them and bounded away.

"Oh, my."

"This water will likely make us sick," he told her, dredging through his memory. "Giardia is the problem, as I recall. If we could boil it…"

She wrinkled her nose. "No stove handy."

"Nope. I don't think symptoms will catch up with us for at least a week or two." He hoped that recollection was accurate. "We'll need to ask for treatment once we have a chance to see a doctor."

If she doubted that time would come, she didn't comment.

Spencer splashed his face to cool it, and wished for a water bottle, too.

If wishes were horses...

His head had begun to throb. He debated taking the

last pill now versus waiting, deciding on the latter. He might need it more come morning.

LEAH'S STOMACH GROWLED. She pressed a hand to it, hoping Spencer hadn't heard. He had enough to worry about, and given the toll his injuries took, he needed fuel for his body even more than she did.

He'd gotten quieter as the day went on, too. Pain tightened his face whenever he didn't remember to hide it. The flush she saw on his lean cheeks above dark stubble made her more uneasy. Even with all the willpower in the world, pushing himself to get back on his feet as soon as he did couldn't have been good for his recovery. She'd known all along that his risk of infection was high. She'd been able to don sterile latex gloves, and the gauze, scissors, needle and suturing material were sterile, too. Unfortunately, the blade of that black-handled knife Joe had used on him wasn't. Then there were the dirty shirts used to stem the bleeding. This was an awful time for the infection to appear. Dumb thing to think—was there a time that would have been *good*? If only there'd been antibiotics in that first-aid kit, or Spencer had stocked them along with the pain meds.

He was capable of going on with a fever, at least for now, Leah convinced herself. But what if they hadn't found their way out of the wilderness two days from now? Three?

He did go on, and on, hours upon hours, until her thighs burned and she'd quit thinking about anything but the next step. She'd thought of taking the lead but decided against it. With Spencer in front, he was more likely to stop when he needed it, while she might misjudge his stamina.

Just then Spencer stopped, Leah stumbling to a halt

just before she walked into him. Blinking, she realized the light had changed without her noticing, deepening into purple.

"We risk getting injured if we continue in the dark," Spencer said, his voice rough. "I'm sorry we didn't come across any berries."

She took the hand he held out. "Going without for a day or two isn't that big a deal. Isn't fasting supposed to be good for you?"

"I've read that. I'm not convinced."

"Me, either." Studying him anxiously, she said, "I should look at your wounds while there's still some light."

"Why?" He let her go and lowered himself to another mossy piece of ground with a few pained grunts he apparently couldn't hold back.

"Why? Because—" She didn't finish.

"I'm not sure we even dare wash the wounds out in a stream," he said wearily. "What if that introduces different microorganisms into my body? And, in turn, I'd be introducing bacteria into the stream that might be deadly to fish or mammals downstream that drink out of it. What's more—" he continued inexorably "—we have no supplies to rewrap my wounds and especially my ribs."

The ribs might be hurting him more than anything, she realized. The binding did offer some support. Yes, she could tear her T-shirt into strips, say, but the knit fabric would be too stretchy to provide the same kind of support.

"I'm sorry." She sank down beside him. "I wish I could do something."

"I'll be okay. I just wish—" He shook his head as if regretting having said that much.

"Wish?" Leah prodded.

"I was sure I'm not leading us astray."

"Short of your watch converting into a compass, I don't see how you can know. You're not Superman, Spencer." Then she stopped again and frowned. "Why am I still calling you that?"

"You don't have to." With a sigh, he rolled his head. "But I might not answer to Alex."

"Really?"

He managed a smile. "No, I'm kidding, but I've even been thinking of myself as Spencer. It's like… Do you speak a foreign language?"

"I'm pretty fluent in Spanish."

"You think in it when you're speaking it, right?"

"Yes."

"When I go undercover, I immerse myself to that extent. I'm not Special Agent Alex Barr. I *am* Spencer Wyatt. I can't slip."

"I can see that," she said slowly, even as she wondered how he could possibly do that. He'd said something once about not being sure who he was anymore, and how he'd done things, bad things, he didn't name. Not raped women, she felt certain. If he'd beaten men to death, or shot them, she believed he'd had adequate provocation.

Apparently losing interest in the subject, he said, "I think I'd like to lie down."

He let her help him, which said a lot about his condition. He encouraged her to join him, and soon they were curled up together. As the temperature dropped with nightfall, he had to be cold on top of everything else—unless he was burning up, of course. Leah rubbed his bare arms and lifted his hands to her skin beneath her sweatshirt. That he didn't protest told her how lousy he felt.

She kept thinking about a man who'd spent—she didn't know—much of the past several years, at least, undercover with violent fanatics who wanted to remake the country into their twisted ideals. She hadn't heard any slurs from him, as she had from some of the other men, but he must know all the right things to say to allow him to blend in.

How jarring it must be to return to his real life, whatever that was. An apartment? How homey was that, when it stayed empty for months on end? He presumably had no pets, he'd said he wasn't close to family and she didn't believe he had a girlfriend or fiancée waiting patiently for him. Spencer Wyatt—no, Alex Barr —wasn't the kind of man to make promises to one woman and have sex with another.

Feeling him relax into sleep, she thought, *I do know him. Of course I do.*

He'd been willing to give his life for her. That said enough about him to erase even fleeting doubts.

Hunger pushed off sleep for another while, but she was exhausted enough to drop off eventually.

Waking suddenly, the darkness unabated, she lay very still. What had disturbed her…? The answer came immediately. A wave of convulsive shivering seized Spencer. His back arched and his teeth chattered before he could clamp them shut.

Terrified, she realized there wasn't a single thing she could do except hold him, and keep holding him.

Chapter Sixteen

A murky haze that made Leah think of smog had settled over the usually crystal-clear silver-gray of Spencer's eyes. Or maybe it was more like a film. All she knew was that he couldn't possibly be seeing as well as usual. He couldn't hide that he was still shivering, too.

She watched as he staggered out of her sight to pee, returning a minute later. His usual grace had deserted him. How could they keep going? If they'd been on a smooth path or the road, maybe, but as it was…

How can we not *keep going?* Leah asked herself bleakly. It wasn't as if he had a twenty-four-hour flu bug. He wouldn't get better until he was on powerful antibiotics. If they didn't reach a hospital, he might die.

Even if they'd both been healthy, each day would be more grueling than the last, considering that they were able to drink only occasionally, and had nothing whatsoever to eat. It surely couldn't be that far before they reached the highway.

"You ready?" he asked gruffly.

Leah nodded. "Let me go first today."

He stared at her for long enough, she wasn't sure whether he was really slow in processing what she'd said, or resisting the idea. But finally, he nodded. Good.

She had to look around before deciding which way

they'd come from, and therefore which way she needed to go. Some feature of ancient geology had formed a shallow dip here, and the forest was dense enough, she couldn't see very far ahead. As they started walking, her thighs let her know when the land tilted downward again.

Once, she said, "Oh, did you see that?" and turned, for a minute not seeing Spencer at all. Her heart took a huge, painful leap.

He plodded around the trunk of one of the forest giants. He hadn't heard her, and the small mammal she'd seen had long since dashed out of sight. His teeth were clenched, his eyes glazed, but he was able to keep moving.

No choice.

From then on she made sure to look over her shoulder regularly to be sure he was still with her.

The pace seemed awfully slow, but she felt sure that raw determination was all that kept Spencer moving.

A distant sound caught her attention. She grabbed Spencer's arm to stop him and listened, momentarily confused. That could be a river, but if it was the Nooksack, that meant they'd also reached the highway that followed it. Of course there were tributaries, like the one that flowed from the side of Mount Baker, running past the resort to meet the larger Nooksack, but the water didn't rush like—

It was a car engine. It had to be.

Traffic on the highway? Or had they unintentionally come close to the resort road?

Leah wished she could be sure where the sound came *from*, but her best guess at direction wasn't even close to precise. It wouldn't be so bad if they spotted the resort road, would it? At least they'd know where they were.

She glanced at Spencer, and fear gripped her. He looked bad. Really bad.

Maybe she should take the gun from him, start carrying it herself. If one of the men suddenly appeared in front of them, was Spencer capable of reacting quickly enough?

Could I? she asked herself, and was afraid she knew the answer. There was a reason cops and soldiers were supposed to spend so much time at gun ranges. *She'd* never fired a weapon in her life. To aim it at a person, one she knew, and pull the trigger—and that was assuming the gun didn't have a safety, which she had no idea how to identify.

Keep going. She had a very bad feeling that, if they took a break and sat down, she might have a hard time getting Spencer up again. She wouldn't be doing it with sheer muscle, since he had to outweigh her by eighty pounds, at least. There had to be a way…but he was still walking.

The light began to seem brighter ahead. They emerged from the trees between one step and the next. Stumps and the kind of mess left by logging told her this land had been clear-cut, probably a couple of years ago. Some scruffy small trees grew, alder and maple, she thought. And a wealth of huckleberry bushes, many growing out of rotting stumps.

"Berries!" she cried.

Spencer bumped into her. For the first time in several hours, comprehension showed on his face. She steered him to a bush covered with purple-blue, ripe berries. Once she saw that he was able to pick them himself and stuff them into his mouth, she started doing the same.

They shouldn't eat very many; the last thing they

needed was to end up sick, but oh, they tasted good, the flavor bursting on her tongue. And she was so hungry!

Within minutes her fingers were stained purple, as were Spencer's. But who cared?

Bushes a short distance away shook. Hand outstretched for more berries, Leah stared. It kept shaking, and that was an odd sound. Sort of…snuffling. Or grunting.

"Spencer," she whispered.

His head turned, his eyes sharp. He had to have heard the alarm in her voice.

He stared at the trembling leaves, and in a move so fast it blurred, had his gun in his hand.

"We need to back away," she murmured.

He nodded agreement.

"Probably won't pay any attention to us," she said, just as quietly.

A stick cracked under her foot. She'd have frozen in place if his hand hadn't gripped her upper arm and kept her moving.

Craning her neck, she saw brown fur. An enormous head pushed between bushes. Supposedly, bears didn't have very good vision, but it was staring right at them. And, oh, dear God, it kept pushing through the growth, canes snapping.

"Not too fast."

The bear wasn't charging, but Leah would have sworn it grew to fill her field of vision. Seeing the hump between the shoulders had her already racing pulse leaping.

"Spencer!" she whispered loudly.

"I see."

Another step, another. The head swung back and forth. Leah would swear the small eyes looked angry.

Suddenly, Spencer cursed, and she, too, heard a deep-throated engine cut off. Car doors slam.

"I see them!" yelled a voice she recognized and detested.

TJ Galt.

The racket off to the right made the bear even more agitated. It took a few steps toward them. Ignoring the two voices Leah now heard, Spencer held her to a slow, steady retreat.

Until the scrubby growth toward what had to be the resort road began to shake and snap as the men trampled through it. One of them yodeled, "Got you now, traitor!"

The grizzly lowered its head and charged.

"Run!" Spencer ordered. She didn't hesitate, racing as fast as she could back the way they'd come. It was a minute before she realized he'd split away, probably intending to draw the bear's attention.

But a gun barked. Again and again. TJ and Arne intended to shoot them down.

She heard a crashing behind her and dared a look back. The bear had stopped and swung toward the two men who were yelling gleefully. One took a shot at her that stung her arm. Spencer… She saw him trip, recover his footing and keep running.

The grizzly charged the men. One of them bellowed, "Bear!"

As if she'd stepped into a noose, Leah pitched forward. She didn't land gently, but didn't even acknowledge pain. Pushing herself to her hands and knees, she twisted to see what was happening.

Gunshots exploded but didn't slow the bear. Screaming, one of the men went down. The other stumbled backward. Even from this distance, she saw his horror.

"Keep going!" Spencer roared.

She used her position like a sprinter on a starting block to run, gasping, hurting, horrified by the snarls and terrible screams she heard behind her.

Leah hadn't gotten far into the woods when she slammed against a hard body. Even as she fought, she couldn't stop herself from looking back.

"Leah! It's me. It's just me."

She was whimpering as she took in his face. If she'd thought he looked bad before, it was nothing to now. He was as sickened as she was by what was happening behind them.

"Come on." He all but dragged her forward. She jogged to keep up with his long strides. Then she realized which hand he gripped her with.

"Your wrist."

"To hell with my wrist." He still held his gun in his right hand. "Let's circle around. If they both went down, we might have transportation."

The words were barely out of his mouth when the engine roared to life. Tires skidded on gravel as the driver floored it.

There was one more strangled scream.

SPENCER'S LUNGS HEAVED like old-fashioned bellows, and his heart was trying to pound its way out of his chest.

He and Leah had slid down an unexpected drop-off and collapsed at the bottom, their backs to a big tree.

She breathed as fast as he did, her eyes dilated, each exhalation sounding like a sob although she wasn't crying. "TJ," she gasped. "That was TJ."

"Yeah," he managed. "And Arne."

"He took off and left him." She sounded disbelieving.

He and she had taken off and left TJ to a terrible death, too, Spencer couldn't help thinking. They'd had more motivation to run even than Arne had, but Spencer also thought sticking around to try to rescue the grizzly's victim would have been useless and possibly a death sentence.

Shaking from reaction or the damn fever or both, he got out, "You okay?"

"I…don't know."

He wasn't a hundred percent sure he hadn't been shot. In fact, he bent his head to search for blood. He saw some, but on Leah, not him.

With an exclamation, he laid down his Sig Sauer and reached for her arm. "Does this hurt?"

She tipped her head to peer dubiously at the bloodstain on her upper arm. "Something stung me."

Yeah, there was a rip, all right. He parted it enough to see that the bullet had barely skimmed her flesh. Its passage might leave a scar, but the blood flow wasn't worrisome. Her face was decorated with some new scratches strung with beads of scarlet like polished rubies crossing her cheek and forehead.

He lifted a hand to smooth her hair, tangled with leaves and twigs. "Damn," he whispered. "I thought that was it."

"Me, too." She blinked against some moisture in her eyes. "TJ sneered at me when I said I was watching for bears. You know, when we were picking berries…"

"We'd better not stick around," Spencer said after a minute. As shitty as he felt, he wanted to kiss her, and maybe more. Nothing like a shot of adrenaline to fire up a man's blood and clear his head. Unfortunately, adrenaline didn't hang around long, and he'd crash when it dissipated. "That bear has to have taken a bullet or two. It'll be mad."

"It won't die?"

"I don't know. Not immediately, I'm guessing. Probably it just thinks it got stung by some yellow jackets."

Gutsy as always, Leah nodded sturdily. She got to her feet faster than he did and picked up his gun for him. Holstering it, he said, "I guess we found the road."

"Yes, and I'm pretty sure we're close to the turnoff."

"We still have to be careful, you know."

Her head bobbed. He had the feeling she was checking to see how *he* was, even as he did the same for her.

She looked like she'd been in a cat fight. Scratches, new and old, on her face and hands. Hair a mess. Her clothes, ripped and dirty, hung on her as if she'd already lost weight. Horror darkened her beautiful eyes.

He hadn't taken very good care of her.

They were alive, he reminded himself. Unlike TJ Galt.

An hour later they had circled around the clear-cut land and saw the resort road. It was paved here, which encouraged him. Not that far to go.

They hiked on, trying to move parallel to it, just near enough they could see it occasionally. Twice they saw a black SUV driving slowly along the road, once heading out, then coming back up.

"They still think they can cut us off," he said.

"What if the driver let off a couple guys who are on foot out here with us?"

The possibility was real, but there was nothing he could do that he wasn't already. He fought to stay in the moment while fighting a blinding headache, chills and a tendency to find himself in other times and places.

A kid, hiding in the woods near his house after his father had used his belt on him. Rage and fear and shame filled him. Sunlight in his eyes, and he was baking in the heat of a street between mud-colored buildings in a village in Afghanistan, feeling eyes on him from every direction. Skin crawling.

Turning his head to see Leah anchored him, so he kept doing it. She needed him. He couldn't let her down.

"I think I see someone," she whispered.

He stared hard in the direction she was looking. Yeah, that desert camo didn't quite work in the green northwest forest.

He nudged Leah, and they very, very quietly retreated, then turned east to parallel the highway, heading toward Mount Baker. Should have known they couldn't pop out right here. Had Higgs sent out his minions to drive up and down the highway, too? Should they hunker down and wait out the day, not try to flag anyone down until morning?

Might be safer...but Spencer bet that by morning, Higgs and the others would have decamped. He would very much like to round them up here and now. Brooding, he thought, yeah, but what were the odds of getting a team here in time?

Even if the sheriff's department had a SWAT unit, could they stand up to the kind of weaponry Higgs's group had? An image formed in his head of the flare of rocket fire followed by a helicopter exploding.

He grimaced.

And, damn, as disreputable as he and Leah looked, how long would it take for police to be able to verify that he was who he said he was, and take action?

What if his head was in Afghanistan or Iraq when they reached a police station? Hard to take a crazy man seriously.

They trudged on, Leah in the lead again.

Her head turned. "I hear a car."

Pulled from the worries that had circled around and

around, he listened, too. That was definitely a car, not an SUV or pickup. Which would have been good news if they'd been close enough to the highway to stick out a thumb. Also, if they could convince some backpacker on his way back down to civilization to hide them on backseat and floorboards so they weren't seen as they passed the resort road.

He realized he'd said that out loud when Leah said, "What if we *cross* the highway and follow it until we're past the resort road?"

It was lucky one of them had a working brain.

HER IDEA HAD sounded practical, but preparing to run across the empty highway, she was almost as scared as she'd been with a grizzly charging after her and bullets flying, too.

She and Spencer would be completely exposed for the length of time it took to slide into a ditch, climb up onto pavement, race across the highway and get across another ditch and into the woods on the far side. SUVs and pickup trucks with powerful engines could approach fast. Yes, but they could be heard from a distance, she reminded herself, even out of sight around a curve.

She stole an anxious look at Spencer. "Ready?"

"Yeah," he said hoarsely. "You say go."

"Okay." She took a few steadying breaths, tensed and said, "Go!"

Side by side, they slid on loamy soil into the ditch, used their hands to scrabble their way up to the road and ran.

Not until they plunged on the other side through dangling ropes of lichen and the stiff lower branches of evergreen trees did she take another breath. They stumbled to a stop, momentarily out of sight from the highway, and Spencer grinned at her.

Her heart gave a squeeze. That smile was delighted and sexy at the same time, and it didn't matter how awful he looked otherwise. When he held out his arms, she tumbled into them, wrapping her own around his lean torso.

She might have stayed longer if he didn't radiate worrisome heat.

"We're not safe yet," she mumbled into his shoulder.

"No, but we're one step closer."

Stupidly teary-eyed, she was smiling, too. Swiping her cheeks on his grungy T-shirt, she made herself lower her arms and back away.

"I don't know about you, but I'm starved. I vote we get going."

The jubilant grin had become an astonishingly tender smile. "I'll second that."

Chapter Seventeen

Two hours later they passed the turn-off to the resort without seeing a single vehicle or any camouflage-clad, armed men hiding in wait. They'd heard a fair amount of passing traffic, but chose not to attempt to stop anyone yet.

Their pace grew slower and slower. The trees weren't as large here, resulting in dense undergrowth. Leah's body had become more and more reluctant. Her legs didn't want to take the next step. She quit diverting to avoid getting slapped by branches. Stumbling, she'd barely catch herself before she did another face-plant. She had never in her life been so tired—and she didn't have a raging fever. She kept checking on him, sometimes slyly so he wouldn't notice. Despite a sheen of sweat on his face and glazed eyes, he plodded on.

Neither of them spoke. What was there to say?

Spencer glanced at his watch. She went on without bothering to ask what time it was. Occasional glimpses of the sun showed it still high enough to give them a few hours before nightfall. If she was wrong…they'd stop. Curl up together and sleep.

"Hey."

Hearing his rough voice, Leah didn't make her foot move forward for that next step.

"Let's get in sight of the road. It's time to flag someone down."

"Oh." How long had it been since she'd seen him check the time? She had no idea. "Okay." She turned right. Just the idea that they might catch a ride and not have to walk anymore inspired a small burst of energy.

It only took a few minutes—five?—to find themselves a spot to crouch barely off the highway, but probably not visible to passing motorists.

The first one they saw coming was traveling east toward Mount Baker. A red Dodge Caravan, it had a rack piled with luggage and kids in the backseat.

They let several more go.

"I'd be happiest with a sheriff's deputy or forest service," Spencer said.

Of course, they had to identify those quick enough to give them time to burst out onto the road, waving their arms and probably jumping up and down.

Vehicles passed. She began to wonder if Spencer was too sick to make a quick decision. Maybe she should make one.

But suddenly he said, "That's it," and launched himself forward.

She stumbled behind, finally seeing what he had. It was a white 4X4 with a rack of lights on the roof. Spencer waved and so she did, too. A turn signal came on, and a siren gave a brief squawk. The vehicle rolled to a stop only a few feet from them. From here Leah could see green trim and the sheriff's department logo.

Spencer didn't wait for the deputy to get out. He jogged along the shoulder to the passenger side. So a passing motorist might miss seeing them, she realized.

The deputy climbed out and circled the front bumper. Probably in his thirties, he looked alarmingly like the men they were fleeing: fit, clothed in a khaki uniform and armed. In fact, his hand rested lightly on the butt of his gun.

That changed in an instant when he saw the gun holstered at Spencer's waist. In barely an instant, the deputy pulled his gun and took up a stiff-armed stance, the barrel pointing at Spencer, who immediately lifted his hands above his head. "Set that gun on the pavement," the deputy snapped. "Do it *now*."

Moving very slowly, Spencer complied. With his foot, he nudged the handgun over the pavement toward the cop. The deputy never took his eyes from Spencer when he moved forward and used his foot to push the gun behind the tire of his SUV.

"You're not a hunter."

"No," Spencer said. "I'm not carrying identification, so I can't prove this, but I'm FBI Special Agent Alex Barr. I was undercover with a violent militia group training at an old lodge near here. Ms. Leah Keaton—" he nodded at her "—recently inherited the lodge from her great-uncle. She decided to check on the condition of the buildings, and surprised the men who'd taken it over. They took her captive."

The guy watched them suspiciously. "You took her and ran?"

"Eventually. One of them found a photo of me online leaving a Chicago courthouse. We were lucky because Leah overheard two men talking about it. We didn't dare even take the time to grab supplies or my phone, just ran. I urgently need to call my team leader. These guys have some serious weapons, including a couple of rocket launchers."

"What?"

Leah spoke up. "I saw one of them. That's when they decided they couldn't let me leave."

"Some of their weapons are US military, stolen by a like-minded active-duty army officer. The leader of this group is a retired air force lieutenant-colonel. We need the FBI to handle this, not local police."

The deputy studied him for a long time. "No way I can verify this story."

"I don't see how."

Leah said, "The resort was called Mount Baker Cabins and Lodge. My uncle's name was Edward Preston. If you're local, you might know about him. He died last fall. I'm his great-niece. I'm…a veterinary technician."

The deputy eyed her. "We drove up to check on Mr. Preston now and again. Annoyed him, but we kept doing it."

"That sounds like him," she admitted. "Mom tried to get him to move to somewhere less isolated, but he refused."

Looking marginally less aggressive, the deputy said, "Special Agent Barr, will you agree to be handcuffed before I give you and Ms. Keaton a lift?"

"Yes."

"He's wounded," she interjected desperately. "He has a knife wound in his thigh, and another between his ribs. I think the ribs are broken, and his wrist, too. He's fighting an infection."

The deputy's eyebrows rose and his gaze snagged on Spencer's wrapped wrist before moving to the blood soaking the upper arm of Leah's sweatshirt. "You appear to be hurt, too."

"Yes, I was shot, but it's just a graze. Spencer's wounds—I mean, Alex's wounds—are infected. He's running a high temperature. It's a miracle he made it this far. Please don't—"

"I'll be okay," Spencer said gently. "We need to get off this road."

He had to explain why she'd called him by two different names, and why it would be a bad thing if they were spotted by any of the men fleeing the lodge.

The deputy cast uneasy glances up and down the highway, patted them both down and made them sit in the back—in the cage, she thought was the right terminology—but didn't insist on the handcuffs. He took Spencer's gun with him when he got behind the wheel, and did an immediate U-turn to head west toward Bellingham and, presumably sheriff's department headquarters. Then he got on his radio.

LESS THAN TWO hours later Alex had set the ball to rolling. In his own imagery, he'd tapped a domino, which would knock down the next and the next, until the last fell.

He was rarely in on the grand finale, although his reasons this time were different. In the past, when he'd completed an undercover investigation, it was just as well not to show up days later as his alter ego, Special Agent Barr.

This wasn't the first time he'd had to jump ship, so to speak, but he'd never before had to help someone else make the swim to shore. It *was* the first time he'd been injured badly enough, he had to be hospitalized.

That partly explained his frustration. He did not like being stuck flat on his back in a hospital bed where he was allowed no voice in how the cleanup was run. He was pretty irked at Ron Abram, who'd delegated much of the response to someone at the Seattle office. Since Alex didn't have his phone, the only update offered to him came via the clunky phone on the bedside stand, and that was from Abram, not the agents who'd joined with the local police to raid the compound—yeah, that was what they'd called it—only to find it deserted. According to Abram, they were packing his and Leah's stuff and bringing it down, as well as having someone bring her car once they figured out how to get it moving.

Alex couldn't help thinking that Jason Shedd could have fixed the car in less time than it had probably taken him to disable it.

The Tahoe Alex had borrowed for this operation from the Seattle office had started, once they reconnected the battery. No surprise it had been disabled. He doubted they intended to return it to him. He guessed he'd have to find his own way to the airport.

Truthfully, he still felt like crap, although the pain meds had helped. He wouldn't be released until morning, at the very soonest. He was on some kind of super-powerful antibiotic being given by IV, along with the fluids the doctor thought he needed. They wanted to see how he responded to the antibiotics before they cut him loose.

What had him antsy was Leah's absence. He wanted to rip the needle out and go looking for her. They'd been taken to different cubicles in the ER and he hadn't seen her since. There wasn't any chance she'd been admitted, too, was there? He couldn't believe she'd leave without finding him. Anyway, she'd need to wait for her purse and phone, even if she was willing to abandon her car for now.

He'd tuned the TV to CNN, but had trouble caring about the latest congressman embroiled in a sexual scandal or tension in some godforsaken part of the world. With a little luck Higgs and company would be rounded up, weaponry confiscated and their entire scheme would become little more than a note on a list of terrorist operations thwarted. No breathless reports on CNN or any other news outlet.

Recognizing the quick, light footsteps in the hall, he turned his head. Since hospital security had been asked to vet any visitors to his room, he wasn't surprised to hear a man's voice and then a woman's. A second later Leah pushed aside the curtain. Her hair was shiny clean and dry, shimmering under the fluorescent lights, and she wore scrubs.

"Spencer?" She sounded tentative, as if unsure he'd welcome her. Then she wrinkled her nose. "Alex."

"I'd really like to shed having multiple personalities," he told her.

She chuckled and visibly relaxed, coming to his side. When he held out his hand, she laid hers in it.

"Will you sit down?" he asked, tugging gently. The minute she'd perched on the edge of the bed, he said, "You saw a doctor. What did he say?"

She reported that, like him, she was being treated for potential *Giardia lamblia*, the microorganism commonly found in otherwise crystal-clear waters in the Cascade Mountains. A dressing covered the bullet graze on her arm, and she was also on an antibiotic for that. Otherwise, she'd been able to shower, a nurse had produced the scrubs for her and she'd been given a chit to pay for a meal in the cafeteria.

"I couldn't eat nearly as much as I wanted," she concluded ruefully.

With a smile lighting her face, she was different. Her eyes sparkled, her mouth was soft, her head high and carriage erect but also relaxed. Seeing her now was a reminder that he didn't know what she'd be like when she wasn't abused and shocked. She could have a silly sense of humor; she might be a party girl; she could habitually flit from one interest to another. Maybe she'd already dropped her determination to go to vet school and come up with another way she could spend any money earned from her great-uncle's legacy to her.

No, not that, he thought. That was unfair. He'd seen her unflagging determination. Her courage. Her strength and intellect.

Her smile had died, and she was searching his eyes gravely. "What about you? What did the doctor say?"

Was that the caring expression of a woman at least halfway in love with a man? Or caring only because the two of them had gone through a lot together?

"Nothing unexpected," he told her. "It was the gash on my thigh that was infected. Strangely enough, this one—" he started to move his free hand to touch his side before remembering that it was now casted "—appeared clean. One rib is broken, one cracked. My ulna is fractured close to the wrist." Rueful, he lifted the casted arm. "They expect a complete healing, but I may need physical therapy once this is off."

"I don't know how you kept going. You saved my life, over and over."

He shook his head. "You saved mine. Over and over."

She didn't seem convinced, and said, "Oh, you mean when I heard Higgs and Fuller talking."

"And when you treated my injures," he reminded her.

"Which you got because you were protecting *me*."

"You also knew enough to find berries to eat, to keep that bear from seeing us as dinner, and you led us to safety when I was too feverish to know which way we were going."

"I don't think any of those measure up to a knife to the—"

He smiled crookedly. "We'll call it even."

Leah laughed. "Not even close."

"Did anyone corner you with more questions?" he asked.

"Oh, yeah. A pair of FBI agents. Apparently, the doctor wouldn't let them go at you, so I got grilled instead."

He was the one to laugh this time. "Grilled?"

Her severe expression melted into a smile. "Okay, asked questions. Only...they wouldn't tell me anything. Do you know what's happening?"

The reminder renewed his irritation. "Not as much as I'd like. As we speculated, Higgs and his crew absconded with all the weapons, down to the last bullet." He told her the rest of what he'd learned, and she appeared relieved to know she'd get her possessions back soon.

"I was worrying about my car," she admitted. "I hated to have to call my insurance agent and say, 'Well, see, these domestic terrorists got mad at me, so they blew it up with a rocket launcher.'"

Laughing, Alex realized he hadn't felt this good since the last time he'd made love with Leah, and then the astonishing pleasure was transitory. They'd both been all too aware of the frightening reality awaiting them.

Before he could say anything else, he heard voices in the hall, followed by one that said, "Knock knock," even as a hand drew back the curtain.

The visitor was Matt Sanford, the deputy who had picked them up off the side of the highway. He had a black duffel bag slung over one shoulder and was pulling a small suitcase with the other hand. "I thought you might like to have your stuff," he said cheerfully.

Leah beamed at him. "Yes, please. Is my purse there somewhere? You do have my phone?"

He let her seize the suitcase handle from him. "I'm told your purse is in the suitcase. The phone, I don't know.

If anything is missing, I'll follow up on it." He looked at Alex. "And I take it this is yours."

"Well, the bag is."

"Do you want your phone?" Leah asked, starting to reach for the zipper.

"Eventually. Unfortunately, I don't dare use it until we know it's clean. Somebody was supposed to bring me—"

The deputy pulled a phone from a pocket. "I'm the somebody."

"Turned you into the pack mule, huh?"

"Beats my average day. You introduced some excitement into our lives."

Alex's eyes met Leah's. "More than I ever want to experience again."

"Amen," she murmured.

"Thank you," Alex added. "You don't know how glad to see you we were."

"That's what they all say," Deputy Sanford joked, but he also smiled. "I'm happy I came on you when I did. Oh, I forgot to say I have an update."

Both focused on him.

"I hear the FBI has caught up with four men. A guy with a Scandinavian name…"

"Arne Larson?"

"That's it. He was with a Robert Kirk."

Leah's hand tightened on Alex's. "I don't remember a Robert."

Alex wasn't surprised. Unremarkable in appearance, Rob had never seemed interested in pushing himself forward.

"The other two were Don Durand—his truck was loaded with rifles, they said—and Garrett Zeigler."

"Those two were together?"

"Not from what I heard."

"I'm glad someone is willing to tell us what's happening."

"Yeah, I figured." Sanford sounded sympathetic. "I put my number in that phone. Call if I can do anything."

They expressed more thanks. He left, leaving silence in his wake.

THIS SILENCE FELT awkward to Leah. She wouldn't try to leave until morning at the soonest, Saturday if it looked like she'd have her car by then, but...should she hang around and keep Alex company now? Or make this breezy but plan to stop by in the morning to say goodbye?

Would she hear from him someday?

"I almost hope Del and Dirk get away," she blurted.

He grimaced. "Me, too, but that won't happen with Del. He got himself in too deep. Dirk... I'll try to keep him from being charged if he followed my advice."

He'd told her about the confrontation with Dirk and what he'd suggested. "If he didn't, there's not much I can do for him."

"How will you know?"

He ran a hand over his rough jaw. "As long as he doesn't have any stolen weapons on him when he's stopped, I'll assume he's running from Higgs, not still taking his orders. Dirk saved us by keeping his mouth shut."

Leah nodded. "They didn't let you shave?"

"Wasn't high on their list of priorities, but, damn it, I itch."

His disgruntlement made her smile. It also, for some obscure reason, made her sad. *Just ask*, she told herself.

"You'll be going back to Chicago, won't you?"

An emotion she couldn't read passed through his light gray eyes. "For the short term," he agreed. "I'm in no shape to be useful here."

"No. Um, I'm expected back at work Monday. So…"

"Have you talked to your parents?" he asked.

She scrunched up her nose. "Yes. Mom was next thing to hysterical. I could hear Dad in the background reminding her that I'm okay."

Annoyingly, amusement curved Alex's very sexy mouth. "Did you mention getting shot?"

Feeling sort of teenaged, she said, "I figured that could wait."

He laughed, but there was something intense in the way he watched her. "Leah…"

"Yes?"

"I don't want to say goodbye."

"I don't want to, either," she whispered, praying he didn't mean that in a "We had quite an adventure, and I'll miss you" way.

"Are you still serious about applying to vet school?"

"Yes, except…there's still the money issue. I suppose I should talk to some real estate agents tomorrow. It might be a while before they can actually take a look at the resort, though, huh?"

"I'm guessing a week or so," he agreed. His gaze never left hers. "I want to keep seeing you."

Her heart did a somersault. "But… Chicago."

"I'm done with undercover work. I can apply for a transfer to be near you."

He meant it. Suddenly, tears rolled down her cheeks. "I was so afraid…"

"I've been afraid, too," he said huskily, tugging her toward him.

Leah surrendered, lifting her feet from the floor so she could snuggle on the bed beside him, her head resting on his shoulder, her hand somewhere in the vicinity of his heart. The familiar position felt *right*. She hated the idea of going to bed without him.

"I had the terrifying thought that you might like nightclubs," he murmured.

She actually giggled at that. "Not a chance. Please tell me you don't bag a deer every year."

This laugh rumbled in his chest. "Nope. Guess that wouldn't go over very well with an animal doc, would it?"

"No." Her cheeks might still be wet, but Leah was also smiling.

"Now that we have that covered, I guess we know everything we need to about each other," he said with an undertone of humor.

"I guess we do." No, he wouldn't be able to go home with her to meet her parents immediately; she could only imagine the kind of debriefing he'd face. "Is there a Portland office?"

"FBI? Yeah, a field office. That's what I'll aim for in the short term. If you want me to."

"I do." She was in love with this man who was willing to make big changes in his life to be with her. The sexiest man she'd ever met. A man who just never quit.

"Good," he said. A minute later his breathing changed as he relaxed into sleep. Apparently, she'd removed his last worry.

Not planning to go anywhere, she closed her eyes, too.

Epilogue

Ten days later Alex strode off the plane at Portland International Airport. Leah had promised to be waiting for him at baggage claim. In part because of the cast he still wore, he carried only his laptop case. He'd taken a two-week vacation, the best he could manage until a transfer came through. This was a "meet the family" trip. Even as alienated as he often felt from his own parents, he supposed he'd be taking Leah to meet them one of these days, too. They loved him, if not in a way he'd want to replicate with his own kids. For the first time he was seriously thinking he'd like to start a family.

Only two days ago he'd gotten word that Higgs had been captured trying to charter a boat in Florida. When the local FBI located the beach cabin where he'd been staying, they'd surprised two other men: Steve Baldwin and Ken Vogel. They'd also found two rocket launchers and a small amount of uranium as well as evidence that the men had been constructing a bomb.

Higgs wasn't talking, but under pressure, Baldwin admitted they'd intended to sail to a Caribbean island where they wouldn't be found until they were ready to make their strike.

Alex felt sick, imagining what might have happened

if the charter operator hadn't had an uneasy feeling he'd seen Higgs's face, and not in a context he liked.

Yeah, the FBI had ended up putting Lieutenant Colonel Edward Higgs on a watch list, and released his photo. This time it had paid off big.

They had also quietly arrested army Colonel Thomas Nash, the man Alex recognized when he and Higgs met the suppliers. Turned out Nash and Higgs had been friends for years.

Of course, the single arrest was the equivalent of peeling open the proverbial can of worms. Nash couldn't have stolen that quantity of weapons on his own. Even with help, procedures were designed to prevent things like this from happening. It was fair to say that army base would be crawling with investigators for months to come, making a lot of people's lives miserable.

Dirk had been picked up and released, at Alex's recommendation. They'd spoken last week, Dirk shaken at his weakness in letting his father push him into something so hateful. He and Helen were getting married and moving to Montana, where he'd found a job with a well-drilling company based in Billings. Alex intended to stay in touch. He and Leah might not have survived if Dirk hadn't listened to his conscience.

Suddenly, he didn't want to think about any of that. The baggage claim carousels were just ahead…and his gaze locked on a woman hurrying toward him, her face alight. Relief and something more powerful flooded him. He let the laptop case drop to the floor and held out his arms.

Leah flew into them, saying only his name. His real name.

* * * * *

THE SHEIKH CROWNS HIS VIRGIN

LYNNE GRAHAM

CHAPTER ONE

ZOE DESCENDED THE steps of her grandfather's private jet and as the sunlight of Maraban enveloped her she smiled happily. It was spring and the heat was bearable but, best of all, she was taking the very first brave step into her new life.

On her own, on her own *at last*, free of the restrictions that her sisters would have attached to her but, most importantly of all, free of the *low* expectations they had of her. Winnie and Vivi had been amazed when Zoe had agreed to move to a foreign country for a few months without freaking out at the prospect. They had been equally amazed when she'd agreed to marry a much older man to fulfil her part of their agreement with their grandfather, Stamboulas Fotakis. Why not? It wasn't as though it was going to be a *real* marriage, merely a pretend marriage in which her future husband made political use of the fact that she was the granddaughter of a former princess of a country called Bania, which no longer existed.

Long before Zoe was even born the two tiny realms of Bania and Mara had joined to become Maraban and apparently her late grandmother, the Princess Azra, had been hugely popular in both countries. Prince Hakem wanted to marry Zoe literally for her ancestry and she would become an Arabian princess and live in the royal palace for several months. There she would enjoy glorious solitude with nobody bothering her, nobody asking how she felt or worriedly enquiring if she thought she should have more therapy to help her cope with ordinary life. Even though she hadn't had a panic attack in months, her siblings had always been on edge around her, awaiting another one.

Zoe adored her older sisters but their constant care and concern had held her back from the independence she needed to rebuild her self-esteem and forge her own path. And taking part in this silly pretend marriage was all she had to do to finally obtain that freedom.

All three sisters had agreed to marry men of their grandfather's choosing to gain his financial help for their foster parents, John and Liz Brooke. Winnie and Vivi had already fulfilled that bargain. But in Zoe's case, no pressure whatsoever had been placed on her and, indeed, John and Liz's mortgage arrears had been paid off shortly after her sister Vivi's marriage had taken place. Yes, she thought wryly, even her extremely ruthless grandfather had shrunk from taking the risk of putting pressure on his youngest granddaughter, having taken on board her siblings' conviction that she was hopelessly fragile and emotionally vulnerable. Nobody had faith in her ability to be strong, Zoe reflected ruefully, which was why it was so very important that she proved for her own benefit that she *could* be strong.

Like her sisters, Zoe had grown up in foster care, and a terrifying incident when she was twelve years old had traumatised her. But she had buried all that hurt and fear, seemingly flourishing in John and Liz's happy home, only for those frightening insecurities to come back and engulf her while she was studying botany at university. Having to freely mix with men, having to deal with friends asking why she didn't want a boyfriend, had put her under severe strain. Her panic attacks had grown worse and worse and, although she had contrived to hide her extreme anxiety from her sisters, she had, ultimately, been unable to deal with her problems alone. Weeks before she sat her final degree exams, she had suffered a nervous breakdown, which had meant that she had had to take time out from her course to recover.

Although she had subsequently completed her degree and worked through the therapy required to put her back on an even track where crippling anxiety no longer ruled her every thought and action, her sisters had continued to treat her as if she could shatter again at any moment. While she understood that their protectiveness came from love, she also saw that their attitude had made her weaker than she need have been and that she badly needed the chance to stand on her own feet. With her sisters now married, one living in Greece and the other in Italy, coming to Maraban was Zoe's opportunity to prove that she had overcome her unhappy past.

Zoe stepped into the limousinc awaiting her, grateful for the reality that her arrival in Maraban was completely low-key. Prince Hakem had insisted that no public appearances or indeed anything of that nature would be required from her. He might be the brother of the current King but he had no official standing in Maraban. Zoe's grandfather should have been travelling with her but a pressing business matter had led to him asking if she could manage alone if he put off his arrival until the following day. Of course, she could manage, she thought cheerfully, gazing out with lively interest at the busy streets of the capital city, Tasit, which was an intriguing mix of old and new. She saw old buildings and elaborate mosques with quaint colourful turrets nudging shoulders with redeveloped areas boasting soaring skyscrapers and office blocks. Maraban was evidently right in the middle of the process of modernisation.

Oil and gas wealth had transformed the country. Zoe had read everything she could find on Maraban and had rolled her eyes at the discovery that nobody appeared to know why her grandmother, Princess Azra, had failed to marry the current King, Tahir, as she had been expected to do. The bald truth was that Azra had run off with Stamboulas Fotakis sooner than marry a man who'd already had three wives. Presumably that story had been suppressed to conserve the monarch's dignity. Luckily, Stam had told her everything she needed to know about his late wife's background.

Darkness was falling fast when the limo driver turned off the road and steered between imposingly large gates guarded by soldiers. Zoe strained to see the enormous property that lay ahead but the limo travelled slowly right on past it, threading a path through a vast complex of buildings and finally drawing up beside one. She was ushered out and indoors before she could even catch her breath and was a little disappointed to find herself standing in a contemporary house. A very *large* contemporary house, she conceded wryly, with aggressively gilded fancy furniture and nothing whatsoever historic about it. A female servant in a long kaftan bowed to her and showed her up a brilliantly lit staircase into an entire suite of rooms.

Her disappointment that she wasn't going to be living in the ancient royal palace slowly ebbed as she scanned her comfortable and well-furnished surroundings. It wasn't ideal that none of the staff spoke her language and that she didn't speak theirs but miming could accomplish a lot, she told herself bracingly as her companion mimicked eating to let her know that a meal was being brought. And long before she went home again, she should have picked up at least a few useful phrases to enable her to communicate more effectively, she told herself soothingly.

A maid had already arrived to unpack her suitcases when a knock sounded on the door. Zoe made it to the door first.

A slimly built young man and a uniformed nurse hovered outside. 'I am Dr Wazd,' the man told her stiffly. 'I have been instructed to give you a vaccination shot. The nurse will assist.'

Zoe winced because she hated needles and she was surprised because she had had all the required shots for Maraban. But then what she did know that a medical doctor would not know better? She rolled up her sleeve and then frowned as she saw the doctor's hand on the syringe was shaking. Glancing up at him in surprise, noting the perspiration beading his brow, she wondered if he was a very newly qualified doctor to be so nervous and she was relieved when the nurse silently filched the syringe from him and gave her the injection without further ado. It stung and she gritted her teeth.

No sooner was that done than a tray of food arrived and she sat down at the table to eat, noting that she was feeling dizzy and woolly-headed and surmising that she was already suffering the effects of jet lag. But while she was eating, she began feeling as though the world around her were slowing down and her body felt as heavy as lead. Feeling dizzy even seated, she rose to go to the bathroom and had to grip the back of a chair to balance. As she wobbled on her heels, blinking rapidly, a suffocating blackness folded in and she dropped down into it with a gasp of dismay…

His Royal Highness, Prince Faraj al-Basara, was in a very high-powered meeting in London dealing with his country's oil and gas production when his private mobile thrummed a warning in his pocket. Few people had that number and it only ever rang if it was very, *very* important. Excusing himself immediately, Raj stepped outside, his brain awash with sudden apprehension. Had his father taken ill? Or had some other calamity occurred back home in Maraban?

Maraban was a tiny Gulf state but it was also one of the richest countries in the world. A terrorist incident, however, would bring the home of his birth to a screeching halt because the security forces were equally tiny and these days Maraban relied on wealth and diplomacy to stay safe. When Raj thought nostalgically of home, it was always of a place of stark black and white contrasts where four-wheel-drive vehicles and helicopters startled livestock in the desert and where a conservative Middle Eastern ethos struggled to cope with the very different mores and the sheer speed of change in the modern world.

It was eight years, however, since Raj had last visited his home because his father, the King, had removed him from his position as Crown Prince and sent him into exile for refusing to go into the army and for refusing even more vehemently to marry the bride his parent had chosen for him. No, he had not been a dutiful or obedient son, Raj acknowledged with grim self-honesty, he had been a stubborn, rebellious one and, unfortunately for him, there was no greater sin in his culture.

That said, however, Raj had, since, moved on from that less than stellar beginning to carve his own path in the business world and there his shrewd brain, intuition and ability to spot trends had ensured meteoric success in that sphere. He had also learned how to steer Maraban into the future from beyond its borders, making allies, attracting foreign businesses and investment while constantly encouraging growth in the public infrastructure required to keep his country up to speed with the latest technology. And his reward for that tireless focus and resolve? Maraban, the home that he loved, was positively booming.

He was pleasantly surprised when he answered his phone and recognised his cousin, Omar's voice. Omar had pretty much been his best friend since the dark days of the military school they had both been forced to attend as adolescents, an unforgettable era of relentless bullying and abuse that Raj still winced to recall. As Crown Prince he had had a target painted on his back and his father had told the staff to turn a blind eye, believing that it would be beneficial for his only child to be toughened up in such a severe environment.

'Omar…what can I do for you?' he asked almost cheerfully, relieved of the anxiety that his elderly father had taken ill because Omar would not have been chosen as messenger for that development. *That* call would only have come from a member of his father's staff. After all, his mother had died while he was still a boy. The memory made him tense for his mother had died in a manner that he would never forget: she had taken her own life. It had taken a very long time for Raj to accept that her unhappiness had surpassed her love for her nine-year-old son and he had never forgotten his sense of abandonment because, once she was gone, everything soft and loving and caring had vanished from his childish world.

'I'm in a real fix, Raj, and I think you are the only person with sufficient knowledge to approach with this,' Omar declared, his habitually upbeat voice unusually flat in tone. 'I've been dragged into something I don't want to be involved in and it's serious. You know I'm a royalist and very loyal to my country but there are some things I *can't*—'

'Cut to the chase,' Raj sliced in with a bemused frown. 'What have you been dragged into?'

'Early this morning I received a call from someone at the palace who asked if I would look after a "package" and keep it safe until further notice. And that's the problem, Raj… I didn't get delivered a package, I got a woman.'

'A *woman*?' Raj repeated in disbelief. 'Are you joking me?'

'I wish I was. All the women in the tribe are outraged and I've been thrown out of my tent to accommodate her,' Omar lamented. 'My wife thinks I'm getting involved in sex trafficking.'

'It could *not* be that,' Raj pronounced with assurance because the penalty for such a crime was death and his father was most assiduous in ensuring that neither drugs nor prostitution gained ground in Maraban.

'No, of course it couldn't be,' Omar agreed. 'But even though the order came from the very highest level of the palace I should not be asked by *anyone* to imprison a woman against her will.'

'How do you know the order came from the very highest level?' Raj demanded.

His cousin mentioned a name and Raj gritted his teeth. Bahadur Abdi was the most trusted military adviser in his father's inner circle and could only be acting at the King's command. That shocking truth shed an entirely different light on the kidnapping because it meant that Raj's father was personally involved. 'Who the hell *is* this woman?'

'You're not going to like the suspicion I'm developing any more than I do,' his cousin warned him heavily. 'But I contacted the palace as soon as I appreciated I was being asked to deal with a *live* package and I was told that she was the last descendant of the al-Mishaal family, which was a shock. Thought they were all dead and buried long ago! Were you even aware that *my* father divorced my mother two months ago?'

Raj was shocked enough by both those revelations

to listen keenly as Omar described his mother's refusal to discuss the divorce and the oddity of her continuing calm over the termination of a marriage that had lasted almost fifty years and had spawned four children and at least a dozen grandchildren. Prince Hakem, Raj's uncle and Omar's father, however, was an embittered and ambitious man, who ever since Raj's exile had been striving to become the recognised heir to the throne in Raj's place. Ironically, Raj didn't even really feel that he could blame his uncle for his ambition because, as the King's younger brother, Hakem had spent his whole life close to the throne but virtually ignored and powerless, his royal brother refusing to grant him any form of responsibility in the kingdom. Furthermore, only the King could name his heir and Hakem had long desired a role of power and the rise in status it would accord him.

'So, what's the connection with this woman?'

Omar shared his suspicions and Raj paled and experienced a spontaneous surge of rage at such a manipulative plot being played out in virtual secret behind the palace walls. 'Surely that is *not* possible?'

'It may not be. I must admit that the woman doesn't look remotely as if she carries Marabanian blood. She's got white-blonde hair...looks like something out of that fairy tale... *The Sleeping Beauty*,' Omar revealed heavily.

Raj parted compressed lips. 'Princess Azra of Bania was the daughter of a Danish explorer, who was blond,' he murmured flatly. 'I don't know much about Azra's elopement with her Greek tycoon, who was working in Maraban when the two countries joined, but I do know her flight with another man created a *huge* scandal.

She was supposed to become my father's fourth wife and instead, she ran off with Fotakis and married him.'

'Didn't know that…but then it's not really my slice of history in the same way as it's yours.' Omar sighed heavily. 'Just give me some diplomatic advice about what to do next because I'm at a standstill. This woman has *obviously* been kidnapped. Our doctor says she's been drugged, so she's unconscious and she arrived with no means of identification. But even if she *is* one of the al-Mishaal family's next generation from that marriage all those years ago I still can't believe that any *young* woman would agree to marry a man as old as my father—'

'It would shock you what some Western women would be willing to do to become an Arabian princess with unlimited wealth at their disposal. Suggest that a crown could also be on offer and there would be many takers of that particular bargain,' Raj breathed with cynical derision, his lean, darkly handsome features clenching hard as he reflected on his own experiences and the shattering betrayal he had endured…and worst of all, only *after* he had destroyed his standing with his father for ever. Even years after that youthful disillusionment, he was grimly aware of the pulling power of his status and wealth in the West. In his radius even seemingly intelligent women frothed and gushed like champagne, desperate to attract and bed him. Sadly for them, he didn't find being chased, flattered or potentially seduced remotely attractive because he preferred to do his own hunting in that field. And, almost inevitably, that shattering act of infidelity following on from his mother's suicide had underlined his growing conviction that women were not to be trusted.

'Possibly not…shocked,' Omar clarified as tactfully as he knew how because he too was probably thinking about that old and demeaning history that still scarred Raj's pride. 'But I *can* tell you that if that is my father's game, very few of our people would like or accept such a marriage. My father is unpopular: he's as old school as your father. I don't know anyone who would be willing to accept him as the heir in place of you, *no*, not even if he *has* somehow contrived to bring back the ghost of the al-Mishaal royal family as a potential bride!'

Raj had been away from palace politics for a very long time but he had not forgotten the scheming games of one-upmanship involved. In the role of Hakem's bride, Princess Azra's granddaughter would be a priceless figurehead, Raj acknowledged grimly. Half the population of Maraban came from Banian roots and all had been seriously dissatisfied forty-odd years ago when the joining of the two states was not matched as had been promised by a marital alliance between Bania's only Princess and Mara's King. All those people had felt cheated by the absence of Banian blood in the royal family tree of Maraban. It would be a triumph for his uncle to marry Azra's descendant and it definitely would increase his popularity, which was precisely why Raj's father would never have allowed such a marriage to take place: King Tahir did not tolerate competition or, for that matter, a little brother he deemed to be getting too big for his boots. After such a publicity-grabbing stunt, Hakem could only have been hoping to be named the King's heir and step into Raj's former position as Crown Prince in his nephew's stead.

Omar broke into Raj's racing thoughts. 'Tell me, what am I to do with her?' he demanded, infuriated that an innocent woman had been kidnapped to prevent a marriage he believed to be wholly inappropriate. 'How do I safely *and* decently rid myself of this appalling responsibility? '

And Raj told him with a succinctness that shook both of them before he powered back into his meeting to apologise and explain that a family crisis demanded his immediate attention. He contacted an investigation firm, who had done excellent work for him in the past, to request an immediate file on his uncle's putative bride. He needed information and he needed it fast yet he was aware that he was struggling to concentrate.

Why?

For the first time in eight years, Raj would be returning to the country of his birth and, although anger was driving him at the prospect of being forced to deal with another unscrupulous and mercenary woman, on another much more basic level he was quietly exhilarated at the prospect of seeing his homeland again...

Zoe surfaced from an uneasy, woozy dream to find someone helping her to lift a glass of water to her lips. Her eyes refused to focus and her body felt limp but she knew she needed the bathroom and said so. Someone helped her rise and supported her—more than one someone, she registered dimly, because her limbs were too weak to carry her. She tried to scan her surroundings but the walls being weirdly bendy spooked her and momentarily she shut her eyes as she was helped back to bed. She had been drugged, taken somewhere, she registered fearfully, fighting without success to stay conscious and focus. She had to protect herself, *had* to protect herself! That self-saving litany rang through her brain like a wake-up call…but even that panic couldn't prevent her from sliding down into oblivion again.

When Raj received the info on Zoe Mardas, he was forced to rapidly rearrange his expectations. Why on earth would such a woman be willing to marry a man almost as old as her grandfather? Clearly, financial greed would be a most unlikely motive for a woman with the billionaire Stamboulas Fotakis at her back. Fotakis was her grandfather and, by all accounts, an extremely protective relative. Other more stressful concerns then started dawning on Raj. The Greek tycoon would scarcely take the kidnapping of his granddaughter lying down. He would not allow it to be hushed up either. Yet, even more strangely, it did look as though Fotakis had been the prime mover and shaker behind the proposed marriage between Hakem and Zoe. What was Stam Fotakis getting out of it? Some lucrative business deal? Or a title for his granddaughter? Raj pondered those unknowns and decided to contact Fotakis direct…

Someone was brushing Zoe's hair when she next woke up, someone murmuring softly in a foreign language. She opened her eyes and saw an older woman, who smiled down at her from her kneeling stance by her side while she brushed Zoe's long mane of pale blonde hair with admiring care. She did not seem hostile or threatening in any way and Zoe forced a smile, her innate survival instincts kicking in. Until she knew what was happening she would be a good little prisoner, playing along until such time as her grandfather came to rescue her; because one thing she *did* know: Stamboulas Fotakis would not be long in putting in an appearance. He would create a huge fuss the instant he realised that Zoe had gone missing and no rock would be left unturned in his search for her, she reflected with a strong sense of relief.

Gently detaching her hair from the woman's light hold, she sat up and the woman stood up and helpfully showed her straight to the bathroom. Even by that stage, Zoe was recognising that she had not been disorientated the night before when she had thought the walls surrounding her looked rather odd. Evidently, she was no longer at the villa in the palace complex, she was in a tent, a very large and very luxurious tent decorated with rich hangings and opulent seating but, when all was said and done, it was *still* a tent! And the connecting bathroom was also under canvas. Zoe felt hot and sweaty and looked longingly at the shower, but she didn't want to risk the vulnerability of getting naked. She freshened up with cold water, dried her face and frowned down at the unfamiliar long white fine cotton shift she now wore in place of the skirt and top she had travelled in. That creepy nervous doctor and his sidekick, she thought in disgust. She would never trust a doctor again!

Why had she been taken from Prince Hakem's villa? Although no one had ever told her that it was *his* villa, she had simply assumed it was. Presumably somebody didn't want this marriage of his to take place, she reasoned reflectively. No problem, she thought ruefully, there had been no need to assault her with a syringe, send her to sleep and ship her out to a tent because she would quite happily go home again without any argument. Furthermore, she rather thought that would be her grandfather's reaction as well because he had demanded very strong assurances from her bridegroom-to-be that she would be safe and secure in Maraban and he would be appalled at what had happened to her. Surely her becoming a princess to follow in the footsteps of her formerly royal grandmother, Princess Azra, would not still be so important to Stam Fotakis that he would expect his granddaughter to risk life and limb in the process?

Two women were setting out a meal when she returned to the main tent and she roamed as casually as she could in the direction of the doorway that had been left uncovered. What she glimpsed froze her in her tracks in instant denial. She saw a circle of tents and beyond them sand dunes that ran off into the horizon. She was in the desert, so escaping would be more of a challenge than she felt equal to because she would need transport and a map at the very least for such a venture. The discovery that she had been plunged into such an alien environment sent her nervous tension climbing higher and she swallowed hard. Where else had she expected a tent to be pitched but in the desert? she asked herself irritably.

Above one of the tents she espied the rotor blades of a helicopter. Was that how she had arrived? Had she been flown in? She shuddered as another far more frightening thought suddenly occurred to her.

Why was she assuming that she had been kidnapped to prevent the wedding taking place in forty-eight hours? Her grandfather was an extremely rich man. It was equally possible that she had been taken so that a ransom demand could be made for her release. That scenario meant that someone laying violent hands on her was a much more likely development, she decided sickly, her tummy hollowing out. As one of the women carefully threaded her stiff arms into a concealing wrap and even tied it for her, Zoe could feel all the hallmarks of an impending panic attack assailing her and she was already zoning out as her thoughts raged out of her control.

She saw a mental image of herself beaten up in a photo for her grandfather's benefit. Her heart raced and she turned rapidly away from the view of the encampment, incapable of even noticing that the two women with her were hastily bowing and backing out of the tent again or that a male figure now stood silhouetted in the doorway. Her throat was tight, making it hard for her to catch her breath. She was shivering in spite of the heat, cold, then hot, dizziness making her sway as panic threatened.

I'm fine, I'm strong, I can cope, she chanted inwardly. But the mantra that usually worked to steady her failed because for several unbearable seconds she was simply overpowered by fear.

A male voice sounded directly behind her and a hand brushed her shoulder. Startled, terrified, Zoe reacted automatically with the self-defence tactics she had spent months learning so that she had the skills she needed to ensure her personal safety.

She spun at speed, her elbow travelling up for a chest

blow and her clenched fist heading for a throat strike while her knee lifted to aim at the groin. Raj was so disconcerted by a woman the size of a child attacking him that he almost fell over in sheer shock and then his own training kicked in and, light as dancer on his feet, he twisted and blocked her before bringing her down on the rug beneath their feet with careful hands.

'Let go of me, you bastard!' she railed at him, clawing, biting and scratching and in the act contriving to dislodge the white *keffiyeh* that covered his head.

Still reeling with disconcertion, Raj backed off several steps because he couldn't subdue her without hurting her and he refused to take that risk. She squirmed frantically away and the sheer terror in her face savaged his view of himself. Her eyes were glassy, her face white as snow.

'You are quite safe here. Nobody is going to hurt you.' Raj crouched down to her level while she wriggled back against a carved wooden chest like a trapped animal and hugged her knees, rocking back and forth. She was tiny and his every instinct was to protect her. 'On my honour, I *swear* that you are safe…' he intoned with as much conviction as he could get into the assurance, because she wasn't listening to him and she wasn't looking at him.

He was annoyed that his cousin had not sent his English-speaking wife, Farida, in to Zoe immediately to explain that there was no threat of any kind against her. But most of all, he cursed his father and the omnipotence he wielded in Maraban, for Raj was convinced that his wily father had ordered the kidnapping of Hakem's youthful bride-to-be. Would his father have counted the cost to the woman involved? Would he even have foreseen that he was unleashing the kind of explosively damaging scandal that no self-respecting country could withstand? No, his father, Tahir, would not have looked at that bigger picture of cause and effect. He would simply have set out to ensure that his ambitious brother's plot to raise his status was foiled while steadfastly refusing to acknowledge the likelihood of unexpected consequences.

In a fierce temper at that frustrating knowledge, Raj sank down beside Zoe Mardas on his knees and began to coax her into attempting a breathing exercise, aimed at calming her down. Extraordinary green eyes, clear as emeralds, skimmed over him and she blinked, long feathery lashes dipping. For a split second he was frozen in place by her ice-cool Scandinavian beauty. He coached her in breathing in, holding her breath and then very slowly breathing out again. She did so and then shot him an exasperated look, *not* the kind of look Raj was accustomed to receiving from young women.

'Yes, I do know how to do that for myself!' Zoe told him sharply as soon as she was breathing normally again. 'Why do you know how?'

'For a while in my teens, I suffered similar episodes,' Raj admitted, startling himself with that candour as much as he startled her; for the severe bullying he had endured at military school had for years afterwards left him damaged. He could only think his candour had been unwisely drawn from him by his glimpse of her at her most vulnerable and a natural need to put her at her ease.

In receipt of that surprising admission, Zoe stared

back at him in wonderment because in her experience men were much less willing to admit to suffering such a condition. But before she could question him further to satisfy her curiosity, he vaulted gracefully upright again. She watched him smooth down his rumpled white buttoned tunic and snatch up the white head cloth she had dislodged in their tussle. And then, strikingly, for the first time in her life Zoe looked at a man with interest because there was no denying it: whoever he was, he was without question the most beautiful creature she had ever seen. Dense silky blue-black curls covered his well-shaped skull while high cheekbones and hollows fed into a truly spectacular bone structure sheathed in olive skin. Dark-as-the-devil eyes glittered below straight ebony brows. A faint shadow of stubble surrounded his wide sensual mouth, his full soft lower lip tensing as he noticed her lingering scrutiny.

Turning pink, Zoe hurriedly glanced away while scolding herself for staring but, really, with looks of that quality, he had to be accustomed to being stared at by women, she reasoned defensively, uneasy with her speeded-up heartbeat and the sudden tightening of her nipples.

She wasn't *that* sort of woman, she reminded herself resolutely. Sex didn't interest her. Basically, men didn't interest her. She had been thrown off the path of normal development at the age of twelve when an attempted rape had devastated her. Ever since then she had held herself apart, avoiding mixed company unless it was family-orientated. She was perfectly happy around her brothers-in-law, Eros and Raffaele, and she hadn't been nervous either when dealing with the male parents at the childcare nursery where she had worked for months immediately after her recovery from her breakdown. Back then a full-time job in her own field of botany had seemed too challenging as a first step back into the real world.

'Who are you?' she asked baldly.

'You may call me Raj. I am no one of importance here,' he intoned in smooth dismissal, for he intended to fly back out of Maraban within the hour because he could not risk discovery and possible arrest. 'But this nomadic base camp is where my cousin, Sheikh Omar, lives at this time of year.'

Zoe bridled as she scrambled upright, wishing for about the thousandth time that she was even a few inches taller, for being only four feet eleven inches tall was not an advantage when it came to persuading people to take her seriously. Unsurprisingly, Raj towered over her but he wasn't quite as tall as her brothers-in-law, both of whom put her in mind of giants when she was around them. 'Is he the man responsible for bringing me here...*against my will*?' she stressed acidly.

'No, he is not,' Raj told her emphatically. 'Nor would he harm a hair on your head but he has kept his distance because he does not speak English.'

'Then who *is* responsible for bringing me here?' Zoe demanded, standing her ground, tensing her spine to keep her back and shoulders straight and her head high. Her favourite self-help book urged that even if you didn't *feel* confident, it was still possible to fake confidence and by so doing actually acquire it.

'I'm afraid I can't tell you that,' Raj countered flatly.

Zoe's green eyes flared as if he had slapped her. *'Why not?'* she demanded.

'It would serve no useful purpose.'

Zoe breathed in very deeply to contain the temper she hadn't known she had until that moment. He was so incredibly patronising, so superior and his attitude affected her like a chalk scraping down a blackboard, setting her teeth on edge. 'That's my decision to make, *not* yours,' she said succinctly.

Engaged in replacing his *keffiyeh*, Raj looked heavenward, involuntarily amused by that argument. She was like a doll with that tiny stature of hers and her phenomenally long blonde hair and she barely reached his chest.

'You're not taking me seriously,' she condemned.

'I'm afraid not,' Raj conceded grudgingly. 'I arrived here to sort this unfortunate mess out and that is what I intend to do.'

'Is it indeed?' Zoe snapped, incredulous that he had simply admitted his inability to treat her like an intelligent individual because, in her experience, most people lied on that score, denying that her diminutive size coloured their attitude towards her.

Raj paced several steps away from her, having discovered that proximity was unwise. His attention kept on dropping to that soft full pink mouth, that shimmering fall of pale hair, the barely noticeable little feminine curves hinting at her physical shape beneath the robe. He shifted, a kick of lust at his groin exasperating him for it was inappropriate and Raj was *always* very appropriate in his reactions to women. He controlled his responses, he did not allow them to control him and he had never understood the intoxicating lust that he had heard other men talk about, because only one woman had ever tested his control and, even then, it had not overwhelmed him.

'I intend to have you conveyed home as soon as it is possible…unless you are unwilling to give up the possibility of marrying my uncle, Prince Hakem, and becoming a princess,' Raj murmured bluntly. 'I suspect my aunt, his wife of many years, whom he recently divorced, would be relieved to have the ingrate back by default, little though he deserves her forgiveness and understanding…'

CHAPTER TWO

'ARE YOU TELLING me that Prince Hakem was already married at the time he agreed to marry me?' Zoe gasped in astonished disbelief, her triangular face tightening and losing colour at that horrendous concept.

'Of course, you were *already* aware of that reality,' Raj informed her with considerable scorn in his tone. 'After all, he has been married for many years. He has four children and a very large number of grandchildren… However, I assume that your grandfather was unwilling to accept a polygamous marriage, so my uncle *had* to divorce his wife before he could be allowed to marry you…'

Zoe was stunned by what she was learning. She wondered if her grandfather had been aware of those same unpleasant facts and then she told herself off for shying away from the unlovely truth that Stam Fotakis had wanted his granddaughter to become a princess regardless of what it would take to achieve that end. Prince Hakem had *had* to divorce his wife to take Princess Azra's granddaughter as a bride! Zoe was appalled and mortified and guilt-stricken, feeling that she should've done her homework better and shouldn't be in the position of finding out such a crucial fact when it was too late to change anything. Hakem's poor wife! Raj was definitely correct in his conviction that her grandfather would never have accepted a polygamous marriage and would only ever have settled for his grandchild becoming the Prince's sole wife.

'I didn't know… I *swear* I didn't know that he was a married man!' Zoe protested vehemently, a guilty flush driving off her previous pallor. 'In spite of what you seem to think, I would never have agreed if I had known that he was getting rid of his real wife just to marry me for a few months.'

Raj had no idea why she was bothering to defend her behaviour by pleading ignorance of the reality that his uncle had been a perfectly happy married man before her availability had ignited his ambition. Zoe Mardas might look convincingly like a storybook princess or a heavenly angel, but Raj had an innate distrust of that level of physical beauty and a cynical view of humanity. Beautiful on the outside but what less than presentable motives were she striving to conceal from him? He had discovered for himself that beautiful on the outside too often meant ugly on the inside.

In any case, Zoe could not possibly be as naïve as she was pretending to be. She *had* to know her own worth in Marabanian terms. Thousands of delighted Banians would flood the streets to celebrate an alliance between a royal Prince and Princess Azra's grandchild. His uncle had come very close to pulling off a spectacular coup in the popularity stakes.

'I assume you are willing to go home now?' Raj queried, marvelling at his own restraint in asking her that question because, frankly, he was determined to get her out of Maraban by any means within his power.

'Of course, I'm willing to go home!' Zoe shot back at him in reproach. 'Good grief, I'm not wanting to marry a man I've never even met, who divorced his wife just to become my bridegroom! Do I look that desperate?'

'I don't know you. I have no idea what your motivations are or, indeed, *were*,' Raj parried with the intrinsic hauteur that came as naturally to him as breathing, his exotically high cheekbones taut, his arrogant nose lifted, his hard jaw clenched.

Zoe's colour heightened, her eyes brightening with anger, for in a couple of sentences, he had cut her down to size, enforcing the distance between them while also underlining his indifference to her feelings about anything. He looked different with that headdress covering his riot of coal-black curls. While the *keffiyeh* framed and accentuated his superb bone structure and those dark deep-set eyes set below slashing ebony brows, it also made him look older and off-puttingly sombre.

'I confess that I am surprised, however, that you have not even met Prince Hakem. While such traditional matches still occasionally occur in Maraban, they are no longer the norm and I would not have thought a woman from your background would have been prepared to accept a husband sight unseen,' he admitted smoothly, dark eyes glittering back at her in cool challenge.

A wild surge of temper rocked Zoe where she stood, thoroughly disconcerting her, and her small hands coiled into tight fists by her side. The derision lacing his intonation and his appraisal was like a slap in the face. He might say that he didn't know her but she could see that, regardless of that reality, he had still made unsavoury assumptions about her character.

'Who the hell do you think you are to talk to me like this?' Zoe suddenly hissed at him, out of all patience and restraint because the way he was looking at her, as though she were some sort of lesser being, infuriated her. 'I came to this wretched country in good faith and my trust has been betrayed. I was drugged, *kidnapped* and subjected to a terrifying experience! Now you start judging me even though you don't know the facts.'

'I agree that I don't know the facts, nor do I need to know them,' Raj countered, disconcerted by the passion etched in her heart-shaped face as she answered him back. He wasn't used to that—he wasn't used to that kind of treatment at all.

He had been reserved from childhood, discouraged from letting his guard down with anyone, continually reminded about *who* he was and *what* he was and exactly what his rank demanded. After his mother's tragic death, he had had to learn to conceal his feelings and his insecurities, had had to accept that such personal responses were out of step with his status. An accident of birth had imprisoned him in a separate category, denying him the relaxation of true friends or freedom. When he had finally broken out of that prison, he had discovered to his consternation that that often icy reserve of his, which kept people at a distance, was as much a natural part of him as his face.

'Well, you're going to hear the facts, whether you want to or not!' Zoe snapped back at him curtly. 'Prince Hakem approached my grandfather to suggest the marriage, *not* the other way round. I didn't meet him beforehand because there was no need for me to meet him when it was never intended to be a normal marriage. I was to go through the ceremony and live quietly afterwards in the Prince's home. He swore that he would treat me like a daughter and that no demands would be made of me. Then after several months I was to go home and get a divorce…'

Raj's spectacular eyes gleamed as darkly bright as polar stars while he absorbed that surprising information. He understood now why his aunt had agreed to the divorce without making a fuss. Hakem must have promised to remarry her once he was free again and, in support of her husband's royal ambitions, Raj's aunt had been willing to make that sacrifice. 'But what was in this peculiar arrangement for you?' Raj persisted with a frown of bewilderment. 'It cannot surely have been enriching yourself when your grandfather is such a wealthy man…'

'Status!' Zoe almost spat out the word as if it physically hurt her and, indeed, it did. 'I would've become a princess and, while that doesn't matter much to me, it means a great deal to my grandfather and I wanted to please him. He's done a lot for me and my sisters.'

'Being a princess wouldn't have been much of a consolation while you were living in Hakem's home,' Raj informed her very drily. 'Hakem's wife and children are well known and well liked and everyone who knew them would have been ready to loathe you on sight.'

'Well, the marriage is not going to take place now, is it?' Zoe cut in thinly, turning away from him to wander across to the far side of the tent. 'After all that's happened, *nothing* short of handcuffs and chains would persuade me to stay in Maraban!'

Raj was disconcerted to find his brain sketching an erotic mental image of her chained to a bed, all flyaway blonde hair, passionate green eyes and little heaving pale pink curves for his private delectation. He stiffened and shifted restlessly while he fought to kill that untimely vision stone dead. But, sadly for him, there was nothing politically correct about his body and within seconds he was filled with desire.

'You know, I don't want to be rude or melodramatic,' Zoe began shakily.

'You may not want to be but you can't help behaving that way?' Raj incised hoarsely, knocked off balance now by his libido, that intimate imagery of her strengthening rather than fading and exercising the most extraordinary power over him.

Zoe spun. 'You're the one being rude!' she condemned, challenged to catch her breath when she clashed involuntarily with his intense gaze. 'Acting like being kidnapped is normal and refusing to tell me who orchestrated this whole stupid charade!'

'I am withholding that information because there is *no* possibility of the man involved being punished,' Raj admitted hoarsely.

What was it about that jet-dark gaze that made goose bumps rise on her exposed skin and sent little shivers running down her taut spine? Why did she suddenly feel so ridiculously overheated? Why did her tummy feel as though butterflies were fluttering through it? Instinctively she pressed her thighs together on the ache low in her core and she blinked in bewilderment and growing self-consciousness, her colour heightening as the explanation for her reaction dawned on her and shot through her like a lightning bolt. It was attraction, simple sexual attraction, and she was experiencing it for the first time *ever.* It made her feel all jumpy and twitchy, like a cat trying to walk across hot burning coals. Sheer shock crashed through her slender frame as she endeavoured to rise above her inner turmoil and focus on the conversation.

'And why is there no possibility of punishment?' Zoe demanded boldly.

'I will not discuss that with you. Please get dressed and we will leave.'

'To go where?' Zoe demanded in surprise.

'We are flying first to Dubai and then on to London, where you will be reunited with your grandfather,' Raj explained. 'As that arrangement is acceptable to him, I assume it is equally acceptable to you.'

'Acceptable?' Zoe echoed and she moved forward with a frown, her astonishment unhidden. 'Are you telling me that you have actually *spoken* to Grandad?'

'Of course.' Raj's intonation was clipped and businesslike. 'He was very angry about your disappearance and I had to reassure him that you were safe and that I would personally ensure that you are restored to his protection as soon as possible.'

But Zoe was still struggling to come to terms with the startling reality that he had already discussed the entire episode with her grandfather because that he should have boldly taken that step was utterly unexpected. Most people avoided Stam Fotakis in a temper and tried to wriggle out of accepting responsibility for anything that annoyed the older man. In fact, the only person she knew who ever stood toe to toe with her grandfather when he was in a bad mood was her sister, Vivi, whose temper matched his. Whoever Raj was, he was fearless, she decided enviously, for when her grandfather started roaring like an angry bull, Zoe simply wanted to keep her head down and take cover.

'I'm in a hurry. We will leave as soon as you are ready. My time here is limited,' Raj admitted flatly, tension tightening his smooth bronzed features. 'I would be obliged if you would be quick.'

'Well, I would need my clothes back to be quick, and I don't know where they are,' Zoe told him thinly, lifting her chin.

With an exclamation, he strode to the doorway and, a moment later, a little woman in tribal dress came running to do his bidding. Zoe's garments were located and laid in her arms, freshly laundered and fragrant. She stalked into the bathroom to look longingly at the shower and then she thought defiantly, What the hell? I'm not putting on clean clothes unless I'm clean as well!

As Zoe stepped beneath the flowing water with a deep sigh of relief, Raj strode out of the main tent, the old rules of polite conduct kicking in even though it felt like a lifetime since he had had to pay attention to such outdated beliefs. She was a single woman and he was a single man and he was in a very old-fashioned place where only his rank had granted him the right to speak to her alone. Even so, he had noted that the females in Omar's family were hovering nearby to ensure that the proprieties were observed. He was relieved that her attack on him had gone unnoticed for that would have very much shocked the tribe, none of whom would have recognised the need for a woman to learn the skills to protect herself. Male relatives were supposed to protect the women in the family.

Evidently, however, Zoe Mardas had not been protected, Raj reckoned thoughtfully, wondering what had happened to her, wondering why she had been so terrified and acknowledging that he would never know. He didn't get into deep conversations of that nature with women. His relationships, if they could be called that, were superficial and consisted of lots of sex and not much else. He doubted that he would ever want anything more from a woman. Why would he? Love had once made him stupid. He had given up everything for love and had ended up with nothing but the crushing awareness that he had made a serious mistake.

'Raj!' Omar gasped as he surged up to him, red-faced from the effort and winded, a small, rather tubby man, who rarely hurried at anything he did. 'You need to leave. One of the camel traders phoned to tell me…a bunch of military helicopters are flying in.'

'Soldiers love to rehearse disasters. It'll be some war game or something,' Raj forecast, refusing to panic. 'I told Zoe to hurry as politely as I could but you know what women are…'

'Raj, if you're caught on Marabanian soil, you could be arrested, *imprisoned*!' Omar emphasised in frustration. 'Grab that stupid woman and get in that helicopter and go!'

The racket of rotor blades approaching made both men throw their heads back and peer into the sky.

'Do you see those colours? That is the royal fleet, which means your father is on board!' Omar groaned in horror.

'It's too late to run. I'll have to tough it out.'

'No, *run*!' Omar urged abruptly. 'Right now…leave the woman here. I think this was a trap. I think she was dumped with me because they knew I was sure to ask you for your help. In the name of Allah, Raj, I will never forgive myself if you come to harm because of my thoughtlessness!'

A trap? Raj pondered the idea and as quickly discarded it. Why would his father, who had considered him a disappointment practically from the day of his birth, seek to trap him in Maraban? Sending Raj into exile, finally freeing himself from a son and heir who enraged him, had been the best solution for both of them, Raj reasoned ruefully.

'My father always warned me that Tahir was very devious, *very* calculating,' Omar breathed worriedly.

'He is,' Raj agreed. 'But he has no reason to *want* to find his son breaking the terms of his exile. Why would he? That would only embarrass him. I'll stay out of sight. Ten to one, he's taken one of his notions to call a tribal meeting and hash over boundaries and camel disputes. He revels in that kind of stuff…it takes him back to his youth.'

'The army craft are encircling the camp to land in advance,' Omar informed him.

'Standard security with the monarch on board,' Raj dismissed.

'No, I'm telling you,' Omar declared in growing frustration at his friend's lack of concern. 'This was a trap and I don't know how you're going to get out of it…'

CHAPTER THREE

THE RACKET OF the helicopters nearby unnerved Zoe and she dressed in haste, flinching from the cling of her clothes to her still-damp skin. When a woman entered the bathroom to fetch her, she was grateful she had hurried and she walked out through the main tent, glad to be embarking on her journey home.

It was a surprise, however, when she was not escorted to the stationary helicopter she had espied earlier and was instead led into another tent, where a group of women were seated round a campfire.

'The King is visiting,' the woman opposite her explained to her in perfect English. 'My husband, Omar, can only receive the King in his tent, which is, unfortunately, the one you have been using, which means that you will have to wait here with us.'

'Your husband?' Zoe studied the attractive brunette, who wore more gold jewellery than she had ever seen on one woman at the same time.

'Sheikh Omar. The King is his uncle. I am called Farida…and you?'

'Zoe,' Zoe proffered, accepting the tiny cup of black

coffee and the plate of sliced fruit she was given with a grateful smile. 'Thank you.'

Hopefully she would be on her way home within the hour, she reasoned, munching on a slice of apple with appetite. 'Where's Raj?' she asked curiously. 'I thought he was in a hurry to leave.'

'Prince Faraj is greeting his father,' Farida framed with slightly raised brows.

Zoe coloured, wondering if her familiar use of Raj's name had offended. 'I didn't know he was a prince,' she said ruefully. 'He said he was nobody of any importance.'

Farida startled her by loosing a spontaneous giggle and turned, clearly translating Zoe's statement for the benefit of their companions. Much laughter ensued.

'The Prince was teasing you. He is the son of our King.'

Zoe's eyes widened to their fullest extent and she gulped. '*He's* the bad-boy Prince?' she exclaimed before she could think better of utilising that label.

'The bad boy?' Farida winced at that definition. 'No, I don't think so. He is my husband's best friend and he took a dangerous risk coming here to see us. '

'Oh…' Zoe noticed that Farida didn't risk translating her comment about Raj being a bad boy and resolved to be much more careful about what she said. According to Raj these people had had nothing to do with her kidnapping and they had looked after her well while she was unable to look after herself. She didn't want to slight them.

After all, she knew next to nothing about Raj, had

merely read that tag for him on a website she had visited, which had contained the information that he had been sent into exile years ago for displeasing his father, the King.

'Risk?' she found herself pressing, taut with curiosity. 'What did he risk?'

'That is for his telling—*if* he has the opportunity,' Farida said evasively. 'But do not forget that the Prince is the King's *only* son, his only child in fact. He was born to the King's third wife when he had almost given up hope of having an heir.'

Zoe nodded circumspectly, unwilling to invite another polite snub and swallowing back questions that she was certain no one, least of all Farida, would wish to answer. Stupid man, she thought in exasperation. Why on earth hadn't he told her who he really was? It was not as though she could have guessed that he was of royal blood. She felt wrong-footed, however, and, recalling how she had assaulted him, gritted her teeth. It was his own fault though: he shouldn't have crept up on her like that.

An adorable toddler nudged her elbow in pursuit of a piece of apple and Zoe handed it over, waving her hand soothingly at Farida, who rebuked the little girl.

'No, my daughter must learn good manners,' Farida asserted.

'What's her name?' Zoe asked as the toddler planted herself in her lap and looked up at her with eyes like milk-chocolate buttons, set beneath a wealth of wavy black hair.

Farida relaxed a little then, and talked about her three children.

* * *

Accompanied by Omar, Raj strode into his cousin's tent where his father awaited him, seated by the fire.

'I thought I would find you here,' his father informed him with a look of considerable satisfaction. 'You are grown tall, my son. You have become a man while you have been away. Omar, you may leave. We will talk later.'

Raj's appraisal of the older man was slower and filled with concern because he could see that Tahir had aged. It was eight years since he had seen his father in the flesh. His parent had been in his fifties when Raj was born twenty-eight years earlier and the agility that had distinguished Tahir then had melted away. From a distance, Raj had watched his father's slow, painful passage to the tent, recognising that the rheumatoid arthritis, which had struck his parent in his sixties, now gripped him hard in spite of the many medical interventions that had been staged. He was still spry but very thin and stiff, the lines on his bearded face more deeply indented, but his dark eyes remained as bright and full of snapping intelligence as ever.

'Sit down, Raj,' the King instructed. 'We have much to discuss but little time in which to do it.'

Raj folded lithely down opposite and waited patiently while the server ritually prepared the coffee from a graceful metal pot with a very long spout. He took the tiny cup in his right hand, his long brown fingers rigid as he waited for one of his father's characteristic tirades to break over his head. Tahir was an authoritarian parent and had become even more abrasive and critical after the death of his third wife, Raj's mother. Sadly, that had been the period when Raj had been most in need of comfort and understanding and, instead of receiving that support, Raj had been sent to a military school where he was unmercifully bullied and beaten up. From the instant Raj had left school, he and his father had had a difficult relationship.

'I knew that Omar would run to you for help. He never had a thought in his head that you didn't put there first,' Tahir remarked fondly. 'We will not discuss the past, Raj. That would lead us back to dissension.'

'I'm sorry, but this woman…' Raj began even though he knew the interruption was rude, because he was so keen to find out why his father had acted as he had and had risked an enormous scandal simply to take his brother down a peg or two.

'You never did have a patient bone in your body.' Tahir sighed. 'Have sufficient respect to listen first. I want you home, Raj, back where you belong, as my heir.'

Raj was stunned. For a split second he actually gaped at the older man, his brilliant dark eyes shimmering with astonishment and consternation.

His father moved a hand in a commanding gesture to demand his continuing silence. 'I will admit no regrets. I will make no apologies. But had I not sent you away, my foolish brother would never have plotted to take your place,' he pointed out grimly. 'For eight years I have watched you from afar, working for Maraban, loyally doing your best to advance our country's best interests. Your heart is still with our people, which is as it should be.'

Raj compressed his lips and gazed down into his

coffee, dumbfounded by the very first accolade he had ever received from his strict and demanding parent.

'Do you want to come home? Do you wish to stand as the Crown Prince of Maraban again?'

A great wash of longing surged through Raj and his shoulders went stiff with the force of having to hold back those seething emotions. He swallowed hard. 'I do,' he breathed hoarsely.

'Of course, my generosity must come at a price,' the King assured him stiffly.

Unsurprised by that stricture, Raj breathed in deep and slow. 'I don't care who I marry now,' he declared in a driven undertone, hoping that that was the price his father planned to offer him. 'That element of my life is no longer of such overriding importance to me.'

'So, no longer a romantic,' his father remarked with visible relief. 'That is good. A romantic king would be too soft for the throne. And it is too late to turn you into a soldier. But your marriage… On that score I cannot compromise.'

'I understand,' Raj conceded flatly, shaking his hand to indicate that he did not want another cup of coffee, for any appetite for it had vanished. Sight unseen, some bride of good birth would be chosen for him and he and his bride would have to make a practical marriage. It would be a compromise, a challenge. Well, he was used to challenges even if he wasn't very good at compromises, he acknowledged grimly. But he would have to learn, and fast, because it was unlikely he would have much in common with the bride chosen for him.

'I should thank Hakem for bringing the Fotakis girl to my attention because I didn't even know she existed,' the King mused with unconcealed satisfaction. 'I was outraged when I realised what my brother was planning to do. I was even more outraged when I realised that I had no choice but to approach Fotakis himself… the man who stole the beautiful Azra from me. But he has given his permission.'

Only then registering what the older man was proposing, Raj threw his head back in shock. 'You're expecting me to marry *Zoe*?'

'And to do it right now, today. I brought the palace *imam* with me,' his father told him bluntly. 'This marriage would be your sign of good faith, your pledge to me that from now on you will act as a sensible son. Marry her and I promise you that nothing will stand in your path.'

'Zoe wants to go home!' Raj pointed out incredulously. 'She will not want to marry me.'

'Her grandfather has given his permission,' the King pointed out with a frown of bewilderment. 'A prince for a prince and a bridegroom less than half Hakem's age, you make an acceptable substitute in Fotakis's eyes. You have no choice in this, Raj. The girl is too great a prize to surrender, a huge gift to our people. No more popular bride than Azra's granddaughter could be found for you. We will have a big state wedding to follow. I believe she is as beautiful as her grandmother. You should be pleased.'

Raj compressed his lips on the reality that his father was insane. He talked as though women still dutifully and happily married the husbands picked by their most senior male relative. But even in Maraban those days were long gone. It was now only men of his father's venerable age who still expected the right to tell their offspring who they should marry.

'Zoe wants to go home,' he repeated steadily.

'You have two hours to persuade her otherwise. I have already prepared an announcement to be made from the palace,' the King told him solemnly. 'Their Prince has come home and done his duty at last.'

'Zoe was expecting to divorce Hakem within a few months,' Raj reminded his parent tautly.

'Yes, you can let her go once the fuss has died down. You can choose your own second wife,' Tahir informed him with the lofty air of a man bestowing a gift on the undeserving. 'I won't interfere, although there is one exception to that rule. That whore, Nabila...you cannot bring her into the family under any circumstances.'

At the mention of that name accompanied by that offensive term, Raj lost every scrap of colour, his eyes lowering, his expression cloaked by his spiky black lashes, for he had just learned that his father *knew* what had happened eight years earlier between his son and his first love. Discomfiture filled him to overflowing but the meeting, Raj recognised by that final warning, was over. He vaulted upright with something less than his usual grace. 'There is no risk of that development. I've not seen her in many years,' he revealed stiffly.

'Go and get ready for your wedding,' his father urged, clearly not accepting the possibility that Zoe might refuse to marry him. 'And send Omar in!'

Having had her breakfast, Zoe was ushered into another tent and left there alone. She checked her watch, shifted her feet, frustrated that she didn't know what the cause of the hold-up was. When Raj entered, she spun fully round to face him and then she froze, remembering uneasily that he was a prince and that she had not treated him as she should've done. But then that was *his* fault, she reminded herself, lifting her chin again. He looked tense, the smooth chiselled bones of his face taut beneath his bronzed skin, his dark deep-set eyes curiously intent on her.

'I thought you were in a hurry to leave,' she reminded him, wondering why even that scrutiny could heat her up inside her skin as if she were being slowly roasted. He made her feel hot and bothered and uncomfortable and if that was sexual attraction, well, then she wanted no part of it. Those physical reactions were affecting her ability to behave like a rational being.

'My father spoke to me *and*...our situation has changed,' Raj admitted, half turning towards the open doorway, avoiding a more direct look at her, lest he lose his concentration.

Any man would've looked though, he assured himself. Her beautiful hair was restrained in a long braid but he still remembered that silken veil unbound. Her shapely legs were exposed by a short skirt. The matching top in soft pastels moulded to her rounded breasts, and on her feet were the most ridiculously impractical heels he had ever seen a woman wear in the desert. Of course, she hadn't known that she would be waking up in the desert, but those towering heels, which still only contrived to lift her a couple of inches in height, were downright dangerous. At the same time, there was something absurdly feminine and cute about those tiny glittery sandals with their plethora of straps. He dragged in a deep breath, gritted his white even teeth. *Cute?* What was he thinking?

That it was safer to look at her feet than her breasts or her legs when his body was behaving as though it belonged to a sex-starved teenager. Since when had he been unable to control his libido? He could not recall ever having that problem before.

Zoe was very stiff, picking up on the undertones in the atmosphere while reading the physical tension he was putting out in waves. '*Our* situation?' she queried, surprised by that designation.

'Ours,' Raj emphasised. 'I don't know how much you know about me.'

'Well, you told me that you were nobody of any importance but Farida told me the truth—that you are the King's son,' Zoe countered in a tone of reproof. 'I also know that you were sent into exile.'

'Eight years ago,' Raj clarified sombrely. 'I refused to marry the woman my father chose for me because I was in love with someone else. There were other factors but essentially that is what caused my long estrangement from my father. You may not be aware of it but in my world a son is expected to be obedient and, to be fair to my father, I was a rebel from day one.'

More than a little disconcerted by that very personal explanation of his troubled relationship with his parent, Zoe coloured, her green eyes clinging to his brooding dark features and the fluctuating emotions he was striving to hide; only those expressive eyes of his continually gave him away, glimmering and glittering, alive with all the passion he struggled to contain. Unwilling fascination gripped her and she gave way to her curiosity. 'What happened with the woman you loved? Did you marry her?'

'No, she cheated on me,' Raj admitted flatly.

'I'm sorry,' she muttered automatically, wishing she hadn't asked.

'You don't need to apologise. It happened a long time ago when I was still young, trusting and naïve. I am not the same man now,' Raj parried wryly.

Because that woman had broken his heart, Zoe registered, recalling her sister, Winnie's heartbreak when she had had to leave the man she loved, after discovering that he was married. Zoe had never experienced anything that intense and she wasn't sure she wanted to either. But then she had never had a boyfriend. After the attempted rape she had fortunately escaped, she had feared and avoided men. She had had one or two male friends at university who had stayed close to her for a while to test her boundaries, hoping she would warm up to them but it hadn't happened. She had stayed apart and untouched and was much inclined to think that that was the best way to live. Without risk, without hurt, without disappointed hopes and unrealistic dreams of some fantasy happy future.

'You said "our" situation,' she reminded him, keen to steer the conversation out of deep waters. 'What did you mean by that?'

'My father has offered me a most unexpected suggestion,' Raj framed with care, brilliant dark eyes locked to her heart-shaped face and the eyes bright as emeralds against her porcelain pale skin. The contrast was breathtaking. 'He has asked me to come home and take my place as his heir again.'

'My goodness, that's wonderful news! I mean…' Zoe hesitated '…if *that* is what you want?'

'I want to come home with my whole heart. This is the first time I have been home in eight years,' Raj admitted harshly, his sincerity bitingly obvious. 'But unfortunately, the King's proposition came with a key stipulation attached. My father has asked me to take Hakem's place as your bridegroom and marry you.'

Zoe blinked several times and continued to stare at him, her heart thumping rapidly enough that it seemed to thunder in her ears. 'But…but why? That's a crazy suggestion!'

'Not if you consider who you are,' Raj pointed out with a wry twist of his wide sensual mouth. 'Half our population are originally from your grandmother's country and they were most resentful when my father and their Banian Princess failed to marry at the same time as the two states allied to become one. As a result, the royal family does not reflect the origins of both countries. If the King's son were to marry Princess Azra's granddaughter, it would be very popular with our people. Principally, *that* is why my father wants us to marry.'

'But I never even met Azra. She died before I was born,' Zoe argued. 'It's just an accident of birth.'

'No, it is your heritage and a vital and proud heritage to those who remember the Princess and a country that now only exists as part of Maraban,' Raj contradicted. 'I should also mention that your grandfather and my father have been in touch—I should imagine only through an intermediary—and this suggestion that you remain here to marry me instead has been discussed by them.'

'Good heavens… Grandad *knows* about all this?' Zoe gasped, already shaken by Raj's serious respect for her ancestry, which was, she realised finally, far more valued in Maraban than it would ever be anywhere else.

'Your grandfather is agreeable to the exchange of bridegrooms,' Raj delivered.

Zoe turned slowly pale with anger. 'But what about me? What about what *I* want?' she demanded starkly.

'That is why I am here…*asking*,' Raj stressed sardonically. 'Your grandfather and my father are quite happy to believe that only their consent is required. I am not that foolish.'

Her anger drained away again. 'Thank goodness, someone here has some sense,' she mumbled.

'You were willing to marry Hakem sight unseen,' Raj reminded her.

Zoe's knees felt weak and she flopped down on a cushioned seat as if her breath had been stolen from her. She was at a crossroads. 'That's different, that was before all this happened and I realised Hakem had abandoned his wife for me and stuff like that,' she argued uncomfortably. 'It was a mistake to agree. Now I just want to forget all this nonsense and go home again.'

'But I am asking you to stay here and marry me,' Raj stated with precision. 'And it is an entirely selfish request.'

Taken aback at that confession, Zoe tilted her head back to look up at him. 'Is it?'

'Yes. It would mean the end of my exile and my estrangement from my father,' Raj pointed out grittily. 'And not only that, my marriage to Azra's granddaughter would delight my people as well. What is in it for you other than the acquisition of an entirely useless title, I don't know, but it would at least be as much as you would have received from my uncle. I can also promise to treat you as well as he would have. He is a decent man, regrettably poisoned by his pointless need to compete with my father.'

What is in it for you? Zoe appreciated his honesty with regard to the advantages to him should he marry her. Even so, her understanding of his position did nothing to stop her brain from whirling with wild indecision. She had been ready to go home and give up on her quest for greater independence but now Raj was offering her another option. Yet somehow marrying him struck her as a far more intimidating prospect than marrying a much older man, who had sworn he would treat her like a daughter. Raj was so much younger, more aggressive, more virile… Her brain ran out of descriptive words as she glanced warily at him.

He was so poised in his long white buttoned tunic, a black cloak folded back over his broad shoulders, his lean, darkly handsome face grave and cool while he awaited her answer, those glorious dark-as-the-devil eyes gleaming with an impatience he was too polite and intelligent to voice. A positive reply would mean a lot to him. She understood that, she really did. She also still yearned for the opportunity to live an independent life, unfettered by the expectations of her family. But most of all, she wanted to prove herself to herself and she wanted to be strong without leaning on anyone else for support. Even less did she want to run home with her tail between her legs and disappoint her grandfather as well.

'What would it take to win your agreement?' Raj pressed, the skilled negotiator that he was breaking cover.

Zoe coloured as if he had turned a spotlight on her and dropped her head. 'Well, I don't know what your expectations would be but I can assure you now that I wouldn't want sex. I'm not into sex. It's something I can live without, but *you*?'

That he couldn't even look at her without thinking about sex was a truth Raj decided he needed to keep to himself. Overpowering curiosity assailed him at the same time. What had put her off sex? One bad experience? An assault? Those were not questions he could ask and he suppressed the urge to probe deeper even as he winced inwardly from the upfront immediate rejection she was handing him. She didn't want sex with *him*. He had never met with that kind of rejection before and he pushed away that awareness, deeming it arrogant and ultimately unimportant in the greater scheme of events.

'I can offer you the exact same marital agreement that persuaded you that you could marry my uncle,' Raj broke in to insist with measured cool.

Zoe tossed her head back in surprise. Little tendrils of white-blonde hair were beginning to cling to her damp brow because she was feeling too warm even in the shade of the tent. Probably because even talking about sex set her cheeks on fire with self-consciousness, but she knew that she had to be frank with him. There was no other way and no room for any misunderstandings if she was candid from the outset. It shook her to acknowledge that she was seriously considering the marriage he was suggesting, for it was unlike her to take a risk. And Raj, her sixth sense warned, would be a risk.

'Unfortunately, you're not old enough to treat me like a daughter!' she told him ruefully.

'But I am old enough not to put pressure on a woman, who doesn't want me, for sex,' Raj retorted without hesitation. 'I appreciate that you would have to take that guarantee on trust but it *is* the truth. I have never had to put that kind of pressure on a woman and I never will.'

'OK,' Zoe mumbled, feeling that they had done the topic of sex and not having it to death. 'I admit that I would like to stay in Maraban and explore a little of my heritage.'

'I could make that possible,' Raj told her.

'Where would we live?'

'In the palace, which is, I must admit, a little dated,' Raj acknowledged, choosing to understate the case because he himself considered his surroundings immaterial as long as the basics were in place.

His father, unhappily, had a great reverence for history and it had proved a major battle to persuade Tahir to allow even modern bathrooms and cooking facilities to be constructed in the ancient building. Guests were lodged in one of the very contemporary villas built within the palace compound to provide convenient accommodation for visitors while preserving his father's privacy.

'I could live with dated,' Zoe muttered uneasily. 'I'm really not very fussy. My sisters and I lived in some real dives before we met our grandfather a couple of years ago and he invited us to move into a property that he owns in London.'

'The palace is not a dive,' Raj murmured with reluctant amusement. 'To sum up, you are prepared to consider my proposal?'

'Thinking about it, wondering if I can trust you.' That admission slid off the end of Zoe's tongue before she could snatch it back and her face flamed with guilt.

'I keep my word…*always*,' Raj proclaimed with pride, dark eyes aglow with conviction. 'You have nothing to fear from me. You would be doing me a very great favour. The last thing I would do is harm you. In fact, if you do this for me, I will protect you from anything and anyone who would seek to harm you.'

He was gorgeous, she thought helplessly, standing there so straight and tall and emotional, *so* very *emotional.* She had never met a man who teemed with so much emotion that he couldn't hide it. She had never met a man she could read so clearly. Reluctant hope, growing excitement and the first seeds of satisfaction brimmed in his volatile gaze. She couldn't take her eyes off his, could still hear the faint echo of his fervent promise to protect her from all threats.

'We would still be able to get a divorce after a few months?' Zoe checked anxiously.

'Of course. We would not want to find ourselves stuck with each other for ever!' Raj quipped with sudden amusement.

And for the very first time in a man's presence, Zoe felt slighted by honesty. She scolded herself for being oversensitive. Naturally, he wouldn't want to stay married for good to a woman he didn't love and neither would she wish to stay with him, would she? He was simply voicing the facts of their agreement.

'Then...' Zoe rose to her feet, suddenly pale with the stress of the occasion and the big decision she was making for herself without consulting her sisters, who probably would've voiced very loud objections '... I will agree to marry you and I can only hope that it brings you the advantages that you believe it will.'

Raj took a sudden step forward and raised his arms and then let them fall again as he stepped back. 'Forgive me, I almost touched you but I am sure you prefer not to be touched.'

'I do.' But Zoe was lying. He had been about to sweep her up in his arms and hug her and she was disappointed that he had recalled her rules and gone back into retreat. He was passionate, a little impulsive, she suspected, the sort of guy who occasionally in the grip of strong feeling would act first, think later. She would have liked the hug, the physical non-sexual contact, the very warmth and reassurance of it, but it was better that he respected her boundaries, she told herself urgently. 'So when will this marriage take place?'

'Today.'

'Today?' she exclaimed in soaring disbelief.

'My father does not trust me enough to allow me to return to the palace without immediate proof that I have changed my ways,' Raj told her grimly. 'This marriage will provide that proof. He brought the palace *imam* here with him.'

'We're getting married here...*now*?' she prompted incredulously. 'What on earth am I going to wear?'

'My father leaves nothing to chance. I would suspect that his wife has brought appropriate clothing for you.'

'Which wife?' she prompted curiously.

'He only has one wife still living. My mother died when I was nine and her predecessor died about ten years ago. The Queen, his first wife, is called Ayshah,' Raj proffered. 'She is pleasant enough.'

Zoe breathed in deep and slow. She was going to marry Raj and make a go of her life all on her own. She would stay in Maraban for several months and there would be no more panic attacks. She would pick up some of the language, learn the history and find out about her grandmother's culture. It would be an adventure, a glorious adventure, she told herself firmly while watching Raj stand by the doorway, quite unconscious of her appraisal. He smiled with sudden brilliance. And gorgeous wasn't quite a strong enough word for him at that moment…

CHAPTER FOUR

'MY FATHER TELLS me that the King is arranging a state wedding to take place in two weeks' time and for that you can wear a Western wedding gown,' Farida informed Zoe in a discreet whisper. 'The King wants to make the most of your entry into the family.'

Apprehensive enough about the wedding about to take place, Zoe could have done without the news that there was to be a second, which would be a public spectacle. Such an event lay so far outside her comfort zone that even thinking about it made her feel dizzy. But she squashed that sensation. Baby steps, she told herself soothingly. She would cope by dealing with one thing at a time, and fretting about the future would only wind her up. Right at that moment it was sufficient to accept that she was about to legally marry a man she had only met for the first time that day.

Marrying Raj's uncle, however, she would have been doing the same, she reminded herself wryly, and at least Raj came without previous attachments such as wives, children and grandchildren. Yes, she had definitely dodged a bullet in not marrying Hakem. Raj was single and refreshingly honest. He had admitted that he had once suffered panic attacks too. He had even admitted to defying his father over the woman he loved and subsequently discovering that she had cheated on him, which must have been a huge disillusionment. Most men that Zoe came across would have concealed such unhappy and revealing facts. That Raj had been so frank had impressed her.

Surrounded by fussing tribeswomen presided over by the elderly Queen Ayshah, who sat in the corner, entirely dressed in black, barking out instructions, Zoe studied her reflection in the tall mirror. She was so heavily clothed in layers and jewellery that she was amazed she could move. A beaten gold headdress covered her brow, a veil covering most of her hair, weighty gold earrings dangling from her ears, hung there by thread. She had very narrowly sidestepped having her ear lobes pierced there and then and she had Farida to thank for tactfully suggesting thread be used to attach the earrings instead. More primitive gold necklaces clanked and shifted round her neck with every movement while rich and elaborate henna swirls adorned her hands and her feet. What remained of her was enveloped in a white kaftan covered in richly beaded and colourful embroidery. Below that were several gossamer-fine silk layers, all of which rejoiced in buttons running down the back. Getting undressed again promised to be a challenge, she thought ruefully.

She had insisted on doing her own make-up though, having run her eyes over her companions, already festooned in their glad rags and best jewellery for the wedding, their faces over-rouged, their eyelids bright blue. Only Farida had gone for the subtle approach. Zoe had used more cosmetics than she normally did and had gone heavy on the eye liner when urged to do so but at least there was nothing theatrical about the end result.

'My wedding celebrations lasted a week,' Farida told her.

'A *week*?' Zoe gasped.

'But yours will only last the afternoon. The King does not wish to spend the night here. The state wedding celebration parties will go on longer, I expect,' Omar's wife chattered. 'Everyone loves these events because they get to see family and friends, but this has been arranged so quickly that it is a very small and quiet wedding—but the jewellery Raj has given you is magnificent.'

'What jewellery?' Zoe whispered.

'Everything you're wearing comes from the royal house. Traditionally, the jewellery is your wedding gift.'

'The King must've brought that with him as well,' Zoe muttered.

'Yes, you were getting married today whether you wanted to or not!' Farida laughed. 'But who could say no to Raj?'

Zoe could feel her face heat and was grateful when the sound of music outside the tent sent all the women to the doorway. She followed them and glanced out to see some sort of ceremonial dance being performed with much waving of swords and cracking of whips. Men leapt over the campfire, competing in feats of daring that made her flinch and at one point close her eyes. A moment later, she was ushered out in an excited procession into another larger tent filled with people. She was led up to the front where a venerable older man appeared to bestow some sort of blessing on her and gave a long speech before handing her a ring. Farida showed her which finger to put it on. In the middle of the speech, she finally glimpsed Raj, resplendent in a sapphire-blue silk tunic, tied with a sash, his lean, darkly handsome features very serious. She tried and failed to catch his eye.

Another, even older man spoke more briefly and then moved forward to flourish a pen over a long piece of parchment, which he duly signed. In fact, several people signed the parchment and then she in turn was urged forward to sign as well, before being led away again without a word or a look exchanged with Raj.

'And now we party!' Farida whispered teasingly in her ear.

'You mean…that's it *done*? We're married now?' Zoe exclaimed in wonderment.

'As soon as you signed the marriage contract, it was done. I would've translated for you but I didn't want to risk offending the King by speaking during the ceremony,' the lithe brunette confided. 'You are now the Crown Princess of Maraban.'

'And I don't feel the slightest bit different!' Zoe confided with amusement, reckoning that her grandfather would be sorry to have missed the ceremony but she assumed he would be attending the state wedding, which was to follow. Her sisters would have to come as well and she smiled at the prospect as Farida guided her into yet another tent full of chattering women where music was starting up in the background.

Introduction after introduction was made and plate after plate of food was brought. There were no men present. Farida explained that the reception after the state wedding would not be segregated but that rural weddings were of a more conservative ilk. Zoe sipped mint tea and watched the festivities as the dancing began. Married, she kept on thinking; she couldn't believe it. But she wasn't really married, she reminded herself wryly, not truly married because she and Raj were not going to live together as a married couple. She wondered how he was feeling. Was he wishing she were his ex-love, who had let him down? Or did the significance of the actual marriage escape him because he was not in love with his bride? Or, more likely, was he simply happy that he was back in Maraban and accepted by his father again?

At one point, Zoe drifted off in spite of the noise and liveliness surrounding her and wakened only when Farida discreetly pressed her hand. She blinked in bemusement, for an instant not even knowing where she was. Darkness had fallen beyond the tent and it was quieter now, only a couple of women dancing, the rest gathered in chattering groups. Slowly her brain fell back into step and she suppressed a sigh, murmuring an apology to Farida for her drowsiness.

'Your body is probably still working on ridding you of the sleeping drug you were given at the palace. Our doctor said it would be a couple of days before you fully recovered from that. I am so sorry that that happened to you,' the other woman said sincerely.

'You were involved in it against your will…not your responsibility,' Zoe pointed out gently.

'And sadly, the instigator will only be celebrating

the reality that he has regained his son,' Farida murmured ruefully.

The last piece of the puzzle fell into place for Zoe and her eyebrows shot up in surprise as she finally appreciated that only Raj's father could have had her kidnapped and remained safe from punishment of any kind. That was why Raj had remained silent about the identity of the perpetrator; that was why he had seemed to feel partially responsible for her ordeal. Clearly the King had been determined to prevent his brother, Hakem, from marrying her.

'It is time for you to retire,' Farida told her, reacting to a signal from Queen Ayshah, who raised her hand and gave her a meaningful look.

That the old lady was still going strong while she felt weary embarrassed Zoe. She lumbered upright, feeling like an elephant in her cumbersome layers of clothing, hoping it was cooler outside than it was inside. But that was a false hope, she recognised when the humid air beyond the tent closed in around her and she was forced to trek across the sand in her wildly unsuitable shoes that dug in at every step. A camel was led in front of her and made to lie down. Farida instructed her to climb into the saddle, which, weighted down as she was by fabric and jewellery, was no easy task, but at last the deed was accomplished and the animal scrambled up again and swayed across the sands in the moonlight, accompanied by whoops from the women crowded round her and with the aid of the herdsman with his very modern torch.

'It is symbolic,' Farida explained. 'Queen Ayshah stands in your mother's place and she is sending you to your bridegroom.'

Zoe rather thought it was more as if she were a parcel to be delivered, although thank heaven, she reflected with a choked giggle, Raj wouldn't be expecting to *unwrap* the parcel. She slid more than she dismounted from the camel and picked herself up off the sand, thinking fondly that she was having an even more exciting wedding day than either of her sisters had enjoyed while wondering when her mobile phone would be returned to her so that she could bring her siblings up to date with events.

She almost staggered into the tent lit by lanterns that awaited her and there she froze in consternation. A large bed confronted her and it dawned on her at last that this was her wedding night, which she was expected to spend in close proximity to her new husband. She wasn't going to get her own tent this time or even her own bed because she was supposed to *share* the bed. In silence she pulled a face because she hadn't anticipated that, although she knew that she should've done.

After all, her agreement with Raj that their marriage would be platonic was a private matter that neither of them was likely to discuss with anyone beyond their immediate family. Grateful when the women retreated again she sank down on the bottom of the low divan and breathed in deep while she waited for Raj to arrive. My goodness, she was getting so hot. She straightened and walked into the primitive bathroom that had been erected alongside and clearly in haste for their comfort. A mirror sat propped up on a chest and piece by piece she removed the heavy gold jewellery and set it on the chest along with the veil.

At that point she heard shouts and catcalls outside and she scrambled up to return to the main tent just in time to see Raj striding in and covering the door again with obvious relief. 'Everyone gets overexcited at weddings,' he said wryly, studying her with fixed intensity.

Colour mantled her cheeks, self-consciousness reclaiming her as she hovered. 'Perhaps they're also celebrating the fact that their Prince is home again,' she suggested.

'It is possible,' Raj fielded with quiet assurance.

He wore confidence like invisible armour and she envied him that gift, wondering how he could ever have suffered the ignominy of panic attacks. He had the innate calm of a man comfortable in his own skin yet, from what little she had already learned, his past was littered with drama and disappointment. Yet he had overcome those realities and moved on, much as she wished to do.

'Do you know where my clothes are? Are they still back at the house I was taken from?' she asked uncomfortably.

'I will enquire for you in the morning,' Raj murmured smoothly.

'I don't even have a toothbrush!' Zoe protested, falling back on trivialities rather than dealing with her insecurities over the situation she was in.

'I will give you one,' Raj informed her in a tone of finality.

Zoe swallowed hard on a burst of angry exasperation. Was she supposed to go to bed naked with all her make-up on? It wasn't his fault that she had been separated from her luggage, she told herself urgently, and she shouldn't take her ire out on him. Deal with it, she instructed herself, and she went back into the bathroom and removed the ornate kaftan before beginning to undo the buttons of the layers beneath. Arms aching, perspiration dampening her face, she stalked back uneasily into the bedroom. Raj was on his phone, black eyes skimming to her instantly. He cast the phone down and studied her enquiringly.

'I'm afraid I need your help with all these buttons,' she framed in considerable embarrassment. 'I don't want to tear anything…'

'No, that would indeed be embarrassing,' Raj conceded. 'It would look as though I ripped the shifts off you.'

Breathing fast, Zoe spun round, presenting him with her slender back. 'I just don't get why it has all those buttons in an absolutely inaccessible place!'

'Because you are not supposed to take it off by yourself,' Raj informed her softly, a faint tremor racking her as she felt the gentle pressure of his fingers against her back as he undid the buttons, because a man had never got quite that close to her before and that he should be undressing her, even though it was at her request, was still a challenge. 'Your bridegroom is supposed to remove the three shifts slowly and seductively. It is a cultural tradition.'

'Oh…' Zoe gasped and then as the ramifications set in, *'Oh,'* she said again.

'You will have Ayshah to thank for the shifts because I don't think most brides bother with this particular tradition these days,' Raj told her huskily, skimming the first shift down her arms and letting it drop to the rug beneath her bare feet before embarking on the next set of buttons. 'That is a shame.'

'Is it? A bridal version of the dance of the seven veils…or whatever?' Zoe heard herself wittering on nervously, cringing even as the words escaped her.

Raj rolled his eyes and gritted his even white teeth because peeling her out of the silk shifts was testing his self-control. Her skin glimmered through the gossamer-fine tissue like the most lustrous of pearls and that close the sweet scent of her, of roses and almonds, was unbelievably feminine and alluring. Raj tugged down the second shift and let it fall before stepping away, carefully not looking at what would now be an enhanced view of her body because he did not require that encouragement.

Bemused, Zoe spun round, registering that he had stopped and walked away. 'I don't want to sleep in this one,' she muttered uncomfortably. 'These shifts are precious to your stepmother. They were put on me with a care that implied they were made of solid gold.'

'She is not my stepmother,' Raj incised curtly. 'She is my father's first wife.'

'Right… OK,' Zoe framed, registering that she had hit a tender spot with that designation, but very much out of her depth when it came to labelling or understanding the doubtless complex relations created in a family consisting of more than one wife. 'But what am I to sleep in?'

Raj was forced to look at her and the image locked him in place. She was so clueless he swallowed hard on impatient words. She might as well have been standing there naked for the thin material hid very little.

The pert little swells of her small breasts were obvious, not to mention the intriguing tea-rose colour of her prominent nipples and the pale curls at the apex of her thighs. Raj sucked in a sustaining breath, hot and hard as hell. 'I will get you something of mine,' he asserted, rather hoarse in tone, his dark deep voice roughening the vowel sounds.

'I'm sorry I'm being such a pain,' Zoe mumbled uneasily as Raj dragged out a leather holdall and opened it to rummage through it.

'I didn't bring much because I didn't think I'd be staying long.' Raj sighed, finally extracting a T-shirt and a pair of boxers for her use.

Zoe grabbed the garments with alacrity and spun round beside him. 'Just undo the last ones, please, and I'll be out of your hair,' she promised.

Raj suppressed a groan, his attention locking on the sweet curvaceous swell of her bottom. Presented with the delights of her in reality his imagination could take flight with ease and he ached with arousal. He grappled with the buttons, no longer deft, indeed all fingers and thumbs as he thought of laying her down on the bed and teaching her the consequences of teasing a man. But even as he thought of such a thing, he was grimly amused by it because he knew she was quite unaware of the effect she was having on him and that he would never touch a woman who had stated so clearly that she did not want to be touched. In fact, he had never been with a woman less aware of her seductive power over a man and, while at first he had found that absence of flirtation and flattery refreshing, now, suddenly, he was finding that innocence of hers a huge challenge.

'Now you can go and take it off and get changed,' Raj informed her thickly.

Zoe turned back to him, catching the harsh edge to his voice and looking up at him to see the dark glow of his eyes accentuated by the flare of colour over his high cheekbones. 'Raj…what's wrong?' she questioned helplessly.

'How honest can I be?' Raj asked.

'I want you to feel that you can always be honest with me. In fact, that's very important to me.'

'Even if it embarrasses you?' Raj prompted.

'Even if it embarrasses me,' Zoe confirmed without hesitation.

'You are half naked and very beautiful,' Raj breathed huskily. 'I have sworn not to touch you but I am still a man and you tempt me. You can still trust me to keep my word but I would be grateful if you…' He fell silent because Zoe had already backed into the bathroom, her face as startled and as red as fire.

Only ten feet from him, separated only by tent walls, Zoe looked at herself in the last shift and she burned all over with mortification. She'd had no idea quite how sheer the shifts were because at no stage had she seen her reflection in them in the mirror. Half naked seemed like an understatement when she was showing everything she had got! Shame and chagrin enveloped her. He had said she tempted him. Dear heaven, did he think her display had been deliberate? No, surely not. She peeled off the last shift, laid it carefully to one side and stepped into the shower, hoping it would cool her off. She didn't want to go back into the bedroom and look him in the eye again.

Cold water drenched her and she stood there as long as she could bear it, before, shivering, she got out and grabbed a towel off the pile. He had been frank with her and she was glad of that, she reflected ruefully. If they were to live in close proximity, she would have to be more careful, more *aware* in a way she had never had to be before. His T-shirt fell past her knees and she put on the boxers, although they struck her as overkill.

'Zoe?' Raj murmured quietly.

She peered into the bedroom and he handed her a toiletries bag.

When even her teeth were clean, she *had* to return to the bedroom but she looked nowhere near him as she crossed to the bed and climbed in straight away.

Raj went for a long cooling shower and tried to remember when he had last had sex. It had been weeks and weeks. He should make more effort in that department, he told himself firmly. Had he formed the habit of regular sex, he was convinced he wouldn't have been so tempted by Zoe. But then, it had been years since he had enjoyed regular sex, he acknowledged ruefully. These days he had occasional one-night stands and he never spent the night because he had discovered that spending too long with the same woman only encouraged the kind of entanglements and expectations that made him feel trapped. 'One and done', he called his routine. He didn't do relationships, he didn't do girlfriends, he didn't do dates. Nabila had sent him flying off such a conventional path.

But Zoe, the wife he could not touch, he was learning to his cost, was a whole new ball game…

Zoe peered out from under the sheet as Raj strode

across the tent, his long, lean, powerful body clad only in boxers. Her eyes widened, drawn by the flex of steel-hard muscle across his bronzed torso. He was a work of art, she thought numbly, barely able to accept that such a thought could be hers and that for the first time ever she was admiring the male body, which had until that moment inspired her only with fear. But then Raj was something else, Raj somehow fell into a totally different category and she didn't understand how that was or even why. Yet he was one of the most masculine men she had ever met. Everything about Raj from his innate poise to the rough stubble now darkening his jaw line and the well-honed strength of his physique screamed male. She closed her eyes tight, blanked her mind and slowly, inexorably fell asleep.

The nightmare that assailed her was an old familiar one. She was sprawled on the floor of an old hut, sneering thugs surrounding her while another cut off her clothes with a terrifyingly sharp knife. She was trapped. Shouting or screaming only earned her another punch and she was already in a great deal of pain because one arm and a leg were broken and, she believed, several ribs. She could barely see out of her swollen eyes but there was nothing wrong with her ears and she could hear every one of the filthy, perverted things they were threatening to do to her. She was petrified, lapsing in and out of consciousness, fighting the sickening effects of concussion…and outside a thunderstorm was crashing and banging like extra evidence that she had been plunged into a living hell.

'It's OK…it's OK,' a vaguely familiar voice was assuring her and she clung to that voice like a drowning swimmer, letting it pull her fully out of the bad dream.

'No,' she croaked in a shaken whisper. 'I'll never be OK again.'

Outside the thunder crashed deafeningly loud and she flinched and gasped, registering that there really was a storm outside, just as there had been the night she had almost been gang-raped. 'I don't like storms,' she muttered, clutching at his warm, solid body for support.

'You were having a nightmare, moaning, shouting for help. I tried to wake you up,' Raj admitted. 'But it took a long time to bring you out of it.'

'The storm confused me, probably woke me in the end… There was a storm in the nightmare too…except it wasn't really a nightmare, it was something that happened to me…but it's been years since I dreamt about it,' Zoe framed shakily. 'I'm sorry.'

'You don't need to apologise. We can't police our dreams,' Raj dismissed, leaning away from her to light the lantern by the bed.

Her anxious eyes widened at the sight of him because being in bed with a half-naked man felt so very alien to her. And Raj was all male as he stretched, that fantasy V-shape flexing across his lower rock-hard abdomen as he shifted to reach for a glass of water and handed it to her.

Colour rising, Zoe gulped down water as if she were suffering from dehydration. She didn't like the way her brain was spewing random sexual thoughts at her. It was scary being that close to Raj and wanting to touch him. *Touch* him? What insanity was attacking her? Since when had she wanted to touch a man? Yet all of a sudden she could imagine *touching* Raj, smoothing a hand over that satin-smooth golden skin laid down over muscle. She sat up and put the glass down just before another deafening crash of thunder boomed and it sent her careening into the shelter and security he offered like a homing pigeon.

Raj had never before found it a problem to have an armful of fragrant woman in his arms. But when the woman was Zoe, it was a major problem. He had heard her shouting for help and saying, 'No, *please…*' over and over again and a kind of unholy rage had gripped him that someone so small and defenceless had been driven to begging, her fear and desperation palpable. Only it became complicated when she got too close to him and his body reacted against his will. He was so hard he dared not leave the bed for fear that she would notice and get scared that he couldn't be trusted. But he was not made of stone.

He closed his arms round her, murmuring soothing things in his own language, doing his best to resist urges that he felt should shame him. 'Were you raped?' he asked in a roughened undertone.

Zoe flinched, her slender body trembling in his hold, and she looked up at him. 'No. I was lucky. I was beaten up but I was rescued before it got that far.'

Raj's level black brows lifted. *'Lucky?'* he derided, not only stunned by what she had told him, but also feeling honoured that she had trustingly bestowed such a terrifying secret on him.

And Zoe laughed and spontaneously smiled. 'Yes, very lucky. I'm a survivor.'

That glorious, utterly unexpected smile was more

than Raj could withstand. Zoe looked up into eyes as bright as liquid starlight and marvelled at the beauty of them. He lowered his head and claimed her soft pink mouth with his.

The thunder boomed beyond the tent. Lightning strafed the ground, lighting up the walls, but Zoe didn't hear or notice any of that because there was a kind of magic in Raj's kiss and it was like no kiss she had ever had before. And yes, she had had kisses before, had tried several times at university to get into the spirit without succumbing to the terror of getting out of her depth with some guy who might then get angry and refuse to listen to her protests. When Raj slid his tongue between her parted lips, an insistent heat she had never felt before flared between her thighs. His hands stroked through her hair and she felt her breasts swell and her nipples tighten and tingle. The warmth of his skin and the weight of him against her led to the discovery that her body liked those masculine aspects of him. Even more did she appreciate the aromatic smell of him, an insanely attractive combination of musky male and designer cologne, which tugged at something very basic inside her. His tongue brushed hers and withdrew, leaving her aching for more, every nerve ending on fire.

And then he set her back from him and dragged in a shuddering breath while still looking at her as though she were the only woman in the universe, a gift of his that yanked at her heart strings. 'I'm sorry,' he breathed in a raw undertone. 'I broke my promise not to touch you.'

'Do you see me running or screaming?' Zoe demanded, shaken by his sudden withdrawal while her body was still humming and pulsing like an unfamiliar entity.

Raj's slightly swollen and very sensual mouth compressed, dark eyes glittering with angry regret. 'I will not make excuses for myself but I assure you that *this* will not happen again. Go to sleep, Zoe. You are safe.'

Since she didn't have much choice, Zoe turned away and snaked back to her own side of the bed, defensively turning her back to him. She had only herself to blame for the way she felt, she thought unhappily. She had told him she wasn't interested in sex, had shown him her fear and, in return, he had sworn not to touch her. Naturally he was angry that he had broken that pledge. Sixth sense told her that Raj didn't usually break promises and probably didn't think much of those who did. But he had warned her earlier that he found her attractive and their current circumstances of false intimacy and mutual dependence only made resistance more difficult.

But for the first time in her life, Zoe had *wanted* a man and she knew that she wasn't likely to forget the crazy buzz of excitement that he had unleashed inside her. She, she reflected in mortification, had been more tempted than he was because he had quickly called a halt.

And what had she wanted to do?

To her eternal shame, she had wanted to snatch him back and *make* him keep on kissing her and, not only that, in the back of her mind she had been well aware that she craved more than that. Somehow, and she really didn't know how or when it had happened, she was finally ready to *try* sex, to experiment, but there was no room for sex in their agreement, particularly in a marriage destined to last only a few months.

When she wakened in the morning, Raj was gone, but one of her suitcases sat in a prominent position near the bed. With a smile of relief, she got up and went to open it before going to freshen up. Clad in light cotton trousers and a pink top, teamed with glittery sandals, she found breakfast awaiting her on her return. She was really hungry and tucked in with appetite, although she was no fan of the yogurt drink included, reckoning it was probably one of those healthy options that she rarely enjoyed.

She walked out of the tent and an explosion of utterly unexpected colour greeted her. A field of flowers stretched before her and she walked in amongst the colourful blooms in wonderment at such a floral display in so seemingly inhospitable a landscape.

'Zoe...stay where you are!' Raj shouted at her, incensed to see her outside and unprotected and wandering with a toddler's absence of caution.

'What on earth—?' she began, glancing up from the pink, purple and mauve blooms she was studying as she crouched.

But Raj, black curls shining, was sheathed in jeans and a T-shirt and already striding towards her, careless of the flowers he crushed beneath his feet, clearly untouched by the beauty of the scene. He scooped her up bodily in his arms, exclaiming in Arabic. 'And what the hell are you wearing on your feet?' he then demanded incredulously.

'Sandals!' she snapped. 'You stood on the flowers

of an *asphodelus fistulosus* and it was the only *one* in this mass of bugloss.'

'There are scorpions and snakes, lying in the shade below the flowers!' Raj bit out, startling her. 'Here you wear only proper footwear that protects you.'

'Oh… OK.' Zoe nodded, recognising concern and superior knowledge when she saw it. 'I didn't know… but the flowers were so beautiful.'

Raj carried her back to the tent, thinking that he would never forget that first glimpse of her in that sea of flowers, white-blonde hair falling to her waist and glittering like highly polished platinum in the sunlight, and those huge green eyes blinking dazedly up at him as he lifted her, full of shock and incomprehension of the risk she had taken. He had trod on pretty flowers and it had bothered her. She was sensitive, also possibly a little ditzy to walk out thoughtlessly into what could be a very hostile environment. But it was his duty to take care of her, watch over her, his job to protect. And the enormity of such a responsibility sat heavy on his shoulders for an instant because he had never been responsible for another human being before.

Nor did he want to be responsible, he told himself staunchly. He would take care of her to the best of his ability without ever forgetting that she was not *truly* his wife and he refused to think of her as such. Zoe was a short-term prospect, not a keeper. He would be ice, he would remain impervious to her charms. He was not about to complicate things by getting too involved with her. He had hard limits and he would observe them, retaining softer feelings, if he could even experience such emotions again, for his future *real* wife. There would be none to waste on Zoe, even if she looked adorable posed amidst flowers. What an asinine thought that was! He surely had more sense than that, enough intelligence to keep his distance, he instructed himself bitterly; he had learned his lesson with Nabila.

Innocent didn't mean she was a virgin. He would never believe a woman's word on that score again! Cute didn't mean trustworthy. Nabila had lied like a trooper and he had not recognised her deceit. Adorable definitely didn't mean loveable. Cute and adorable were words that should never feature in his vocabulary because caring about the wrong woman hurt like hell and he wasn't revisiting that mistake for anybody!

CHAPTER FIVE

WITHIN AN HOUR a brief flight in the helicopter returned them to the palace.

Zoe walked through an ancient porticoed entrance and instantly felt as though she had been transported into another world and another time. An awe-inspiring giant hallway full of pillars and elaborately tiled walls greeted her as well as a wealth of fawning servants, some of whom were in actual tears welcoming Raj back to his home. Brushing off their blandishments with palpable embarrassment, Raj hurried her on into the building while a cohort of attentive staff fell in behind them.

'My father has placed us in the oldest part of the palace, which is…unfortunate,' he told her in a clipped undertone. 'It is, however, where the Crown Prince always has his apartments, so I cannot fault him for following tradition.'

'Why's it unfortunate, then?' she queried uneasily, even while her eyes fled continually to her surroundings. She was enthralled by the exotic quality of the internal courtyard gardens she espied from the stairs and the fabulous views out over the desert, not to mention the stonework, the domed roofs and the stern palace guards, dressed as though they had stepped out of a medieval painting, armed with swords and great curved knives. The palace was everything she had dreamt of when first coming to Maraban but far more grand and mysterious than she had naïvely expected.

'Only one bedroom has been prepared for us,' Raj breathed curtly, his strong jaw line clenching. 'It will be difficult to give you privacy.'

'We'll manage,' Zoe told him with an insouciance she could not have contemplated before meeting him in the flesh. She knew in her very bones that she could trust Raj, believed that he would never try to force her into anything, but when she pondered that conviction, she was challenged to understand why she had such faith in him. He'd shown her empathy, tenderness, kindness the night before, she reminded herself ruefully.

'That is very generous of you but not strictly within our agreement,' Raj pointed out, refusing to be soothed.

'Can't be helped,' Zoe murmured, breathless from trying to keep up with his long stride as he traversed long corridors at speed and mounted flights of stone stairs with lithe ease. 'This is a very large building.'

'But *not* modernised,' Raj retorted grimly, throwing wide a door before a hovering servant could reach for it and guiding her into a simply vast room in which a bed hunched apologetically in one corner.

'Plenty of space though!' Zoe carolled like Job's comforter.

The remainder of her cases were already parked along with the one that had travelled out to the desert encampment. A maid glided up and tilted one suggestively, looking eager to unpack, while Raj stalked across the huge Persian rug, like a jungle predator at bay looking for something else to complain about.

A connecting room, she quickly learned, contained cavernous wardrobes.

'This suite was last occupied by my father fifty-odd years ago,' Raj informed her grimly. 'You can tell.'

'You didn't use these rooms when you were younger?'

'No. Before my marriage I was expected to live in my father's household.'

Zoe passed on into a ridiculously gigantic bathroom with a great domed roof studded with star tiles. The bathroom fittings huddled somewhat pathetically against the walls. 'It just needs more furniture,' she told Raj with determined cheer. 'We could have one of those fainting couches in the middle and I could lie there like Cleopatra eating grapes.'

His starlit eyes focused on her without warning, an intensity within that look that made something quiver and burn low in her pelvis. *'Naked?'*

'Whatever turns you on,' Zoe mumbled, face burning, outclassed in her attempt to be light-hearted and dropping her head even while she pictured herself lying there naked for Raj's enjoyment. A ridiculous fantasy, she scolded herself, for there would be nothing particularly sexy or seductive about her very small curves on display.

'I have staff to introduce you to now,' Raj announced, biting back the comment that seeing her naked in any circumstances would work a treat for him. There would be no flirtation between them, he instructed himself harshly, no foolishness.

'Staff?' she exclaimed in dismay.

'Principally my PR team, but you will have your own PA to keep you well informed of events. My father has made certain requests. He would like you to give an interview to our leading newspaper.'

Zoe had frozen. 'An...*interview*?' she yelped in dismay.

'Saying how you feel about arriving in your grandmother's country and being on the brink of a state wedding. My team will advise you and remain with you during it. There is also a fashion stylist, who will recommend a suitable wedding dress and new clothes.'

'I brought a wedding dress and an entire wardrobe with me,' she informed him helpfully.

'It would be distasteful to me were you to wear the dress you purchased for the marriage you planned to make to my uncle,' Raj delivered succinctly. 'You will wear nothing bought for that purpose.'

Zoe just couldn't see why it should matter what she wore. 'Don't you think you're being too particular?'

Raj settled hard black eyes on her, startling her. 'No. I know what I like. I know what I *don't* like. The concept of you wearing anything chosen with another man in mind offends me.'

Zoe sucked in a sustaining breath, deciding that he was more sensitive to her past history than she had appreciated. She returned to supervising the maid hanging her clothes because it seemed safer to keep her head down.

'You will be kept very busy over the next few days

choosing wedding apparel,' Raj informed her from the doorway.

'Can I use your phone for a few minutes?' Zoe asked abruptly. 'Mine needs charging and I want to catch up with my sisters and my grandfather.'

'Of course.' Raj dug out his phone, cleared the password and handed it to her. 'I will see you later.'

And then, just like that, he was gone and she was staring at the space where he had been, all black silky curls with his dark, devastatingly beautiful face taut and uninformative. She had wanted him to stay with her, had wanted *more*. For a charged moment, she couldn't cope with seeing that large gap between reasonable expectation and sheer idiocy for, naturally, Raj wasn't planning to hover over her like a protective and loving spouse because he wasn't really her husband in the truest sense of the word. No, he was genuinely offering her what she had told herself she needed and craved: an independent life in which they would live separate in mind and body. So why did that sensible arrangement now seem much less inviting? Why did his attitude currently feel like something of a rejection? She shook off that strange notion and told herself to stop overthinking everything before she drove herself mad.

Her grandfather was delighted to hear from her and eager to be assured that Raj was treating her properly, while adding that he would be arriving for the wedding, the fierce pride in his voice as he mentioned 'state' wedding so strong that it made her roll her eyes and swallow back a sigh. Winnie and Vivi were far less accepting of the change of bridegroom.

'He's a lot younger than the oldie,' Vivi warned her

worriedly. 'Make sure he doesn't try to get too friendly because he may have a different agenda.'

And when Zoe protested about how kind and considerate Raj had been so far, Winnie snorted. 'He's a prince, a future king—obviously he'll be full of himself. And I looked him up online…he's incredibly good-looking. Watch out for him trying to change the terms of your agreement.'

But when Zoe went to bed that night there was no sign of Raj being full of himself or looking to change the terms of anything. He had joined her earlier for dinner out in their private courtyard, a space shaded by towering and somewhat neglected trees and shrubs, and he had then excused himself to work. She had been measured up for a new wardrobe, had looked at length at designer dresses on a screen and had stated her preferences. By the end of the day she was too exhausted to stay awake, wondering where Raj was.

Raj worked late into the night before bedding down on the sofa in his office. It was the safe option. A vision of Zoe naked troubled his rest and at four in the morning he was on his phone trying to find out what a fainting couch was; for some reason he was determined to buy one regardless of cost. He groaned out loud at the conflict tearing at him. He didn't want to get involved. He didn't want to have sex with her…except when his resistance was at a low ebb. Why the hell would he buy a fainting couch for her to pose on? He found a purple velvet one hung with tassels and pictured her with a driven exhalation of breath before he thumped the cushion beneath his head. No couch, no flirtation, no sex, no intimacy whatsoever, he reminded himself grimly.

* * *

'Well, I couldn't say much for the accommodation,' Vivi remarked with a decided sniff.

Zoe bit back a tart response because her sister had been making critical comments ever since she had arrived the night before and it was starting to annoy her. 'It's very comfortable and Raj says I can take furniture from any of the unused rooms in the palace or buy new stuff, but contemporary wouldn't really work in surroundings like these. I haven't had time yet to change anything with all this wedding craziness going on.'

'That monster bathroom is just ridiculous,' Vivi opined snarkily.

'Raj's father wouldn't agree to any structural alterations when the bathrooms first went in. As far as he can, the King wants to preserve the palace as it was when he took the throne and I can understand that. It's a very old and historic building and he feels more like the custodian for future generations than the owner who has a free hand,' Zoe pointed out.

'You've got more confident…that's clear and I definitely approve of that,' her eldest sister, Winnie, said warmly. 'Here you are giving interviews and the like. I never thought I'd see the day.'

'Oh, the interview was easy,' Zoe carolled. 'Raj's PR team headed off any too personal questions for me and advised me on what to wear and all the rest of it.'

'But you picked your own wedding gown,' Winnie said knowingly, scrutinising the tiny glittering figure of her youngest sister. The dress was an elegant sleeved sheath with a modest neckline. Elaborate embroidery sewn with crystals and pearls adorned the lightweight tulle and it was the perfect fit for her petite frame. 'It's very chic.'

'Oh, stop changing the subject, Winnie,' Vivi cut in curtly, keen to cut through the chit-chat to what she believed was truly important, which was *protecting* Zoe. 'You know that you're as worried as I am. We *talked* about it last night.'

'And we're not going to talk about it any more,' Winnie declared, throwing her fiery sibling a pleading look. 'It was Zoe's decision to do this and the deed is done. They're already married.'

'With *one* bedroom in a palace the size of a small city!' Vivi interrupted worriedly, seriously suspicious of that development. 'How's she going to fight off a guy twice her size?'

Zoe paled at the tenor of the conversation. 'I won't have to fight him off. Raj sleeps elsewhere. We haven't had to share a bed since that first night I told you about, and that was kind of unavoidable and he apologised for it.'

'Raj is smooth, sophisticated, *predatory*,' Vivi outlined in condemnation, finally speaking her mind, for she had taken one look at Raj in all his good-looking, silkily soft-spoken glory and seen him as a major threat to the terrifyingly innocent and fragile little sister she loved. How could such a very handsome and wealthy man *not* be predatory? Zoe's near rape had almost destroyed her and Vivi didn't want her sister plunged into any situation that could threaten her peace of mind. 'I would imagine he is never stuck for the right word in a difficult situation.'

'He's not predatory,' Zoe argued with distaste. 'He's been kind. He's courteous and considerate and that's all we need right now.'

'Leave it, Vivi,' Winnie said ruefully. 'All you're doing is putting more pressure on her.'

Zoe's hand shook a little as she reapplied her lipstick. She was furious that Vivi had called Raj predatory after only meeting him for an hour over the formal dinner that had been staged the night before. Stam Fotakis, her grandfather, had been grudgingly impressed by Raj, pointing out to her with satisfaction that, unlike her sisters' husbands, Raj had never been tagged a womaniser.

Diamonds flashed with every movement of her body. Raj had sent her jewel cases containing a tiara, a necklace and earrings. She didn't know whether they were family heirlooms or bought specially for her use and she hadn't had the chance to ask him because she had barely seen Raj since their move to the palace two weeks earlier. He joined her for dinner every evening but his manner was formal and distant and she didn't know how to break through that façade.

And although she had tried to penetrate that barrier to establish a friendlier vibe, Raj remained resolutely detached and very, *very* polite. His attitude frustrated the hell out of her. She didn't know what the matter with him was or what was travelling through his brain. The warmer, milder, more approachable side of Raj had vanished as though it had never been.

Although she could have had no suspicion of the fact, Raj's attitude was frustrating his royal parent even more.

'Any normal man would want to *keep* her!' King Tahir was proclaiming to his stony-faced son.

'I have no intention of keeping Zoe as a wife,' Raj asserted quietly. 'You knew that going into this.'

'She's a beautiful, gentle girl. Everyone who has met her has talked highly of her. She could be a tremendous asset to you with her personality and ancestry,' his father fumed. '*Why* are you sleeping in your office with a beautiful wife in your bed? Have you forgotten how to woo a woman?'

The obstinacy that ran through Raj like a steel backbone flared and he gritted his teeth. 'She agreed to a fake marriage and I will abide by that agreement as I will abide by the one I made with you.'

The King paced the floor and silence fell. It was the silence of unresolved differences and residual bitterness that most often distinguished meetings between father and son. It took effort for the older man to persist. 'I loved your mother. I *know* she was unhappy as my wife but I loved her very much and the mode of her death devastated me,' he bit out harshly. 'I have to live with my regrets and my mistakes but I still remain grateful for the time I had with her.'

Raj swallowed hard, unable even to look at his father and utterly taken aback by that confession. He had never realised that his father actually loved his mother but he did recall that, after her passing, the older man had lived like a hermit for over a year. Not guilt so much as grief, Raj adjusted now, his view of the past softening the trauma of loss just a little.

Ironically, even appreciating that could not lift his gloom because there was nothing to celebrate when marrying a very beautiful woman who appealed to him on every level but who would ultimately leave him. His mother had left him by taking her own life, Nabila had left him through betrayal of all that he held dear. But then, hadn't he *agreed* that Zoe would ultimately leave him? Hard cheekbones colouring at that timely recollection, he reminded himself that he was in control of events and walking the path he had chosen. By the time Zoe walked out of his life again, he would surely be glad to reclaim his freedom.

The state wedding was so official and serious that Zoe's face ached with her set and determined smile. Being the cynosure of all eyes was taxing for her, but she wouldn't let herself dwell on that reality because she was well aware that all brides were subject to close scrutiny. Instead she reminded herself that she was lucky enough to have her grandfather, her sisters and their husbands with her for support. Sadly, the formality of the event had persuaded her sisters that their young children were better left at home and she suppressed a sigh. Winnie's son, Teddy, was a very lively little boy and her toddler daughter was full of mischief while as for Vivi's twin boys, sitting still for any length of time was a massive challenge for them, but Zoe was still disappointed not to have had some time with her nephews and niece because she had always adored children and had grieved over the truth that she was unlikely to have any of her own.

Yet her recognition of her attraction to Raj and her enjoyment of that amazing kiss had made her think that just maybe there was hope for her in the future. Maybe some day, after all, she would be able to have a relationship with a man like any normal woman, and if that happened then she just might have children of her own to love and care for eventually. More than anything else, what she had learned about herself since arriving in Maraban had convinced her that staying in her grandmother's country was the very best thing she could do to steer herself back into the land of the living. There was a whole world out there waiting to be discovered and for the first time in years she was filled with hope and optimism.

In the short term, however, she acknowledged wryly, there was the marrying, the constant smiling and the solemn bridegroom to contend with at their reception. If a smile had cracked Raj's face once she must not have been around to see it. A half-smile would play about the corner of his full sensual lips in the most infuriatingly tantalising way and she would watch and watch those lean, darkly beautiful features of his, but the real thing never quite made it, even for the authorised wedding photographs, which had proved to be an exercise in rigid formality.

Yet everywhere in Raj's radius, a virtual party was in swing, his return to being Crown Prince clearly a development that was celebrated by the many important guests attending, who ranged from visiting royal connections to business tycoons, top diplomats and local VIPs. His popularity was undeniable, although he was quick to dampen comments that tactlessly suggested that some day he would take Maraban forward in a different way from his father. Zoe sat through a lot of business talk before escaping back in the direction of her sisters.

She had already done her stint with Queen Ayshah, who had employed Farida as a translator and had embarrassed the other young woman greatly by insisting on passing on her convictions of what it took to be a good royal wife. A feminist would have had a field day with those rules, Zoe reflected with strong amusement, but then the elderly Queen had grown up in a different world where a woman's happiness and even her life could be utterly dependent on retaining her husband's favour. Thankfully, Raj would have no such power over her, Zoe thought fondly as she took a detour towards the cloakroom before approaching Winnie and Vivi.

In the big anteroom surrounding the cloakroom, a tall, slender woman rose from a chair and addressed her. 'Your Royal Highness?' she murmured with modestly evasive eyes. 'May I have a word?'

Zoe looked up into one of the most beautiful faces she had ever seen: a flawless oval graced by almond-shaped brown eyes with remarkable lashes, a classic slim nose and a pouty full mouth. The woman wore a sophisticated silk suit, tailored with precision to show off her well-formed figure and falling to her ankles while still toeing the line of local mores on modest dress. The pale golden hue of the outfit set off her glowing olive colouring and her wealth of tumbling black wavy hair to perfection.

'I am Nabila Sulaman,' she revealed in a very quiet voice. 'I was Raj's first girlfriend and, as I'm sure you're aware, it ended badly between us.'

Thoroughly disconcerted by that introduction, Zoe merely gave an uncertain nod while her mind raced to understand why the wretched woman would want to approach her.

'I run one of your grandfather's construction firms and he brought me here with his party of business people. I would definitely not have received an invite on my own behalf,' Nabila admitted, startling Zoe even more with that freely offered information. 'I'm very much a career woman and I don't want past mistakes to taint my future now that I've returned to Maraban to work. My parents suffered a great deal over my short-lived relationship with Raj. My father is a diplomat but he has been continually passed over for promotion since I blotted my copybook with the royal family. I am speaking to you now because a lot of time has passed since then and I was *hoping* that you could persuade Raj to bury the hatchet.'

Zoe winced at that bold suggestion. 'I'm sorry but I don't think I'm the right person to intercede for you. I don't interfere with Raj's life and he doesn't interfere with mine.'

'How very modern he must have become,' Nabila remarked with a dismissive toss of her beautiful head and an amused smile. 'Well, I think you should know that I'm in charge of the Josias project as CEO of Major Holdings, and that Raj and I will be working together in the near future. Please make him aware of that. I'm leaving now.'

'But Raj is here. You could speak to him yourself,' Zoe pointed out.

'No. I don't want to put him in an awkward position and surprise him in front of an audience,' Nabila declared with assurance. 'We haven't seen each other since we broke up.'

'Oh…' Bemused, Zoe watched the poised brunette walk away again and she entered the cloakroom with a lot on her mind. Nabila was gorgeous, clever and successful and had once been the woman Raj loved and wanted to marry, Zoe reflected ruefully. Loved and wanted to marry *a long time ago*. Eight years back, she reminded herself, practically pre-history in date. But even though that was her mindset she still headed straight for her grandfather to check out his opinion of the brunette.

'Nabila Sulaman? She's one tough cookie, a real go-getter,' Stam opined. 'Had to be to get so far in the construction field. She's Raj's ex?' Her grandfather grimaced. 'I wouldn't have included her in my party if I'd been aware of that.'

'Oh, it doesn't bother me,' Zoe hastened to proclaim just as her sisters joined them and then, of course, the entirety of her short conversation with Nabila had to be recounted.

'She's got some brass neck!' Vivi declared. 'I wish I'd been with you. Didn't you learn anything from us growing up?'

Zoe blinked and studied her sibling's exasperated expression. 'What do you mean?'

'You don't tangle with an ex. You certainly don't give her any information… I mean, what you were thinking of, telling her that you and Raj don't interfere in each other's lives?' Vivi demanded ruefully. 'How normal does that sound? You *want* the ex to think you're the love match of the century.'

'Put a sock in it, Vivi,' Winnie cut in. 'Zoe doesn't have to pretend if she doesn't want to. It's a marriage of convenience and both of them know and accept that. It's not personal for them the way it was for you and me.'

Zoe had lost colour. No, it was *not* personal, she repeated staunchly to herself, because, unlike her sisters and their husbands, Zoe had had no prior relationship with Raj before their marriage. Yet even in acknowledging that truth she was taken aback by the revelation that she would have liked to have scratched Nabila's beautiful eyes out because Nabila had *hurt* Raj. A long time ago, she reminded herself afresh, and he was perfectly capable of looking out for himself.

When the festivities were almost at an end, Zoe went to change into more comfortable clothing for their journey. They were to be out of the public eye for two weeks and she couldn't wait to reclaim some privacy. Apparently, the royal family owned a very comfortable villa by the Gulf on the Banian side of Maraban, and Raj had already promised to show her the beauties of her grandmother's birthplace, which was greener and less arid in landscape. She pulled on a light skirt and T-shirt, teaming them with a pair of glitzy high sandals, one of the many, many pairs she harboured in her wardrobe but had never previously worn. She had a serious shoe fetish and knew it.

'We're fortunate to be making so early an escape,' Raj remarked, sliding into the limo beside her, a lean, lithe figure in jeans and a shirt, his black curls tousled as though he had changed out of his wedding finery in as much of a hurry as her. 'If my father wasn't so eager to pack us off on a honeymoon, the celebrations would have lasted all week.'

'Farida mentioned that weddings usually last for days here, but then it was our *second* time round the block,' she pointed out before pressing on, doing what her conscience told her she had to do, which was to warn Raj that he would be working with his ex on some project that she didn't recall the name of. 'I met your ex-girlfriend, Nabila, at the reception.'

Raj's arrogant head turned, a frown building, his lean, darkly handsome face forbidding. 'That is not possible. She would not have been invited. Nabila is a common name in Maraban.'

'Apparently she came in my grandfather's party of guests,' Zoe persisted. 'She's the CEO of some company called Major Holdings and she asked me to warn you that you would be working with her on some project.'

'The Josias hospital project.' Raj's intense dark eyes shimmered almost silver in the fading light. 'But I need no warning. I am not so sensitive,' he breathed with roughened emphasis.

And then he didn't say another word for what remained of the fairly lengthy journey that took them to the airport and a flight and, finally, a bumpy trip in a SUV. And, unfortunately that brooding silence told Zoe everything she didn't want to know or surmise about the exact level of Raj's sensitivity. He was like a pot of oil simmering on a fire but all emotion and reaction was rigidly suppressed by very strong self-control that acted like a lid. But knowing that, accepting that she hadn't a clue what he was thinking, didn't make Zoe feel any happier. For the first time with Raj, she felt very alone and isolated…

CHAPTER SIX

WITH DIFFICULTY, RAJ emerged from circuitous thoughts laced with outrage at the prospect of being exposed to Nabila's deceitful charm again and stepped out of the SUV. He expected to see the sprawling nineteen-twenties villa that his family had used as a holiday home since his childhood. He blinked in disbelief at the very much smaller new property that now stood in its place and signalled the army major in charge of their security to seek clarification of the mystery. A couple of minutes later he returned to Zoe's side.

'Apparently, my father had the old villa demolished several years ago because it was falling into disrepair and he thought it was too large to renovate,' Raj explained. 'It was built by your great-grandparents at a time when the Banian royal family had half a dozen daughters. My family used it rarely after your mother's father died. My father likes the sea but the Queen does not.'

Relieved that Raj was talking again, Zoe murmured, 'Did you come here much as a boy?'

'Often when I was very young with my parents. My mother loved it here.' His lean strong face tightened, his perfect bone structure pulling taut beneath his bronzed skin. 'I remember her skipping through the surf and laughing. No worries about etiquette or protocol or who might be watching and criticising her behaviour. She could be an ordinary woman here again and she loved it.'

'An *ordinary* woman?' Zoe queried, puzzled by that label.

Momentarily, Raj turned away to evade the question because he disliked talking about past traumas. In his experience a trouble shared was not a trouble halved and he preferred to gloss over such issues. Without skipping a beat, he deftly changed the subject. 'My father should have told me that there was a smaller property here now,' Raj breathed. 'As he only comes here alone, there may only be one bedroom.'

'Oh, let's not get into *that* debate again!' Zoe carolled with a comically exaggerated shudder that locked his eyes to her animated face. 'We're adults, we'll get by, even if you make me sleep on the floor!'

Her green eyes could dance like emeralds tumbling in sunlight, Raj noted abstractedly, settling a hand to her spine to guide her down the path because it was dark and she could hardly move in her high heels without stumbling on the stony surface beneath their feet. He had watched her throughout the day, had been forced to watch her teeter and sway and steady herself on furniture every time she lost her balance. She might continually wear high heels but had evidently not yet learned how to comfortably walk in them. The idea of her falling and hurting herself made him want to go into her wardrobe and *burn* every one of those preposterous shoes. It was an odd thought to have and he tagged it as such and frowned in bemusement.

'You know, I wouldn't do that.'

'You're not sleeping on the floor either!' Zoe warned him as they approached the well-lit front door. A lovely wrap-around veranda fronted the building and their protection team surged ahead of them to check that the house was safe. 'Where have you been spending the night since we got married?'

'My office.'

'Is there a bed there?'

Raj shrugged a broad shoulder. 'A sofa,' he admitted grudgingly.

Zoe gritted her teeth in annoyance. 'Are you *that* scared of me?'

Dark colour scored the hard, slanted lines of Raj's spectacular cheekbones and his stunning eyes flashed gold with angry disbelief. At that optimum moment the protection team reappeared to usher them inside. It didn't take long to explore the interior of the beach house. There was a surprisingly large contemporary ground-floor living area and a winding staircase led upstairs to a spacious bedroom and bathroom.

'There's no kitchen!' Zoe exclaimed abruptly, glancing out at the walled swimming pool beyond the patio doors. 'How are we supposed to eat here?'

'The staff stay in a new accommodation block built behind the hill and cater to our needs from there,' Raj told her. 'Meals will be delivered. It's not a very practical arrangement but my father enjoys his solitude.'

'I'm starving,' Zoe admitted.

'I will order a meal.'

'I'll go for a shower and change into something more comfortable,' Zoe said cheerfully.

She was halfway up the stairs when Raj spoke again. 'I am not scared of you, nor was I implying that you would choose to tempt me into breaking my promise,' he assured her levelly. 'But it annoys me that my father is making it so difficult for me to offer you the privacy I swore to give you.'

'And why *is* he doing that?' Zoe prompted, tipping her head to gaze down at him, her cheeks warm from his misapprehensions about her. No, she wouldn't ever set out to deliberately tempt him but she was painfully conscious that she wanted him to make some kind of move on her because she was keen to explore the way he made her feel. It was just sex, she told herself guiltily, sexual urges tugging at her hormones, and there was nothing more normal than that, she told herself in urgent addition, nothing to be ashamed of in such fantasies. It was simply her bad luck that she was married to an honourable male who believed in keeping his promises and not taking advantage. Luckily for her, she could not even imagine a scenario where she would tell him honestly how she felt and, for that reason, the humiliation of making a total fool of herself over him was unlikely.

In the meantime, all she could freely do was glory in the sheer physical beauty of Raj, his wonderful broad-shouldered, lean-hipped and long-legged physique that magnetically glued her attention to him, the dark deep-set eyes that were silver starlight when he stared up at her, his perfect golden features taut. Heaven knew, he was gorgeous and it was little wonder she was obsessed, she conceded ruefully. He had broken through her barriers, made her experience feelings she had never known she could feel, but he hadn't intended to do that and now she was stuck with the rules according to Raj, which had about as much give in them as steel bars.

'My father believes you could be my perfect *for ever* wife. He's hoping for more than a pretend marriage from us and obviously he's doomed to disappointment,' Raj extended drily.

'Oh…' Deprived of speech by that piece of bluntness and stung by the assurance that she was safe for ever from being asked to entertain the idea of something *other* than a pretend marriage, Zoe sped on into the bedroom.

There was so much she didn't know about Raj, she reflected. All she had were the bare bones of his background and the fact that his first love had cheated on him. At least, she was assuming that Nabila had been his first love but, really, what did she know? Little more than was available on the Marabanian website about the royal family. And ignorance was *not* bliss. Raj had frozen and backed off the instant she'd asked about his mother. Nabila wasn't the only no-go zone; his mother clearly was as well. Zoe heaved a sigh as she showered, wondering what had made Raj quite so complex and reserved.

Raj glanced up from his laptop as Zoe reappeared downstairs, clad in some kind of pastel floaty dress that bared most of her shoulders and a slender length of shapely leg. Not even the most severe critic could have deemed the outfit provocative, but her pert little breasts shifted as she completed the last step and he went instantly hard, cursing his libido and the fierce desire he was holding back that was becoming harder and harder to contain. Most probably he would need her covered from head to toe not to be affected, he conceded wryly, and what good would that do when he had already seen her virtually naked and could summon up that mental image even faster? He clenched his teeth together, hating the sense of weakness she inflicted. It was weak to want what he knew he shouldn't have. He prided himself on being stronger and more intelligent than that.

Nabila had been enough of a mistake to scar a man for life, a warning that his judgement wasn't infallible, that people lied and cheated to get what they wanted or merely to make a good impression and cover up the less presentable parts of their character. But, at least, he no longer carried resentment where Nabila was concerned, he reflected absently. Time had healed his bitterness and maturity had taught him more about human nature. Even so, the very prospect of having to deal with Nabila in any form, most particularly in a professional capacity in the company of others, was deeply distasteful to him. It was even more offensive to him that Nabila had dared to approach his wife and introduce herself. That had been brazen and, although he knew that Nabila could be utterly brazen and calculating, he could not begin to understand why she had made such an inappropriate move.

'Wow…look at the food!' Zoe whispered in wonderment as she glimpsed the array of dishes spread across the low table in front of him. 'You should've started without me.'

'I do have *some* manners,' Raj told her huskily, amusement glimmering in his shrewd gaze.

'I never said you didn't,' she muttered in some embarrassment, lifting a plate to serve herself and watching him follow suit. 'But I did take ages in the shower.'

Raj could have done without that visual of her tiny, delicately curved body streaming with water. 'I had a shower before we left the palace.'

'I didn't have time and it was so warm in that car even with the air conditioning.' She sighed. 'So, I'm about to ask you to be straight with me on certain issues because if you aren't I could slip up and say something embarrassing to the wrong person,' she pointed out, trotting out the excuse she had come up with in the shower to make Raj talk about what he didn't want to talk about. 'Who was your mother?'

Raj tensed and swallowed hard. 'She was a nobody in the eyes of most. Ayshah and my father's second wife, Fairoz, were both royal princesses from neighbouring kingdoms and my father married them to make political alliances when he was in his early twenties. Since *he* did *his* duty in the marital line you can understand why he expected me to be willing to do the same eight years ago.'

'Yes, but he grew up during a very unsettled period of Maraban's history when there was constant war and strife. It was different for you because you didn't live through any of those wars or periods of deprivation,' Zoe told him calmly, her retentive memory of what she had read about Maraban's history ensuring that she had a clear picture of past events. 'Now tell me about your mother and why she was nobody in the eyes of others.'

'She was a commoner, a nurse. My father had heart surgery in his fifties and she looked after him in hospital.'

Zoe smiled in approval. 'So, it was a romance?'

'Well, no, for most of my life I assumed he simply took my mother as a third wife in the last-ditch hope that a much younger woman could give him a child,' Raj confided with a twist of his full sensual mouth. 'That was the perceived reality. It never occurred to me that he had fallen in love with her until he admitted that to me only a few days ago. Now I am shamed by my prejudice but, in my own defence, my mother was a very unhappy wife and I remember that too well.'

'Why was she unhappy?' Zoe pressed.

'Picture the situation, Zoe,' Raj urged with rueful emphasis. 'Two childless older wives of many years were suddenly challenged by a much younger new arrival and they didn't like it. They didn't think my mother was fit to breathe the same air as their husband and when she quickly fell pregnant, as they had failed to do, their resentment and jealousy turned to loathing. They bullied her cruelly and treated her like dirt. My father likes a quiet life in his household and he did not interfere between his wives. He ignored the problems.'

'I'm *so* sorry,' she murmured, registering that Raj must have been old enough to understand how his mother was being abused and that his troubled relationship with his father and Ayshah probably dated from that period.

'By the time I was nine years old, she was so depressed that she took her own life with an overdose. It happened here in the old original house. Perhaps that is also why my father had it demolished,' he admitted in a driven undertone. 'There, now you know the whole unhappy story of my childhood.'

Zoe reached for him, her small fingers spreading to grip his much larger hand in a natural gesture of sympathy, finger pads smoothing over the sleek brown skin. 'Thank you for telling me,' she whispered. 'I wouldn't have pushed so hard if I'd known it was a tragedy.'

'She was a wonderful, loving mother but it was many years before I could forgive her for leaving me,' Raj confessed in a rueful undertone.

'I have no memory of either of my parents. I was only a baby when they died in a car crash,' Zoe told him with regret. 'Cherish the memories you have, try and build a bridge with your father. Everybody needs family, Raj.'

'I prefer not to need *anyone*. Independence, in so far as it is possible, is safer. Do you want something sweet to finish?' Raj enquired in casual addition. 'There is a fridge hidden in that cupboard over there. The maid filled it with desserts.'

Listening to him, Zoe had lost much of her appetite, but she scrambled upright and fetched the desserts to serve, knowing that Raj would welcome that distraction. It seemed that she always, *always* put her foot in it with him. She should have been more patient, should have waited until he was willing to talk, instead of forcing the issue. Beating herself up for her nosiness soon led to her faking a yawn and saying she was going up to bed.

Raj worked on his laptop for an hour, giving Zoe time to fall asleep. He mounted the stairs as quietly as he knew how and then he saw her, lying on the bed in something diaphanous, the pool of light surrounding her veiling her entire body in soft gold. She looked up from her book, green eyes wide, little shoulders tensing, petite breasts pushing against the finest cotton to define the pointed tips and that was the moment that Raj finally lost the battle. Hunger surged through him with such power it virtually wiped out conscious thought. She was there, she was where he wanted her to be and, in that moment, she *was* irresistible.

Zoe was fiercely disconcerted when Raj simply stalked like a prowling jungle cat across the room and bent down to snatch her up into his arms. 'Raj?' she exclaimed uncertainly, all the breath from her body stolen by that action.

'I want you… I *burn* for you,' he breathed rawly. 'Tell me to put you down and I will walk away. I will not try to railroad you into anything you don't want.'

Zoe stared up into his silvered eyes and her entire body clenched while her heart pounded in her ears. 'I want you too,' she admitted breathlessly, barely able to credit that she had the nerve to admit that and yet if he could admit it, why shouldn't she?

As he cradled her in his arms, a faint shudder of relief racked his lean, powerful frame and he claimed her parted lips with so much passion he took her by storm. Head swimming, mouth swollen, she plunged her fingers into his silky black hair, revelling in the crisp luxuriance of his curls and holding him to her. There was no sense of fear, no sense of threat and she rejoiced in that freedom, pushing up into the heat of him as he brought her down on the bed. She yanked at his shirt as he reached for her nightdress, their combined movements ending up in a tangle.

'We're behaving like teenagers!' Raj rasped in disbelief, gazing down, nonetheless, at her flushed and lovely face with ferocious satisfaction. He had never craved anything as much as he craved her hands on his body and he leant back from her to pull his shirt up over his head and discard it.

Zoe looked up at him, secretly thinking that she was behaving like a teenager because her experience of men was probably about that level. She truly was a case of arrested development, cut off from normality at the age of twelve when everything to do with men and sex had frightened her into closing down that side of her nature. Now she wondered if she should warn him that she was a virgin, but wasn't there a strong chance that her inexperience would turn him off? Or, at least, make him pause to consider whether they should be having sex in the first place? She didn't want Raj to stop and ESP warned her that if cautious, logical Raj got in charge again, her desire to have sex for the first time could be thwarted.

Raj, however, chased away all her apprehensive thoughts simply by taking his shirt off. As he leant back over her to toss it away, his abdominal muscles flexed like steel girders and she gazed up at his superb bronzed torso with helpless appreciation. Heat flowered low in her pelvis, making her press her thighs together on the resulting ache. Exhilaration flooded her at the knowledge that she was finally feeling what other women felt when they desired intimacy with a man.

'I thought you didn't like sex,' Raj breathed in a driven undertone.

And then I met you.

But she wasn't going to frighten him off by telling him *that*, was she?

'It's time I tried again,' she muttered obliquely.

'I will endeavour not to disappoint you,' Raj growled, his lips ghosting in a whisper of a caress across her collarbone that made her shiver, lean brown hands tugging up the nightdress inch by inch, fingertips lightly glossing over her slender thighs and finally her narrow ribcage. The butterflies fluttering in her belly took flight.

The nightdress fell away and Zoe sat up to embark on his jeans. It might be her first time but she wasn't about to lie there like some petrified Victorian virgin and let him do everything, she told herself squarely. Her hands were shaking so much though that she could hardly get the zip down and he closed a steadying hand over hers, pressing her fingers against him before arching his hips to snake lithely out of his jeans. His boxers went with them and she stared at the evidence of his arousal and then, dry-mouthed, reached out to stroke him, her heart already racing as though she had run a marathon.

The instant she touched him, Raj tugged her up against him with a hungry groan and crushed her mouth under his again, his tongue prying apart her lips and skating across the roof of her mouth before colliding with hers. Another burst of heat shot through her, tightening her muscles, and she shifted closer still, wanting the hard heat of him plastered to every inch of her. He was so passionate and she loved that passion, could feel it surging through his lean, powerful body to meet her own.

He laid her back and shaped her breasts with sensuous hands, smoothing, massaging, moulding, before dipping his head to catch a straining pink nipple in his mouth and swirl his tongue round the throbbing peak until her spine arched and a stifled gasp was torn from her. She was much more sensitive there than she had ever realised and little tingling thrills began to dart through her, trickling down into her pelvis to create a hot liquid pool between her thighs.

Her hips arched up of their own volition, her body controlling her responses, and all the time the nagging craving at the heart of her was building to an unbearable level and she was making little impatient sounds she couldn't quell. When he finally touched her where she most needed to be touched, her body jackknifed and a wild flood of sensation seized hold of her, provoking a cry from her lips. It was her very first climax and the sheer intensity of it took her by surprise.

Raj smiled down at her and kissed her even more hungrily. 'You are so receptive,' he husked.

Lying there dazed by the experience, Zoe reached up to explore him, palms spreading across his chest, captivated by the strength and heat of him before sliding lower to encounter a restraining hand.

'Not now,' Raj grated out. 'I'm too aroused and I need to be inside you. Are you protected?'

For a split second she didn't know what he was talking about and then comprehension sank in and she shook her head in an urgent negative. With a groan, Raj sprang off the bed naked and dug into his luggage, spilling out everything on the floor in wild disarray and then leafing through the tumbled garments to retrieve a wallet and extract a foil packet.

'I only have a few. I will need to buy more. I have not been with anyone recently and we must be careful.'

Warmed by his admission that he had had no recent lovers, Zoe frowned.

'Careful?' she queried.

Surprised by the question, Raj glanced at her. 'In our situation, a pregnancy would be a disaster...not that it's very likely. Look how many years it took my father to produce a child!' he urged wryly. 'For all I know a low sperm count runs in the royal genes.'

'But contraception is pretty much foolproof these days...surely?' Zoe pressed.

'Nothing's foolproof in that line. Accidents and surprises still happen,' Raj pointed out, coming back down on the bed with a smouldering look of hungry urgency silvering his stunning eyes. 'But it will *not* happen to us.'

Zoe reddened, disconcerted to find herself in the very act of picturing a little boy or girl with his spectacular dark eyes. Some day in the future, she promised herself, and most definitely she would become a mother with someone she had yet to meet. Raj would just be an experience she recalled with warmth, she told herself; nothing more, nothing less was due to the man who had rescued her from her fears.

She stretched up, winding her arms round his neck to draw him down to her and she kissed him, enjoying that freedom and that new confidence to do as she liked, and it all came from the reassuring, delightful discovery that Raj appeared to want her every bit as much as she wanted him.

He tugged at her lower lip with the edge of his teeth, sent his mouth travelling down the elegant line of her slender neck and that fast conversation was forgotten as another cycle of arousal claimed her. Her temperature rose, a fevered energy gripping her limbs as her heartbeat quickened and her breathing fractured.

Excitement quivered up from her pelvis when she felt him surge between her thighs, sliding into her inch by inch, sending the most exquisitely unexpected sensations sizzling through her.

'You're very small and tight,' Raj ground out breathlessly.

And then with a final shift of his lean hips he forged his passage and her whole body jerked with the pain of it and she cried out.

Raj stilled. 'What's wrong?'

Mortified that she had made a fuss, Zoe grimaced. 'It hurt more than I was expecting. It's my first time.'

As shock clenched Raj's lean, darkly handsome features and he began to withdraw from her, Zoe grabbed his shoulders. 'No, don't you dare stop now!' she told him. 'I've been waiting such a long time to experience this.'

The deed was already done, Raj rationalised, but anger was roaring through his taut body and it was only with difficulty that he swallowed it back because he didn't want to risk hurting her any more…even if she had chosen to have sex with him as though he was an adventurous new experience much like a day out behind the wheel of a supercar, he reflected wrathfully.

'Raj, please…don't make a fuss,' Zoe urged, studying him with huge green eyes that pleaded.

And Raj did what every nerve ending in his body urged him to do and surged deeper into the welcome of her, a low growl of sensual pleasure wrenched from him. And from that point on, no further encouragement was required. A wondrous warmth began to rise low in her pelvis, building on the visceral ache for fulfilment, making her fingernails dig into his long smooth back as excitement seized her and held her fast. The feel of him over her, inside her, all around her sent rippling tremors of joy spiralling through her and when she hit the heights again, it was explosive.

In the aftermath she felt as though she were melting into the bed in a boneless state and the very last thing she needed then was Raj freeing himself from their entangled limbs and springing off the bed to breathe rawly, 'You've got some explaining to do. You *lied* to me!'

CHAPTER SEVEN

GRABBING THE SHEET to cover herself, Zoe hauled herself up against the tumbled pillows, watching Raj yank on his jeans. Going commando, she noticed, colour flaring in her face. It was as if her mind weren't her own any more. She couldn't take her eyes off his lithe bronzed body, couldn't concentrate.

'I didn't lie,' she reasoned stiffly.

'You *lied*,' Raj repeated wrathfully. 'You said it was time you tried sex *again* when clearly you had never had sex before—'

'Well, I may have blurred the edges of the truth a bit,' Zoe mumbled defensively.

'You lied and I detest dishonesty!' Raj shot back at her fiercely.

'So what?' Zoe fired back, her temper sparking in answer to his.' It was *my* decision to make—'

'And mine. I wouldn't have touched you had I known I would be the first!' Raj bit out curtly. 'But you chose to withhold that knowledge, which was unfair—'

'Oh, for goodness' sake…' Zoe thrust the blonde hair falling round her hot face back off her damp brow. 'It was just sex. Why are you making such a production out of it? We're consenting adults, neither of us is in another relationship.'

Raj skimmed scorching dark eyes to her. 'I don't do relationships.'

'Well, I'm afraid you're *stuck* in this one,' Zoe told him with unashamed satisfaction. 'You can't have it both ways, Raj. If you don't do relationships, then you should be quite happy to have had no-strings-attached sex.'

Dark colour scoring his superb cheekbones, Raj shot her a blistering look of derision and strode out of the room. She listened to his bare feet thumping down the wooden stairs and then the slam of the front door signifying his exit from the house. Switching out the lights, she got out of bed to walk over to the window and finally picked him out striding down onto the beach. Moonlight glimmered along the hard line of his broad shoulders and danced over his curls.

Mortification gripped Zoe, who was conscious she had said stuff she didn't actually believe to hit back at him because she had felt humiliated by his annoyance. It *had* been her decision to have him as her first lover, hadn't it? But she wasn't liberal enough to plan to have casual sex with anyone, even if she had made it sound as though she were. She had simply wanted that experience, had wanted *him*. Was that so bad? But it also felt wonderful to no longer fear the act of sex, to no longer feel that she was somehow less than other women and missing out on an experience that others enjoyed.

Uneasily aware then of the ache at the heart of her from that first experience, she went into the bathroom and ran herself a bath to soak in. She had messed up, brought sex into their platonic relationship…but, hey, hadn't Raj been the one to make the first move? Why hadn't she thrown that at him? It was *his* fault they had ended up in bed. Why, in his eyes, would it have been acceptable to become intimate if she had had more experience? How had it somehow become wrong because she had been inexperienced?

Throwing on a cotton wrap and stuffing her feet into flip-flops, Zoe left the house and trudged across the sand to where Raj was walking through the whispering surf.

Raj heard her approach. There was nothing stealthy about Zoe crossing sand. He breathed in deep and slow, rising above his angry discomfiture and the guilt she had inflicted him with.

'All right, I'm sorry I didn't tell you beforehand, but you're the one who dragged *me* into bed,' Zoe reminded him flatly, her face burning. 'Regrets now are a bit late in the day and they're not going to change anything.'

'In my culture a woman's purity is highly valued and respected. That may seem outdated to you—'

'Very much so. Why should a woman be any more restricted with what she does with her body than a man is?' Zoe slung back at him half beneath her breath.

'I feel guilty that I took that innocence from you,' Raj admitted harshly.

'Even if it's what I wanted? It's not like I'm still a teenager in need of protection,' Zoe argued vehemently, surprised herself to realise how strongly she felt about the decision she had made. 'I just wanted to be like everyone else and know what it was all about instead of feeling…feeling odd,' she framed grudgingly.

'You deserved more than I gave you. It wasn't special...it *should* have been special,' he asserted with conviction.

'Was your first time special for you?' Zoe demanded, cutting in.

Disconcerted by that unexpectedly bold question, Raj gritted his teeth and opted for honesty. 'No.'

'Well, there you are, then, once again you didn't practise what you preach.'

A reluctant laugh was torn from Raj and he turned to look at her, so tiny she barely reached the centre of his chest and yet in so many ways she was absolutely fearless in her outlook, happy to express her views even when they conflicted with his. She was also too stubborn and independent to even acknowledge his point that if she had valued herself more she would not have entertained surrendering her innocence to him. People rarely confronted Raj with his mistakes or criticised him but Zoe had no such filter. She was quite correct: *he* had dragged *her* into bed.

'And I'm sorry if you don't feel the same way,' she added stiffly, 'but what we shared *did* feel special to me.'

Disconcerted, Raj sent her a gleaming glance and then his lashes dropped low. 'I'm sorry if I upset you but I do hate lies,' he murmured grimly.

'I'm usually very honest but I didn't want you to back off,' Zoe completed unevenly.

'You were curious,' Raj commented, wondering if he had ever had such an extraordinary conversation with a woman before, a conversation in which he was painfully honest and she was as well. He didn't think so and there was something remarkably refreshing about the experience.

'Yes, sorry if that makes you feel a bit like an experiment...but I suppose you were, rather, a new experience, I mean,' she mumbled apologetically.

Exactly like having a day out behind the wheel of a supercar, Raj thought again with relish, and he burst out laughing. No, no woman had ever dared to tell him before that he was an experiment, but then none had ever used that word, special, for what they had shared with him either. 'Am I allowed to ask how I scored?'

'No. That would be bad for your ego...' Zoe gazed up at him, encountering moonlit dark eyes that shimmered, and her heart skipped a beat.

'You were amazing...and special,' Raj murmured, lifting his hands to gently comb her tousled mane of hair back from her cheekbones, the pads of his fingers brushing the petal-soft skin of her face, sending a quiver of awareness arrowing through her. 'But I shouldn't have touched you. I had no right.'

'We're married.'

'In name only,' he reminded her with scrupulous accuracy, and for some reason she wanted to kick him. 'It's not meant to be real but it's starting to feel very real, which is worrying.'

'Why worrying?' she prompted.

'It wasn't supposed to be like this. We were supposed to live separate lives and make a few public appearances together and that was to be that.'

'So, we departed from the set script. But we're not hurting anyone,' she whispered, her hands settling to his lean waist, her fingers rubbing over smooth, hot skin, feeling the ripple of the muscles of his abdomen pull taut at even that slight touch.

'I don't do relationships,' he reminded her stubbornly even as he leant down to her, drawn by the ripe pink swell of her mouth.

'You're right in the middle of a relationship with me…stop kidding yourself!' Zoe countered. 'Do you think you're about to wake up some morning and find yourself handcuffed to the bed and trapped?'

Raj scooped her slight body up into his arms as if it were the most natural thing in the world to carry her and trudged back up the beach towards the house. 'If it was you cuffing me to the bed, I wouldn't fight and I wouldn't feel trapped,' he muttered huskily.

'That's probably the nicest thing you've ever said to me, but I've got to tell you that cuffing you to the bed looms nowhere on my horizon. If you don't want to be there, you can sleep on the floor,' she told him roundly.

'You said you weren't up for that option.'

'Guess I lied again,' Zoe trilled. 'I could happily consign you to the floor now.'

'And if I *want* to share the bed?' Raj left the question hanging as her lashes opened to their fullest extent, revealing emerald-green enquiry.

'You're welcome,' she said gruffly as he set her down and she kicked off her flip-flops. 'I think sex makes me hungry… I'm starving again!'

And Raj threw back his head and laughed, stalking over to the concealed fridge, discovering it was packed with prepared food in readiness for such an occasion. Zoe stiffened, marvelling at how relaxed she now felt with Raj. Barriers had come crashing down when they had shared that bed, she acknowledged, but now that she felt closer to him and no longer separate, she was more likely to get hurt. What had happened to her defences? What had happened to her belief that she was only in Maraban to become stronger and more independent? Now she was involved with Raj on a level she had never expected to be and her emotions were all over the place and making her feel insecure.

Zoe froze, frowning as she surveyed the room. 'All the dinner dishes have been cleared away.'

'The staff have been in. Our protection team probably let them know the coast was clear. The bed's probably been changed as well,' Raj forecast.

Zoe gulped. 'It's after midnight, Raj. Don't the staff sleep?'

'They work rotation shifts. Invisible service is a matter of pride to them.'

They ate snacks and she went up to bed first, the exhaustion of the long day crashing down on her all at once. She pillowed her cheek on her hand and watched Raj strip off his jeans and go for a shower, enviably indifferent to any form of self-consciousness. But then maybe had her body been as flawlessly beautiful as his she would've been equally blasé, she thought sleepily. Instead she was blessed with short legs, tiny boobs and a bottom that was a little big for the rest of her.

'What are we doing tomorrow?' she whispered when he joined her.

'It is already tomorrow,' he pointed out. 'I'm taking you to the old palace where your grandmother grew up and afterwards there'll be an informal meet-and-greet session with the locals and official photographs. My father is making as much possible use of your time in the family as he can.'

'I suppose that was the deal,' she muttered drowsily. 'It'll be interesting seeing where Azra grew up... It was almost as interesting watching your father and my grandfather politely avoid each other at the wedding, and then I was steering clear of your uncle Hakem and he was staying well away from me as well.'

Her brow furrowed at that recollection. Prince Hakem had proved to be a rather colourless little old man and she had been astonished that such a seemingly nondescript personality could be burning underneath with thwarted royal ambitions.

A husky laugh fell from Raj, his breath warming her shoulder. 'My father made a fuss about having your grandfather at the wedding but I talked him round. Stam is, after all, the man who ran off with the Banian princess my father was supposed to marry.'

'But my grandmother, Azra, and your father hadn't even met when she met Stam and fell for him,' Zoe whispered.

'My father still felt it was an insult and it rankled. Go to sleep,' Raj urged. 'This will be another long day but, after the palace visit, we are off the official schedule for the rest of our stay.'

And Zoe thought tiredly of how anxious she had been about having to make any public appearances when she'd first arrived in Maraban and of how inexplicably Raj's presence by her side, or even in the same room, soothed her apprehensions. Somehow, he made her feel safe, protected, as if nothing bad could happen while he was around. It was so silly to endow him with that much importance, she conceded ruefully, and then she slept.

What they had *was* a relationship, Raj recognised with considerable unease. It had become one the minute he married her and intimacy had only deepened the ties and made it more complex. Truly it had been naïve of him not to foresee that development, given the level of attraction they shared Zoe had said it was 'just' sex. Could he believe that, accept that? Was she really sophisticated enough to make that distinction? And could they keep it at that casual level? And in time go their separate ways without regret? It would be like a very long one-night stand, he reasoned while even his brain told him that that was a foolish misconception. He didn't want to treat Zoe the same way he treated his occasional lovers, being distant, keeping it impersonal, always hiding his true self. He felt much more comfortable with Zoe. He wanted to make her happy. For the first time ever with a woman, he would just go with the flow…

Zoe wakened in the morning in Raj's arms. 'Hey, your only body temperature seems to be hot as the fires of hell,' she complained, striving to slide away to cool off.

Raj pulled her back to him with ease and the thrust of his arousal against her stomach made her eyes widen. She looked up at him, all bronzed and in need of a shave, with blue black curls, and he was to die for and there was no denying that she was willing. 'Oh…' she said in entirely another voice.

'If it would be uncomfortable for you…?' he husked, hitching a perfect ebony brow in enquiry.

It probably would be a little bit, she acknowledged,

but there was a hungry tingle of awareness heating up between her thighs that made her hips shift with longing. 'No, it wouldn't be,' she lied shamelessly. 'But I need to clean my teeth.'

'No, you don't…you smell like strawberries and woman,' Raj framed thickly, cupping her cheekbones and devouring her mouth as though his life depended on it.

And that was that for Zoe, her heart thumping fit to burst from her chest as her body ratcheted up the scale of arousal as though it had been doing it all her life. When he kissed her, he set her on fire, when he touched her, exploring her urgently sensitive nipples and the tender flesh between her thighs with those long skilful fingers of his, the fire began to blaze out of control and she was turning and twisting, downright writhing with tormented pleasure. By the time he hooked one of her legs over his hips and plunged into her, Zoe was surging towards a climax at an unstoppable pace and the raw, hot excitement of that passionate invasion sent her flying with a choked gasp into the horizon.

'Let's see if you can do that again,' Raj growled as she thrashed under him and he surged into her afresh in a timely change of pace, aiming for long and slow rather than fast and furious.

And she caught her breath again and barely with a quivery little inhale, blonde hair lying in a mad tangle around her head as he rose over and looked down at her, black starlit eyes intent and riveting, her body still singing and pulsing from his last onslaught. His rhythm was sensual, calculated, letting the erotic tension build again and inexorably she shifted from melting to craving. His passion compelled her, and her hands slid over his back, rejoicing in the hard, smooth strength of him as rippling waves began to clench at her pelvis. A wildness took hold of her and she wrapped her legs round him and that final thrust made her soar in an excess of pleasure to the heights again.

Afterwards, he brushed her hair off her damp face and kissed her. 'I hate to hurry you when I've made you late in the first place, but we have to be out of here in an hour if you want to see the palace before we have to face the official welcome…'

'An hour?' she gasped incredulously.

'I'll call your maid and get out of here,' Raj told her helpfully. 'Am I allowed to say that you make a great friend with benefits?'

Was *that* what she was? Zoe thought about that in the shower and pulled a face. It sounded a lot bolder and a lot more laid-back than she believed she was, but who was to say she couldn't change? Wasn't that what her stay in Maraban was aimed at? Finding out who she really was without her sisters and her grandfather wrapping her in cotton wool and watching over her all the time? She was in a brave new world, she reminded herself, and aspects of it were likely to be unfamiliar and scary. Or *sobering*, she conceded ruefully, because her gut instinct was that she didn't want to be a friend with benefits for any man…even Raj.

Her maid had apparently accompanied her from the palace and already had an outfit laid out for her when she reappeared from the bathroom. Zoe cast an eye over the pale green tailored dress and decided it would do very well. At her request her hair was braided, which was cooler in the heat, and when she descended the stairs dead on time, she was smiling, thinking that a maid with hairstyling skills was an invaluable asset and a luxury she had better not become too accustomed to having. It was *all* temporary, she reminded herself, like a winning prize ticket that took her off on an extravagant holiday. Raj was, also, simply a temporary presence in her life. Maybe that was what made the 'friends with benefits' concept meaningless and possibly a little slutty. She winced at that self-judgement.

'You can't wear those shoes trekking round an old building!' Raj exclaimed, engaged in staring at her feet in what appeared to be disbelief.

Zoe sent him a dirty look. 'I'm crazy about shoes, but I'll bring a pair of flats and change into these later,' she conceded reluctantly. 'But don't you get the idea that you have the right to tell me what I should and shouldn't wear… I'm not having that!'

An unholy grin slashed Raj's often serious features as he awaited her reappearance.

The one-time home of the former Banian royal family was huge and sprawling and, although the building had been carefully conserved, it was not used for any purpose other than to house a small museum on the history of Bania and provide the public with the chance to tour Princess Azra's former apartments.

'I wish she hadn't died before I was born.' Zoe sighed, studying old black and white photos of a youthful blonde in local dress. 'Grandad showed me pictures of her. He totally adored her, you know,' she told Raj cheerfully. 'He cast off my father for refusing to do a degree in business and come and work for him. My grandmother told him he was doing the wrong thing and that he should let my dad make his own path but Grandad was too proud and stubborn to listen.'

'It is a challenge for one generation to understand what drives the next. It was years before I could appreciate that in demanding that I marry a woman he chose my father was only asking me to do what he had done himself.'

'But you were in love with someone else,' Zoe reminded him. 'You couldn't possibly have married another woman and made a success of it. You would've been full of bitterness and resentment.'

'My father believes that in our privileged position emotions cannot be allowed to make our decisions for us. I learned the hard way that he was correct,' Raj completed with a harsh edge to his voice.

'You still have to tell me about you and Nabila,' Zoe told him.

'I thought women didn't like a man to talk about previous affairs,' Raj countered in surprise, shooting her a disconcerted glance.

'I'd have to be in love with you to mind that sort of thing and all jealous and possessive and I'm *not*,' Zoe pointed out calmly. 'I'm just being nosy.'

Raj nodded, although the concept shook him because he was unconsciously accustomed to women wanting more from him than he was willing to give, which was why his sensual past consisted of more fleeting encounters than anything else. 'I studied business at one of the Gulf state universities. That's where I met her. Have you ever been in love?' he heard himself ask with

is from a different generation. He does not understand female liberation. In his day a woman's main claim to fame was her purity and a decent woman didn't give it up for anything less than a wedding ring.'

'Gosh, I was cheap,' his bride chipped in, her face suddenly on fire. 'Because as you pointed out, we're not really married in the truest sense of the word.'

'You weren't cheap,' Raj breathed as the museum custodian nervously watched their progress round the exhibits from the other side of the room. Long fingers stroked down her face and lingered below her chin to lift it. 'You were totally incredible and I was unworthy of the gift.'

'That's just flannel,' Zoe informed him, her face warming even more as she connected with brilliant dark eyes that sent butterflies fluttering in her tummy. 'We did what we did because we wanted to.'

'And every time I look at you,' Raj confided thickly, 'I want to do it again.'

'You were telling me about Nabila,' Zoe reminded him doggedly, tiny tingles of arousal coursing through her slight taut length while she fought to suppress those untimely urges. 'Not trying to turn me into a sex maniac.'

'Could I?' Raj asked in a roughened undertone, those gorgeous eyes pinned to her with a feverish intensity that scorched.

'It's possible,' she downplayed in haste. 'Nabila?'

'She told me she was a virgin because she probably assumed that that was what I wanted to hear. But it wasn't, I wouldn't have cared,' Raj admitted ruefully. 'So naturally I respected what she told me and I was prepared to wait until we were man and wife, but she got bored.'

'Hard to be set on a pedestal and to pretend to be something you're not,' Zoe put in thoughtfully.

'Yes, I did have her on a pedestal.' Raj grimaced. 'I was very idealistic at the age of twenty.'

'You were too young for that size of a commitment,' Zoe commented. 'What happened?'

'I refused to give her up and my father exiled me. It was my final visit and I left Maraban in a hurry. Nabila had given me a key to her apartment and my sudden return was unexpected. That was when I found her in bed with one of her so-called friends. It was clearly a long-standing arrangement and what an idiot I felt!' Raj relived, his superb cheekbones rigid. 'I had surrendered everything for her and there she was, the absolute antithesis of the woman I believed her to be—a shameless cheat and a liar, who only wanted me for my status!'

'And your body, probably,' Zoe told him abstractedly, winning a startled sidewise scrutiny. 'You must've been devastated. I'm lucky. I've never been hurt like that, don't want to be either.'

Raj stared down into her beautiful expressive face and wondered why it was so very easy to talk to her about Nabila, whom he had never discussed with anyone before. It was because she didn't have a personal stake in their marriage, at least not one that he understood, because from what he had observed her new royal status and the awe it inspired meant precious little to her. 'The meet and greet downstairs starts in thirty minutes. You can put on the skyscraper heels if you must.'

'If I *must*?' Zoe queried, slinging him a look of annoyance.

'You struggle to walk in very high heels,' Raj pointed out bluntly.

'Because I never went out anywhere until I came to Maraban. I had this fabulous collection of gorgeous shoes and my sisters borrowed them and I never got to wear them until now,' Zoe told him hotly. 'I'll *learn* to walk in them!'

'Obviously,' Raj countered, realising that he had been tactless in the extreme. 'But why didn't you go out anywhere?'

'I panicked if men came onto me, couldn't handle it,' she confided reluctantly. 'But you don't do that to me for some reason.'

'Maybe because you're not falling for me,' Raj suggested glibly, while cherishing the obvious fact that she felt safer and more protected in his company.

'Yes, that could well be it,' Zoe responded cheerfully as she slid her feet into her high heels while leaning on both his arm and a door handle to balance. 'You wouldn't believe how much more confident I feel standing a few inches taller.'

Watching her sip coffee and smilingly chat by his side only minutes later, Raj decided it had nothing to do with the stupid shoes. He remembered their first meeting and her panic attack and marvelled at how much she had already changed. He had merely met her at a bad moment in a scenario that would have frightened any woman, he recognised. His fingers splayed across her spine and he concealed a grin, thinking about the scratches on his back, badges of pride for a man who knew he had satisfied his woman. Not *his* woman, he immediately corrected himself. Well, she sort of *was* his for the present, an acceptance that somehow lightened the cloud threatening his mood.

It seemed no time at all to Zoe before they were being posed in the palace's grand reception room for the photographs and then they were done, and it was a relief to not be on show any more and know that they had only a holiday ahead of them, she reflected sunnily. They were walking back to the car when a photographer popped out from behind some trees and shouted at them. Half of Raj's security team took off in pursuit of him. At the same time Raj's phone started shrilling and one of the diplomats she had met at the reception emerged with a grim face and moved in their direction with something clutched in his hand.

'What the hell?' Raj groused only half under his breath, pulling out his phone while ensuring that Zoe was safely tucked into the car awaiting them.

She watched as the diplomat proffered the magazine to Raj, saw him glance at it with patent incredulity and then compress his lips so flat they went bloodless. After that he strode back and forth in front of the car talking on his phone, his lean brown hands making angry gestures, his whole stance telegraphing his tense, dissatisfied mood.

'What's happened?' Zoe asked anxiously when he finally came off the phone and climbed in beside her.

CHAPTER EIGHT

'A STORM IN a teacup but it's put my father in a real rage.' Raj expelled a stark breath, impatience and exasperation lacing his intonation. 'Last year my father drove Maraban's only gossip magazine out of the country. Now they're based in Dubai and what they publish about us has steadily become more shocking. He should've left them alone. He has to accept that these days everything we do is watched and reported on and our family cannot hope to keep secrets the way we did when he was a boy.'

'I guess he's a bit behind the times. The press are more disrespectful of institutions nowadays. So, what's in that magazine?' she prompted, thoroughly puzzled. 'Some forgotten scandal?'

'Not even a scandal, merely an intrusion.' He had crushed the magazine between his hands and now he smoothed it out with difficulty and handed it to her. 'Of course, you can't read it but the photos are self-explanatory and this article coming out the same week as our wedding, suggesting that I wasn't allowed to marry the woman I loved because she was a commoner, may be embarrassing for my father but it is also an absurd allegation.'

Dry-mouthed now, Zoe stared down at the splash of photographs, depicting Raj with Nabila. *Old* photos, of course. She could see that they were younger but what she had not been prepared to see was the look of adoration in Raj's face as he gazed down at the other woman. He was studying Nabila as if she'd hung the moon for him and for some reason, Zoe registered, seeing those youthful carefree photos of them holding hands, larking about beside a fountain and smiling at each other *hurt*. She couldn't explain why those photos hurt but the instant she scrutinised them in detail she felt as though someone had punched her hard in the stomach because the pain was almost physical in its intensity.

What the heck was wrong with her? Was she starting to care for Raj? Was she suffering from jealousy, despite her earlier reassurance to him that she felt no such emotion concerning him? Those questions made her feel as shaky as if the ground had suddenly disappeared from under her feet. Yes, she was starting to care in the way you did begin to care more for someone when you got closer to them, she reasoned frantically and, yes, she had been jealous when she saw those photos. But none of that meant that she was necessarily falling for him.

'She was my first love and that was all,' Raj continued, wonderfully impervious to his bride's pallor and her silence. 'Very few people marry their first love and what does it matter anyway what I was doing *eight* years ago? It's a really stupid article but it *is* revealing a relationship that only our families knew about to the public. What I can't understand is how they got a hold of such private photos. I had copies but I destroyed them after we parted and the friend who took the photos—Omar—would never have shared them with anyone.'

'You said it was an absurd allegation,' Zoe recalled dully. 'How so when it's true? Your father wouldn't agree to you marrying her.'

'Not because of her parentage but because I suspect he had had her checked out and knew a great deal more about her than I knew at the time,' Raj admitted wryly. 'At least he had the consideration not to throw what he had found out in my face.'

'As you said…a storm in a teacup,' Zoe remarked rather stiffly, because all of a sudden she was tired of hearing about anything that related to Nabila and she could only marvel at her previous curiosity. Just then she thought she would be happier if she never heard the wretched woman's name spoken out loud again. As for seeing those stupid photos of her with Raj regarding her as if he had been poleaxed, well, that had been anything but a pleasure for a woman already labelled as a friend with benefits. No doubt that was why she had felt envious of the other woman.

No doubt, right at this very moment Raj was thinking about Nabila, remembering how much he had loved and wanted her, positively *wallowing* in sentimental memories! And on that note, Zoe decided that she would be very, very tired that night, in fact throughout the day, so that Raj would not dare to think she was in the mood to provide any of those benefits he had mentioned!

'You still haven't told me how it happened,' Raj reminded Zoe stubbornly.

Raj was like a dog with a bone when he wanted information, he just kept on landing back on that same avoidance spot of hers, an area of memory where she never ever travelled if she could help it. She breathed in deep, a little bit of a challenge when he was still flattening her to the wall of the shower. Shower sex? Yes, she had gained a lot of experience she had never expected to have over the past two weeks. Resolving to keep her paws off Raj hadn't worked when he was behaving like lover of the year. It was the only analogy she could make when she refused to let herself think of him as a husband.

But there it was: her watch broke, so a new one studded with diamonds arrived within the hour; phone kept on running out of charge, and a new phone was there by bedtime so that she could talk to her sisters as usual. She preferred flowers growing in the ground to those cut off in their prime and stuffed for a short shelf life into vases, and so he took her into the hills of Bania to stage a luxury picnic beside a glorious field of wild flowers. That had been only one of the blinders Raj had played over the past fortnight. He hated her high heels, seemed to be convinced she was going to plunge down steps and, at the very least, break her neck, *but* he had still bought her shoes, the dreamiest, absolutely over-the-top jewel-studded sandals with soaring heels. She had worn them out to dinner last night in a little mountainside inn, where everyone around them had pretended—not very well—not to know who they were to give them their privacy.

The only problem for Zoe, who was blossoming in receipt of such treatment, was that it was a constant battle not to start caring too much about Raj. She kept on reminding herself that none of this was real. Yes, he was her husband, but this was a convenient arrangement that they'd both agreed to. At best, he was just a friend, an intimate friend certainly, but beyond that she knew she dared not go. She was terrified of falling for him and if she made that mistake, she would be rejected and her heart would be broken.

'Zoe...' Raj growled, nipping a teasing trail across the soft skin of her nape to her shoulder with his lips and his teeth, sending a shudder of response through her that even very recent fulfilment could not suppress. 'I want to know how it happened.'

'And I don't want to revisit it.'

'It would be healthier for you to talk about it,' Raj told her doggedly.

'Like you talk about being bullied at military school!' Zoe flung even as she wriggled back into his lean, powerful body, registering that he was ready to go again while conceding that there was nothing new about that because Raj appeared to be insatiable. 'I practically had to cut the story out of you with a knife at your throat,' she reminded him with spirit. 'And by the way, Raj, it wasn't bullying. What you and Omar went through was abuse of the worst kind!'

'If I talked you can talk too,' Raj traded, running a long-fingered hand down over her spine, setting her alight without hesitation.

'This is sexual torture,' she told him shakily.

'All you have to do is say no,' Raj whispered, nipping at the soft lobe of her ear, flipping her long hair over his shoulder as he had learned to do, lost in the magic of her and her response for, as he had learned, it was enthralling to have that much power over a woman, as long as he never ever looked at the other side of the coin and acknowledged the reality that it was mutual.

Zoe straightened her shoulders and breathed, 'Right… I'm saying no…but you're not allowed to look at me like that!'

'Like what?' Raj prompted.

Those stunning dark silvered eyes of his shimmered with hunger and a tiny hint of hurt, and even a hint of hurt on show grabbed Zoe's heart hard and squeezed the breath out of her. She wanted him; every time she looked at him she wanted him.

But that was fine, absolutely fine, she told herself soothingly. It was just sex. She'd had a friend at university who went on a girls' holiday once purely to have sex with a lot of different men. That had been Claire's idea of fun: Raj was Zoe's idea of fun. And the world of sensual freedom she had learned to explore with Raj was the best reward of all. After the shocking attack she had survived as an adolescent, she had never dreamt that she could aspire to such freedom in her own body. Now she could only look back with a sigh when she recalled the frightened, broken young woman she had still been when she'd first met Raj.

'OK… I'll tell you,' she conceded, stepping out of the shower, surrendering to his demand but unable to do so when he was still touching her, something in her shying away in revulsion at any association between making love with Raj and what had happened to traumatise her when she was still a complete innocent.

Zoe settled down on the side of the vast bed, still

wet and dripping and not noticing. But Raj noticed, pale beneath his bronzed skin, his sculpted bone structure rigid because he was worried that he had pushed too hard for her confidences. Lifting her up, he carefully wound her like a doll into a giant fleecy towel, but when he tried to keep a soothing hold on her body, she broke away from him and dropped down into a bedside chair instead.

'There was an older boy, well, not much older, he was fourteen and I was twelve,' she trotted out shakily. 'In the same foster home. We used to play video games together… I thought he was a friend. There was a film I wanted to see, a stupid romantic comedy, and my foster mum said he could go with me, look out for me…but he didn't take me to the cinema.'

'You don't have to tell me if you don't want to,' Raj incised in a hoarse undertone.

'No, my sisters used to say I needed to talk about it, which is why I went to therapy. He didn't take me to the cinema. He took me what he said was a shortcut across wasteland and there was this old hut…and I was complaining because there was a storm and I was getting soaked.'

Her breathing was sawing noisily in and out of her struggling lungs.

'In the hut all these boys were waiting. They were a gang and the price of his entry into the gang was to bring a virgin, any virgin. They beat me up when I tried to get away and I was so badly hurt I couldn't move. They cut off my clothes with a kn-knife…and I had nothing even for them to see b-because I was a l-late developer,' she muttered brokenly, almost back there, reliving the terror, the pain and the shame of that public exposure.

Raj grasped both her trembling hands to pull her back into the present. 'It's in the past, and it can't hurt you now unless you let it… And, as you've already told me, you were lucky—you're a survivor.'

'Yes…' Her voice was stronger when she encountered shimmering dark-as-night eyes that seemed full of all the strength and calm she herself so often lacked. 'Yes, you're right. You have to be wondering how I escaped being raped. The police forced their way in to arrest one of the gang and I was rescued. But now you know why I suffer the panic attacks and why I eventually had the nervous breakdown at university—because I hadn't really dealt with what had happened to me. That was when I went for therapy and it helped enormously.'

Raj lifted her fingers to his mouth and kissed them. His hands were unsteady. All his emotions were swimming dangerously close to the surface and he was fighting to suppress them with every breath in his body. Hers was a distressing story and he now more than understood her fear of men, but there was no need for the rage inside him at those who had been ready to prey on a child for a few moments of vicious entertainment. She had been saved and they had been punished by the law. Only it wasn't enough, he thought fiercely, nowhere nearly enough punishment for the damage that had been inflicted on Zoe. In Maraban, the punishment would have been the death penalty.

As they travelled back to the palace, their honeymoon, as such, at an end, Zoe could see that telling Raj what had happened to her had made him settle back in behind his former reserve. Her small face tightened and her hands gripped together hard. She was questioning why she had shared all her secrets with him and anxious about why she was allowing herself to feel so close to him. Wasn't she acting foolishly? Wasn't it unwise in the circumstances to let every barrier between them drop?

'A surprise awaits you on your return to the palace,' Raj announced, trying to sound upbeat about what he was about to reveal, but failing miserably because he was no idiot and Vivi's cold reaction to him at the wedding had told him all he needed to know about how *he* was viewed by Zoe's family.

'A surprise?' Zoe queried.

He would have to hope that his own surprise went unnoticed while her sister was present. Dark blood highlighted Raj's exotic cheekbones as he thought about the fainting couch he had succumbed to buying and he had to wonder how he had drifted so far from his original intentions. Logic, good judgement and self-control had gone out of the proverbial window the minute he'd laid eyes on Zoe. It was that simple, that *basic*, he acknowledged grimly.

'Raffaele, Vivi's husband, is apparently attending a business meeting in Tasit and your sister accompanied him to visit you.'

To his surprise, Zoe's mouth down-curved and her chin came up, scarcely the display of uninhibited delight he had expected to see in receipt of such news. After all, she was in daily contact with her siblings, revealing a very close bond with them.

* * *

Zoe's rarely stirred temper was humming at the prospect of seeing Vivi. Vivi was only coming to visit to check up on her.

'This is a lovely surprise,' Zoe said, smiling and lying through her teeth as she hugged her older sister, wondering when her redheaded sibling would finally accept that she was a grown woman but, by nature, Vivi, a forceful personality, was very protective of those she considered weaker. It stung Zoe's pride to see herself as weak and breakable in Vivi's eyes.

'I wanted to see how you were managing.'

'My phone calls should've reassured you on that score,' Zoe pointed out as a maid brought in coffee and tiny cakes.

Vivi winced. 'Well, to be frank, they had the opposite effect because you sound so gosh-darned happy all the time.'

'My goodness, when did being happy become a sign that there was something to worry about?'

'It's a sign because I've never really heard you this happy before,' Vivi admitted ruefully. 'You can smile and laugh and seem happy on the surface but it's usually very brief and *now*, all of a sudden, when nobody's expecting it…'

'Have you noticed all the changes I've made around here?' Zoe interrupted abruptly, setting down her cup and springing up to indicate all the additional furniture in the room. 'The staff took photos of the unused rooms and sent them while we were away and I made selections. It's a big improvement, don't you think?'

'If medieval makes you hot to trot,' Vivi remarked with a sniff, strolling across the room to flick a heavily carved piece that in her opinion would have looked fabulous in a horror movie of some creepy old house.

'Let me show you around,' Zoe urged, willing to do anything to evade Vivi's curiosity, because in truth she *was* happy and she didn't really want to think too deeply about why.

Vivi glanced into the bedroom, her attention locking straight onto the male and female apparel currently being unpacked by staff. 'So, what happened to the—?'

In haste, Zoe thrust open the bathroom door, although she hadn't yet added anything to its décor, and then froze at the sight of the very opulent tasselled purple fainting couch in the centre.

'Oh, I like *that*...it's sort of sexy and decadent!' Vivi carolled, walking over to smooth a hand across the rich buttoned upholstery and flick a braided gold tassel.

Zoe was recalling her conversation with Raj and her face was burning hot as hellfire even while a little flicker of heat at her core flamed at the gesture... the *challenge*. Would she or wouldn't she? He would be wondering all day about that, she knew he would be, and a dreamy smile at the knowledge of that erotic prospect removed the tension that Vivi's arrival and awkward questions had induced.

'You know, I don't even need to ask you any more.' Vivi sighed as she returned to her coffee. 'Obviously, the separate bedroom deal crashed very quickly and you're sleeping with him. Whose idea was that? I hardly think it was yours! If you get too involved with Raj, Zoe...there will be consequences, because what you have together isn't supposed to last…and where will you be when the marriage ends?'

'It doesn't matter whose idea it was,' Zoe argued quietly. 'All that matters is that there isn't a problem of any kind with Raj and I, and our present arrangements are our private business.'

Vivi groaned out loud. 'You're besotted with him. It's written all over you,' she condemned, her concern palpable. 'That smooth bastard took advantage of you just as I feared he would!'

'Vivi!' Zoe blistered across the room in a furious voice her sister had never heard from her before. 'You do *not* talk about Raj like that!'

'I'm not saying anything I wouldn't say to his face!' Vivi shot back at her defensively. 'I'm trying to protect you but it looks like I got here a little too late for that. Damn Grandad, this is all his fault, his wretched snobbery pushing you into this marriage, and now you're going to get *hurt*.'

Zoe drew herself up to her full unimpressive height. 'There is no reason why I should get hurt.'

'I know what I saw in your face…you're in love with this guy, who only married you to please his father and use our fancy-schmancy grandmother's ancestry to enhance his standing.'

'I'm *not* in love with him,' Zoe argued fiercely. 'It sounds slutty but we're just having sex for the sake of it!'

Vivi unleashed a pained and unimpressed sigh. 'And what would you know about a relationship like that?'

Zoe lifted her head high. 'I'm learning as I go along, just like every other woman has to. I need that freedom, even if I make mistakes… It's part of growing up,' she reasoned.

'You're definitely growing up,' Vivi conceded ruefully. 'I never thought there would come a day when *you* would fight with *me*.'

'Even Winnie fights with you!' Zoe laughed and gave her much taller sister a hug, relieved the unnervingly intimate dispute was over.

After Vivi had been picked up an hour later, Zoe walked thoughtfully back to her suite with Raj. *Not. In. Love. With. Him.* She was simply happy and there was nothing wrong with being happy, was there? Zoe hadn't enjoyed much happiness in her life and she was determined to make the most of every moment.

She studied the fainting couch set out like a statement, an invitation, and she smiled before she wandered down the steps to the private courtyard around which their rooms ranged, which allowed them complete privacy.

And all around her she could see the proof of Raj's desire to please her and make her happy, for the once dark courtyard had been replanted during their absence into a spectacular jungle of greenery amongst which exotic flowers bloomed. Even the fountain she had admired, which had long since fallen out of use, was now working again, clean water sparkling down into the brightly tiled basin below. He hadn't mentioned a word about his intentions, but then he never did. He never looked for thanks either. Gifts simply appeared without fanfare, gifts like the wonderful transformation of an outdated, neglected courtyard garden.

She didn't need him to love her as he had loved

Nabila, she only needed the proof that he *cared*, Zoe reflected fiercely. And care he did with amazing efficiency and resolve. How could she expect any more than that in a pretend marriage? After all, he was already giving her much more than she had expected to receive. It wasn't going to last, she knew that, *accepted* that and that was her choice, her choice to live for today and worry about tomorrow only when it arrived…

CHAPTER NINE

Zoe sat up in bed and her head swam and her tummy rolled.

Worry gripped her. She had believed she had caught a virus when the symptoms first started but weeks had passed since then and the unwell feeling was lingering, despite the careful diet she had observed. Raj had wanted to get the palace doctor in but she had stalled him once a greater concern began to nag at her nerves.

Zoe grimaced at her pallid reflection in the bathroom mirror. She had lost weight and her eyes looked too big for her face. As soon as the dizziness had evaporated, she went for a shower, striving not to agonise *again* over the reality that she had not had a period since she'd arrived in Maraban. After all, she couldn't possibly be pregnant even if the light head, the nausea and her tender breasts reminded her of what her sisters had experienced during pregnancy. How could she be pregnant when Raj had not once run the risk of getting her pregnant? But, she did recall once, weeks ago in the shower when he had overlooked the necessity and she had meant to mention it but hadn't been worried enough to do so.Now she wished she had pointed out that oversight.

Of course no method of birth control was infallible, another little voice nagged at the back of her head. And how on earth was she to put her worries to rest when the acquisition of a pregnancy test in secret had so far proved beyond her capabilities. She never got the opportunity to leave the palace alone. She was surrounded by security and all too many helpful people when she went out. Let's face it, Zoe, she thought forlornly, the Crown Princess of Maraban cannot be seen buying a pregnancy test without causing a furore. It was ironic that what would have thrilled the population filled Zoe with sick apprehension because she couldn't forget Raj saying that such a development would be a disaster in their situation.

Of course, it would be when it was only a pretend marriage and if she had a boy, he would be next in line to the throne. If she was pregnant and it was a boy, she would have to live in Maraban for at least the next twenty years as Raj's ex-wife and she certainly didn't fancy that option as a future. She would have to sit on the outskirts of his life, watching him marry another woman and have a family with her. Naturally, Raj would move on after their marriage ended but she certainly didn't want to sit around nearby to actually *watch* him doing it.

When she emerged from her bedroom, dressed in a pastel-blue dress with her hair in a braid and her make-up immaculate, Bahar, her PA—or social secretary, as Zoe preferred to think of the young attractive brunette—awaited her with a list of her appointments. It pleased her tremendously that after three months away from home she had now acquired the confidence to handle visiting schools and such places without having to drag Raj everywhere with her for support. Coming to Maraban and marrying Raj had been the best decision she had ever made when it came to getting stronger and moving forward with her life.

As her breakfast was brought to the table, Zoe's stomach lurched even as she looked at it and she pushed the plate away and settled for a cup of tea. After all, she couldn't afford to eat if she was going out to an official engagement where her succumbing to a bout of sickness in public would be a serious embarrassment, she reflected with an inner shudder at the prospect. She would catch a snack later, by which time hopefully the nausea would have subsided.

Walking down the last flight of stairs, she was wondering whether or not to call in on Raj in his office when she broke out in a cold sweat. Her legs wobbled under her and she snatched at the stone balustrade to stay upright but the sick dizziness engulfing her was unstoppable and as she lurched to one side, dimly conscious that someone was seizing hold of her from behind, she passed out.

When Zoe came around slowly, she winced at the sensation of a needle in her arm and gripped the hand that was holding hers in dismay. Her eyes fluttered open as Raj leant down to her saying, 'Don't try to get up in case you faint again. Dr Fadel decided a blood test would be a good idea…sorry about that.'

The very quietness of his voice made her scan the room behind him, which seemed to be filled to the brim with anxious-looking people. Mortification made her close her eyes again and do as she was told because she had a clear recollection of almost tumbling down that last flight of stairs.

'I'll be late for my appointment,' she protested.

'You will not be leaving the palace today.'

'But...'

'Not until the doctor has diagnosed what is wrong with you,' Raj spelt out more harshly, in a tone she wasn't accustomed to hearing from him.

In shock at that attitude, she glanced up at him, but he had already moved away to speak to the older man closing a doctor's bag on the desk. She registered that she was in Raj's office on the sofa he had slept on when they were first married, and very slowly and carefully she began to inch up into a sitting position.

Raj stalked back to her. 'Stay flat and lie still,' he told her wrathfully.

He was furious with her, Zoe realised in consternation, wondering why. Possibly the uproar her faint had caused, she reflected unhappily, because the room was still crammed with staff all trying to speak to Raj at once in his own language, so she could only follow one word in three that she was hearing and those were the simple ones. Her ambition to learn Arabic was advancing only slowly. Finally, the room cleared and they were alone again.

'May I sit up now or are you going to get angry again?' Zoe murmured.

Raj gazed across the office at her and then moved forward before hovering several feet from her as though an invisible wall had suddenly come down between them. 'I apologise. I was not angry with you, I was angry with myself for neglecting your health,' he admitted tautly. 'I knew you were unwell but I listened to you when you refused to let me call the doctor in. I *shouldn't* have listened!'

'Raj, that was *my* fault, this stupid virus, and I'm not awfully fond of medics.'

'You will want to express thanks to your bodyguard, Carim. He saved your life when he prevented you from falling down the stairs. At the very least you would have been badly hurt with broken limbs,' Raj framed jaggedly, his hands clenching into fists by his side. 'But such a fall could definitely also have killed you and nothing is worth that risk.'

'Of course, it isn't,' Zoe agreed soothingly because she was shaken as well by the accident that she had so narrowly escaped. 'OK, you were right and I was wrong.'

'I swore to look after you and I have failed in my duty,' Raj informed her hoarsely.

Zoe paled. 'It's not your duty, Raj. I'm a fully grown adult and I made an unwise decision when I chose not to consult a doctor. Please don't blame yourself for my mistake.'

'How can I do anything else?' Raj shot back to her with seeming incredulity. 'You are my wife and you are in a country foreign to you. Who else should stand responsible for your well-being?'

I'm not your *real* wife. The declaration sprang to her lips but she didn't voice it, belatedly recognising that whether Raj viewed her as his real wife or otherwise he would still feel that it was his duty to ensure her well-being. Three months ago she would happily have flung that declaration of independence at him but now she knew him a little better, knew the crushing weight of responsibility he took on without complaint. As his father, the King, suffered increasing ill health and days he was unable to leave his quarters, more of his obligations were falling on Raj's shoulders. Unsurprisingly, Raj didn't have an irresponsible bone in his lean, beautiful body and he was infuriatingly good at blaming himself for any mishap or oversight.

'I'm sorry if I seemed to speak rudely and angrily,' Raj breathed tautly, silvered dark eyes locked to her lovely face. 'But I was very concerned.'

'I understand that and I'm fine. In fact I think I'm recovered enough now to make that appointment.'

'No, they will have to settle for me doing it in your place,' Raj sliced in forcefully. 'You're not going out anywhere until we have heard from the doctor—'

'Raj, for goodness' sake, I'm fine,' she told him again, swinging her feet down onto the floor to punctuate the statement.

'We'll see,' Raj asserted with tact as he reached for her hand to help her upright, tugging her close to him, his stunning dark deep-set eyes below his straight black brows roaming over her delicate face. 'But we will not see today...however, I am free this evening, and if you were to feel strong enough to welcome me home on that couch, I would be extraordinarily pleased.'

Zoe gurgled with laughter and stretched up on tiptoe to taste his wide sensual mouth with her own. And that was that, he was magically distracted from his overwhelming anxiety about her welfare. Her heart hammered and her fingers closed into his shirtfront because she wanted to rip it off him. Against her, she could feel him hard and ready and hunger coursed through her, turning her wanton with need.

With an enormous effort, Raj set her back from him. 'We *can't*. People are waiting for my arrival,' he reminded her raggedly. 'But it is one of those occasions when I wish I had the freedom to tell everyone but you to go to hell!'

Zoe flushed, censuring herself for tempting him merely to distract him because it had been a selfish move and he was never selfish, which made her feel bad. On the other hand, the couch invitation was welcome, she acknowledged with a tiny shiver of anticipation, wondering what had happened to the genuinely shy young woman she had been mere months earlier. She wasn't shy with Raj. In fact, she was doing stuff with Raj she had never dreamt she would ever do with any man, once alien things like purchasing very fancy lingerie and posing in it, revelling in the rush of powerful femininity his fierce desire for her and his equally audacious appreciation gave her every time. She had discovered a whole new self to explore and secretly it thrilled her.

Outside the office door, she thanked the guard who had saved her from falling and he grinned at her, telling her in broken English that he would have died sooner than let anything happen to her on his watch. His undeniable sincerity shook her and she climbed the stairs, thinking that until now she hadn't quite grasped how the people around her and those she met during engagements viewed her as Raj's wife, certainly hadn't taken that level of care and concern as seriously as they did. It struck her that many of those same people would be disappointed when she and Raj split up. But then there was nothing she could do about that, was there? She was a sham wife but *they* didn't know that, didn't know that she was nothing more than a glossy convenient lie foisted on the public, she ruminated unhappily.

She was having lunch when the middle-aged doctor she had glimpsed in Raj's office called to see her. Dr Fadel was King Tahir's doctor and resident in the palace and, fortunately for her, he had qualified in London and spoke excellent English.

After the usual polite pleasantries, he asked if he could dismiss the hovering staff and she nodded acquiescence with a slight frown, her tension rising. Of course, he was about to tell her that her hormones were all out of kilter, which was the most likely diagnosis, and she didn't want to discuss her absent menstrual cycle with an audience either.

'I am blessed to be the doctor to break such momentous news,' he then informed her with a beaming smile. 'You have conceived, Your Royal Highness…'

'Conceived...?' Zoe repeated as if she had never heard the word before, and she tottered back down into the seat she had vacated to greet him, so great was the shock of that announcement. That her deepest fear had been confirmed rocked her world to its foundations.

'The blood test was positive. Of course, it is impossible for me to tell you anything more without a further examination.' He looked at her enquiringly. 'Would that be in order? Or would you prefer another doctor, perhaps a specialist, to give you further information? I'm not inexperienced. I do have many female patients in the royal household.'

Zoe was in a daze. She pushed her hands down on the table to rise again. *Pregnant?* she was screaming inside her head, still wondering if it could be a mistake and willing to subject herself to any check-up that could possibly reveal his diagnosis *was* a mistake, she reasoned fearfully as she followed him from the room and he lamented the lack of lifts in the palace. A lift would have to be installed immediately, the doctor began telling her, particularly when her near accident earlier was taken into consideration. A pregnant woman couldn't be expected to run up and down flights and flights of stairs, particularly not a woman carrying a child he described as 'so precious a child for Maraban'.

It wouldn't be precious to Raj, Zoe thought miserably, not to a man who had frankly referred to such an unlikely event as a *disaster*. Suddenly she was in total conflict with herself and split into two opposing halves. On the one hand she adored children and she very much wanted her baby if she did prove to be pregnant, but on the other, she was sort of guiltily hoping that the doctor's verdict was wrong because of the way Raj would feel about it and that felt even more wrong.

A glimpse of the trim and determined little nurse who had jabbed her with a syringe the night she was kidnapped was not a vote winner in the troubled mood she was in, but Zoe refused to react, deeming her potential pregnancy more important as she lay down on an examination couch and an ultrasound machine was wheeled in. An instant later she heard the whirring sound of her baby's fast heartbeat and she paled, feeling foolish for thinking that the doctor could have been in error. It was an even greater surprise to discover that she was already three months along and almost into the second trimester, which meant that she had conceived very early in their marriage.

The doctor happily dispensed vitamin tablets and congratulated her on her fertility, studying her literally as if she were a walking miracle. She supposed in comparison to the last generation of the royal family, she did strike him that way because it had taken over thirty years and three wives to produce Raj.

'The King will be overjoyed,' he told her cheerfully.

'Oh, but…' Zoe hesitated, questioning if it was even possible to keep a lid on such a revelation within the palace.

'The King needs this good news, with his health as precarious as it has been,' his doctor assured her with gravity.

'Then my husband can tell him after I have *first* told *him*,' Zoe countered firmly.

But on one level she thought she was probably wasting her breath because the cat was out of the bag and there was nothing she could do about that: the doctor, the nurse and whoever had done the blood test already knew of her condition. Just how fast the news had spread was borne out only minutes later when she returned to her room and was ushered into the bedroom where tea, a ginger biscuit and the book she had been reading awaited her by the bed like a heartfelt invitation to rest as pregnant women were so often advised to do. Smothering a groan, she lay down, ironically worn out by the day she had had. Off came her shoes and then her dress and she lay back, confronted by the daunting evening lying ahead of her because she had no choice other than to tell Raj immediately. Would it sound better if she did the couch thing first? Or would that look manipulative?

In the event, she didn't get to make that decision because she slept through most of the afternoon, only wakening when the sound of a door closing jolted her awake. She opened her eyes on Raj striding towards the bed and the slumberous expression in his shimmering dark scrutiny as he looked at her lying there in her flimsy underwear. He sank down on the edge of the bed. 'How are you feeling now?'

'OK—hungry now that the sickness has taken a break. Dr Fadel said that with a little luck that should start fading soon,' she told him tightly. 'You see, I'm *not* ill as such. I'm pregnant…'

As she hesitated, her nerves getting the better of her for a moment, she studied Raj; his lean, darkly handsome features had locked tight, his jaw line clenching hard.

'I think it must've been that time in the shower just after the wedding. You forgot to use anything. I should've said something then but I really didn't think anything would come of it,' she acknowledged uncomfortably, wishing he would say something.

Raj blinked because for an instant his surroundings had vanished; what she had told him had to be the very last development he had expected, but it also led to a revelation that hit him even harder. He turned pale, in the matter of a moment recognising the situation he was in.

'We've barely got out of bed to eat for three months,' Raj breathed in a rueful undertone. 'What can I say? I was in charge of contraception and I forgot. So, we are going to become parents…forgive me, I am stunned by the concept of something so surprising.'

'You said it would be a disaster if I became pregnant,' Zoe reminded him uncertainly, still unable to read his mood, particularly when he sprang upright again and started pacing across the floor, clearly too restless to stay seated.

'A disaster more from your point of view than from mine,' Raj qualified with level clarity. 'We agreed to part but I cannot agree to let you leave me carrying our child and I do not want our child raised without either one of us. Surely we are doing well enough together for you to stay in our marriage for some time to come?' A straight ebony brow lifted enquiringly, intense dark eyes scanning her triangular face for an answer. 'Could you accept that? If we remain married, we can raise our child together.'

A quivery little breath ran up through Zoe, allowing her lungs to function again. The backs of her eyes prickled and stung. Until Raj had asked her to *stay* married to him, she had not realised how horribly tense she had become and the painful tension slowly ebbed out of her stiff muscles.

'So, we just go on as normal?' Zoe checked.

'Why not? Are we not both content as we are?' Raj prompted tautly.

Zoe nodded but couldn't help wishing he could be a little more emotional about staying married to her. There she went again, wanting what she couldn't have, she scolded herself, because she knew herself better now. She could look back and recognise the raging jealousy that had assailed her after seeing those photos of Raj with Nabila that had so clearly depicted his love for the beautiful brunette. There was nothing she could do about such feelings except keep them under control and hidden. And considering the circumstances in which they had married, each for their own very practical reasons, it was illogical and pathetic to long for Raj to fall in love with her as well.

'You said…"stay in our marriage for *some time to come*",' Zoe recited tightly. 'What sort of time frame were you considering?'

At that question for further clarification, Raj stiffened and raked long brown fingers through his tousled black curls. 'Must we be so precise?'

Zoe swallowed hard at the edge of reproof in his tone. 'Well, it would be easier for me to know how *you* see the future.'

'With you and our child together. I would impose no limits. I would like to throw away *all* the boundaries we agreed and make this a normal marriage,' Raj spelt out without hesitation. 'I still can't believe that you're pregnant.'

'Neither can I,' Zoe revealed, scrambling off the bed only to be immediately caught up into his strong arms.

'I didn't think it could happen that easily…it is a brilliant accident,' Raj murmured with husky conviction as he came down on the bed with her. 'Are we still allowed to share this bed?'

'Of course, we are. I've been fully checked out.' A kind of sick relief combined with dizzy happiness was filtering through Zoe as she dimly acknowledged that he was giving her what she most wanted. She wasn't going to have to give him up like the salted caramel ice cream she had recently become addicted to, she was going to get to *keep* him. Of course, it wasn't perfect, she conceded reluctantly, not when he only wanted her to stay married to him because she was pregnant. Even so, being accepted as a normal wife was a huge upgrade on being labelled a friend with benefits.

'What are you thinking about?' Raj chided, lying back on the bed with his gorgeous dark eyes fiercely welded to her reflective face.

'Nothing remotely important,' she told him, and she meant it when she said it even if she dimly understood even then that sooner or later she would once again fall into the trap of craving more than he had to give her.

He toyed with her mouth, soft and gentle, and then nipped wickedly at her bottom lip with the edge of his teeth. Her hands lifted and her fingers speared into his black curls, liquid heat pooling in her pelvis as he deliberately snaked his lean hips into the junction of her thighs, the thrust of his arousal unmistakeable. He was always so hot for her. It was enough, it was more than enough to be desired, cared for, appreciated. Even if she felt as though she was keeping him by default? She crushed the thought, burying it deep. She already had more with him than she had ever thought she would have, so craving anything else would be greedy.

'I want you so much,' Raj confided rawly, sitting up over her to wrench off his shirt, yank roughly at his tie. 'Knowing my baby is inside you is so sexy…'

Zoe blinked. It *was*? He was lifting her to deftly undo

her bra, groaning with satisfaction when her small pouting breasts came free to hungrily claim an engorged nipple with his mouth. A gasp was wrenched from her as he teased the other with his fingers. 'You're more sensitive there than ever,' he husked. 'I love your body.'

She knew he did: he never left it alone. He couldn't walk past her without touching her in some way and if they were alone, it almost always concluded in their bed, although they had succumbed to christening his office sofa a time or two and they had once had sex in a limousine on a long drive. He had an astonishingly strong sexual appetite. Anyone watching him could have been forgiven for thinking he hadn't had the freedom to enjoy her for a couple of days at least but that was not the case.

He tugged off her panties and yanked down the zip in his trousers, shedding his clothing with an impatience that never failed to add to her excitement. There he was, all sleek and golden and beautiful, and he was finally hers to keep like a precious possession she had been fighting for without even appreciating what she was doing or even what was happening inside her own head. She had wanted love but then what woman didn't? If *he* could settle for less, she could settle, she reasoned as he snaked down her body with darting little kisses and caresses that set her on fire, ultimately settling between her spread thighs to pleasure her in the way he enjoyed the most.

As a rippling spasm of pleasure gathered low in her body, she clutched at his hair, writhed, squirmed, begged until at last she climaxed in an explosive surge that certainly didn't feel in any way as though she were settling for less. Raj shifted over her then, hungrily kissing her, and the excitement began to rocket again as he sank into her with delicious force, pushing her legs back to deepen his penetration. Definitely not less, she told herself as she rose breathlessly to meet his every thrust, every move instinctive and raw with the excitement she could barely contain. There was more and then even more of that insanely thrilling pleasure before he sent her flying into a wild breathless climax that shattered her senses and her control, leaving her slumped in a wreck of heavy, satiated limbs in the aftermath.

She hadn't heard a phone ring, had been too far gone, but she surfaced when she realised that Raj wasn't holding her close as he usually did. She turned over, saw him talking urgently on his phone while he strode about, naked and bronzed and muscular, and she propped her chin on the heel of her hand, enjoying watching him. That enjoyment gradually faded when he went on to make several other quick calls in succession, alerting her to the knowledge that something must have happened, and because his expression changed from smiling to grim she couldn't tell whether what had happened was a good or bad thing.

'I'm afraid I'm going to have to leave you for the night,' Raj told her with a frown. 'The construction workers have stumbled on archaeological remains at the Josias site.'

'The hospital project in the capital of Maraban?'

'It's potentially a very exciting discovery but it means that the site has to close until we can get an official inspection done tomorrow, and that throws the whole project and the work crews into limbo. I'm flying out there now to meet with the managers and look at contingency plans. It is possible that we won't be able to build there at all,' he concluded gravely. 'And the hospital is very much needed in that area.'

Recalling that Nabila was the CEO of the construction firm involved, Zoe sat up, her pale hair falling round her flushed face, because she knew he was undoubtedly about to meet the other woman again for the first time in eight years and she very much wanted to be in the vicinity. 'I could come with you!' she said in sudden interruption.

'No, not this time. What would be the point? I'm likely to be in meetings most of the night and certainly all of tomorrow, sorting this out,' he told her dismissively as he strode into the bathroom.

'I would still like to have gone,' Zoe confided in a small voice to an empty room.

But did she really need to cling to him like glue? she reproved herself. There were few things more distasteful to a man than a clingy, needy and jealous woman and Raj would quickly get tired of her if she started acting paranoid and suspicious purely because he was mixing with his ex-girlfriend in a business environment. She had to grow up, she told herself urgently, not react to her stabbing insecurity with adolescent immaturity. After all, nothing was likely to change in the short term. She was pregnant and *really* married now.

And how did Raj truly feel about that development? It shocked Zoe to accept that she had not the smallest idea of how *he* felt, and the instant she registered that worrying truth, another little brick of security tumbled down from her inner wall of defences. Sadly, there was no ignoring the truth that the closest Raj had actually come to expressing his personal feelings was the assurance that he regarded her being pregnant with his child as…sexy. Although he had labelled her conception a brilliant accident, which did suggest he was pleased.

Zoe grimaced. Why couldn't he simply have said so, openly? In reality, now that she was recalling that conversation, she realised that Raj had not expressed a single emotion, which for an emotionally intense man of his ilk was not reassuring, she reflected worriedly.

Were duty and a sense of responsibility for his child all that had driven Raj's request that she stay married to him?

And if that *was* the case, what could she possibly do about it?

CHAPTER TEN

RAJ'S PHONE RANG constantly right up until he left the palace. He was feeling guilty because Zoe had been very quiet when he left. But there was no way he would have considered dragging her across country late at night, especially now that she was pregnant and he had no idea where he would be staying. Zoe looked frail for all her lack of complaint. She had lost her appetite, dropped in weight. Yet even though he had noticed he had said and done nothing because it had not even occurred to him that she could be pregnant. What kind of husband was he? Not a very good one, he decided grimly.

And now he was to become a father. A dazzling smile flashed across his lean dark features. That was a marvellous development, a near miracle in their circumstances.

His phone rang again as he awaited his limo in the forecourt of the palace and he dug it out, only to freeze in surprise as the caller identified himself for, although he had met the man, his royal status ensured that he wasn't especially friendly with anyone in that profession, and the warning the journalist gave Raj astonished him. He immediately called Omar and passed it on to him and Omar announced that he would be travelling to the hospital site as well.

In the early hours of the following morning, having dealt with a torch-lit visit to the site and with wildly excited archaeologists, who were hopeful that the legendary lost city built by Alexander the Great had been discovered on Marabanian soil, Raj was more than ready for his bed. He walked into the comparatively small hotel closest to the site. He was relieved that he hadn't succumbed to the temptation of bringing Zoe because he did not think the level of comfort on offer sufficient for a pregnant woman. As his father had remarked in wonderment when he had phoned him earlier to break their news, Zoe would have to be treated from now on like the Queen she would one day be.

Raj was smiling at the memory and sharing it with his cousin, Omar, who was beside him as he pushed open the door of his room. And then quite forcibly the warning he had received, and begun to discount because he had yet to even *see* Nabila, was revived because Nabila sat up in the bed that should've been his, the sheet tumbling to reveal her bare breasts. Filled with angry distaste at her brazen display, Raj averted his eyes, unimpressed by the expression of seemingly embarrassed innocence she had put on when she glimpsed Omar by his side.

'For goodness' sake, tell Omar to *leave*,' Nabila urged Raj.

'I'm staying,' Omar delivered with satisfaction, never having liked the brunette even when Raj had been in love with her. 'But it is gratifying to discover that you can sink even lower than I expected.'

Raj strode to the foot of the bed. 'What the hell are you playing at?' he demanded.

Deciding to ignore Omar, Nabila focused her eyes on Raj with blatant hunger. 'I want you and I really don't care what I have to do to get you this time around. Isn't that enough?' She treated him to a look of languorous enticement. 'Don't tell me you're not still curious about what it would be like between us.'

Raj's mouth curled with disgust and he swung round to stalk back to the door and address his protection team in the corridor. 'Get her out of here…and find me another room,' he ordered impatiently.

'I'm not asking for marriage this time around,' Nabila crooned behind him. 'I would be your mistress…your every secret fantasy.'

'My *wife* is my every secret fantasy,' Raj countered drily as he strode out.

At dawn, Raj was enjoying a working breakfast on the terrace at his hotel with Omar and the management team of Major Holdings, including the CEO, Nabila, who had contrived to take a seat opposite him. He ignored her to the best of his ability, barely even turning his head when she spoke.

'Raj!' she exclaimed, startling him while simultaneously reaching for his hand.

For a split second, he was so disconcerted by that unanticipated over-familiarity and the pleading expression she wore on her face that he did nothing and then he freed his fingers with a sudden jerk and leant back in his chair, cursing himself for not having reacted more immediately to the threat. For Nabila *was* a threat, he acknowledged in a sudden black fury, a threat to his marriage. At that moment, he had not the slightest doubt that a photographer was hiding somewhere in the vicinity, most probably one with a telephoto lens, and had captured that image of them holding hands and that that stolen photo was intended for publication with the presence of their companions eradicated.

A couple of hours later, because she was sleeping in, Zoe turned over in bed, drowsily wondering what had wakened her and failing to notice that her mobile phone was flashing on the cabinet to one side of her. She stole her hand across to the other side of the bed and then remembered that Raj was gone for the night. With a dissatisfied sigh, she dragged her fingers back from that emptiness and reminded herself that it was mortifyingly clingy to want him there *every* night. She could be perfectly happy without him, of course she could be! With no suspicion of just how soon that assumption was to be tested, Zoe went back to sleep.

Zoe wakened in astonishment to find her sisters beside her bed and blinked in disbelief. 'What are you two doing here at this hour of the day?' she demanded.

'We were shopping in Dubai so we didn't have far to come,' Winnie explained stiffly. 'We want you to come home with us. Grandad agrees.'

Zoe sat up. 'Why on earth would you want me to come home with you?'

'*Because*,' Vivi said bluntly, 'Raj is playing away behind your back and you're in love with the rat!'

Zoe frowned. 'No. Raj wouldn't do that to me,' she

said with perfect assurance because, in that line, she trusted him absolutely.

Winnie shoved a mobile phone in front of her gaze. Her lashes fluttered in bewilderment and then she focused and saw Raj with the *one* woman in the world she wouldn't trust him with. Raj in a photo holding hands with Nabila, his lean, darkly handsome features very serious, her face beseeching. Beseeching *what* from him? Zoe broke out in a sudden sweat and then just as quickly, as familiar queasiness assailed her, was forced to leap out of bed and push past her sisters to make it to the bathroom in time to be sick.

'Where did you see that photo? Raj only left last night,' she reasoned when she was able to respond, wondering exactly *when* that photo had been taken and then questioning whether the timing even mattered.

'That photo was offered to Grandad for sale first thing this morning,' Winnie told her in disgust. 'I imagine it was taken by some greedy paparazzo, who worked out what that picture would be worth on the open market.'

As Zoe drooped over the vanity unit brushing her teeth, still weak with nausea and dizziness, Vivi tugged her gently away and settled her down on the fainting couch. 'Take a deep breath and keep your head down. What's the matter with you? Are you ill?'

'Pregnant,' Zoe whispered, still in shock at that photo, fighting to withstand the great tide of pain threatening to engulf her. Raj had refused to take her with him the night before...*no wonder*! Had he known even then that he wanted the freedom to be with his ex-girlfriend?

'Pregnant?' Vivi gasped and her sisters engaged in a lively argument above her head, which Zoe was content to ignore because infinitely more important decisions loomed ahead of her, she grasped dully.

How could she remain married to a man in love with another woman and already seeing her behind her back? Holding hands with her? Although that was the least that had probably gone on between them, she recognised sickly, for it was unlikely that Raj and Nabila would not finally have taken the opportunity to have sex. Particularly not when, in that photo, they were staring at each other like long-lost lovers reunited.

'I'll be frank,' Vivi murmured with surprising quietness. 'You're in love with Raj and he's hurting you and we love you enough that we can't just stand back and allow that.'

'I'm *not* in love with him,' Zoe lied, her eyes watering in a last-ditch effort to save face with her sisters.

But there it was: the truth she had suppressed and refused to face except in the secret depths of her heart. She had fallen madly in love with her fake husband and for all the wrong reasons. Reasons like his smile and the sound of his voice and the raw power of his body over hers in bed. Reasons like the English breakfast tea he had ordered on her behalf and the glorious shoes he'd bought her and had put in the dressing room without even mentioning the purchases. Reasons that encompassed a hundred and one different things and many that she would have found hard to put into words.

Winnie's eyes were also brimming with tears. 'Come back with us to Athens...*please*!'

And Zoe's first reaction was to say no, until she considered the alternatives. She could confront Raj and he would probably admit the truth, which would not be a comfort to her. She could pretend she hadn't seen the photograph and silently agonise over it and that prospect had even less appeal. Or she could take advantage of a breathing space in which to decide what she would do next, she reasoned bravely. It wouldn't be running away, she ruminated, it would be giving herself the time to control her emotional reaction and behave like an adult and deal with the situation. If she stayed, she might cry and let him see that she had been hurt, and what was the point of that?

But what if Raj had not actually cheated on her? Raj was not by nature a cheat, she reasoned, wondering if she was clutching at straws when she thought along such lines. Naturally she didn't want to think he could've been unfaithful, but Nabila was different, Nabila was in a class of her own because once Raj had *loved* her. Could he have resisted the chance to finally be with the woman he had once loved? And wasn't hoping he might have resisted only proof that Zoe was weakly willing to make excuses for him? Shame drenched her pale cheeks with hot pink and she decided to listen to her sisters, who had much more experience than she did with men. If Winnie and Vivi both believed that Raj had succumbed to Nabila's wiles, they were probably right. She trusted their judgement more than she trusted her own because she was all too well aware that her feelings for Raj coloured her every conviction and that she wasn't capable of standing back and making an independent call.

Zoe had her maid pack only one suitcase, because

there was no advantage in advertising the fact that she was leaving and would probably never return to the royal palace. She would send for the rest of her stuff later but when she thought about that, thought about the wardrobe Raj had bought her, thought about his favourite outfits, she as quickly decided that she wanted nothing that would only serve to keep unfortunate memories alive.

Her protection team accompanied her to the airport and flatly refused to leave her there. Suppressing a sigh, she let them board her grandfather's private jet with her, knowing that Raj would recall them later after he had read her note and had seen the photo she had sent to his phone. He wouldn't require any other explanation for her departure because he was definitely not stupid.

When that photo came up on his phone, forwarded by Zoe, Raj succumbed to a rage that almost burned him alive and it took Omar stepping in to prevent him from telling Nabila in front of an audience what he thought of her filthy tactics. Omar's intervention ensured that he did what he had to do at the site, which was his duty, and went home as soon as he possibly could to talk to his wife. A single-line note informing him that she would never 'share' a man greeted his return.

The discovery that she had been removed by her siblings and flown to her grandfather's home in Greece came as a complete shock. It was closely followed by a terse phone call from Stamboulas Fotakis, who accused him of disrespecting his grandchild in a grossly offensive public disregard of his marital status. And as if those punishments were not sufficient, he was summoned by his father, who in his ineffable highly efficient way knew exactly what was happening in his son's marriage and pointed out that his son only had himself to thank for allowing a harpy like Nabila within a hundred yards of him.

'When you bring your wife home again, I will have Nabila thrown out of the country,' the King pronounced with satisfaction.

'Let us hope I can bring Zoe home,' Raj breathed with difficulty, mastering his temper but only just in the face of that provocation, for throwing Nabila out of Maraban would only create a scandal that Nabila would relish.

His arrival in Greece late that night was punctuated by further unwelcome attacks. Zoe was in bed and not to be disturbed, according to Stam Fotakis. 'She's fragile,' he told Raj in condemnation. 'She needs protection from those who would use her soft heart against her.'

'I would not use…'

Her sister, Vivi, walked into her grandfather's office and proceeded to try and tear strips off Raj but Raj wasn't taking that from anyone, least of all Zoe's fiery sibling, and an almighty row broke out before Stam ran out of patience and demanded that both of them go to bed. 'If you must, you may speak to Zoe in the morning,' he informed Raj in a ringing tone of finality.

But Raj wasn't about to be steered in a direction he didn't want to go. He let himself be shown to a guest room without any intention of *waiting* until he could see *his* wife. As soon as he was alone, he learned where her room was by the simple measure of contacting her protection team.

Zoe was curled up on a lounger on the balcony beyond her room, watching the sea silver and darken in the moonlight. Misery felt like a shroud tightly wrapped round her, denying her the air she needed to breathe. She had still to accept the concept of a life empty of Raj. Every time she contemplated that terrifying prospect, she felt as though someone were flaying the skin from her bones, only the pain was internalised. How had one man become so important to her survival that her entire world had begun to revolve around him? It both shocked and incensed her that she could have been weak and foolish enough to fall in love with a man she had known from the outset would never be hers on any permanent basis.

When the patio doors behind her slid open, she flinched, expecting it to be one of her sisters, come yet again to offer depressing advice. She didn't want the assurance that she would get over Raj. She didn't want to be told that there would eventually be another man worthier of her love in her future when just then, and against all reason and logic, all her body and her brain cried out for *was* Raj.

'Zoe…?'

In astonished recognition of that dark deep accented intonation, Zoe was startled and she leapt off the lounger and spun round. *'Raj?'* she gasped incredulously.

'Hush…' Raj put a finger to his lips in warning. 'I wouldn't put it past your family to try and drag me out physically and I don't want a fight breaking out between my protection team and your grandfather's. But I will allow no man on earth to tell me *when* I can see my wife.'

'But I'm not your wife—not really your wife,' Zoe protested. 'And I *never* was.'

Raj studied the pale triangle of her face in the moonlight and guilt cut through him because it was *his* fault that she had been hurt and upset. 'I have to explain what happened with Nabila.'

'No, you don't owe me any explanations!' Zoe cut in hastily. 'But you can't expect me to live with you and turn a blind eye to an affair either!'

'Why would I have an affair with Nabila? Have you asked yourself that?' Raj demanded, moving forward to scoop her gently up into his arms and return her with care to the lounger before stepping back to lean back lithely against the balcony wall.

'Because you still love her…' Zoe muttered ruefully.

'Why would I still love a woman who slept with another man behind my back?' Raj asked gently. 'Do you honestly believe I am so stupid that I would still blindly love a woman who was unworthy of my love and respect?'

Zoe reddened and her eyes evaded his. 'I'm not saying you're stupid, just that sometimes people can't control their feelings even when they *know* they should,' she framed uncomfortably.

'But that is not the case with Nabila. My love died the instant I realised how poorly I had judged her character. She was my first love,' Raj admitted grittily. 'At the age of twenty I also believed she would be my last love but I was very young and I was wrong. I couldn't continue to love a woman who lied and cheated once I saw her for what she was. I couldn't love a woman who only wanted me because I am wealthy and one day I will be King.'

'Well, if that's all true what were you doing holding hands with her?' Zoe demanded baldly, influenced against her will by the obvious sincerity of his self-defence.

'Before I left the palace yesterday, I received a phone call from a journalist and it was most illuminating… yes, I *know* you are impatient for an explanation but please bear with me to enable me to tell you the whole story,' Raj urged when she made a frustrated gesture with one tiny expressive hand. 'I learned from that call that Nabila had personally contacted him and given him the photos that proved the existence of our youthful romance.'

'*She* was behind the release of those photos to the gossip magazine?' Zoe exclaimed in surprise.

'Yes. I assume she wanted that information publicised as a first move in her desire to come back into my life. Evidently she assumed there would still be a place for her in my heart.' Raj's wide sensual mouth compressed. 'The journalist involved called to warn me yesterday that she was planning to wreck my marriage and had a photographer lined up in readiness.'

'Journalists love scandal. Why would he have warned you?' Zoe pressed suspiciously.

'Zoe…' Raj murmured softly. 'The gossip magazine was quite happy to publish old photos of a romance few people knew about but the owner, the journalist I mentioned, is a loyal Marabanian and he refused to get involved in framing me with Nabila in a seedy scheme likely to damage my marriage. That was a step too far for him and, instead of playing along, he warned me of her ambition to cause trouble.'

'Well, it doesn't look like the warning did you much good,' Zoe said drily.

'It put me on my guard and I took Omar with me on the trip. When I went to my hotel room that night, she was waiting for me in the bed and I had her removed. We didn't have a conversation either because I have nothing to say to Nabila,' Raj told her doggedly.

'Nothing?' Again, Zoe looked unimpressed by his claim but she was already thinking of the stunning brunette waiting in his bed for him. 'Was she undressed?'

Raj nodded.

'And you weren't even tempted?' Zoe prompted helplessly.

'No, but I think my protection team were,' he remarked wryly. 'Omar can confirm that nothing happened. He was also present at the table when she grabbed my hand.'

'Grabbed?' Zoe queried with a frown. 'But how could Omar have been there when you were alone with her?'

'I wasn't alone with her. The photo is deceptive. Three of Nabila's colleagues were also at that table with us.' Raj dug out his phone and brought up the photo for her appraisal. 'And if you look…*there*…you can just about see the sleeve of the man sitting beside me.'

Her heart thumping hard at getting that close to him again, Zoe stared down at the photo and squinted until she too registered that there was indeed a tiny glimpse of what could only have been another arm at the very edge of the picture.

'Nabila arranged for her photographer to take that photo to suggest an intimacy that does not exist between us. When she grabbed my hand, I was so disconcerted I didn't react fast enough to evade the photographer. I was too *polite* to say what I wanted to say in front of other people,' he derided with sudden visible annoyance. 'I believed I had dealt with her in the hotel room the night before and that she would leave me alone, resenting the fact that I had rejected her invitation… I was wrong, for which I am heartily sorry. But I have *nothing else* to apologise for.'

'So you say…' Zoe muttered, fixedly studying his lean, darkly beautiful face while her brain sped over everything that he had explained, seeking a crack or a hole in his account of events. 'And how do you feel about her now?'

'What would I feel but heartfelt relief that she showed me what she was before I made the mistake of marrying her?' Raj countered wryly. 'Omar is downstairs waiting to act as my witness.'

Zoe swallowed hard on that assurance before an involuntary giggle was wrenched from her. 'Raj, if you killed someone, Omar would bury the body for you! You two are *that* close. Omar in the guise of a reliable witness is a joke!'

Raj dropped fluidly down on his knees beside the lounger and studied her with raw frustration. 'Then I will produce the other people at that table for your examination,' he swore with fierce determination.

Zoe adored him in that moment because she believed him, believed that he would go to any embarrassing length to prove his innocence. He had been warned about Nabila's plans and had assumed that he had taken sufficient precautions to protect himself but the devious brunette had still contrived to catch him out. He simply wasn't sly enough to deal with a woman that shameless, he was too honourable, too loyal, too honest, and that Nabila had attempted to use his very decency against him infuriated Zoe.

'No, that won't be necessary,' Zoe told him tenderly. 'You don't need to embarrass yourself that way.'

'It wouldn't embarrass me if it gave *you* peace of mind,' Raj argued. 'That is all that matters here—'

'No, what really matters,' Zoe murmured with a new strength in her quiet voice, 'is that I *believe* you.'

'But you said Omar is no good as a witness,' he reminded her in bewilderment.

'I was sort of joking,' Zoe muttered in rueful apology. 'I *do* believe that you have told me the truth.'

'Allah be praised,' Raj breathed in his own language.

'How long did it take you to get over Nabila?' Zoe asked then with helpless curiosity.

'Not very long once what I realised what an idiot I had been!' Raj confessed in a driven undertone. 'But the whole experience damaged me, and even before I met her I was already damaged by my mother's suicide. That made it difficult for me to trust *any* woman.'

Zoe ran soothing fingertips down from a high masculine cheekbone to the hard angle of his taut jaw. 'Of course, it did,' she whispered sympathetically. 'You were badly hurt when you were still a child and then hurt and humiliated by what happened with Nabila. I can understand that.'

'But you will probably *not* understand that I never

had another relationship with a woman until I met you,' Raj admitted harshly. 'All I allowed myself was a succession of grubby one-night stands.'

'Grubby?' She questioned his wording.

'It *was* grubby when I compare those encounters to what I have found with you,' Raj confessed.

'And what have you found with me?' she whispered, her gaze held fast by the silvered darkness of his, heart pounding with anticipation, because in those eloquent eyes of his she saw what she had long dreamt of seeing but barely credited could be real.

'Love,' he said simply. 'Love like I never felt for anyone, certainly not for Nabila. That was a boy's love, this is a man's and you mean the whole world to me. I don't know how else to describe how very important you are to me…'

'You're doing great,' she mumbled encouragingly when he hesitated.

'I hate being away from you. I missed you when I went to bed last night and when I woke up this morning. Wherever you are feels like home. Whenever you smile, my heart lifts. At the beginning,' he breathed hoarsely, 'I believed it was only sexual attraction and I tried incredibly hard to resist you…but I couldn't. What I've learned since is that you are the very best thing that has ever happened to me and you make me amazingly happy.'

Zoe breathed in slow and deep and it was a challenge when her lungs were struggling for oxygen. He had just made all her dreams come true. He had just blown her every insecurity out of the water but she still had some questions. 'So why, when I told you that I was pregnant, didn't you tell me then how you felt?'

'Because I didn't know how you felt about me,' Raj responded as though that were an obvious explanation. 'And I had messed everything up with you from the start. I was worrying about you wanting to leave me and going back to the UK to get the divorce I had stupidly promised you, and wondering how I could possibly prevent that from happening. I have never been more relieved than when our unexpected but very much welcome baby gave us the excuse to stay together.'

'I didn't need an excuse,' she told him then. 'I didn't want to leave you…well, probably since the honeymoon, maybe even sooner, I'm ashamed to admit. I fell in love with you weeks and weeks ago and knew it but I wasn't going to tell you that *ever*.'

Raj sprang gracefully upright and lifted her up into his arms to sit back down on the lounger holding her tight, as if he feared she might make a sudden leap for freedom. 'I denied my feelings for a long time and tried to hold back but you give me so much joy it is hard to hide it from you,' he confided huskily. 'That you return my love is almost more than I could ever have hoped for because I love you so much it burns in me like a fire…'

A knock sounded on the patio doors. Raj rose with her in his arms as the door opened.

'What the hell—?' Vivi began in shock when she saw them.

'Bad timing, Vivi,' Zoe interrupted sharply. 'My husband loves me and I'll see you at breakfast.'

Behind her Winnie laughed and tugged Vivi back. 'Yes, breakfast promises to be fun, Raj…with Grandad grouching and Vivi giving you suspicious looks, but if Zoe trusts you, you have my trust too.'

'You turncoat!' Vivi gasped but Winnie was inexorably dragging her out of the room.

'So, where were we?' Zoe prompted as Raj deposited her on the bed and went straight across the room to lock the bedroom door in a sensible move that delighted her. 'Ah, yes, you were saying that your love is like a fire.'

'More of an eternal flame,' Raj assured her poetically. 'You've got me for life.'

'Thank goodness for that. You see, I'm not a changeable woman,' she murmured softly, eyes gliding possessively over his lean, powerful length. 'I expect and demand for ever and ever, like in all the best fairy tales.'

'Perfect,' Raj murmured hoarsely, framing her flushed face with reverent hands as he stared down at her with unashamed adoration before claiming her pink pouting lips with passionate hunger.

And it was perfect for both of them as they left behind their doubts and fears and rejoiced in their newly discovered closeness and trust. Passion united them as much as love, every sense heightened for them both by the fear that they could have lost each other.

'I love you so much,' he breathed in a hoarse groan in the aftermath.

'I love you too,' she whispered, both arms wrapped possessively round him, a glorious sense of peaceful happiness powering her with a new surge of confidence.

EPILOGUE

EIGHTEEN MONTHS LATER Zoe laughed as she watched her year-old son lurch like a tiny drunk across the floor to greet his father, because he had only begun walking for the first time the day before. Raj had been really disappointed to miss those very first steps because he had been in Moscow on business and the video Zoe had sent had only partially consoled him. Now, he swept the toddler up into his arms with noisy sounds of admiration so that Karim's little face literally shone with his sense of achievement and his delight in his father's appreciation.

Raj was a great father, keen that his son would grow up with few of the royal restrictions and traditions that had held him back during his often lonely childhood. Karim was encouraged to play with other children and he was fortunate that his many cousins on both sides of the family were regular visitors. Even King Tahir unbent in Karim's energetic and sunny presence, but then the whole of Maraban was still reacting to Karim's birth as though he were an absolute miracle. That level of interest was a big weight for one little boy to carry on his shoulders and Zoe did everything she could to ensure that his upbringing was as normal and as unstarry as she could make it, even though they lived in a royal palace. Karim also had a pair of grandfathers, who sought to outdo each other with the very lavishness of their gifts.

Zoe was blissfully happy in her marriage. Raj made every day they were together worth celebrating. He loved her as she had never dreamt she would ever be loved and he gave her amazing support with everything she did. He had even made an effort to strengthen his relationships with her occasionally challenging family and was now her grandfather's favourite grandson-in-law, while Vivi had apologised for her initial doubts about Raj's suitability as a husband and fully accepted him, so that Zoe could relax and mix freely with her sisters and their husbands.

Zoe's fingers slid down to press gently against the very slight swelling beneath her sundress that signified that in a few months Karim would have company in the royal nursery. She had had an easy pregnancy and an easy birth with her son and was keen to have her children close together and complete their family while she was still in her twenties. Raj had wanted her to wait a little longer but she had persuaded him because Zoe adored babies and she hadn't wanted to wait when there was no good medical reason to do so.

'You look like a splash of sunlight when you wear yellow,' Raj murmured huskily as Karim was borne off by his nanny for his bath and he intercepted his wife before she could follow them. 'Our little Prince will manage without his parents for one bathtime.'

'But—' Zoe began.

'My son has to *share* you with me,' Raj pointed out, appraising her beautiful smiling face with all-male hunger. 'And this evening when your sisters arrive to celebrate your birthday with you, it'll be giggles and girl talk and I won't get a look-in.'

'Well, if you would just wait until bedtime that wouldn't be the case,' Zoe teased.

'I waited for bedtime the last time!' Raj groaned as he bent her back over one strong arm to engage in kissing a trail across her delicate collarbone that sent a highly responsive quiver through her slight body and flushed her cheeks. 'And you didn't come to bed until *three* in the morning!'

Zoe grinned. 'That'll teach you patience!'

'I'm no good at waiting for you,' Raj confessed, bundling her up into his arms with ease and heading for their bedroom. 'I'm not any better at not missing you when I'm away and I'm even worse at getting by without you in my bed.'

'You've only been away two days, but I missed you too,' Zoe confided with a helpless sigh of contentment as he brought her down on the bed. A little ripple of positively wanton anticipation gripped her as he began to remove his business suit, revealing that long bronzed, lithe and powerful physique she adored.

'I wonder if it's normal to have sex as often as we do,' she muttered abstractedly.

'It's a great healthy workout,' Raj assured her with unholy amusement. 'And wonderfully rewarding if done right.'

'No wonder I love you,' Zoe teased him back with dancing eyes. 'You always do it right!'

'But only with you.' Raj groaned with pleasure as she skimmed her hands over him, and kissed her with a raw, passionate love that made further discussion impossible.

*****

BOUND TO HER DESERT CAPTOR

MICHELLE CONDER

This is for Robyn, who is always warm and welcoming no matter what.

Thanks for taking care of my dad.

CHAPTER ONE

'I'M SORRY, YOUR MAJESTY, but there has been no further information as to your sister's whereabouts.'

Jaeger al-Hadrid, King of Santara, nodded once then turned his back on his silver-haired senior aide. He stared out of the arched windows of his palace office on to the city of Aran below. It was early, the dawn sun bouncing off the Gulf of Ma'an and bathing the sleepy capital of Santara in a golden glow. The pale pink palace perched on the crest of a hill faced the once industrious port that had recently been transformed into a tourist mecca: hotels, restaurants and shopping outlets, tastefully designed to blend the old with the new. It was just one of Jaeger's successful attention-grabbing visions to boost the local economy and showcase the changing face of his kingdom.

He didn't see any of it right now, his mind locked down by the worry brought about by his sister's disappearance.

Where was she? And, more importantly, was she all right?

A week ago he had returned from a business trip to London to find a note on his desk.

Dear Jag,

I know you won't like this but I've taken off for a few weeks. I'm not going to tell you where I'm going be-

cause this is important to me. That's why I haven't taken my cell phone.

No doubt if I did you'd figure out where I'm going before I even get there! But don't worry, I'll be fine.
I love you,
Milena xxx

Don't worry? Don't worry? After what had happened three years ago, how could he do anything but worry?

He reached for the note on his desk, now enclosed in an evidence bag, and had to force himself not to crumple it in his fist. So far the only thing his elite security team had been able to find out was that she had taken a flight to Athens and then disappeared with a man. A man who had been identified as Chad James. An employee, no less, whom Jaeger had personally allowed his sister to work alongside for the past six months.

His jaw hardened and he had to force himself to breathe deeply. Chad James was a brilliant graduate who had been recruited from the States last year to work for his pet company, GeoTech Industries. The company only employed high-energy, intelligent men and women who could think outside the box to create leading-edge technologies that rivalled anything coming out of Silicon Valley. A week ago the young graduate had put in for one month's leave without pay.

Had he coerced Milena into going with him for some lovers' tryst? Or, worse, kidnapped her and planted the note, planning to ask for a ransom any day now?

Jag cursed silently. Since becoming King a decade ago he'd done his best to keep his siblings safe from harm. How had he failed so extraordinarily in that endeavour? How had he got it so spectacularly wrong? Again! Because it *was* his fault. He'd put his sister in harm's way, even if he hadn't known it at the time, and he held himself *fully responsible.*

And it couldn't have come at a worse time.

For the past decade he had worked tirelessly to pull Santara out of the economic and political quagmire his father had inadvertently left it in, and, right when he was on the verge of having Santara recognised as an integral political powerhouse on the world stage, his sister went missing.

The worry was eating him alive.

'How is it possible,' he growled in Tarik's direction, 'that in this day and age no one can find out where she is?'

The elderly man Jag had known since his boyhood shook his head. 'Without her mobile phone or computer there's no way to track her,' Tarik answered, not telling him anything he didn't already know. 'We have accessed security footage in and around the ports of Piraeus, Rafina and Lavrio, as well as the local train stations, but so far we have come up empty-handed.'

A knock at the door cut off Jag's vicious string of curse words. His PA entered, and murmured something to Tarik before casting him a quick, sympathetic glance.

Jaeger's heart thumped into his throat. Please don't let his sister be in trouble.

Noticing his granite-like expression, Tarik shook his head. *No, not the Princess.*

Jag let out a rough breath. Only his tight inner circle knew that Milena was missing. Together they had mobilised a small taskforce of elite soldiers to hunt for her and Chad James, demanding absolute silence in the meantime. Jag hadn't even alerted his brother to Milena's disappearance and he didn't plan to until he had something concrete to give him. Nor had he alerted the Crown Prince of Toran whom Milena was due to marry in a month's time.

The last thing he needed was a scandal of this magnitude, a week out from hosting one of the most important international summits in Santara's history. Leaders from all over the globe would be descending on Santara for four days to discuss world matters including environmental affairs, world health issues, banking and trade deficits. It would be the largest summit of its kind; a pinnacle moment in Santara's rebirth, and his staff had worked tirelessly to see that it came off without a hitch.

'Tell me,' he demanded, noticing the slight hesitation on his aide's pale face.

'I have just been informed that Chad James's older sister landed in Santara an hour ago.'

Jag frowned. 'The sister he emailed the day before he disappeared?'

'I believe so. A report on her has been sent to your inbox.'

Jag sat down at his desk, touching the mouse pad on his computer to awaken the screen. Quickly he found the relevant email, scanned it, and opened the attachment. It was a dossier of sorts.

Name: Regan James
Age: Twenty-five

Height, weight and social security number were all there. Her eyes were brown, her hair brown, and she worked at some posh-sounding school as a teacher. According to the report, she lived alone in Brooklyn, and volunteered at a bereavement centre for kids. No pets and no known convictions or outstanding warrants for her arrest. Parents deceased.

Which Jag already knew from the file that had been compiled on her brother. She also had a photography website. Jaeger flicked to the next page. On it was a photo of

Regan James. It was a half-body shot of her standing on a beach somewhere, her hair tied back in a low ponytail, wisps of it caught by the breeze on the day and flattering her oval-shaped face, her hand raised as if to keep it back. She was smiling, a full-faced smile, showing even white teeth. A camera hung around her slender neck, resting between her breasts. It was a photo of a beautiful woman who didn't look as if she would hurt a fly. And her hair wasn't brown. Not in this photo. It was more auburn. Or russet. And her eyes weren't just brown either, they were…they were… Jag frowned, caught his train of thought and shut it down. They were brown, just as the report said.

'Where is she now?'

'She booked into the Santara International. That's all we know.'

Jag stared at the photo that shimmered on his screen. This woman's brother had taken his sister somewhere and he would move heaven and earth to find them and bring Milena home.

He only hoped Chad James had an army to help him when he finally got his hands around the bastard's scrawny neck, because nothing else would be able to.

'Have her followed,' Jag ordered. 'I want to know where she goes, who she talks to, what she eats and how often she goes to the bathroom. If the woman so much as buys a packet of gum I want to know about it. Is that clear?'

'Crystal, Your Majesty.'

Regan knew as soon as she walked into the shisha bar that she should turn right back around and walk out again. All day she'd trudged around the city of Aran looking for information on Chad, but the only thing she'd learned was that there was hot and then there was *desert* hot.

Despite that, she knew that she would have fallen in

love with the ancient walled city if she were here for any other reason than to find out what had happened to her brother. Unfortunately the more she had searched the city for him the more worried she had become. Which was why she couldn't follow her instinct now and leave the small, dimly lit bar Chad had frequented, no matter how tempting that might be.

The dinky little bar was dressed with various-sized wooden tables and chairs that looked to be filled with mostly local men playing cards or smoking a hookah. Sometimes both. Lilting Arabic music played from some unknown source and the air seemed to be perfumed with a fruity scent she couldn't place. Not wanting to be caught staring, she straightened the scarf she had draped over her head and shoulders in deference to the local custom, and wound her way to the scarred wooden bar lined with faded red leather stools.

The truth was this place was almost her last resort. All day she'd been stymied either by her own sense of inadequacy in trying to navigate the confusing streets of Aran, or by the local people she met who were nowhere near as approachable as the travel-friendly propaganda would suggest. Especially Chad's weasel-like landlord, who had flicked her with a dismissive gaze and informed her that he would not open the apartment without permission from the tenant himself. Having just come from GlobalTech Industries, where she couldn't get anyone at all to answer her questions, Regan hadn't been in the mood to be told no. She'd threatened to sue the shifty little man and when he'd responded by informing her that he would call the police she had said not to bother—she'd go there herself.

Unfortunately the officer on duty had told her that Chad hadn't been missing long enough to warrant an investigation and that she should come back the next day. Everything in Santara functioned at a much slower pace than she was used to. She remembered it was one of the things Chad enjoyed most about the country, but when you were desperate it was hard to appreciate.

Utterly spent and weighed down by both jet lag and worry, she'd nearly cried all over the unhelpful officer. Then she'd remembered Chad mentioning this shisha bar so after a quick shower she had asked for directions from one of the hotel staff. Usually when she went out in New York it was with Penny, and right now she wished she'd persuaded Penny to come with her because she didn't feel completely comfortable arriving at an unknown bar alone. She felt as though everyone was watching her and, truth be told, she'd felt like that all day.

Most likely she was being overly dramatic because she was weighed down by a deep-seated sense of dread that something awful had happened to her brother. She'd felt it as soon as she'd received his off-the-cuff email a week ago warning her not to try and contact him over the next little while because he would be unreachable.

For a man who was so attached to his phone that she often joked it was his 'best friend', that was enough to raise a number of red flags in her head and, try as she might, she hadn't been able to dispel them. A spill-over effect, no doubt, from when she'd had to take over parenting him when he was fourteen. Still, she might have been able to set her worry aside if it hadn't been for her friend and work colleague, Penny, who had regaled her with every morbid story she could remember about how travellers and foreign workers went missing in faraway lands, never to be heard from again.

For two days Regan had ignored her growing fear and tried to contact Chad, but when she'd continued to have no luck Penny had almost bought her the plane ticket to Santara herself. 'Go and make sure everything is okay,' Penny had insisted. 'You won't be any good to the kids here until you do. Plus, you've never been on a decent holiday in the whole time I've known you. At best you'll have a great adventure, at worst…' She'd left the statement unfinished other than to say 'And for God's sake be careful,' which hadn't exactly filled Regan with a lot of confidence.

As she cast a quick glance around the bar as if she knew exactly what she was doing, her gaze was momentarily snagged by a shadowy figure in the far right corner. He was dressed all in black with a *keffiyeh* or *shemagh* of some sort on his head, his wide-shouldered frame relaxed and unmoving in a rickety wooden chair, his long legs extending out from beneath the table. She wasn't sure what it was about him that gave her pause but nor could she shake the feeling that he was dangerous.

A shiver raced down her spine and she told herself not to be paranoid. Still, she felt for the can of mace in her handbag and, satisfied that it was there, pinned a smile on her face and turned towards the bar. A man as big as a fridge stood behind the counter, drying a glass, his expression one of utter boredom.

'What'll it be?' he asked, his voice as rough as chipped cement. As far as greetings went it fell far short of the welcome mark.

'I don't need anything,' Regan began politely. 'I'm looking for a man.'

The bartender's brow rose slowly over black beetled eyes. 'Many men here.'

'Oh, no.' Regan fumbled in her pocket when she realised how that had sounded and pulled out a recent photo of Chad. 'I'm looking for this man.'

The bartender eyed the photo. 'Never seen him before.'

'Are you sure?' She frowned. 'I know he comes here. He said so.'

'I'm sure,' he said, clearly unamused at being questioned. He reached for another glass and started drying it with a dishtowel that looked as if it hadn't seen the inside of a washing machine for days. Maybe weeks. 'You want hookah? I have strawberry, blackberry and peach.' Which would explain the fruity scent she'd noticed when she'd first walked in.

'No, I don't want a hookah,' she said with a note of defeat in her voice. What she needed, she realised, was some sort of guide. Someone who could help her navigate the streets and widen her search for Chad.

She'd thought about hiring a car while she was here but the Santarians drove on the opposite side of the road to what she was used to and, anyway, Regan's sense of direction was not one of her strong points. Some might even call it one of her worst. At least Chad would. Remembering how he had often teased her about how he could turn her in a circle and she wouldn't know which way was north made a lump form in her throat. The thought of never seeing her brother again was too much to bear. He'd been her lifeline after their parents had died. The one thing that had kept her total despair at losing them at bay.

'Suit yourself,' the human fridge grumbled, ambling back down the bar to a waiting customer in local dress. In fact, most of the patrons were dressed in various forms of Arabic clothing. Everyone except the man in the corner. She cast a covetous glance in his direction to find that he was still watching her. And he hadn't moved a muscle. Was he even breathing?

Determined to ignore him, she strengthened her resolve and shoved a dizzying sense of tiredness aside. She was here to find Chad and no oversized bartender, or man in black, was going to put her off. Feeling better, she clutched Chad's photo tightly in her hand and started to move from table to table, asking if anyone knew him or had seen him recently. Of course, no one knew anything, but then, what had she expected? It was just a continuation of the theme of the day. As she grew more and more despondent it wasn't until she had stopped at a large table of men playing baccarat that she realised that the low-level conversation in the bar had dwindled to almost nothing.

Suddenly nervous, she smiled at the men and asked if any of them knew Chad. A couple of them smiled back, their eyes wandering over her. Regan felt the need to cover herself with her hands but knew that she looked perfectly respectable in cotton trousers and a white blouse, the scarf covering her unruly brown hair. One of the men leaned back in his chair, his tone suggestive as he made a comment in Santarian. The other men at the table laughed and Regan knew that whatever he'd said, it hadn't been pleasant. She might be on the other side of the world but some things were universal.

'Okay, thanks for your help,' she said, giving them all her stern schoolteacher look before turning her back and quickly moving to the next table.

Which, unfortunately, was *his* table.

Her gaze skimmed across the table with the untouched hookah on it to his hands folded across his lean abdomen. From there it travelled up the buttons of his shirtfront to his tanned neck and square jaw. Moistening her lips with the tip of her tongue, Regan vaguely registered a sensual unsmiling mouth, a hawk-like nose and the most piercing sapphire-blue eyes she had ever seen. And that was as far as she got. As if she was caught in the crosshairs of a predator's glare she stood frozen to the spot, her gaze held prisoner by his. His eyes glittered with a lethal energy that was startling and Regan had the sudden realisation that she'd never come across a more dangerous-looking or unapproachable man in her life. Her heart palpitated wildly inside her chest as if she'd just stepped in quicksand and was about to sink.

Run! echoed throughout her head but, try as she might, she couldn't make her body obey. Because not only was he dangerous-looking, but he was also sinfully good-looking, and, just as that thought hit, so did a wave of unbridled heat that raced through her whole body and warmed her face.

Good lord, what was she doing noticing his looks at a time like this?

She blinked, her sluggish brain struggling to register her options. Before she could come up with something plausible he moved, kicking the chair opposite him away from the table and blocking her avenue of escape. The sound of the chair scraping across the stone floor made her jump, and once more her heart took off at a gallop.

'Sit down.' His lips twisted into a mocking smile. 'If you know what's good for you.'

His voice was deep and powerful, commanding her to obey even though she knew it was stupid to do so.

This close she could see that he was far more physically imposing than she'd first thought, and completely, unashamedly male. He looked strong enough to be able to pick her up one-handed and take her wherever he pleased. With a start she realised she might not be completely against the idea. A ripple of excitement coursed through her, making her feel even more light-headed than the jet lag.

This was insane.

This *thinking* was insane. She did not react to men like this. Especially not men who looked as if they meandered on the wrong side of the law and won. Every time. Still, what could possibly happen to her in a bar full of patrons? Patrons who were still watching her with curious eyes.

Driven by the need to get out from under those curious glances, she chased off the inner voice of doubt and did as the man suggested, taking a seat and perching her handbag on her lap as some kind of shield between them. He glanced at it as if he'd guessed its purpose and his lips tilted into a knowing smirk.

Feeling exposed under his steady gaze, she somehow defeated the urge to jump back up and leave. It wasn't as if she had many alternatives right now. After this bar she had nowhere to go except back to her hotel room, and then possibly back to Brooklyn. Defeated. She wouldn't do that. Ever.

'Like what you see?'

His deep voice slid over her skin like the richest velvet, making her realise that she'd been caught staring at his mouth. Alarmed, she realised that the tingly sensation swamping her senses was some sort of sexual attraction she couldn't remember ever experiencing before.

A betraying jolt went through her and his lazy, heavy-lidded gaze told her that he was too experienced to have missed it.

Flustered and appalled at her own lack of sense, she dragged her eyes to his. 'You speak English.'

'Evidently.'

His droll tone and imperious gaze made her feel even more stupid than she'd felt already, and she grimaced. 'I meant you speak English *well*.'

His only response was to raise one eyebrow in condescension. Regan got the distinct impression that he didn't like her. But how was that possible when she had never even met him before?

'What are you doing here, American?' His voice was low and rough, his lips curling with disdain.

No, he didn't like her. Not one little bit.

'How do you know I'm American? Are you?'

She hadn't been able to place his accent yet.

He gave her a humourless smile. 'Do I look American to you?'

No, he looked like a man who could tempt a nun to relinquish her vows. And he knew it. 'No. Sorry.'

'So what are you doing here?'

She let out a breath and pulled herself together. She didn't know whether to hold the photo of Chad out to him or not. Despite his relaxed slouch, he looked as if he was ready to pounce on her if she so much as blinked the wrong way. 'I'm…looking for someone.'

'Someone?'

'My brother.' Deciding there couldn't be any harm in showing him the photo, she extended it across the table, making sure their fingers didn't connect when he took it. His eyes held hers for a fraction longer than necessary as if he knew exactly what she was thinking. Which she hoped wasn't true because she was still stuck on the whole sexual attraction thing. 'Have you seen him before?'

'Maybe. Why are you looking for him?'

Regan's eyes widened. Hope welled up inside her at the thought that she might have finally found someone who would be able to help her. 'You have? Where? When?'

'I repeat, why are you looking for him?'

'Because I don't know where he is. Do you?'

'When was the last time you heard from him?'

His tone was blunt. Commanding. And suddenly she felt as though he was the one looking for Chad instead of her.

'Why won't you answer my questions?' she asked, her instincts warning her to tread carefully.

'Why won't you answer mine?'

'I have.' She shifted uncomfortably in her seat. 'How do you know my brother?'

'I didn't say I knew him.'

'But you did…you said…' She shook her head. What exactly had he said? She lifted her hand to her head where it had started to ache. 'Look, if you don't know him just say so. I've had a long day and I'm really tired. Not that you care, I know, but if you know where he is I'd really appreciate you telling me.'

He looked at her for so long she didn't think he was going to say anything. 'I don't know where he is.'

Something in his tone didn't sound right but her brain was so foggy she couldn't pick up on what it was. All she could focus on was a growing despair. After the surge of hope she'd felt moments ago it seemed to weigh more heavily on her than it had all day. 'Okay, well—'

'When was the last time you heard from him?' he asked for a second time.

Regan paused before answering him. She didn't know this man from Adam. He didn't know her either for that matter. So why was he asking her so many questions? 'Why do you want to know that? You already said you don't know where he is.'

He shrugged his broad shoulders. 'I don't. But I didn't say I wouldn't help you.'

Their eyes clashed and Regan had a sudden image of a lethal mountain lion eyeing off a prairie rabbit. 'Help me?'

'Of course. You look like a woman who is almost out of options.'

She *was* a woman who was almost out of options. But how did he know that? Did she look as desperate as she felt?

He smiled at her but it held not a hint of warmth. 'Are you going to deny it?'

Regan's brows drew together. She wanted to deny it but

she couldn't. And really she *could* use some help right now. Especially from someone who was a local and knew the area well. Someone who might even know Chad. But this man had already admitted that he didn't, and frankly he unsettled her. She'd thought he was dangerous when she'd first spotted him from across the room and, while closer inspection might have confirmed that he was incredibly good-looking, it hadn't shifted her initial impression one bit. Which was strange because he hadn't made a single threatening move towards her. Still, she listened to her instincts and there was something about him she didn't trust. 'Thanks anyway, but I'm good.'

'Good?' He gave a humorous laugh. 'You're a foreign woman in a bar, alone at night in a city you don't know. Exactly how are you good, America?'

She pursed her lips at both the nickname he had given her and the element of truth behind his words. When she'd first set out it had been early evening and she hadn't given much thought to the time. All she'd considered was finding information that might lead to Chad. But she wasn't completely vulnerable, was she? She had her mace. 'I just am. I'm from New York. I know what I'm doing.'

'Really? So what's your plan now? You going to go bar-hopping and hold up your little photo to every person you come across?' He made the only idea that had come into her head sound ridiculous. 'That's fine if you're looking for trouble as well as your brother.'

'I'm not looking for trouble,' she retorted hotly.

His gaze narrowed at her haughty tone, his inky black lashes making his blue eyes seem electric. It was totally unfair that she should have brown hair and brown eyes while this man was one of the most beautiful creatures she had ever seen in the flesh.

'Take a look outside. You have been in my country for

less than twenty-four hours and you know nothing about it. You should be glad that I'm offering my assistance.'

Regan narrowed her eyes suspiciously. 'How do you know how long I've been in Santara?'

'Any longer and you would know not to swan into a bar in this part of town without an escort who could take on fifty men.'

Regan felt a trickle of unease roll down her spine. She glanced around the room to find it even busier than before. 'I'd like my photo back, please,' she said, standing to go.

He watched her, unmoving. 'Where are you going?'

As if she was silly enough to tell him that. 'I've taken up enough of your time,' she said briskly, 'and it's getting late.'

'So you're just going to turn around and walk out of here?'

'I am,' she said with more bravado than she felt. 'Do you have a problem with that?'

'I don't know, America; can you take on fifty men?'

Regan shivered at the husky note in his voice, her body responding to him in a way she really couldn't fathom. Their eyes clashed and something raw and elemental passed between them. Again, he hadn't moved but she got the distinct impression that he was a bigger threat to her than fifty other men could ever be.

Not wanting to put that to the test, she gave him a tight smile. 'We'll have to see, won't we?'

Once more conversation slowed as curious eyes surveyed her and Regan stuck her hand in her bag, palming her can of mace, before turning and striding towards the entrance of the bar as if her life depended on it.

Relieved when she made it outside without incident, she sighed and hailed a cab that by some miracle pulled into the kerb in front of her.

'Hello? Are you free?' she asked the pleasant-looking driver wearing some sort of chauffeur's hat.

'Yes, miss.'

'Thank heavens.' She jumped in the back and gave the driver the name of her hotel, only feeling as though she could fully relax when the dark car started moving. Which was when she realised that the stranger in black hadn't given Chad's photo back to her.

She glanced out through the rear window, half expecting to find him standing on the pavement watching her, but of course he wasn't. She was being silly now. And the photo didn't matter. She would print off another one tomorrow.

CHAPTER TWO

JAG STOOD OUTSIDE the door to Regan James's hotel room and questioned the validity of his actions. He'd been doing that the whole drive over.

After meeting her in the bar it was clear that she knew nothing about her brother's whereabouts. She also seemed to know nothing about his sister being with him. But then she had grown cagey when he'd probed her about the last time her brother had contacted her, and he didn't know if that was because her sense of self-preservation had kicked in, or whether she had something to hide.

Regardless, she was his only link to Chad James and she would undoubtedly have a wealth of significant information about her brother that could lead him to find his sister.

A predatory stillness entered his body as he raised his hand to knock at the door. Regan James had been a revelation at the bar. He'd been right when he'd first seen her photo. Her eyes were not brown, they were cinnamon, and her hair was a russet gold that reminded him of the desert sands lit by the setting sun. Her voice had also been a revelation; a husky mixture of warmth and pure sex.

She had evidently reminded some of the other men in the bar of the same thing because Jag had noticed the sensual speculation in more than one male gaze as she had moved through the bar. She had a slender grace that drew the eye and her smile was nothing short of stunning. Even his own breathing had quickened at that first sight of her, and when she'd stood in front of his table, her doe eyes wide and uncertain, he'd had the shocking impulse to reach across the table and drag her into his lap.

It had been a long time since he'd responded to a woman with such unchecked desire and the only reason he was even here was because he'd realised that he couldn't interrogate her in the bar. As it was, some of his people had started to recognise him despite the fact that he'd shaved off his customary neat beard and moustache. He rubbed his hand across his clean-shaven jaw, quite liking the sensation of bare skin. Instantly the thought of rubbing his cheek along Regan James's creamy décolletage entered his head and altered his breathing.

He scowled at the unruly thought. It had been a long time since he'd been influenced by his emotions rather than his intellect as well; some might have said never. Milena often accused him of having ice running through his veins, of being inhuman. He wasn't. He was as human as the next man, as his physical reaction to Regan James earlier had proven.

The fact was, Jag had learned to control his emotions at an early age and he didn't see anything wrong with that. As a leader it was essential that he keep a cool head when everyone else was losing theirs. He had certainly never let a pretty face or a sexy body influence his decision-making process and he never would.

Irritated that he was even pondering emotions and sex, he raised his fist to bang on the door.

He heard the sound of water being shut off and a feminine, 'Just a minute.'

He let out a rough breath. Excellent; she was just out of the shower.

The door opened wide and he found himself staring into

Regan James's gorgeous eyes. Seconds seemed to lengthen into minutes as his eyes automatically travelled down her slender form.

'You!'

'Me,' Jaeger growled, his voice roughened by the swift rise of his body at the sight of her in a cotton dressing gown and towel around her head. He pushed past her into the room before she had a chance to collect herself and slam the door in his face.

'Hold on. You can't come barging in here.'

Jag didn't bother to point out the obvious. That he already had. Instead he scanned the small room, looking for any signs that might clue him in as to where her brother might be.

'Did you hear me?' She yanked on his arm to turn him towards her and the move was so unexpected, so shocking that he did indeed turn towards her, a frown on his face. Nobody touched him without first being given permission to do so. Ever.

His eyes narrowed as she clutched the lapels of her robe closed, making him acutely aware that she was naked beneath the thin cloth. He wanted nothing more than to wrench the garment from her body and sink into her feminine softness until he couldn't remember what it felt like to be burdened by duty. Until he couldn't remember what it felt like to be alone. But no one could escape destiny and one night in this woman's arms wouldn't change anything. Duty and loneliness went hand in hand. He'd learned that from watching his father.

Savagely tamping down on needs that had materialised from who knew where, he scowled at her.

'I heard you.'

'Then…' She lifted her chin in response to his brusqueness. 'What are you doing here?'

Jag glanced at the photo of her brother in his hand before flicking it onto the coffee table. 'You left this behind.'

Her gaze landed on the photo. 'Well…thanks for returning it, but you could have left it with the front desk downstairs.'

Ignoring her, Jag raised the flap of her suitcase and peered at the contents. 'Is this all the luggage you have?'

Frowning at him, she crossed the room and slammed it closed. 'That's none of your business.'

Deciding that he'd wasted enough time humouring this woman, Jag gave her a look that usually sent grown men into hiding. 'I asked you a question.'

This close, he dwarfed her in height and form, but her instincts for survival must have been truly lost because she still didn't move back from him.

'And I asked you to leave,' she shot back.

Jag's lip curled. He would have thought her much braver than she looked if not for that pulse point throbbing like a battering ram at the base of her neck.

'I'm not leaving.' His voice held a dark warning. 'Not before you've told me everything you know about your brother.'

'You do know my brother, don't you?' Finally she took a quick step backwards. 'Do you also know where he is? Did you lie about that?'

'I ask the questions. You answer them,' he stated coldly.

She shook her head. 'Who are you?'

'That is not important.'

'Do you have my brother?' Her voice held a fine tremor of panic. 'You do, don't you?'

Jag's lip curled into a snarl. 'If I had your brother, why would I be here?'

'I don't know.' Those cinnamon-brown eyes were riveted to his. 'I don't know what you want or why you're here.'

She swallowed heavily and Jag felt his chest constrict at her obvious fear. The need to soothe it—the need to soothe her—took him completely by surprise.

Knowing this would go a lot easier if she were relaxed he tried for a conciliatory tone. 'There's no need to be afraid, Miss James. I merely want to ask you some questions.'

His saying her name seemed to jolt something loose inside of her. He saw the rise of panic in the way her eyes darted to the side, clearly searching out an avenue of escape. Before he could think of how to placate her, to put her at ease, she darted, quick as a whippet, towards the hotel room phone.

If he'd wanted to alert hotel security to his presence he'd have called them himself and he had no choice but to stop her, wrapping his arms around her from behind and lifting her bodily off the ground.

She fought him like a little cat with its tail caught in a door, her nails digging into his forearms, the towel around her head whipping him in the face before falling to the ground.

'Keep still,' Jag growled, wincing as her heel connected with his shin. For a little thing she had a lot of spunk in her and if he wasn't so irritated he'd be impressed. 'Dammit, I'm not—' Jag grunted out an expletive as her elbow came perilously close to connecting with his groin.

Deciding to put an end to her thrashing, he spun her around to face him and gripped her hands behind her back, bringing her body into full contact with his. Her flimsy robe had become dislodged during the struggle and this new position put her barely constrained breasts flat up against the wall of his chest. His traitorous body registered the impact and responded as if it belonged to a fifteen-year-old youth rather than a thirty-year-old man who was also a king.

She panted as she glared up at him, her wet hair wild around her flushed face. Jag's breath stalled. Like this, with her cheeks flushed, her lips parted, her breathing ragged, she looked absolutely magnificent. And that was *absolutely* irrelevant.

'I'm going to put you down,' he said carefully. 'If you run again, or go for the weapon in your handbag, I'll restrain you. If you stay put this will be a lot easier.'

For him at least.

Her fulminating glare told him she didn't believe him, but at least she'd stopped struggling.

He shook his head when she remained stubbornly silent and released her anyway. He was twice her size; if she ran again he'd stop her again. Only he'd prefer not to. It was most likely due to the stress of his sister's disappearance, but being this close to Regan James was playing havoc with his senses.

'Where is your phone?'

He'd check to see if she'd received any calls during the day and move on from there. He glanced into her angry face when she didn't immediately answer. By the set of her jaw she had no intention of doing so.

'Miss James, do not infuriate me again by making this more difficult than it has to be.'

'Infuriate you! That's rich! You follow me to my hotel, barge into my room and then attack me. And you're the one who's infuriated?'

'I did not attack you,' Jag said with all the patience of a saint. 'I restrained you and I will do so again if you run again. Be warned.'

She folded her arms across her chest, a shiver racing down her body. 'What do you want?' She lifted her chin at a haughty angle.

'Not you,' he grated, 'so you can rest easy about that.'

She looked at him as if she didn't believe him and he could hardly blame her after the way he'd handled her. Still, it was true. He preferred his lovers sophisticated, compliant and willing. She was none of those three. So why was he so affected by her?

'Take a seat,' he growled, 'so we can get down to what it is that I do want. Which is information about your brother.'

When she remained stubbornly standing Jag sighed and sat himself.

'A week ago your brother wrote to you. Have you spoken to him since?'

'How do you know he wrote to me?'

'I ask the questions, Miss James,' he reminded her with forced patience. 'You answer them.'

'I'm not telling you anything.'

'I would seriously advise you to reconsider that approach.' His voice was steely soft. She might not know it but there wasn't anything he wouldn't do to find his sister, and the reminder that this woman's brother had her reignited his anger. She looked at him as if she wanted to bite him and he felt another unbidden surge of lust hit him hard.

'No, I haven't heard from him,' she finally bit out.

'What made you come to Santara?'

Her lips compressed and for a moment he thought she might defy him again. 'Because he lives here. And I was worried when he didn't answer his cell phone.'

'He did live here.' He wasn't going to for much longer.

She shook her head. 'He wouldn't move without telling me.'

'I take it you're close.'

'Very.'

The soft conviction in her voice jolted something loose inside his chest. He had once been that close to his own siblings. Then his father had died in a light-aircraft crash that had made him King. There hadn't been time for closeness after that. There hadn't been *room* for it.

'What do you know about what your brother has been up to lately?'

'Nothing.'

'Really?' He watched the flush of guilt rise along her neck with satisfaction.

'I don't,' she said, shifting from one foot to the other, her eyes flashing fire and brimstone at him as she fought her desire to defy him. He would have been amused if he didn't find her audacity so invigorating. So arousing.

'I mean, I know that he was enjoying work, that he liked to explore the countryside on weekends, that he had just bought a new toaster oven he was particularly proud of, and that he had a new assistant.'

'A new assistant?'

'Yes. Look, I'm not answering any more of your questions until you answer mine.' She planted her hands on her hips, inadvertently widening the neck of her robe. 'Why are you so interested in my brother?'

Dragging his gaze up from her shadowy cleavage, he savagely tamped down on his persistent libido. 'He has something of mine.' His jaw clenched as he wondered how Milena was. Whether she was okay, or if she was in trouble. If she needed him.

'He stole from you?'

The shock in her voice pulled his mouth into a grim slash. 'You could say that.'

Regan noted the subtle shift in his muscles when he answered her, the coiled tension that clenched his jaw and his fists at the same time. Again she thought of a mountain lion ready to spring. Whatever her brother had taken it was important to this man. And that, at least, explained his interest in Chad. But, while her brother had gone through a couple of rough years after their parents died, he wasn't a bad person. He was smart, much smarter than her, which was why she had worked so hard to make sure he finished high school, finally fulfilling his potential with a university degree in AI at the top of his class. An achievement that had brought him to this country that was, from the little she had seen, both untamed and beautiful.

Much like the stranger in front of her who left her breathless whenever he trained his blue gaze on her as if he was trying to see inside her. Possibly she hated that most of all; the way her body responded to his with just a look.

He was watching her now and it took all her concentration to ignore the sensations spiralling through her. If he hadn't touched her before, grabbed her and held her hard against him it might have been easier.

Regan's nipples tightened at the memory of his arm brushing over her. He was built like a rock, all hard dips and plains that had been a perfect foil for her own curves. And she was in a hotel room alone with him. A man who outweighed her by about a hundred pounds.

'It wasn't Chad,' she said fiercely, forcing her mind back on track.

'It was.'

'My brother isn't a thief,' she said with conviction. 'You've made a mistake.'

'I don't have the luxury of making mistakes in my line of work. Which I have to get back to. Where's your phone?'

'Why do you want my phone?'

Thick black lashes narrowed so that the blue of his eyes was almost completely concealed. 'I've humoured you enough, Miss James. Where is it?'

He uncoiled from the sofa, all latent, angry male energy, and she instinctively stepped back. He noticed, causing her temper to override her anxiety. 'First tell me who you are. You owe me at least that for scaring the life out of me before.'

'Actually I don't owe you anything, America.' His gaze travelled over her with blatant male appraisal. 'I am the King of Santara, Sheikh Jaeger Salim al-Hadrid.'

'The King?' Regan clapped a hand over her mouth to stifle a laugh. The man might have an expensive-looking haircut, now that she could see it without the headdress he'd worn earlier, but with his dark clothing and scuffed boots he looked more like a mercenary than a king. And then another thought struck. Had he been hired to kill Chad? Did he think she would inadvertently lead him to her brother? 'I doubt that. Who are you really?'

She saw instantly that laughing at this man was the wrong thing to do. His blue gaze pinned her to the spot, his body going hunting-still. 'I am the King,' he said coldly, taking a step towards her.

'Okay, okay.' Regan held her hand out to ward him off. 'I believe you.' She didn't but he didn't need to know that. As long as he left—and soon—that was all she needed him to do.

She forced her brain to forget about the perfect symmetry of his face and start thinking more about surviving. He was clearly a madman—or a potential killer—and she was alone with him in her room.

Fresh fear spiked along her spine. She tried to remember that everyone said she had a gift for communicating but this was no recalcitrant seven-year-old with a smartphone hidden beneath his desk.

'You think I'm lying?' he said softly.

'No, no.' Regan rushed to assure him, only to have him bark out a harsh sound that was possibly laughter.

'Unbelievable.'

He shook his head and Regan briefly measured the distance from her to the door.

'Too far,' he murmured, as if reading her mind. Probably not difficult, since she was staring at the door as if she was willing it to open by itself. Which she was.

'Look—'

He moved so quickly she barely got one word out before he was in front of her. 'No more questions. No more games. Give me your phone or I'll tear everything apart until I find it.'

'Bathroom.'

His eyes narrowed.

'I was taking a shower when you turned up,' she said. 'I like to play music while I'm in there.'

'Get it.'

Nearly demanding that he say 'please', Regan decided that the best thing she could do was to stay quiet. The sooner he got what he was looking for, the sooner he would leave.

Moving on wooden legs, she walked towards the bathroom, coming up short when he followed her. Staring back at him in the bathroom mirror, she saw just how big he was, his wide shoulders filling the doorway and completely blocking out the view of the room behind him.

Their eyes connected and for a brief moment awareness charged the air between them, turning her hot. Flustered, she dropped her eyes and picked up her phone. She handed it to him, crossing her arms over her chest in a purely protective gesture.

'Password?'

Heat radiated from his body, surrounding her, and she wished he'd move back. 'Trudyjack,' she said grudgingly.

'Your parents' names?' He gave her a bemused look. 'You might as well have used ABC.'

Regan's eyes flashed to his. How did he know they were her parents' names? *How did he know so much about her?*

'Who are you?' she whispered, frightened all over again.

'I told you. I am the King of Santara. I knew everything about you less than an hour after your plane landed in my country.'

Regan swallowed hard and pressed herself against the basin behind her. Could he really be who he said he was? It didn't seem possible, and yet he did have an unmistakable aura of power and authority about him. But then so did killers, she imagined.

She watched him scroll through her contact list and emails, his scowl darkening in the lengthening silence.

'Chad's phone is switched off,' she said, unable to keep her vow of silence from moments ago. She couldn't help it. She'd never been good with silences and when she was nervous that only became worse. 'I know because I've tried to call him daily.'

'He doesn't have his phone with him.'

'Then what are you searching for on my phone?'

'A burner number. An email from an unknown source.'

'How do you know he doesn't have it with him?'

Ignoring her question, he asked another one of his own. 'Does he have a second phone?'

Regan frowned. Why would Chad not take his phone with him? His phone was his lifeline. 'No. But I wouldn't tell you even if he did.'

His blue eyes melded with hers, a zing of heat landing low in her belly.

'You like to provoke me, don't you, Miss James?'

Regan's heart skipped a beat at his warning tone. No, she didn't like to provoke him. She really didn't.

With a look of disgust he pocketed her phone. She wanted to tell him that he couldn't keep it because her phone was her lifeline too, but at this point she'd do almost anything to placate him and make him go away.

'Satisfied?' she asked, the word husky on her lips.

'Hardly.' His gaze raked down over her again and she became acutely aware of her nudity beneath her robe. The small room seemed to shrink even more and the air grew heavy between them, making it nearly impossible for her to breathe. The man had a dire effect on her system, there was no question about that.

'Why were you so keen to jump on a plane and fly here after that one email?'

'I…' Regan swallowed. 'I was worried. It's not like Chad to be out of contact.'

'So you rushed over here because you thought he might be in trouble? Do you always put your brother first, or is it that you like to feel indispensable?'

Regan's pride jolted at his words because there was some truth to them. Becoming Chad's guardian and throwing herself into the role had helped to fill a void in her life and move on from her grief.

Hot colour flamed in her face. 'You don't know me.'

'Nor do I want to. Get dressed,' he ordered before turning and walking back into the main room.

Regan exhaled, willing herself to be calm. She moved to the doorway to find him going through the photos on her camera. Instantly she went into panic mode. 'Hey, don't touch that. It's old and I can't afford to replace it.'

She lunged to retrieve her precious camera and he held it aloft. 'I'm not going to break it,' he snapped. 'Not unless you keep trying to grab it.'

Snatching her hand back from where it had landed on the hard ball of his shoulder, she slapped her hands on her hips. 'I don't care who you are, you have no right to go through my things.'

He gave her a dismissive glance to say that he had every right and even if he didn't there wasn't a damned thing she could do about it. 'There isn't anything I won't do to get my sister back, Miss James. You'd better get used to that idea.'

His sister?

Regan frowned. 'What has your sister got to do with anything?'

Slowly his gaze returned to hers, the blue so clear and so cold she could have been staring into a glacier. 'Your brother has my sister. And now I have his.'

'That's insane.'

'For once we agree on something.'

'No, I mean you're insane. My brother isn't with your sister. He would have told me.'

'Really?'

Maybe. Maybe not. 'Are they in a relationship or something?' If they were she was a bit hurt that he hadn't told her. They had always shared everything in the past.

'You'd better hope not. Now move. My patience is at an end. I need to return to the palace.'

Wait? Was he really the King of Santara?

'I'm… I'm not going anywhere with you.'

'If you insist on going as you are I won't stop you. But you'll get far more looks than you did earlier, parading around in tight jeans and a flimsy shirt.'

'My clothes were perfectly respectable, thank you very much.'

'You have five minutes.'

'I'm not going with you.'

'That's your choice, of course, but the alternative is that you remain in this room until your brother returns.'

Regan frowned. 'You mean as in *locked* in here?'

'I can't afford to have my sister's disappearance become public knowledge. With you asking questions and wandering around on your own you'll only draw attention to yourself. And, no doubt, get yourself into trouble in the process.'

'I won't say anything. I promise!'

Regan knew she sounded desperate and she was. The thought of being locked in a hotel room for who knew how long was not acceptable. If what this man said was true she wanted freedom to find Chad and figure out what was going on. Preferably before this man found him.

He shook his head. 'Make your decision. I don't have all night.'

'I'm not staying here!'

'Then get dressed.'

Regan's mind was spinning out of control. Her head, already fuzzy from lack of sleep, was struggling to keep pace with the rate at which things were moving. 'I need more time to think about this.'

'I gave you five minutes. You now have four.'

'I don't think I've ever met a more arrogant person than you. Actually, strike that: I know I haven't.'

He folded his hands across his chest, his muscular legs braced wide, his expression hard. Like this he looked as if he could take on fifty men blindfolded and win.

'Your telephone service will be disconnected and I will have guards posted outside your door. I do not advise you to try to leave.'

'But how do I know you are who you say you are?' she said on a rush. 'You could be an imposter for all I know. A murderer. I'd be crazy to go with you.'

'I am not a murderer.'

'I don't know that!'

'Get dressed and I'll prove it to you.'

'How?'

He heaved an impatient sigh. 'You can ask any member of the hotel staff downstairs. They will know who I am.'

For the first time since he had barged into her room Regan saw a way out. If he was really going to take her downstairs then she had a chance of alerting someone as to what was going on.

'Okay, just…' She grabbed a clean pair of jeans and a long-sleeved shirt from her case. 'Just give me a minute.'

Locking herself in the bathroom, she very nearly didn't come back out but decided that he'd most likely break the door down if she aggravated him too much. He had the arms for it.

Concentrating more on his abundant negative qualities, she opened the door to find him propping up the opposite wall, looking at his watch. 'One minute early. I'm impressed.'

Arrogant jerk.

Regan grabbed her handbag and walked ahead of him out the door. She waited as he stabbed the elevator button. 'If you're really a king, where are all your guards?'

'I rarely take guards with me on unofficial business. I can take care of myself.'

Convenient, she thought.

'And why was it that no one in the shisha bar knew your identity? If you're really the King I would have expected some bowing and scraping.'

The slow smile he gave her told her he wouldn't mind making her bow and scrape for him. 'I've found that people rarely see what they're least expecting.'

Regan raised a brow. She couldn't argue with that. She might have thought he looked dangerous when she had first seen him, but she hadn't expected him to turn up at her door making outrageous accusations about her brother. Nor had she expected him to tell her he was the King. Though whether or not that was true still remained to be seen.

'How's the headache?' he asked, watching her in the mirrored wall. Regan slid her gaze to his. 'Don't bother denying it,' he continued. 'You're so pale you look like you're about to pass out.'

'My head is fine.' She wasn't about to admit that he was right. She wasn't sure what he would do with the information. She wouldn't put it past him to try to make it worse.

When they arrived at the lobby Regan felt a surge of adrenaline race through her. Glancing around, she was disappointed to find that the large lobby was mostly empty. Before she could make a move in either direction her arm was gripped, vice-like, and she was towed along towards the reception desk.

The smile on the young man's face faltered as he took them in. They probably looked quite a sight, she thought grimly. Her with her fast-drying hair no doubt resembling a wavy cloud around her head, and her unwanted companion with a scowl as dark as his clothing.

'Ah, Your Majesty, it is an honour.' The man bowed towards the desk, his expression one of eternal deference. Then he said something in Santarian that her companion answered. The younger man's eyes went as big and as round as a harvest moon.

'But…' He gave her a panicked look. 'Miss James, this is His Majesty the King of Santara.' The words almost came out in a stutter, as if he couldn't quite believe he was saying them.

Frankly, nor could Regan. 'How do I know you haven't just set this up?' she said with disdain. 'One man's opinion is hardly folk law.' Turning back to the concierge, Regan said, 'Actually, I'd like to report—'

She didn't get any further as the stranger beside her growled something low under his breath and then towed her further into the lobby, veering off towards the sound of a pianist playing a soulful song. Through French windows Regan saw a room full of people.

Stopping just inside the entrance, they stood waiting until finally most of the room grew silent, staring at the two of them. Then half of the occupants stood and bowed low towards the man still holding her arm.

Regan shook her head, her brain refusing to compute the evidence that he really was the King of Santara. Which meant that if he was right then maybe her brother was with his sister, *Princess* Milena, his new research assistant. She swallowed, swaying on her feet.

Clearly worried she was about to do something girly, like swoon in his presence, the King snaked a hand around her waist, pulling her up against him. Regan set her hand flat against his chest to stop their bodies colliding. Her head fell back on the stem of her neck as the heat from his body sapped the last of her strength. She could feel his heart pounding a steady rhythm to match her own but all she could focus on was the blue of his eyes, indigo in the soft light. Time seemed to disappear as he looked back at her with such heat Regan's thoughts ceased to exist. It didn't matter who she was or what he was. All that mattered was that he kiss her. Kiss her so that the ache building inside her subsided.

A soft growl left his throat, his eyes devouring her lips, and for a brief moment she thought he *would* kiss her.

But then his eyes turned as sharp as chipped jewels and his hand tightened on her hip. 'Satisfied?' he murmured, throwing her earlier question back at her.

Regan shook her head, her balance precarious despite his firm hold. She heard the word 'no' coming from a long, dark tunnel right before she did something she'd never done before. She fainted.

CHAPTER THREE

Two nights later Jag sat behind his large desk brooding over the voice message he had received from Milena.

'Hi Jag. I know you're worried—you're you—and I'm sorry I can't tell you where I am, or what I'm doing, but I want you to know that I'm with a friend and I'm fine. I'll explain everything when I return. I love you.'

'Any idea where the call originated from?' he asked Tarik.

'Unfortunately not. It was likely made from a burner phone and it was sent through several different carriers. Whoever scrambled the transmission is good.'

Chad had scrambled the transmission, of that Jag was one hundred percent certain; he'd hired the kid in the first place because he was a borderline genius with technology. Anger coursed through him, a hot and welcome replacement for the impotence he'd felt since she'd gone.

He turned to stare outside the window, brooding. On the one hand he was happy that his sister was safe and well, but the reality was that she could have been forced into making that phone call. Not that she'd sounded forced. She'd sounded full of vigour. Almost buoyant. A state he hadn't seen her in for quite a while. A state he would welcome if the memory of what had transpired three years ago wasn't like a smoking gun in his mind.

Then there was the obvious assumption that if she hadn't

been forced to leave Santara then she'd gone somewhere with Chad James of her own free will, and that raised a whole host of ugly questions Jag didn't want to consider. Questions like, what were they doing together that Milena wasn't able to tell him about? Like maybe she was considering not going through with the marriage to the Crown Prince of Toran? Questions like, was she unhappy, and, if so, why hadn't she come to him the way she used to when she was a child?

He rubbed his fingers hard across his forehead. Well, of course she'd been coerced. There was no other way to look at this. Just as he had coerced Regan James into coming to the palace. He recalled the moment she had fainted when she had discovered that he was actually the King, the dead weight of her body as she'd slumped in his arms. He'd had a lot of reactions from women in the past when they'd found out he was royalty—everything from obsequious preening to outright manipulation—but he'd never had a woman faint on him before. Which had been a good thing because right before that he'd nearly given in to an urge he'd been fighting all night and leant down and kissed her. In public! He didn't know what bothered him about that the most: the fact that his inimitable self-control had taken a long hike, or that he would have shocked the hell out of those watching.

Shocked himself, he'd quickly scooped her into his arms and taken her out to his waiting SUV. She'd come to fairly quickly in the car, demanding that he return her to her hotel, but he had calmly reminded her that it had been her choice to come with him and that she was now out of options.

Well aware that his behaviour had been less than stellar with regard to the American woman, he pushed thoughts of her, and his sister, from his head and picked up the raft of reports he needed to sign off. 'These can go to Helen to have the corrections worked up, these can go back to Finance, and this one I still have to read. Tell Ryan I'll get to it later tonight.'

'Very good.'

He rubbed the back of his neck. 'For once I hope that's it for the night.' He gave Tarik a faint smile and saw the old man hesitate. It was only the slightest of movements but Jag knew him too well to miss it. His body immediately shifted into combat mode. 'What is it? And please tell me it has nothing to do with the American.'

As much as he had been trying to keep her presence in the palace under wraps, she had been trying to stop him. Banging on the door of her suite, demanding that she be given her phone and her computer, demanding that she be released, demanding that he come to her. But Jag didn't want to go to her. Already her voice and the memory of her scent had imprinted themselves on his brain. He couldn't imagine that seeing her was going to make that any better.

'Unfortunately it does. She is refusing to eat,' Tarik said.

'Refusing to eat?' Jaeger felt his stomach knot. 'Since when?'

'Since last night, sir. She did not eat her evening meal and today she has rejected all food.'

Jag's jaw hardened. If Regan thought she was going to make herself ill by not eating she had another thing coming.

Trying not to overreact, he pushed himself to his feet. 'What time is her evening meal due to be delivered?'

'It has been delivered. She sent it away.'

Jaeger scowled. 'Have my dinner taken to her suite in half an hour.'

He made to leave but again Tarik hesitated.

'Please tell me you've left the best to last,' Jag drawled.

Tarik grimaced. 'Not exactly, Your Majesty, but I have it in hand.' He passed Jaeger a printout from a local news website. On it were two photos of himself and Regan standing close together. They must have been snapped by one of the patrons in the hotel, the camera perfectly capturing the moment she had discovered he was the King: her eyes wide, lips softly parted, wild mane cascading down her back like a silken waterfall. The next was right before she'd fainted. Jag had tangled his fingers through her hair to cup the nape of her neck, his other hand tight around her waist. Her face had been upturned, her mouth inches from his own. Would those pink lips have tasted as pure and sweet as they looked? Would the skin of her abdomen feel as soft beneath his fingertips as the nape of her neck? Would—?

Tarik cleared his throat. Jag inhaled deeply, uncomfortably aware that his trousers were fitting a little snugger than they were before. What the hell was wrong with him?

'Fortunately they were taken down before any damage was done,' Tarik informed him. 'And the woman's name was not discovered. But I thought you should be informed.'

'Of course I should be informed.' He glanced at the images again, an idea forming in his mind at rapid speed. If he was going to detain Regan James until her brother returned then by damned he would make her useful to him. 'Republish the photos.'

'Your Majesty?'

'Make sure her name is attached and that the images are picked up by the international Press. If the sight of her in my arms doesn't bring her brother out of the woodwork, I don't know what will.'

Tarik looked at him as if he wanted to protest but Jag wasn't in the mood to listen. He wanted a hot meal, a cool shower and a peaceful night's sleep. Since meeting her the American woman had interfered with the latter; now it seemed she would be interfering with the first two as well.

* * *

Regan's stomach grumbled loudly in the silent room and she pressed her palm against her belly. 'It's been one day,' she told her objectionable organ. 'People can survive a lot longer than that without food, so stop complaining.'

She didn't know exactly how long a human being could survive without food, but she recalled various movies about survival and knew it was more than a day.

Mind you she was starving and her errant brain advised her that food would help to keep her strength up. And that the arrogant ruler of Santara wouldn't care about her eating habits anyway.

But it wasn't just the lack of food bothering her. It was the boredom and worry. She'd come to Santara to make sure Chad was okay. Not only was she not doing that but she wasn't doing anything at all. She'd never had so much time on her hands and she was going crazy. The first day she had kept herself busy taking photos of the amazing garden suite she was imprisoned in; the arched Moorish windows, the Byzantine blues and greens that were used to colour the room and the amazing studded teak doors, the one keeping her locked in being the most beautiful of all, which she refused to see as ironic in any way.

Then there was the garden with the swaying palm trees, and deep blue tiled pool. The whole place was stunning and she itched to download her images onto her laptop and play around with the lighting and composition. If she'd been in this magical place under any other circumstances she doubted she'd want to leave.

But more than that she wanted to see the King again. Not because she wanted to see him per se, but because she wanted to know if he had an update on Chad. She hadn't realised when she'd made the choice to leave her hotel room that she'd be swapping one prison for another. Perhaps if she hadn't been so tired and strung-out, if he'd given her more time to consider her options, she would have made a different choice. She certainly wouldn't have thought about what it would feel like to kiss him!

She groaned softly in mortification as she recalled the moment he'd held her against him in the hotel lobby, the moment he'd held her inside her hotel room, his hot eyes on her cleavage, their bodies melded together so tightly she was convinced she'd felt… *Don't go there*, she warned herself. Bad enough that she'd recounted those times second by second in her dreams. The man might be stunningly attractive, but he was holding her against her will and accusing her brother of a terrible crime.

A crime she was even more convinced, now that she'd had some sleep, that he would never commit. If only that blasted King would give her the time of day so she could explain that to him. Explain what a gentle soul her brother was. Explain that Chad was the type to save baby birds in their back garden, not stomp on them.

When her brother had finished university and taken the prestigious opening at GeoTech Industries she'd thought her days of worrying about him had come to an end.

She'd been eighteen when their parents died and she'd been thrust into the role of parent. And she'd thought she'd done okay. But if Chad really had run off with the King's sister… She rubbed at her bare forearms, chilled despite the humid warmth of the night air. She couldn't take the King's claim seriously. Chad just wouldn't do something like that, she knew it. She knew him!

Sensing more than hearing a presence behind her, Regan slowly turned to find the man who had taken her captive standing in her living area. Her heart skipped a beat before taking off at a gallop. He looked magnificent in a white robe that enhanced his olive skin and blue eyes to perfection. He wasn't wearing a headdress tonight, his black hair thick and a little mussed from where it looked as though he had dragged his fingers through it countless times during the day. The glow from the elaborate overhead chandeliers threw interesting light and shadows over his face, making him even more handsome than she remembered.

'Miss James.'

Her name was like thick, rich treacle on his lips and she shivered, hiding her unwanted reaction by stepping forward. 'So you've finally decided to show up,' she grouched, instinct advising her that attack was the best form of defence with a man like this. 'How kind of you.'

He gave her a faint smile. 'I understand you're not eating.'

A small thrill of satisfaction shot through her. So her self-imposed starvation had worked. 'Yes. And I won't until you release me.'

He shrugged one broad shoulder as if to say that his care factor couldn't be lower. 'That's your choice. You won't die.'

'How do you know?' she shot back.

'It takes three weeks for a person to starve to death. You're in no danger yet.'

Resenting his sense of superiority, Regan frowned as he clapped his hands together and two servants wheeled a dining cart into the room. One by one they set an array of platters on the dining table near the window.

'Will that be all, Your Majesty?'

'For now.'

Regan gave him a look as they bowed and exited the room. 'Don't expect that clapping trick to work with me,' she warned. 'I'm not one of your minions.'

His silky gaze drifted over her and she wished she were wearing more than a pair of shorts and a T-shirt. If she'd thought he might actually show up she'd have pulled a curtain from the wall and draped herself in it. Anything so that she didn't feel so exposed.

'No, that would take far more optimism than even I have for that to occur.'

He moved to the dining table and took a seat, inspecting the array of stainless-steel dishes the servers had laid out.

'No matter what you say,' she advised him, 'I won't eat.'

He gave her a long-suffering look. 'Believe it or not, Miss James, I do not wish for you to have a bad experience during your stay in the palace. I even hoped that we might be...friends.'

'Friends?'

He shrugged. 'Acquaintances, then.'

Regan couldn't have been more incredulous if he'd suggested they take a spaceship to Mars. 'And you say you're not optimistic.' She scoffed. 'The only thing I want from you is for you to release me.'

'I can't do that. I already told you that I will do whatever it takes to have my sister returned home safely.'

'Just as I would do whatever it takes to have my brother returned home safely as well.'

He inclined his head, a reluctant smile tugging at the corners of his mouth. 'On this we understand each other.'

Not wanting to have anything in common with the man, Regan set him straight. 'What I understand is that you're an autocratic, stubborn, overbearing tyrant.'

He didn't respond to her litany of his faults and she narrowed her eyes as he uncovered the small platters of delicious-smelling food. His imperviousness to her only made her temper flare hotter.

Then her stomach growled, making her feel even more irritable. She watched him scoop up a dip with a piece of flatbread, his eyes on her the whole time. His tongue came out to lick at the corner of his mouth and a tremor went through her. 'You look ridiculous when you eat,' she lied. 'Can't you do that somewhere else?'

Expecting him to become angry with her, she was shocked when he laughed. 'You know, your disposition might be improved if you stopped denying yourself your basic needs. Hunger strikes are very childish.'

Stung to be called childish, Regan stared down at him. 'My disposition will only improve when you release me and stop saying awful things about my brother.'

His eyes narrowed when she mentioned Chad, but other than that he didn't show an ounce of emotion; instead he scooped up more food with his fingers and tempted her with it.

Irritated, she thought about moving outside but then decided against it. If he was going to antagonise her she would do the same back.

'You cannot think to stick with this plan,' she said, wandering closer to him.

Curious blue eyes met hers. 'What plan?'

'The one to keep me here until my brother returns with your sister.'

He leaned back in his chair, wiping his mouth with his napkin. As he regarded her Regan's eyes drifted over the hard planes of his face, those slashing eyebrows and his surly, oh, so sinful mouth. He would photograph beautifully, she thought. All that dominant masculine virility just waiting to be harnessed… It gave a girl the shivers. She could picture him astride a horse, outlined against the desert dunes with the sun at his muscled back. Or asleep on soft rumpled sheets, his muscular arms supporting his head, his powerful thighs—

Regan frowned. Sometimes her creative side was a real pain.

'Is that my plan?' His deep voice held a smooth superiority that set her teeth on edge.

'Well, obviously. But I already told you that I wouldn't say anything about your sister being missing. I'm even willing to sign something to say that I won't.'

'But how do I know I can trust you?'

'Because I'm a very trustworthy person. Call my boss. She'll tell you. I never say anything I don't mean or do anything I say I won't.'

'Admirable.'

'Don't patronise me.' She gripped the back of the carved teak dining chair opposite him. The smell of something delicious wafted into her sinuses and she nearly groaned. 'You're really horrible, you know that?'

'I've been called worse.'

'I don't doubt it. Oh…' She clenched her aching stomach as it moaned again, and glared at him. 'You did this on purpose, didn't you?'

'Did what?' he asked innocently.

'Brought food in here. You're trying to make me so hungry that I'll eat despite myself. Well, it won't work.' She glared into his sapphire-blue eyes. 'You can't break me.'

She wheeled away from the table, intending to spend the rest of the night in the garden until he left, but she didn't make it two steps before he stopped her, wrapping his arm around her waist and hauling her against him.

Regan let out a cry of annoyance and banged her fists down on his forearms.

'Stop doing that,' she demanded. Already her skin felt hot, her unreliable senses urging her to turn in his arms and press up against him. 'I hate it when you touch me.'

'Then stop defying me,' he grated in her ear, yanking the chair she'd just been gripping out from the table and dumping her in it.

'You like doing that, don't you?' she accused, rubbing her bottom to erase the impression left behind from being welded to his hard stomach. 'Using your brute strength to get what you want.'

He picked up his fork and pointed it at her. 'Eat. Before I really lose my temper and ask the palace doctor to get a tube and feed you that way.'

'You wouldn't dare.'

The smile on his face said he would, and that he'd enjoy it.

'I'm only doing this because now that I know you won't let me go I'm going to need my strength to escape,' she said, snatching up a delicate pastry from a silver platter and shoving it into her mouth. It dissolved with flaky deliciousness on her tongue, making her reach for another. She murmured appreciatively and blushed when she found him staring at her. 'What?' she grouched. 'Isn't this what you wanted all along?'

'Yes.' His voice was deep and low, and turned her insides to liquid.

Not wanting him to know just how much he affected her, she decided to take another tack. 'This is preposterous, you know?'

He glanced at her. 'The food? My chef will not be pleased to hear that.'

'Keeping me here.' She picked up her fork and stabbed at something delicious looking. 'It's the twenty-first century and you appear to be an educated man.' Though that was popular opinion, not hers. 'A ruler, for heaven's sake. You can't just impose your will on others whenever you feel like it.'

He gave a short bark of laughter. 'Actually I can.' He piled more food onto his plate. 'And I am aware of the century. But in my country the King creates the laws, which pretty much gives me carte blanche to do what I want, whenever I want.'

'That can't be true.' She frowned. 'You must have checks and balances. A government of some sort.'

'I have a cabinet that helps me govern, if that's what you mean.'

'And what's their job? To rubber-stamp whatever you say?'

'Not quite.'

'They must be able to order you to let me go.'

'Not quite.'

Completely exasperated, Regan put down her fork. 'Look, you're making a big mistake here. I know my brother is innocent.'

His eyes narrowed on hers. 'We've had this conversation. Eat.'

'I can't. The conversation is killing my appetite.'

'Then stop talking.'

'God, you're impossible. Tell me, what makes you think that my brother has taken your sister? Because it's not something my brother would do. He's not a criminal.'

'He stole a car when he was sixteen and copies of his finals exams when he was seventeen.'

'Both times the charges were dropped,' she defended. 'And how do you even know this? Those files are closed because he was a minor.'

He gave her a look and she rolled her eyes. 'Right, you know everything.' She took a deep breath and let it out slowly. 'Chad got into the wrong crowd with the car thing and he stole the exam papers to sell them to help me out financially. We had a hot-water system to replace in our house and no money. He didn't need to steal the exams for himself. He's a straight-A student. Anyway, that's a lot different from *kidnapping* someone,' she shot at him.

'To say that you've been kidnapped is a trifle dramatic. You came to my country of your own free will. Now you are being detained because you're a threat to my sister's security.'

'I had nothing to do with your sister's disappearance!'

'No, but your brother did,' he pointed out silkily, 'and as you've already confirmed he has the capability for criminal activity.'

'He was young and he was going through a hard time,' she cried. 'That doesn't mean he's a career criminal.'

'Why was he having a hard time?'

'I'm surprised you don't know,' she mumbled; 'you seem to know everything else.'

He handed her a warm triangle of pastry. 'I know that your parents both died of cancer seven weeks apart. Is that what you're referring to?'

'Yes.' Emotion tightened her chest. 'Chad was only fourteen at the time. It hit him hard and he didn't really grieve properly… I think it caught up with him.'

'That must have been hard to have both parents struck down by such a terrible disease. I'm sorry.'

'Thank you.' She shook her head and bit into the food he'd handed her, closing her eyes at the exquisite burst of flavours on her tongue. 'This is delicious. What is it?'

'It is called a *bureek*, a common delicacy in our region.' He frowned as he dragged his eyes up from her mouth. 'Who looked after the two of you when your parents died?'

'I was eighteen,' she said, unconsciously lifting her chin. 'I deferred my photography studies, got a job and took care of us both.'

He frowned. 'You had no other family who could take you in?'

'We had grandparents who lived across the country, and

an aunt and uncle we saw on occasion, but they only had room for Chad and neither one of us wanted to be parted.'

His blue eyes studied her for a long time, then he handed her another morsel of food. She took it, completely unprepared for his next words. 'I lost my father when I was nineteen.'

'Oh, I'm sorry,' she said instinctively. She missed her parents every day and her heart went out to him. 'How did he die?'

'He was killed in a helicopter crash.'

'Oh that's awful. What happened to you?'

'I became King.'

'At nineteen? But that's so young.'

He handed her another type of pastry. 'I was born to lead. For me it wasn't an issue.'

Wasn't an issue?

Regan stared at him. He might say it wasn't an issue but she knew how hard it was to take on the responsibility of one brother, let alone an entire country. 'It couldn't have been easy. Did you have time to mourn him at least?'

She noticed a flicker of surprise behind his steady gaze. 'I was studying in America when his light aircraft went down. By the time I arrived home the country was in turmoil. There were things to be done. Try the *manakeesh*.' He indicted the food she forgot she was holding. 'I think you'll like it.'

That would be a no, then, she thought, biting into a delicious mixture of bread, spice and mince. His slight grin told her he knew that she'd enjoyed it. She shook her head, trying to make sense of their conversation.

He might sound as if he were talking about little more than a walk in the park, but Regan could tell by the slight tightening of the skin around his eyes that his father's death had affected him very deeply. 'How old was your sister at the time?'

'My sister was eight.' He tore off a piece of flatbread and dipped it in a dark purple dip. 'My brother was sixteen.' He handed her the bread.

'You have a brother?'

'Rafa. He lives in England. The *baba ganoush* is good, yes?'

'Yes, it's delicious.' She licked a remnant of the dip from the corner of her mouth, frowning when she realised what he was doing. 'Why are you feeding me?'

His piercing gaze met hers. 'I like feeding you.'

Something happened to the air between them because suddenly Regan found it hard to draw breath. She reached for her water glass. Their conversation had taken on a deeply personal nature and it was extremely disconcerting.

'I can't stay here,' she husked. For one thing, she needed to find Chad, and for another…for another, this man affected her on levels she didn't even know she had and she had no idea what to do about it.

'You have no proof that my brother did anything wrong.'

His gaze became shuttered. 'That topic of conversation is now closed.'

Agitated, Regan stared at him. 'Not until you tell me what makes you so certain Chad has taken your sister.'

Leaning back in his chair, he took so long to answer her she didn't think that he would. 'We have CCTV footage of them together and after she'd gone my sister left a message on my voicemail informing me that she was with a friend.'

Regan frowned. 'That hardly sounds like someone who has been taken against her will.'

'Milena is due to marry a very important man next month. She would not have put all of that at stake if she wasn't forced to do so.'

'Maybe she doesn't want to marry him any more.'

A muscle jumped in the King's jaw. 'She agreed to the marriage and she would never shirk her duties. Ever.'

His sister might have agreed, Regan mused silently, but having to marry out of duty would make most women think twice. 'Does she love the important man she's going to marry?'

'Love is of no importance in a royal marriage agreement.'

'Okay.' Regan thought love was important in *any* marriage agreement. 'I'll take that as a no.'

'You can take it any way you want,' he ground out. 'Love is an emotional concept and does not belong in the merger of two great houses.'

'Merger? You make it sound like a business proposition.'

'That is as good a way of looking at it as any.'

'It's also harsh. What about affection? Mutual respect? What about *passion*?'

She had no idea where that last had come from—she'd meant to say *love*.

His gaze narrowed in on her mouth and a hot tide of colour stung her cheeks. 'Those things can come later. After the marriage is consummated.'

'That's provided you marry someone nice,' Regan pointed out. 'What if this important man is horrible to her?'

'The Crown Prince of Toran will not be horrible to my sister or he will have me to answer to.'

'That's all well and good in principle, but it doesn't mean your sister *wants* it. I mean, don't get me wrong, there isn't anything I wouldn't do for my family, but when it comes to marriage I'd like to choose my own husband. Most women would.'

'And what would you choose?' His voice was deep and mocking. 'Money? Power? Status?'

His questions made Regan feel sorry for him. Clearly he'd met some shallow women in his time, which went some way to explaining his attitude. 'That is such a cynical point of view,' she replied. 'But no, those things wouldn't make my top three.'

'Let me guess,' he said, a sneer in his voice. 'You want kindness, a sense of humour, and someone to want you just for you.'

Surprised that he'd hit the nail on the head, Regan was flummoxed when he started laughing.

'I don't see what's so funny,' she griped. 'That's what most women want.'

'That's what most women *say* they want,' he retorted with masculine derision. 'I've found that those things fall far short of the mark unless money and power are involved.'

'Then I'd say you've been dating women far short of the mark. Maybe you need to raise your expectations.'

'When I marry, Miss James, it will not be for kindness, love or humour.'

'No,' Regan agreed, 'I'm sure there'll be nothing funny about it. Or loving.'

His lips tightened at her comment. 'I don't need love.'

'Everyone needs love. Believe me, I see the kids in my classroom who aren't properly loved and it's heartbreaking.'

'I agree that a parent should love a child,' he rasped, 'but it's irrelevant in a marriage.'

'I disagree. My parents were deeply in love until the day they died. My father was someone who showed genuine love and affection to all of us.'

'No wonder you have a fairy-tale view of relationships.'

Regan tilted her head, wondering where his *un-fairy-tale-like* view had come from. 'What about your parents? Were they happily married?'

'My parents' marriage was a merger.'

'Not a surprise, I suppose, given your attitude, but I didn't ask why they married, I asked if they were happy.'

One minute he was sitting opposite her and the next he was standing at the windows, staring out at the darkening sky. He took so long to respond to her question, and was so still, Regan would have assumed he'd gone to sleep if not for the fact that he was standing up. Just as she was wondering what she could say to break the tension in the room he turned back to her, a scowl darkening his face. 'Whether my parents were happy or not is unimportant. But actually they weren't. They rarely saw each other. My mother found that she didn't have the stamina to be a queen and spent most of her time in Paris or Geneva. My father was King. A job that leaves little time for anything else. He did what needed to be done. As my sister will. As my brother will, and as I will.'

His words painted a somewhat bleak picture of his early years.

'That sounds a bit cold. Maybe your sister wants something different. Maybe she and my brother are in love. Have you considered that?'

If the muscle jerking in his jaw was any indication, then yes, he had considered it. And not happily.

'You'd better hope not,' he growled.

'Why not? What if they're in love and want to get married?' God, what if they were *already* married? This man would probably skewer Chad like a pig on a spit-roast. 'Would that be such a big deal at the end of the day?'

The look he gave her was dangerous. Dangerous and uncompromising. 'Milena is already betrothed,' he bit out softly. 'And that betrothal cannot be broken. It *will not* be broken.'

'Tell me,' she said, narrowing her eyes, 'are you concerned about your sister's welfare because she's your sister or because she might ruin your precious plans with this so-called Crown Prince?'

'Are you questioning my affection for my sister?' he asked with deadly softness.

'No. I'm saying that if it's true and she and Chad are in love, what can you do about it? I mean, it's not like you can punish my brother for falling in love with your sister. You might not think it's important but falling in love is surely not a crime. Even here.'

The smile he gave her didn't reach his eyes. 'You don't know my country very well at all, Miss James, do you?' He stalked towards her and leaned over her chair, caging her in with his hands on either armrest.

Regan's heart knocked against her chest so loudly she thought he'd be able to hear it. She wasn't afraid of him, although perhaps if she had any sense she would be, because the look in his eyes could chill lava. 'I can have your brother executed for just looking at my sister.'

Regan drew in a shocked breath. 'You cannot.'

His mouth twisted into a grim smile. 'You have no idea what I'm capable of.' His eyes drifted over her face and down to her body. Regan's breath hitched inside her chest. He was so close, his scent filled her senses and started acting like solvent on her brain. She wanted to tell him that she didn't care what he was capable of but neither her brain nor her body seemed to be functioning on normal speed.

'But all that is irrelevant. If you and your brother are as close as you claim to be then he will come running soon.'

With that arrogant prediction he straightened away from her, giving her body enough respite that she could finally drag air into her lungs.

'Goodnight, Miss James. I hope you enjoyed your dinner.'

Discombobulated by his nearness and the vacuum left by

his sudden departure, Regan jumped to her feet and went after him, grabbing hold of the sleeve of his robe. 'Hold on a minute.' She blinked a few times to clear her head. 'What do you mean by that? Why will my brother come running?'

'Because hopefully he's seen the photos I've had released of the two of us.'

'Photos?'

'Yes.' His blue eyes glittered down into hers. 'It seems you and I were photographed together in the hotel lobby. By now they should be splashed all over the European news networks with your name attached.'

'You're using me as bait,' she whispered on a rushed breath.

'I like to think of it as insurance.' His superior smile did little to ease her rising temper. 'When your brother finds out you're here I'm hoping those familial connections you spoke so movingly about will have him scurrying out of the woodwork.'

'Oh, you are t-truly awful,' she stammered furiously. 'Your sister has run away because you're mean and trying to marry her off to someone who is probably just as horrible as you, and you're going to scare my brother in the process.'

'Your brother will pay for his sins, Miss James, and if you two are as close as you say you are he'll come running.'

Regan shook her head. 'I've never met a man as cold and heartless as you. Something you're no doubt very proud of.' She shoved her hands on her hips and stared him down. 'You can't keep me here like this. When I tell the American consulate what you've done you'll be an international pariah.'

The look he gave her was cold and deadly, not a shred of compassion on the stark planes of his beautiful face. 'Are you threatening me, Miss James? You do know it's a crime to threaten the King?'

Regan tossed her hair back from her face. 'It's no doubt a crime to hit him as well but if I had a baseball bat handy, Sheikh Hadrid, or King Jaeger, or whatever your title is, I'd use it.'

She saw his nostrils flare and she suddenly realised how close together they were standing. If she took another step forward they'd be plastered up against each other. She told herself to do the opposite and step back but once again her body and her brain were on divergent paths.

'The correct title is *Your Majesty*,' he said softly. 'Unless we're in bed. Then you can call me Jaeger, or Jag.'

Oh, God, why had he said that?

And why was he looking at her as if he wanted to devour her? As if he wanted to kiss her as much as she wanted to kiss him?

This is stupid, Regan, she warned herself. *Step back. Step back before it's too late.*

But she didn't step back; instead she poked the bear. Quite literally, with her pointer finger. 'Like that will ever happen,' she threw at him. 'I hate you. The only time I would *ever* sleep with you is in your dreams.'

'Is that so?'

He grabbed hold of the finger she was using to jab him and brought it to his mouth. Regan's breath backed up in her lungs as he ran the tip of her finger back and forth across his lower lip. Heat raced through her, consuming every ounce of good sense she'd ever owned. 'Don't do that,' she begged, her voice husky.

He looked down at her, his blue eyes blazing. 'Don't fool yourself. You don't hate me, little America. Far from it.'

CHAPTER FOUR

THE FOLLOWING MORNING Regan was still incensed by the King's high-handedness. Clearly nothing was beyond him: imprisonment, trickery, *sexual domination.*

'Don't fool yourself. You don't hate me, little America. Far from it.'

She did hate him. Of course she did. He was autocratic… arrogant… He was… The memory of the way his warm breath had moistened the tip of her finger, hinting at the dark heat of his mouth, made her shiver. He was unbelievably sexy!

Not that she was thinking about that. Or her response. She liked men who saw themselves as equal with women. King Jaeger obviously saw himself as equal with no one. Not even the gods!

'I make the rules here,' she muttered under her breath, completely oblivious to the beautiful, sultry day outside. 'You'll do as I say.'

How could she find a man like that sexy? Stress. Lingering jet lag. Inconvenient chemistry.

If only he were a rational man you could reason with. But he wasn't. He had decided her brother was guilty, and appealing to reason wasn't going to work.

Which left her with no option but to get away, or at the very least get word to Chad that she was fine and that he needn't worry about her. As much as she wanted to find out what was going on with him, she couldn't bear it if he panicked and did something crazy. Such as put himself in King Jaeger's path.

She glanced around the high walls that surrounded the gardens. She had thought about scaling them but had almost immediately dismissed the idea. They were about twenty feet high and smoothly rendered. There wasn't a foothold anywhere. She had also tried brazening it out and simply walking out of the door on the first day but it was always locked. The only time it wasn't was when the maid was cleaning, as she was now, but on those occasions a security guard was stationed outside the door.

Regan knew because she had tried to sneak out the day before and been met with his implacable, blank stare. Maybe the King trained them personally.

Frustrated at how utterly helpless she felt, she strode back inside. Had the photo of her in the King's arms been released to the media yet? Probably. She hated the thought that Chad had seen it and was worried about her, but more, she hated the thought of what would happen once King Jaeger got hold of her brother.

Good God, what had her brother been thinking, running off with a princess? Was he personally involved with her? And could the King really have him executed? More importantly, would he? He definitely seemed ruthless enough to do it but something told her that he wasn't as bad as he made out. Closed, yes. Bad…no.

Regan fought back a wave of helpless frustration, absently watching the maid enter something into her tablet before picking up the feather duster again. Regan didn't know what she could possibly be dusting—the room was immaculate. The maid was young, no more than twenty, at a guess, and seemed sweet enough. Unfortunately she spoke limited English, totally clamming up that first day when Regan had informed her that she wasn't a guest of the King and needed to leave the palace as quickly as possible.

The girl had given her a confused, shy smile and told her in broken English how wonderful the King was, at which point Regan knew she wouldn't be getting any help from her direction.

But if King Jaeger thought she would sit back while he planned her brother's demise he was very much mistaken. As soon as she was free she would contact the American Embassy and demand that they…that they…what? Put in place economic sanctions against Santara? Ban tourism to the smaller nation? Most likely Jaeger would laugh and shrug those impossibly broad shoulders with a care factor of zero.

Irritated, she watched as the maid returned to her trolley and retrieved a cloth and cleaning agent before heading into the bathroom, leaving the trolley behind. Wandering around the room like a caged tiger in need of exercise, Regan passed the trolley and abruptly stopped when she realised that the maid had not only left her trolley unattended, but she'd left the tablet on it as well.

Heart thumping, she glanced towards the bathroom, where she could hear the maid singing softly to herself, and grabbed the electronic device. Praying that it wasn't password-protected, she nearly gave a cry of relief when the screen lit up at her touch.

Ignoring her sweaty palms, she quickly connected to the internet and chewed on her lip as she thought about what to do next. Not having expected to get access to the web, she had no idea who to contact. The American Embassy? Did they have an emergency email on their website? But even if she contacted them they would have no way of telling Chad that she was fine. That she wasn't at the mercy of King Jaeger. Worse, they might not even believe her.

Thinking on her feet, she pulled up her social-media account and had a brainwave. Rushing over to a sun lounger, she quickly unbuttoned her shirt so that her bra looked like a bikini. With trembling fingers she angled the tablet, plastered a bright smile on her face and took a photo of herself with the pool in the background. Then she quickly captioned a message underneath.

Having fun chez King Jag. Hope you are too. The King is a wonderful host! ❤❤❤

She grinned as she added the three heart emojis. They were a fun joke between her and Chad that she had started when he had been an easily embarrassed teenager. It was something her mother would have taken great joy in doing to both of them.

Before she could reconsider her actions she hit 'post' and watched it come up on her home page. It wasn't much, and she had no guarantee that Chad would check the site, but it was a way they had kept up with each other's lives after he'd gone to university. With any luck he would check it before panicking about what the heck she was doing in the King's arms.

Spiked with adrenaline at having outsmarted His high-and-mighty Majesty, she was about to write Chad a private message when she heard a noise in the room. Not wanting to alert the maid to what she had done, Regan quickly closed down the page she was on and strolled back inside, the tablet behind her back.

The maid didn't even look her way and Regan only realised that her whole body was shaking after she quickly put the device back on the trolley. She exhaled a rushed breath and tried to calm her heartbeat. The tablet wasn't in the same place as where she'd found it, but with any luck the maid would think that she had moved it herself.

Glancing at Regan quizzically, the young girl returned to the trolley and gave her a small smile as she wheeled it out of the room.

A shiver snaked its way down Regan's spine. She had managed to thwart the King. She only hoped he never found out. A small smile touched her lips. But, even if he did, it wasn't as if he could do anything about it. The man didn't control the world.

Jag pounded his opponent so hard the man's knees nearly buckled beneath him.

He should never have gone to her suite. Never have argued with her and certainly never have brought her fingers to his lips.

He swung hard again, grunting as his gloved fists connected with solid muscle.

From now on she would stay on one side of the palace and he would stay on the other.

His opponent groaned loudly. 'Either I'm in really poor form, or you're in extremely good form today, boss-man.' Zumar winced as he prodded the side of his jaw. 'If I'm lucky I might get out of this bout still standing.'

Jag rolled his aching shoulders and waited for Zumar to resume his fighting stance. Zumar was six feet six, built like an iron tank, and the head chef in the palace. He'd once been a black belt in karate and a kick-boxing champion before injury had forced him into another career as a street fighter. Many years ago Jag had assisted him in a five-against-one street brawl and given him a second chance. Zumar had studied as a chef, and could now run a Michelin-star establishment if he so chose. He didn't. Instead he'd made a life for himself in Santara and remained loyal to Jag. Loyal until they faced off in the ring during their regular training sessions.

'Stop complaining,' Jag growled. 'I can't help it if you're going soft on all those pastries you bake.'

'Soft, is it?' Zumar laughed. 'Bring it on, boss-man.'

Jag did…taking out his pent-up energy and frustration in the ring rather than on the woman currently occupying his garden suite.

He still couldn't believe how close he'd come to kissing her again last night. The woman did things to his equilibrium he didn't want to contemplate. Because, for a man who was used to being in the utmost control at all times, it was a sad indictment to admit that when he'd taken one look at her in those cut-off shorts he'd nearly forgotten his own name.

Then there was all her talk of love and happiness…as if they were goals that motivated his life!

What did motivate him was success, position, power. Providing for his country and his family. Making sure everything ran smoothly and that Santara would never be in an inferior political position with its neighbours—Berenia and Toran—again. And if that made him a—what had she called him?—a stubborn, autocratic, overbearing tyrant, then so be it.

Usually steady on his feet, he felt Zumar's fist connect with his right cheekbone. He staggered sideways and scowled at his chef's ecstatic expression.

'Lucky shot,' he growled.

'I'll take it, boss-man,' Zumar chortled, raising his fists again.

Jag feinted a right hook to his jaw and then did a kickboxing manoeuvre that brought the other man down.

'You learn too fast,' Zumar complained. 'I'm calling time.'

‘You can’t,’ Jag stated. ‘I’m not finished.’

‘You want to cook your own meal tonight, boss-man?’

Jag grunted, wrapping his gloved hand around Zumar’s and hauling him to his feet. He glanced around the basement gymnasium many of his senior officers also used, to see if there was anyone else who would help him work off some steam.

Regan James might, his recalcitrant libido whispered, *though that would be a very different type of workout from this.*

Ignoring that unhelpful thought, he tried to catch the eye of a few of his army officers. Unfortunately Jag had never been known to employ idiots and every man in the room kept his gaze averted. It wasn’t hard to sense that their leader wasn’t quite himself right now.

‘What’s up with you anyways, boss-man?’ Zumar asked, wiping the sweat from his brow with a sports towel. ‘This big-deal summit tying you up in knots?’

‘It’s not the summit.’

‘A woman, then.’

‘A woman?’ Jag gave him a baleful look, yanking his gloves off. ‘Why would you say that?’

The Nigerian shrugged. ‘When a man is as worked up as you are it usually means trouble of the female variety.’ He gave Jag a knowing grin. ‘But there is no escape, huh? The heart knows what the heart wants.’

The heart?

‘What about your parents? Were they happily married?’

From out of nowhere, Regan’s unexpected question from the night before dredged up unwelcome memories of his childhood. He still couldn’t fathom how he had become embroiled in a conversation about his family with her. He never talked about his parents, not his father’s death, nor his mother leaving them when they were young. It had happened, he'd dealt with both events and moved on, as was befitting for the as then future King of Santara.

And no, he hadn't mourned his father's death. He hadn't thought to. He had respected his father and always done his duty by him, but he hadn't really known the man, other than as his King. And as for his mother…she had never asked for Jag's love and never wanted him to give it.

His throat thickened. Regan James didn't know what she was talking about with her fairy-tale ideas about life. She'd never known duty or hardship. She had never… He frowned. Actually, she had known duty and hardship. And still she remained soft and open. Trusting that people behaved the way that they should. *Little fool.*

Yes, he would be on one side of the palace, she on the other. Because whenever he was around her she managed to twist logic and common sense into something unrecognisable. And really, why would he see her again? She was a means to an end. When that end came about they'd part company and never see each other again. And wasn't that a cause for celebration?

He gave Zumar a hearty slap on the back. 'Thanks, Chef.'

Zumar blinked. 'What for?'

'For helping me realise what was wrong.'

Zumar cracked his jaw. 'Next time I'd appreciate you working that out *before* we get into the ring, boss-man.'

Jag laughed. It felt good to be on solid ground again. Back in charge.

Last night…the chemistry between them, the way she made him question himself… Gone. Completely gone.

At least it was right up until Tarik burst into his dressing room thirty minutes later, his forehead pleated like an accordion.

Jag immediately stopped whistling. 'Milena?'

'No, no, I have no updates on Milena, Your Majesty.'

Jag let out a relieved breath, pulling on his trousers. 'Then it's something to do with the American. I can see the signs of frustration on your face. Don't let it bother you. I imagine she has that effect on everyone she meets.'

'Yes, sir, it is the American woman.'

'What has she done now? Tied her bed sheets together and scaled the palace wall? Planned out my demise in three easy steps? Whatever it is,' Jag assured him as he pulled a white shirt from its hanger, 'I'm not going to let it ruin my good mood.'

'She connected to the internet and uploaded a picture of herself at the palace.'

'Say what?' Jag nearly tore a new armhole in his shirt as he thrust his arm through it. 'Let me see.'

Tarik turned the tablet around so that the screen faced him. He scanned the photo that showed way too much of Regan's sexy cleavage in an ice-blue bra.

Jag knew five Santarian dialects and he swore in all five of them. 'Isn't that the pool in the garden suite?' he bit out.

'Yes, sir. This is a social-media post from the palace.'

He went still. 'The palace is not on social media.'

'No, sir, but Miss James is.'

'Miss James does not have a phone or any other device with her.'

'No. But she somehow got access to one and two hours ago she uploaded this post.'

'She got access to one?' Jag repeated softly. 'How?'

'The IT department is working on obtaining that information. They should know very soon.' There was a touch of desperation in Tarik's voice and Jag knew that his aide was trying to handle him.

'Take it down before anyone sees it,' he ground out. Like

her brother, whom he had no doubt had been the troublesome woman's intended audience.

'I already ordered it to be taken down, Your Majesty.' Tarik swallowed heavily. 'Unfortunately it has already been seen.'

Jag paused in the process of buttoning his shirt, a sense of foreboding turning his powerful frame tense. 'By whom?'

'The post has been shared across various multimedia outlets six million times, sir.'

'Six mill…' Jag scowled. 'How is that possible in so short a time frame?'

'You are a very popular monarch, Your Majesty, especially since the world is expecting you to announce your betrothal to Princess Alexa this weekend. And, with all eyes on Santara at present because of the impending summit, I'm surprised it's not more.'

Jaeger cursed viciously. He had completely forgotten about Princess Alexa.

'Quite,' Tarik agreed. 'But, speaking of your prospective engagement, I have King Ronan on the phone. He is furious that it seems you are entertaining a *concubine*—his words, sir—after agreeing to marry his daughter. He is threatening to call off the engagement and boycott the summit.'

Jag stared at Tarik. For the first time in his life his brain was struggling to keep up with the turn of events. As beautiful as Princess Alexa was, Jag had no real desire to marry her other than the convenience of it. She understood his world and, from what he knew of her, she was as logical and pragmatic as he was. She was also polished and poised. Any leader would be fortunate to have her on his arm. Not only that, but marrying her would strengthen ties with Berenia, Santara's third neighbour.

'Miss James is *not* my live-in mistress,' he bit out. 'And I have *not* formally agreed to marry Princess Alexa.'

'I know, Your Majesty, but King Ronan is clearly of the impression that you have.'

'That's because King Ronan is a pushy bastard who tries to manipulate people.'

'Of course, sir. But it is important that you have a plus-one this weekend. If King Ronan is not pacified he will not allow Princess Alexa to attend as your escort. And you know it is never a good idea to attend these events alone.'

Yes, he did, but he had more pressing matters to consider right now than a plus-one. He dragged a hand through his still damp hair. By rights he should be furious with Regan for this stunt—and he was—but part of him couldn't fault her ingenuity. Hell, he might even admire it if she wasn't causing him so much grief in the process.

'King Ronan is holding for you, Your Majesty. He wants to speak with you personally.'

'Of course he does.' Jag snatched up his cell phone from his dresser. 'Transfer the call to my personal number,' he ordered, his brain having gone from sluggish to full-on alert as he went into automatic problem-solving mode.

'Yes, sir.' Tarik flicked his finger quickly across the screen on his tablet. 'And Miss James?'

Jag scowled. 'Leave Miss James to me.' He'd strangle her as soon as he placated the volatile King of Berenia and made a decision about whether or not to marry the Princess.

Striding down the marble staircase en route to the garden suite, he brought his phone to his ear. 'King Ronan,' he said smoothly. 'I believe we have a small problem.'

CHAPTER FIVE

'COME ON, JUST sit still,' Regan crooned. 'Please, just for another few seconds.'

Her camera shutter clicked as she photographed a pair of olive and yellow birds with elegantly turned-down beaks. It was clear by the way they danced around each other and rubbed their beaks together that they were a couple, and their antics made her smile. They reminded her of hummingbirds back home, and she'd always had a soft spot for photographing couples—both animal and human. Everyone loved the notion of finding their soulmate, and she found that 'couples' sold well as stock photos.

She checked her viewfinder, satisfied that the pretty pair would be very popular when they were uploaded onto her website. The light was magnificent in Santara, making the exotic colours of this timeless land pop. Just looking at the sweeping sands of the desert beyond the palace made her itch to explore it.

As concentrated as she was on capturing a shimmering mauve dragonfly hovering above the azure-blue of the pool with her lens, there was no mistaking the moment the King stormed into her suite. She heard the heavy door to her room bang forcefully against the wall, and turned to see a small cloud of white powder float to the floor from where the ornate handle had gouged the plaster.

Regan moved to the arched doorway and then blinked.

King Jaeger stood inside her room, dressed in a pair of tailored trousers that hugged his powerful legs, an unbuttoned pristine white shirt, and that was it. His legs were braced wide, his hands held loosely at his sides, and he wore an expression on his face that could level a mountain. Regan couldn't prevent her eyes from running down the darkly tanned strip of flesh from his neck to the trousers that sat low on his hips. Dark hair covered his leanly muscled chest, arrowing down to bisect abdominal muscles you could probably bounce a coin off.

Her mouth ran dry as her gaze continued on down to his feet.

'I think you forgot your shoes,' she said, appalled to find that she even found the sight of his bare feet sexy.

The door closed behind him with a thud.

'And possibly your sense of humour,' she added, trying to lighten the mood and stop herself from obsessing about his body.

'If I were you I'd be very worried right about now,' he drawled menacingly.

She was. Worried that she couldn't stop thinking about sex whenever he was around. It was becoming insidious.

'About?' she asked, deciding to brave out his obviously bad mood. It wasn't possible that he'd found out about her post so quickly. Not unless he had ESP, or security cameras in her room. She cast a quick glance at the corners of the ceilings. Nothing there. Thank heavens.

'How did you do it?' he asked softly.

Damn. He did know. 'Do what?'

'Don't play cute with me—it won't work. How did you access the internet?'

'Oh, that…' She strolled further into the room until she'd put the protection of the sofa between them. He didn't have the look of a man who was about to do her physical harm, and indeed, every time he had restrained her she'd felt him leash his physical strength so as not to hurt her, but she suspected that if his temper ever did blow it would make Mount Vesuvius look as innocuous as a child throwing sand.

'Yes. *That.*' He came towards her, with animal grace, the muscles in his abdomen rippling with every silent footfall. Regan swallowed, her own stomach muscles pulling tight at the sight. A rush of excitement shot through her. *Excitement?* Was she completely daft? The man looked as if he was coming up with new ways she was going to die!

He stopped in front of the sofa, his eyes briefly scanning it before returning to her. It wouldn't be enough, she thought wildly; the Great Wall of China wouldn't be enough to keep her from him if he wanted to get to her.

'So I accessed the internet,' she murmured vaguely. 'I didn't write anything negative. I actually implied that I liked you. Which I don't, in case you get any ideas.'

Or, at least, any more ideas...

'You implied a lot more than that,' he muttered furiously.

'You're just unhappy because I countered your move and foiled your horrible plan to worry Chad. How did you find out so quickly, by the way? Do you have cameras in this room, watching my every move? That would be truly creepy if you did.'

'I do not have cameras in here, though I might after this,' he bit out. 'But, in answer to your question, your post has been shared a number of times.'

'Good,' she said. 'I hope Chad has managed to see it.'

'I know Chad was your intended audience.' His thick dark lashes narrowed, making his blue eyes seem impossibly vibrant. 'Unfortunately you picked up a few more *interested* parties.'

Regan frowned at his deceptively light tone. 'How many more?'

'Six million more.'

'Six mill—! That can't be true. I only have forty-eight followers and most of those are work-related.'

'You might not be popular, Miss James, but I am.'

'Lucky you,' she retorted, wishing he'd worn more clothing. 'Don't you want to button your shirt?' she said, inwardly cringing at the husky note in her voice when she'd been aiming for cool. 'It's quite chilly today.'

'It's forty degrees in the shade. And I'll button my shirt when I'm good and ready.' His voice became a lethal purr. 'Unless it's bothering you…'

'No. Not at all.' She waved off his suggestion as if it were ludicrous. 'I was just thinking that it didn't look very… *kingly*.'

His smile said that he knew she was lying. 'Good, because I'm not feeling very *kingly* right now.' His eyes drifted to her lips and Regan barely resisted the urge to moisten them. Sexual tension arced between them like a tightrope, and she had no idea what to do with all the jittery energy that coursed through her. She felt like a small child in a room full of sweets who had been told to stand in the corner and not touch anything.

Heat suffused her cheeks and she tried not to think about how warm and resilient his skin would feel if she were to slide her hands inside his open shirt. 'Of course, how you walk around the palace is entirely up to you. Don't mind me.'

She bit into her lip to stop the nervous chatter. She hoped the sharp little pain would also stop all the inappropriate thoughts running through her head.

'Thanks for the memo,' he bit out tautly. 'Now stop prevaricating and tell me how you did it.'

'I can't.' One thing she wouldn't do was get the lovely girl who cleaned her room into trouble.

A muscle ticked in his jaw. 'Miss James, I am two seconds away from strangling you with my bare hands and feeding your body to a lake full of alligators. I suggest you don't push me any further.'

'There are alligators in the desert?'

'Regan!'

She jumped as he bellowed her name. He'd never used her first name before and it scattered her thoughts. 'Calm down.' She didn't know if she was referring to him or herself, but it didn't matter. 'I was only asking. But…' She couldn't think of any more stalling tactics, so she just went with honesty. 'I have no intention of telling you how I accessed the internet, so stop asking me.'

'If someone in my employ helped you they will be punished.'

Regan planted her hands on her hips. 'It wasn't her fault.'

Jaeger's blue eyes narrowed, assessing. 'The maid helped you.'

'She didn't help me. She had a tablet and I…borrowed it.'

The muscle in his jaw flexed rigidly.

'If you punish her I'll never forgive you,' she said earnestly, 'because it wasn't her fault.'

'I have no doubt it wasn't her fault but it is obvious she was negligent.'

'I took advantage.'

'Believe me, I'm in no doubt about that.'

'So you won't do anything to her?' she implored. 'Because I can't allow it.'

'*You* can't allow it?'

He coughed out a laugh and Regan folded her arms across her chest. 'No. It wouldn't be fair. And you strike me as a very fair man.'

'Stop playing to my vanity.' He shook his head. 'It

hasn't worked with women before you; it won't work for you either.'

'I was only—'

'Quiet,' he growled. 'I need to think.'

He might need to but she could really use some air.

'Where are you going?'

Regan looked over her shoulder to find him watching her. 'There's no need to shout,' she grouched. 'I'm right here. And you clearly don't need me to think.'

'I never shout,' he corrected her. 'At least, I didn't before I met you.'

Seriously unnerved by the effect his near naked body was having on her Regan's heart hammered inside her chest. 'You know how to fix that,' she said faintly. 'You can let me go.'

He laughed. 'I wish I could. Believe me, you're a nuisance I could well do without.'

For some reason his words hurt. For all the unconventional nature of their meeting, and their missing siblings, Regan couldn't deny that he was the most exciting man she had ever met. Since her parents had died she'd become cautious and responsible. She always played it safe. One look at this man, one touch, made her feel electrified and more alive than she'd felt in so long. The feeling was at once thrilling and completely appalling. The man didn't *do* love and that was all she knew how to do.

He let out a rough breath that brought her eyes back to his. 'You have no idea what you've done, do you?' he muttered.

Something in his tone stayed her. 'Should I?'

'No. I suppose not.' He dragged a hand through his hair, mussing it further. 'In your world, posting a provocative image on social media would barely raise a ripple. Here it is very different. Here we have morals and ethics.'

'We have morals and ethics in America,' Regan said a little defensively. Well, they used to, at least, and most still did.

'Be that as it may, what you have done, Miss James,' he said with palpable restraint, 'is create a diplomatic crisis I am now in a position to have to fix.'

'A diplomatic crisis? I don't see how.'

'I have probably the most important summit my country has ever hosted starting tomorrow and a raft of people wondering who the American woman is I'm entertaining in my palace.'

'You're hardly entertaining me.'

'Further, I am now without an escort for the next four days.'

'I fail to see what this has to do with me.'

'Then let me explain it to you.' His blue eyes glittered down into hers. 'Since you have created this issue, you will become the escort you made me lose.'

'I didn't make you lose anyone,' she denied hotly. 'And there's no way I'm going to be your escort.' She gave a shaky laugh. Just the thought of it made her hot. 'Do you know what people would think if they saw us together?'

His eyes turned smoky and he leant against the back of the sofa, one bare foot crossed over the other, his eyes on her denim shorts. 'I think that horse has already bolted, *habiba*.'

Regan swallowed heavily. 'Well, I don't intend to make it worse by being seen on your arm. And anyway, this is all really your fault for bringing me here in the first place.'

'I agree. But that horse has also bolted, and now we deal with the consequences.' His eyes turned hard. 'Usually Milena would step in during these situations, but we both know why she can't do that, don't we?'

Regan grimaced. 'My brother had nothing to do with

your sister going AWOL! But okay,' she added quickly when she noticed the betraying muscle clench in his jaw. 'I think the best thing we can do now is leave things as they are. I won't cause any more problems,' she promised. 'And soon enough everyone will forget all about my little photo.'

'No one will forget you're here after that *little* photo. But even if they did, that doesn't solve all of my problems.'

'Surely you have women on speed dial all over the world who could play hostess—escort—for you. Probably any one of them would jump at the chance to do it.'

'I'm sure you're right.' His gaze travelled over her in blatant male appraisal. 'But the women I have on speed dial fulfil a very different function from hostessing, *habiba*.' His lazy drawl left her in no doubt as to what that function was. 'And I don't want to spend the weekend with a woman who might think that I'm more interested in her than I am. With you I know that won't happen.'

'Oh, you can count on that.'

A smile played around the edges of his mouth, amusement lighting his eyes. 'Why is it you're the only person who ever has the gumption to argue with me?'

'Probably if someone else had we wouldn't be in this dilemma because you'd have developed a sense of reason.'

'Oh, we'd be in it.'

'You might be,' she said irritably. 'But I wouldn't. I work at a prestigious private school. I have my reputation to think about, and once this is all over I'll be returning to my normal life and I'm not doing that as some hot desert king's mistress!'

'Hot?'

'As in temperature,' she said, her face flushing. 'You're like a furnace.' He laughed, which only irritated her more.

'Probably my friend, Penny, has already left me a tonne of messages on my phone asking me what's going on. Not that I'd know about those.'

'She has. My staff have replied on your behalf.'

'Oh…!' Her lips pressed into a flat line. 'I promised myself I wasn't going to let you make me angry again, but I'm struggling.'

'Good to know. And I understand your dilemma.'

'You do?'

'Yes. Which is why I won't present you as my partner, or escort. I'll present you as my fiancée.'

'Your *what*?'

Ignoring her shocked outburst, he paced back and forth. 'Yes, this is a much better solution. It will not only satisfy the curiosity of those wondering why you're in my palace, but, since the photo of you in my arms didn't bring your brother running to your rescue, news of our betrothal might do that job too.'

'You're as ruthless as a snake,' she spluttered. 'But it won't work. Chad would never believe it.'

'He doesn't have to believe it.' His bright blue eyes connected with hers. 'He just has to bring my sister back unharmed.'

Regan frowned. If Chad knew she was engaged to the King there was no doubt he'd come running. And maybe that was for the best. Then this whole situation would be resolved and she could go home. 'And if it doesn't work?'

'It has to work.'

'Why? Because your mightiness has decreed that it will?'

He stopped pacing to stare at her. 'You like challenging me, don't you, Regan?' His gaze lingered on her lips and her pulse jumped erratically in her throat.

'Yes, you should look wary,' he murmured. 'Right now

I want to put my hands on you and I'm not sure if I want to make it pleasurable or painful.'

Regan jumped away from him, her insides jittery. 'We were talking about my brother,' she reminded him huskily. 'The whole reason you're here.'

He slowly prowled towards her, crowding her to the point where all she could think about was him. How tall he was. How big. How the stubble on his jaw would feel beneath her fingertips.

'Stop thinking of our betrothal in the romantic sense,' he advised. 'It's a business arrangement and it's temporary.'

'Two things you're obviously exceptionally good at.'

His jaw hardened and his gaze dropped to her mouth. 'I'm good at a lot of things, Regan, and if you're not careful you'll find out which of those things I'm *particularly* good at.'

Regan's mouth went dry at the sensual threat and once more she was acutely aware that he *still hadn't buttoned his shirt.*

He shook his head. 'Your desperation not to marry me serves you well, but it only reinforces that this is the right thing to do. My personal aide has been insisting for years that I need a partner at these major events, and having you by my side will mitigate any potential fallout from your ill-timed photo—'

'*My* ill-timed photo?'

'—And stop any untoward gossip from developing about the Western woman residing in my palace.'

'Residing?' She huffed out an astonished breath. 'You mean imprisoned.'

'If you were imprisoned you'd be in jail.'

'But this is all one-way. This is all about you and what you want. But what about what I want?'

'You're not in any position to make demands.'

'Actually, I am.' She threw back her head and stared at him. 'If you want my co-operation this weekend then I want something too.'

His body went preternaturally still and Regan got the distinct impression he thought she was going to ask him for money or jewels or something. 'You must have really dated some shallow women if the look of dread that just crossed your face is anything to go by.'

His eyes flashed blue sparks at her. 'Don't keep me waiting, Miss James; what is it you want?'

'A deal.'

'Excuse me?'

'Since deals are the only thing you seem to understand, I'll make one with you. I'll agree to be your escort, or rather, your partner this weekend if you let Chad go when he returns.'

'Absolutely not.' He swung away from her and then back. 'Your brother has my sister. That will not go unpunished.'

'But you don't really know what's happened or why they're together.'

'I will. And when I do your brother will be in serious trouble.'

'Fine; then you'll have to pull out your little black book and explain why you've locked me up some other way.'

He stalked over to the window and dug his hands into his pockets. Regan did her best not to notice the way the fabric of his trousers pulled tight across his well-defined glutes.

They're just muscles, she told herself, *just like the ones in his arms, his chest, his thighs...*

'Deal.'

What?

Her head came up, a betraying blush burning her face when she realised he had caught her staring.

'I'm agreeing with you. You become my fiancée for

three nights and four days and when your brother returns, as long as my sister is unharmed, I'll let him leave the country. Unharmed.' He prowled towards her and she unconsciously backed up a step at the light of battle in his eyes. 'Rest assured, though.' He stopped just short of touching her. 'If my sister is hurt in any way I'll kill him, are we clear?'

'Rest assured,' Regan fired back at him. 'If my brother has caused your sister harm in any way you won't have to kill him—I will. But he won't have,' she added softly. 'Chad isn't like that. He's not a macho kind of guy who takes what he wants. He's kind and considerate.'

'Unlike me?' he suggested silkily.

'I didn't say that.'

'You didn't have to, *habiba*; your face is very expressive.'

God, she hoped not.

'Like for the last half hour,' he murmured, taking another step towards her, 'you've been wondering what it would be like to kiss me.'

Regan sputtered out some unintelligible noise that might have had the words 'massive' and 'ego' in it, her hands coming up between them to press firmly against his hard, *naked* chest. She bit her lip against the urge to slide them up that warm wall of muscle and twine them together at the nape of his neck. 'You're wrong,' she husked.

A light came into his eyes that turned her lips as dry as his dusty desert land. 'I'm not wrong. Your pupils are dilated and your pulse is hammering, begging for me to put my mouth on it.'

His words caused hot colour to surge into her face. 'That's fear.'

His eyes lifted to hers. 'Fear of what?' he asked softly. 'That I will kiss you, or that I won't?'

Regan started to shake her head, a soft cry escaping her lips when his hands threaded into her hair and framed her face. His gaze held hers for an interminable second and then something coalesced behind his blue eyes and his head lowered to hers.

Regan's body jerked against his, her hands gripping his wrists with the intention of dragging them away from her, but it didn't happen. His mouth moved on hers with such heat and skill she went still beneath the onslaught. He gave a husky groan as his tongue traced the line between her lips, urging them to part. Sensation rocked through her and without any conscious thought her lips were shaping themselves to his, her mouth matching his hungry intensity.

With consummate skill, he completely controlled the kiss, one of his hands tunnelling further into her hair, angling her head so he could deepen the contact, the other pressed to the small of her back, urging her lower body to fit against his.

At the feel of his rock-hard desire, Regan moaned, wrapping her arms around his shoulders, her senses spinning out of control as she moved against him, her neck arching for the glide of his lips and tongue scraping against her skin.

He made a growling noise in the back of his throat that she felt deep in her pelvis, making her ache.

'Regan, I...' His lips returned to hers, his tongue exploring her mouth with a carnal intimacy that shocked her, the kiss going from hot to incendiary within seconds.

Regan heard herself moan, felt awash with sensations she couldn't contain. Her breasts were heavy and aching, desperate for relief, and her pelvis felt hollow. Beyond thought or reason her hands kneaded his shoulders, her fingers pushing aside his shirt to stroke his heated flesh.

He vibrated against the contact and his own hands must

have moved, because suddenly he was cupping her breast, his thumb strumming the hard nub of her nipple, drawing a keening sound from deep inside her. She felt the need in him ramp up, his movements hungrier, more urgent as his hands skimmed over her body, his fingers tugging on her blouse to release the row of buttons, revealing the upper swell of her breasts to his lips and teeth.

Regan's hands gripped fistfuls of his hair, urging him closer. 'Jaeger… Jag. Please…' His name on her lips seemed to shift something in both of them. He lifted his mouth from her body, his breathing hard, his eyes almost black.

She sucked in a breath, tried to clear her head. She saw shock register on his face and knew instantly that he regretted what had just happened.

'Why did you do that?' She touched her fingers to her tender lips, swollen from the force of his kisses.

His eyes narrowed on her, somehow a lot clearer than hers. 'I've wanted to taste you since the first moment I met you. Now I have.' He stepped further away from her, his eyes mirroring the mental distance he was placing between them as well as the physical. 'Tomorrow you will be provided with a wardrobe that should cover everything you need for the next four days. As long as you stick to your side of the agreement, I'll stick to mine.'

With that he pivoted on his feet and walked out of the door.

As soon as it clicked closed Regan let out a pent-up breath and pressed her hand to her abdomen.

'I've wanted to taste you since the first moment I met you. Now I have.'

Her hand trembled as she pushed her hair back from her face.

Was he serious?

How could he kiss her like that and then walk away?

How was that possible when she felt as if her world had been tipped upside down and shaken loose?

Well, because he must have kissed a thousand women to the half a dozen men she had kissed, most of which had occurred in high school before her parents had died. She'd never been great with boys and as she'd matured she hadn't been great with men either. The ones who liked her she had zero interest in, and the ones she thought had potential were not interested in a woman raising a teenage boy. Even if that boy was her brother. No way had anyone ever kissed her with the sensual expertise she'd just experienced with King Jaeger. But maybe kings were good at everything. Jag certainly claimed to know everything.

She shook her head, pride fortifying her spine. If he could walk away from that kiss without a backward glance then so could she.

Unconsciously her fingers went to her mouth and stroked down the side of her neck along the same path his lips had taken. When she realised what she was doing she dropped her hand and picked up her camera.

Reliving whatever it was that had just happened between them was not conducive to forgetting it. And forgetting it was exactly what she needed to do. She wasn't here for him. She was here for Chad. And now a deal she'd made on the fly.

A deal with the devil.

A deal she knew she could *never* go through with.

CHAPTER SIX

JAG KNEW AS soon as he spotted her in the small anteroom beside the grand ballroom that she was going to renege on their deal. And really he should let her. He didn't really give a damn about having a plus-one for the weekend. He'd done hundreds of these events before on his own. What would one more matter? And as to her unexplained presence in the palace…that was tougher to handle, but not impossible.

He paused for a moment, just watching her. She was pacing back and forth, her teeth delicately worrying her lower lip. A lower lip he had taken gently between his teeth not twenty-four hours earlier.

She looked astonishingly beautiful dressed in a slender column of burnished copper silk overlaid with a sheer organza bodice that accentuated the long line of her neck and hinted at the delicate swell of her breasts. The colour perfectly matched her hair, as he'd known it would, and turned her skin to polished ivory. Skin that was as soft as it looked.

Regan paused in front of the ornate mirror above the fireplace, tucking a strand of hair back behind her ear. Their gazes met in the mirror, her wide cinnamon eyes bright and lovely, her luscious lips painted a subtle pink. With her hair piled on top of her head in an elaborate style, she looked like an ethereal queen from a bygone era, and in that moment he knew he couldn't release her from their deal. Not yet.

Unwilling to analyse his motivations for that decision too closely, he leaned against the doorjamb. 'It's too late to change your mind, *jamila*,' he said gruffly.

She turned towards him with a suddenness that made the skirt of her gown swirl around her body, outlining her long legs before resettling. 'How do you know I want to change my mind?' she asked, her eyes gliding down over his body as if she couldn't help herself. He knew the feeling.

'Body language.'

He only hoped she wasn't as good at reading it as he was. If she was she'd know his was shouting, *I want you. Now.*

Uneasy at the depth of his primal response to her, he reminded himself that he'd already had this discussion with himself in the shower and it wasn't going to happen. He was not going to touch her again, or kiss her, and if that was all he could think about, well, that was just too bad. He wouldn't allow himself to complicate an already complicated situation. It wasn't logical. Just as kissing her hadn't been. One minute he'd been staring into her beautiful, expressive eyes and the next his hands were in her hair and his lips were soldered to hers.

She was like a magnet, and in that moment he'd had all the willpower of a metal shaving. It wasn't something he liked to acknowledge, even to himself.

Pushing away from the door, he strolled into the room. 'We have a few housekeeping issues to sort out before we—'

'Your Majesty, wait. Please.' She drifted closer and his nostrils flared as he picked up her delicate jasmine scent. He'd made sure that she'd been kept busy all day with spa treatments and massages, and just the thought of how supple her scented body would be was a sweet torture he could well do without.

'It's Jaeger,' he reminded her. 'Or Jag. Remember?'

She blushed a becoming shade of pink and pursed her lips. 'I'm trying not to.'

'Look, if this is about that kiss yesterday—'

'It's not about the kiss,' she cut him off quickly. 'I know what that was. You've already said. You wanted to know what it would be like to kiss me, you found out, and now you don't want to repeat the experience. We can move on from that.'

Move on? He wasn't sure that he could.

'The fact is, there's no way I can pose as your fiancée. I'm not royal, or a supermodel. I'm an ordinary schoolteacher. Everyone will know instantly that I'm a fraud.'

'You're not ordinary and I don't want you to pretend to be anyone but yourself. As a teacher you must be used to standing in front of large groups of people. I'm sure this won't be any different.'

He paced away from her, his mind still spinning at what she'd just said to him. Should he correct her misconception that he didn't want to repeat their kiss, or would it be easier to let it stand?

Unable to form a decision about that on the spot, he shelved it for later.

'I'm used to standing up in front of primary-school children,' she explained, 'which is not the same as what will be expected of me this weekend. And honestly, I'm a better behind-the-scenes person. I don't do well when the focus is directly on me. I get nervous.'

'Why?' Jag had dealt with crowds and attention his whole life. He was so used to being scrutinised from afar he didn't even give it a second thought. It was being scrutinised from up close that made him uncomfortable.

'I think it stems from all the impromptu interviews from the child-protection services I had to undergo in the early years. Whenever I was under the spotlight there was always the chance that Chad would be taken away from me. I never wanted to let him down by not being good enough and as a result I really dislike surprises and I especially dislike being the centre of attention.'

Shocked that she would tell him something so deeply personal, Jag felt something grip tight in his chest. 'I promise you that you won't be the centre of attention.' He reached out to stroke the side of her face and thought better of it. 'Don't forget, this is a political summit, not a day at Royal Ascot. That means I'll be the one in demand.' He kept his voice deliberately light, wanting to put her at ease and erase the vulnerability he saw in her expression. Vulnerability led to pain and the last thing he wanted was for her to suffer because of him. 'Now, the first part of housekeeping…' he reached into his pocket and pulled out a matte red box '…is for you to wear this.' He opened the box and turned it towards her.

'Oh, my God. It's as big as an iceberg,' she said, snatching her hands behind her back. 'I can't wear that.'

Jag smiled at her response. 'It was the biggest one I could find. Give me your hand.'

'No.'

Ignoring her small act of rebellion, he gently took hold of her left forearm and dragged her hand out from behind her back. 'I hope it fits. I had to guess the size of your fingers. They're so slender the jeweller thought I'd made a mistake.'

They both stared down at the intricately cut diamond glowing on her finger as if it had its own light source. 'But of course you didn't,' she said huskily. 'Are you sure it's not loaded with some beacon so you always know where I am?'

'Don't give me any ideas, *jamila*.'

She blinked up at him. 'You called me that before. What does it mean?'

'Beautiful.'

'I'm not—'

'Yes, you are.'

Awareness throbbed between them and Jag fought with the need to drag her into his arms and ruin her pink lipstick.

'Your Maj—'

'Jag,' he growled.

'This is too much,' she said thickly, keeping her eyes averted from his. 'I hope it's not real. I'll be afraid someone will rob me.'

'Nobody is going to rob you. Not in this crowd, but if it makes you feel any better my security detail will not let you out of their sights.'

'Are you sure that's not so I won't run off with it myself?'

'You won't run off with it. If you did I'd catch you. And yes, it is real.'

She pressed her lips together, staring at the ring, and he had to curb another powerful need to soften the strain around her mouth with a kiss.

'There are three other items of housekeeping to go through,' he said briskly. 'Protocol demands that you always walk two paces behind me, and you also cannot touch me.' He noticed her tapered brows rise with astonishment, and he nodded. 'Santarians do not go in for PDAs.'

'Not ever?'

'Sometimes with children. If the family is a tactile one.'

'Wow, my parents would have been locked up, then. They were always hanging all over each other. And us. Chad and I definitely inherited their affectionate nature. Oh…' She gave him a disconcerted look. 'You probably didn't want to hear that.'

No, he hadn't. But more because he couldn't stop thinking about how wild she'd been in his arms the night before. And of course he didn't want to entertain the idea that

Milena was having a relationship with Chad. *She wouldn't be strong enough to cope if it turned bad.* 'The third item is that I do not intend to spend the evening talking about your brother or my sister. It is a topic that is off the table from this moment on. Understood?'

'Perfectly. And I agree. It wouldn't look good if we started arguing in front of your guests.'

'My lords, ladies and gentlemen, *mesdames et messieurs*, I give you Sheikh Jaeger al-Hadrid, our lord and King of Santara, and his intended, the future Queen of Santara, Miss Regan James.'

Regan gave a small gasp at the formal introduction. She stood two steps behind Jag, waiting for him to descend the grand staircase, craning her neck to see over his wide shoulders to the room below. What she could see took her breath away. The room looked like a golden cloud, the walls gilt-edged and inlaid with dark turquoise wallpaper. Ancient frescoes and golden bell-shaped chandeliers adorned the high ceilings, while circular tables, elegantly laid with silverware and crystal, filled the floor space. Beautifully dressed men and women, some in military garb and traditional robes, milled in small groups and stared up at them with eager, over-bright eyes. Some, mostly the women, were craning their own necks to get a look at her, and it made Regan shrink back just a little more in the shadows.

When Jag had first informed her that she would have to walk two steps behind him at all times she'd been offended. Now she wondered if that wasn't a blessing. It might mean that she went unnoticed the whole night!

She twisted the egg-sized diamond on her finger, eyeing the endless row of steps they needed to descend with mounting dread. She just hoped she didn't trip over the beautiful gown she'd been squeezed into. It was the most delicate, the most exquisite piece of clothing she had ever worn and it made her feel like a fairy princess.

Queen, she amended with a grimace. Had Tarik really needed to introduce her as the future Queen? Couldn't he have just said her name? Or, better yet, nothing at all?

She noticed Jag shift in front of her and her heartbeat quickened. *Here we go*, she thought, preparing to follow him down the staircase. Only that didn't happen. As if sensing her unease, he turned towards her, his hand outstretched.

Regan glanced up to find sapphire-blue eyes trained on her with an intensity that made her burn. And just like that she was back in his arms with his mouth open over hers. She moistened her lips and saw his eyes darken in response. His chest rose and fell as he took a couple of deep breaths and she wondered if he wasn't thinking about the same thing. Then he gestured for her to approach him.

She took a small step, then another. 'What?' she whispered self-consciously. 'Why have we stopped?'

'The thing is…' A wry grin curled one side of his mouth and he looked so impossibly handsome in that moment she could have stared at him forever. 'The thing is, I've always hated protocol.' He drew her to his side and clasped her hand.

A low murmur rippled through the crowd as he raised her hand to his lips, a sexy smile lighting his eyes. It was a chivalrous gesture. A gesture meant to impress, and it did, melting Regan's heart right along with every other woman's in the ballroom.

Do not get caught up in all this, she warned herself, instantly suppressing the shiver of emotion that welled up inside her. This was not a fairy-tale situation. She was not Cinderella, and Jag was not going to be the Prince—or

King—who promised to adore her for ever. Real life didn't work out that way. Real life was often a painful slog.

She gave him a faltering smile, wondering why he was still stalling. 'It's too late to change your mind now,' she whispered, throwing his earlier words back at him.

His smile widened. 'I have no intention of changing my mind, my little America.'

Regan told herself not to get lost in that smile. Or the nickname that sounded too much like an endearment. He had walked away from their kiss last night without a backward glance. The only interest he had in her was with regard to thwarting diplomatic crises and getting his sister back. That settled in her mind, she took a deep breath and concentrated on not tripping.

Unbelievably the night went much faster than Regan had expected. The people she met were mostly lovely and interesting, and Jag never let her very far out of his sight, instinctively sensing when she was feeling out of her depth and coming to her side.

'He's divine,' more than one woman had said with unabashed envy throughout the night, giggling like schoolgirls when Jag paid them personal attention. She watched with fascination at how he skilfully worked the room and put the people around him at ease. It was such a contrast to the way they had met, and yet she saw both elements of him in the superbly tailored tuxedo that did wicked things to his body. He was at once incredibly sophisticated and also inherently dangerous. Not physically. At least not to her. No, King Jaeger's danger was in the masculine charisma he exuded with unassailable ease. It made everyone in the room want to be near him. Especially her.

Realising that the wife of a Spanish diplomat had just spoken to her, Regan smiled apologetically. She cast a sideways glance at Jaeger, watching the way he easily com-manded the conversation in the small group of delegates clustered around him. A stunning woman at his side leaned close to him and whispered something in his ear, her hand placing something into his trouser pocket so effortlessly Regan nearly missed it.

'You are very lucky,' the woman, Esmeralda, said again, forcing Regan to refocus.

'Lucky?' Regan murmured, wondering what they were talking about now.

'Yes. He is a king amongst kings.' She gave Regan a knowing smile. 'Although I'm not sure I could handle all that latent sexuality, and I'm Latin.'

Regan's face flamed as she recalled the sexual skill with which he'd kissed her, the way his hands had moulded her to him and stroked her breasts.

'Ooh-la-la…' Esmeralda chortled. 'I can see that you can.'

'Can what?' Jag asked smoothly, placing his arm around Regan's waist.

'Just girl talk, Your Majesty,' the older woman said, raking her eyes over his torso as if she wished it were her blood-red fingernails instead.

But Regan was embarrassed, knowing for a fact that the woman's assumptions were completely wrong. She didn't have the experience, or the expertise, to handle someone of Jaeger's sexual nature and she never would.

Excusing them both, Jag led her towards their table.

'What's in your pocket?' Regan asked, leaning close to him so no one could overhear.

He stopped and looked at her, stepping to the side to avoid anyone else following in their path. His eyes glinted with amusement at her. 'I suspect it's a phone number. I haven't looked.'

Regan's mouth fell open. She wasn't sure what astonished her the most. That he hadn't looked or that a woman would slip a man her phone number in plain sight of anyone who happened to be paying attention.

'But you're engaged,' she said on a rush. 'At least, that woman thinks you are.'

'She's also married.' His eyes twinkled as they gazed into hers.

'That's terrible. I don't know who to feel sorry for more—her or her husband. She's clearly not happy in her marriage.'

'Some people just want the excitement of being with someone new.'

'Well, I wouldn't. If I committed to someone I'd always be faithful to them.'

'As would I, *habiba*.' His voice was rough, as if he were speaking directly to her and not in generalities.

Her heart bumped inside her chest. 'So you do have scruples,' she said huskily.

'Just because I don't let anyone mess with my family, that doesn't make me the bad guy you think I am, Regan.'

He settled his hands on her waist and Regan's pulse leapt in her throat. 'I didn't think Santarians were into public displays of affection,' she murmured breathlessly.

'We're not,' he confirmed, leading her back towards their table. 'But I figured I'd already broken protocol once tonight and the sky didn't fall in.'

She shook her head. 'You're a real rebel, aren't you?'

He laughed softly. 'Actually I'm not. I was always the child who did the right thing and toed the line growing up.'

'The dutiful son. Was that because it was expected of you as the first born?'

'That and because it was the only thing that made sense.'

'Love makes sense,' she said softly.

'For you, not for me.'

'Why do you think that?'

'Because I know how the world works. Both my parents were emotional. Their relationship unbearably volatile. Whenever emotion took over my mother left and my father worked harder. If there's one thing I've learned from watching my parents it's never to let emotion get in the way of making decisions.'

'But how do you control that so well?'

Right now all she could think about was wrapping her arms around his neck and dragging his mouth down to hers. It was actually frightening, the amount of times she thought about touching him. It felt as if she'd been in a deep sleep for a long time, only to waken and imprint on him like a baby bird.

'Practice.' He smiled at her, his teeth impossibly white against the dark stubble that had already started shading his jaw, taking him from merely handsome to outrageously gorgeous.

'Okay, well, I'm going to start practising emotionlessness right now. If you'll excuse me, I'm going to freshen up.'

'Don't be long.'

Regan let out a ragged breath as his gaze held hers. For a split second his eyes had been on her mouth and she could have sworn they had turned hungry. Most likely wishful thinking on her part.

She really didn't want to like him after the way he had threatened her brother and detained her as bait, but she knew that she did. Maybe if he hadn't kissed her she'd feel differently. But that wasn't entirely true. She'd found herself drawn to him even before she knew he kissed like a god. But he wasn't the only one who tried not to let their emotions dominate their decisions. She'd had to put her own aside after her parents died. And worse, she knew no one was indispensable, so why put yourself out there in the first place?

'Excuse me.'

'Oh, I'm sorry.' Regan smiled at a beautiful dark-haired woman as she exited the ladies' room. She stepped to the side so the woman could enter but she shook her head.

'I'm not going in.'

'Okay.' Regan smiled again and was about to return to the ballroom when the woman took a hesitant step forward. A prickle of unease raised the hairs on the back of Regan's neck. 'Is something wrong?'

'No, I—'

'Have you been crying?' Regan stepped closer to her. 'Your eyes are damp.'

'I'm fine.' The woman sniffed, clearly not fine. 'I just wanted to get a closer look at you.'

During the night many guests had wanted to get a closer look at her, and, while it hadn't been as daunting as she'd first thought, she still didn't like it.

'Why are you crying?'

'I'm Princess Alexa of Berenia.'

'I'm Regan James.'

The woman gave a brief laugh. 'I know.'

'Well, at least I made you smile.' She frowned with concern. 'Has someone hurt you? Are you feeling ill? Why don't I take you back to your table so you can—?'

'No. I don't want to go back to my table.' She gave her a hard look. 'You don't even know who I am, do you?'

Getting an uneasy feeling in the pit of her stomach, Regan shook her head. 'Should I?'

'Considering I was the King's fiancée up until yesterday, I would have thought so. I can't believe he would keep you in his palace and then *marry* you.'

Regan felt as if someone had poked her in the stomach with a sharp stick. 'Do you mean King Jaeger?'

'Who else?' Tears welled up in her eyes again. 'My father thinks you have bewitched him. He blames me, of course.'

'I haven't bewitched anyone,' Regan said vehemently, feeling sick. 'It's just… I mean… I can't explain it to you but I'm really sorry this has happened to you.'

'He loves you. It's obvious by the way he looks at you.' More tears leaked out of her eyes and she valiantly tried to hold them back. 'The way he touches you.'

Regan agreed that he had touched her a little too much. It had kept her in a heightened state of awareness all night. But she knew for a fact that he didn't love her. 'I don't know what to say to you.' Her own emotions felt as if they were being buffeted in a fierce wind. She was at once upset for this woman, who clearly cared for the King a great deal, and incredibly angry at Jag's obvious insensitivity. Why hadn't he told her about his engagement? Why hadn't he warned her that his ex might show up and approach her? Because surely he had known Alexa was invited? He'd signed off the guest list.

'There's nothing you can say.' The Princess raised her regal chin in a show of bravado that only made Regan feel worse for her. 'I tried to tell my father that those photos didn't matter, that you were nothing to the King, but I was wrong.'

'You're not wrong.' Regan bit her lip, anger making her muscles rigid. 'Look, I can't be sure but…maybe things will still work out for you. Maybe you should keep your fingers crossed. You never know what can happen in a couple of days. But if I were you, and I wanted him as much as you seem to then I *wouldn't* give up hope.'

The Princess looked at her as if she was crazy. She wasn't. She was just really angry.

'Are you going to talk to me at all about what's bothering you or are you going to continue to give me frostbite?'

Regan had been giving him the cold shoulder for the last hour until Jag had finally had enough and called it a night.

'Why have we stopped here?' she asked curtly, brushing aside his question and glancing along the unfamiliar corridor.

'You've been moved from the garden suite to the one adjoining mine.'

She glared up at him, her mouth tight. 'I don't want the room adjoining yours.'

Growing more and more irritated because he'd actually enjoyed what was usually a tedious formal evening, he pushed the door to his room wide open. 'Too bad. The garden suite is now occupied by the King and Queen of Norway. Feel free to join them if you like.'

She looked at him with such venom he thought she'd decide to do it. But then she lifted her dainty nose in the air and swept past him into the room. Sighing heavily, he followed her into his private living room, wondering what had gone wrong in the last hour.

'You don't need to accompany me,' she said; 'I know how to undress myself.'

Jag's eyes dragged down over her lush body and all the way back up. A flush of colour tinged her cheeks and heat surged through his veins. Graphic images of her spread out on his elegant sofa wearing nothing but her delicate gold stilettos drove his frustration levels higher. 'You sure about that?' He shrugged out of his jacket and tossed it across the back of said sofa. 'I'd be happy to lend a hand if you need it.'

'Oh, I'm sure you would.' She folded her arms over her chest. 'I'm sure you've helped many women out of their clothing in your time. Women like Princess Alexa perhaps. Your *ex-fiancée*.'

Ah…suddenly the reason for her cool hauteur made sense. 'Princess Alexa was not my fiancée. Whoever told you that is mistaken.'

'She did,' she said, challenge lighting her golden-brown eyes. 'In between bouts of crying.'

Jag stared at her. He'd spoken to King Ronan personally ahead of the opening dinner, reminding the elderly King that he had never actually committed to marrying his daughter and now he wouldn't be.

'Princess Alexa and I—'

'Please.' Regan held up her hand dismissively, cutting him off. 'Don't feel as if you have to explain anything to me. It's none of my business. I'm only the stand-in. Lucky that you find women so interchangeable, no doubt it's water off a duck's back for you.'

'I *do not* find women interchangeable.'

'No, you just see them as part of a package deal to be moved about according to your needs and political machinations. Is this her ring?' She tugged at the diamond he had given her earlier. 'She stared at it long and hard when she saw it. Did you choose it together?'

'Would you stand still and listen to me?' Her pacing was starting to give him whiplash.

'It doesn't matter. I find I can't abide wearing another woman's ring, even if it is just a prop.'

She held it out to him and Jag gritted his teeth, locking his hands around her wrists and jamming the ring back on her finger. 'That is not Alexa's ring. It is yours. I never chose a ring for Alexa.' Unused to explaining himself to anyone, Jag found himself in unfamiliar territory. 'A few months ago King Ronan approached me about marrying his daughter. I believed the idea had merit and said I would consider it. In the meantime someone from the Berenian Palace has been feeding information to the Press to create speculation and, I suspect, a way to encourage me to seal the deal.'

'As far as I could tell, it was definitely sealed for her. She sounds as if she's in love with you.'

'I met the woman twice. Do you really believe that's enough time to fall in love with someone?'

She hesitated a fraction of a second before staring down her nose at him. 'Clearly it was for her.'

'I doubt that. The woman is more in love with the idea of being Queen than being my wife, and her father wants easy access to Santara's wealth.'

'I find that hard to believe. She was incredibly upset.' She tugged at her wrists and he released her to put some much-needed space between them. 'But just say your version is the correct one and she's only marrying you for political gain, I would have thought that was right up your alley. No messy emotions involved to muddy the waters.'

His jaw ached from clenching it so hard. Tarik had pointed the same things out to him the day before. So why, with all the political advantages it also offered, had he killed the idea completely? 'I have explained as much as I am willing to explain to you.'

'Oh, right, because I'm just one of your minions. I suppose you're about to clap your hands next to make me disappear.'

'Don't tempt me,' he grated.

'I think it was really insensitive of you not to tell me about her. You knew that I was nervous about meeting all those people and you just threw me to the wolves.'

'I did not throw you to the wolves. I made sure you were

by my side the whole night. And I am not happy that Alexa approached you, but in the end no harm was done.'

'To you maybe,' she said, clearly not placated by his response. 'But that's because you don't care about people. You're so caught up in your duty and your wheeling and dealing you've forgotten the human element. You should make sure you donate your body to science after you die—you'll be the only person in the world who has been able to exist minus a heart.'

'I am not heartless and at the end of the day this is not about you and me as a couple. We're not a couple. We are a means to an end.'

'Yes, my brother's end.'

Feeling an overload of emotion, Jag walked away from her. 'I refuse to get into this with you.'

'Why?' she volleyed at him. 'Because you're selling Milena off the way King Ronan is his daughter?'

'I am not selling my sister off.'

She gave him a look as if to say 'dream on' and Jag's hands balled into fists. This woman was driving him crazy. 'I'm getting very tired of you questioning my decisions regarding my sister.' He watched as her eyes widened when he paced towards her. 'When Milena was sixteen she became infatuated with an international farrier that had come to work at the royal stables. I assumed it was harmless. I *assumed* he would be a gentleman, given her station and her age. I was a fool. He tried to seduce her even though he was married and he ended up breaking her heart.' He took a slow even breath, anger returning along with his memories. 'Not long after he left she stopped eating and lost an enormous amount of weight. Then I found her with a bottle of sleeping pills clasped in her hand.' He still remembered that feeling of having his heart in his mouth when he'd realised how gravely ill his sister had become, and he'd do anything to ensure that she was never hurt like that again.

'Oh, poor Milena. And poor you.' Regan's sympathy was a tangible force that threatened to wrap around him and never let him go. 'No wonder you're so protective of her. I assumed it was just for political reasons.'

Jag moved away from her so that he couldn't absorb any more of her warmth. 'The political aspect *is* vital. But more than that Milena has always struggled with the need to feel wanted, to feel of value to anyone. She has always blamed herself for our mother's defection. What she fails to realise is that our mother was never maternal. When this marriage arrangement was first presented to me I believed it would give Milena the stability and sense of purpose her life has always lacked. The last thing I need is you coming along and making me second-guess myself.' Shocked to realise how much he kept revealing to a woman who was virtually a stranger, he strode to the windows and stared out at the black, starless night.

'I'm sorry I probably brought back bad memories for you when I refused to eat the other day.' Hearing the deep emotion in her voice, Jag couldn't stop himself from turning to look at her. He'd never met a woman so open with her emotions and so willing to take ownership of her actions. 'And I'm sorry for saying you were heartless. I can see that you really do care very deeply for your sister and it was wrong of me to suggest otherwise.'

'I don't need your sympathy.' Put on the spot by the raw emotion in her voice that paradoxically tugged at his own, Jag put the brakes on the conversation. What he needed was her to get naked so he could work off some of the excess energy coursing through him, not to feel even more than he already did.

He heard her murmur a soft goodnight before she disappeared through one of the closed doors. As he was about to tell her that she'd entered his bedroom instead of her own she returned, red-faced. 'I think I just went into your room. It smells like you.'

Jag's jaw clenched. 'You did.' He pointed to the door on the far side of the room. 'You can access your bedroom through there.'

She ran her hands down the sides of her dress and threw him a nervous smile. 'Okay. Take two.'

Needing to lower his tension levels with something other than her, Jag headed for the bar. He'd just picked up the crystal decanter when she screamed.

Striding through the connecting door, he pulled up short when he found Regan standing on the bed, holding a stiletto sandal in her hand and wearing nothing but a nude-coloured slip. A very short nude-coloured slip.

'Sp-p-pider,' she stammered, her lovely eyes as wide as dinner plates. 'I swear it's as big as a wildebeest.'

'Where?'

'In the…in the wardrobe.'

Finding the offending arachnid, he had to concede that the spider was indeed huge. Maybe not a wildebeest, but if you'd never seen a camel spider before it probably looked as bad as one. Retrieving an empty glass from her bathroom, he captured the spider and tossed it outside the window, closing it after him.

'Technically it's not a spider,' he informed her, returning to find her still on the bed, her long, lithe legs braced apart. 'It's known as a *Solifugae*.'

'As long as it's technically gone I don't care what it's known as. Are there any more?'

Jag checked around the bed, welcoming the diversion from her legs. 'All clear. I'll make sure the staff do a regular sweep of the rooms tomorrow. But rest assured, we don't tend to see very many of them inside the palace. They prefer the open desert.'

'This one got lost,' she said, still warily eyeing the carpet as if she expected to see an army of them come out of the woodwork.

'Come.' He held his hand out to her, even though he told himself not to touch her. 'I'll help you down.'

Still in a state of shock, she took his hand without argument, becoming unbalanced as she stepped off the bed.

Jag caught her in his arms, her body fitting against his like a silken glove, her arms winding around his neck, her legs wrapping around his hips.

Somehow her bottom, round and firm, was cupped in the palms of his hands.

The kiss from the night before spiralled through his head, taking over.

'You wanted to know what I tasted like and now you don't want to repeat it.'

At one point during the night he'd wanted to repeat it so badly he'd nearly cleared the grand ballroom. Part of the problem was that her taste was damned addictive.

The air-conditioning whirred overhead.

Was she breathing?

He wasn't.

Her body was open to his, clinging, her scent winding him up. He was so aroused, he shook with it. All it would take was for him to bunch her silk slip a fraction higher, test her readiness with the tips of his fingers, release himself from his trousers and bury himself deep inside her.

His hands moved to her thighs, tightening on the soft resilience of her skin, then he inhaled raggedly, letting her slide down his torso until her feet touched the floor, biting back a groan.

She stared up at him, as dazed as he was, her eyes dark

with unslaked lust. Her nipples were hard, her breathing as uneven as his, and he knew if he put his hand between her legs he'd find she was equally turned on.

A muscle ticked in his jaw. She wasn't here for this. He hadn't asked her to pose as his fiancée so that he could satisfy a hunger for her he was barely able to comprehend. He'd done it to avert an international crisis; he'd done it to get his sister back. How would it look if he threw sex into the mix for the hell of it?

If Chad James was out there having sex with his sister he'd kill him. He'd expect no less in return. He took a step back from her, called himself ten types of a fool and headed for the door before he could change his mind.

CHAPTER SEVEN

REGAN WAS ALREADY up when breakfast arrived on the King's private terrace. She'd showered and changed into her own clothes—jeans and a T-shirt—ignoring the beautiful items the King had provided for her, since she had no idea what would be expected of her today. She thought about the woman who had slipped him her phone number the night before and wondered if he had gone to find her after he'd walked away from her. And then reminded herself yet again that she didn't care.

She stared at the selection of local pastries and fruits and thought about his revelation concerning his sister the night before. She honestly hadn't thought he had the potential to feel anything on a personal level, but after the disclosure about Milena was torn from his chest she could see that he did. He felt things incredibly deeply and she was coming to understand that the way he had coped with taking control of a family and a country so young was to close down his emotions and just get on with it.

She recalled the way he had fed her in the garden suite when she'd gone on a hunger strike. At the time she'd assumed that he'd fed her for purely selfish reasons, but had he done it because deep down he was a nice person? Somehow she preferred the first option. It made it much easier to dislike him if she thought he was a hard-hearted tyrant.

She spied the food now and tried to stop thinking about

him so that she could figure out if she was hungry or not when he walked through the glass doors and joined her.

Smoothing the napkin on her lap, she told her heartbeat to settle down.

'You were right last night,' he said quietly, his eyes on her face. 'It was insensitive of me not to have informed you about the situation with Princess Alexa. I hadn't looked at it from your point of view, and I also genuinely believed that Alexa would not be overly disappointed if the betrothal didn't go ahead. I'm sorry I put you in that position.'

Not expecting him to apologise, Regan felt taken aback. 'I probably overreacted a little,' she admitted, knowing that really, she had overreacted a lot because she'd been unexpectedly jealous of the other woman. Something that didn't make sense at all given their circumstances. 'But it's okay.' She forced a lightness into her voice. 'I told Princess Alexa not to give up hope.'

His brows drew together. 'Why would you tell her that?'

'Because I felt sorry for her. She was really upset and she's perfect for you.' That thought had kept her up a lot during the night. 'She's beautiful and poised *and* royal. In terms of matches you'd make beautiful babies together. You should definitely go ahead with it.'

He moved towards the table and picked up a peach, testing it for ripeness. She hadn't realised how much she wanted him to deny her advice until he didn't. 'You're always looking for the silver lining, aren't you?'

'I prefer silver linings to thunderclouds. Life's tough enough without always waiting to be rained on.'

'That's a romantic way of looking at the world. If you're not careful you'll be blindsided when you least expect it. And you hate surprises.'

'I hate bad surprises.'

'Is there any other kind?'

Well, there was her reaction to his kisses. That was definitely a thundercloud because, as intoxicating as they were, as much as they made her burn for more, she would never be what he was looking for in a woman.

'Good point,' she agreed, frowning as a thought came to her. 'You're not going to say anything to Princess Alexa, are you? I wouldn't want her to get into trouble for approaching me.'

'First you protect my staff, and now the Princess? Who are you going to protect next? Because I don't ever see you protecting yourself and you make yourself vulnerable in the process.'

'That's not true.'

'It is true.' He leant against the table beside her. 'You didn't even realise how much danger you were in that night at the shisha bar, or walking around a strange city alone. Anything could have happened to you.'

'It didn't,' she said, feeling the need to defend herself.

'All evidence to the contrary,' he said, bringing a slice of peach to his mouth. His eyes held hers and the air in the room grew unbearably hot.

'How is it you can eat that and not spill a drop?' she began on a rushed breath. 'Did you go to a special etiquette school for royals or is it something you're born knowing how to do?'

'I'm careful.'

'Well, if I was eating that I'd have juice all over me by now. When I was younger my mother used to secure a tea towel around my neck whenever I sat down to a meal.' Aware that she was babbling because he made her so nervous, and he was so close, she stopped when he deftly sliced a sliver of peach and held it out to her. 'Open,' he ordered softly.

Open?

Without thinking she parted her lips and the sweet, fragrant fruit slipped inside. Regan's tongue came out to capture it and her heart beat a primal warning through every cell in her body as his eyes lingered on her sticky lips.

Kiss me, she thought. *Please, please, just kiss me before I die.*

'Your Majesty?' A male voice interrupted the awareness sparking between them as brightly as the Christmas lights at Macy's.

Tarik walked into the room, bowing formally. 'Excuse me,' he murmured, seeming to sense that he had interrupted something he shouldn't have. 'You asked me to brief you here and… I did knock.'

'That's fine.' The King recovered from the moment a lot quicker than she did and yet again Regan got the impression that he affected her a lot more than she affected him. 'You didn't interrupt anything important.' He moved away from the table and sat in the seat opposite her. 'What have you got for me?'

'The agenda for the day.' Tarik handed them each a one-page document. 'There have been a few amendments made to yours, sir, that I need to run through with you.'

Jag poured himself a short black coffee and held the pot aloft in question to Regan. She shook her head, hoping that she wasn't blushing in the process. She really had to stop letting him feed her.

'Okay, Tarik, tell me what I need to know.'

The older man ran through a list of morning meetings Jag was required to attend that made Regan feel exhausted just listening to it. 'After the round-table meeting on international banking reform, you're supposed to open the new sports complex at the local primary school followed by a tour of the facilities to drive more economic investment in the area. Unfortunately we've had to reschedule the meeting on foreign policy and counter-terrorism, which you shouldn't miss either, and there's no chance you can do both.'

Jag paused and poured himself another coffee. By the sound of his schedule he'd need to have a jug of the stuff on standby. Regan glanced at her own schedule, which consisted of another day of pampering in preparation for another dinner that evening. She frowned. 'Excuse me, I don't like to interrupt but is there any way I can help out?'

Both men looked at her as if she'd grown an extra head.

Regan rolled her eyes. 'Surely, as your supposed fiancée, I can be of more use to you than window dressing and keeping other men's wives at bay.'

His lips quirked at her attempted joke. 'What did you have in mind?'

'Well, I am a teacher. Is there any way I can do the school tour so that you're free to attend the other meeting? I mean, I would offer to attend the counter-terrorism meeting but other than just tell everyone to love each other I'm not sure what I can offer.'

He shook his head at the incongruity of her comment, his eyes sparkling with amusement.

'What do you think, Tarik?' he surprised her by asking the older man. 'I broke with protocol last night. Would this be stretching it?'

'Not really,' Tarik said slowly. 'I mean, if Miss James were really your fiancée it would be highly acceptable, even delightful, for her to take on a task such as this. It's not as if she needs to contribute anything specific. And her presence would add credence to your pet project, given that you're unable to attend.'

The morning sun glinted off the King's tanned face and made his blue eyes seem impossibly bright. 'Are you sure you want to do this, *habiba*? You know if I'm not there all the attention will be on you and you alone.'

Regan shook her head. 'Pretty much all the attention was on me last night anyway—as you knew it would be. But, as you can't be in two places at once, I'm happy to do it. Seriously, there are only so many times you can get your nails and hair done, and I'm not used to having so much time on my hands. It doesn't sit well with me.'

'If you're sure, then…thank you.' Something sparked behind his eyes, some emotion that Regan couldn't identify but then he blinked and it was gone. 'Tarik will accompany you. If at any time you think it's too much for you, tell him and he will return you immediately to the palace.'

Jag paced around his room and checked his watch for the hundredth time in half an hour. Regan should have been back an hour ago. Tarik had sent him a text saying they were on their way. So what was keeping them?

About to contact the security detail he had sent along with them, he heard quick footsteps racing down the marble hallway and knew immediately who it was.

Regan burst into the room, her cheeks rosy with exertion, Tarik hot on her heels. They were both laughing at some shared joke and his eyes narrowed. 'Is either one of you aware of the time? We are expected downstairs at the dinner in thirty minutes.'

Immediately Regan stopped smiling. 'It's my fault,' she assured him. 'Tarik told me that I had to finish up earlier but it was really hard to leave.'

'Miss James was magnificent, Your Majesty.'

Jag watched her roll her eyes at his aide in mocking rebuke. 'That's not true. If anyone's magnificent this man is. I can't believe he's seventy years old. He was kicking a soccer ball around with ten-year-olds.'

'As were you, my lady.'

'I'm just glad I wore flat shoes for the occasion,' she said, pulling the band from her ponytail and letting her glorious mane of hair swirl around her shoulders. 'I'm dead on my feet after today.'

'You're hardly going to be any use to me dead on your feet, Miss James.'

Stark silence greeted his blunt statement and, as Jag became aware that he was experiencing an unexpected jolt of...jealousy...at the obvious camaraderie between his aide and his temporary fiancée, his agitation levels rose. 'I don't remember seeing soccer on the itinerary.'

'It wasn't,' she said demurely. 'Again, that was my fault. We were touring the new gymnasium and sports grounds, which are incredible by the way—hats off to you because I know it was your vision to provide such an amazing space for the kids—and one of the boys rolled the ball my way. I returned it and noticed that the girls were sitting on the sidelines and I encouraged them to join in. Before we knew it we were all playing.'

Tarik was looking at him oddly and Jag drew in a deep breath. 'It's fine. Regan, you need to go and get ready for the dinner. We have...' he consulted his watch '...twenty-five minutes before it's due to commence.'

'Oh, right, of course.' She ran a hand through her hair, tousling it more. 'Oh, Tarik, if it's not too much of a bother, do you mind providing me with the postal address of the school? I have a lot on my mind but I don't want to forget.'

'Of course, my lady.'

'Hold on,' Jag said, feeling his irritation levels rise even higher at their unexpected mutual-appreciation society. 'Why would you need the postal address of the school?'

Regan gave him a faint smile. 'It's nothing. I promised one of the teachers I'd send them some art supplies because it's the one area in the school that isn't flourishing and it's really important.'

'I'm sorry?' Jag was finding it hard to keep up with her.

'The curriculum is really strong on maths, science and English, which can be a bit limiting, particularly for really young kids. They need music and art and lots of time to play so that their love of learning doesn't wither and die in the later years.'

'The reason the curriculum is set up that way is because when I took over as King the school system was in an appalling state.'

'I heard. All the teachers, and local dignitaries, were singing your praises. Apparently ten years ago Santara was in the bottom three percent for literacy and now it's only in the bottom twenty-five percent.'

Jag winced. That was mainly due to the remote country schools that were slow to keep pace with changes made in the cities, but he'd have liked things to be further along than they currently were. The problem was that he couldn't be on top of everything, as Tarik was wont to tell him.

As if reading his mind, his loyal aide raised a brow, seeming to remind him that he wasn't an island, and he scowled.

'Anyway, I said I would send some specialist supplies I know my kids back home love to use.'

Jag shook his head. He should be used to women taking advantage of his position and thinking they could spend his money out of hand. Just because she was spending it on kids didn't make him feel any more generous towards her. In fact, the disappointment that she was like so many other women, who couldn't wait to get their hands on a man's money, made his tone harsh.

'Next time you think to abuse my generosity and allocate palace funds you might care to run it by me.' His eyes were cool as they held hers. 'I will, of course, honour your promise this time, but next time I won't.'

A heavy silence filled the air and just when he was feeling that he had everything in hand Tarik moved to correct him.

'Your Maj—'

'Tarik, please don't.'

Surprisingly Tarik did as Regan requested and Jag stared from one to the other. 'What were you going to tell me, Tarik?'

Before his aide could speak Regan lifted her eyes to his. 'He was going to tell you that I was planning to pay for the art supplies myself.'

Another silence followed her statement. This time a fulminating one. Jag dragged a hand through his hair. 'How is it that you always seem to wrong-foot me, Miss James?'

'I don't know. Maybe it's because you're always looking for the worst in people.'

'That would be because I've seen the worst in people.' He sighed. 'And you will not be spending your money on supplies for the school.'

'But—'

'The palace will provide whatever is needed. Education is of vital importance to our nation. Write up a list of what you want and give it to Tarik.'

'Really?' Her face lit up and she gave him a smile that stopped his heart. 'You don't know how happy that makes me to hear a world leader speaking that way about education. Too often governments just pay lip service to education issues and it's completely debilitating for those who work in the industry. Do you have enough funds set aside for musical instruments too? From what I could tell, they're woefully under-represented as well.'

At the term 'lip service' Jag's gaze dropped to her sexy

mouth and he reminded himself that he was not an untried fifteen-year-old boy but a grown man in full control of his faculties. 'Don't push your luck, *habiba*.' If she did he wouldn't be responsible for his actions. 'And now you only have fifteen minutes to get ready. Should I tell them to hold dinner?'

'No, no.' Regan pivoted on her light feet and raced towards the connecting door to her room. 'Give me ten minutes. And thank you. You've made me really happy.'

Swamped by emotions he couldn't pin down, Jag immediately poured himself a stiff drink.

'Everyone loved her today, Your Majesty; she's—'

'Here temporarily,' Jag reminded Tarik, cutting off what was sure to be an enthusiastic diatribe as to Regan's virtues. 'Or have you forgotten that?'

'No, Your Majesty, it's just—'

'I think you're needed elsewhere, Tarik,' Jag informed him, not at all in the mood to hear any more. 'I'm quite sure I can await my fiancée's reappearance on my own.'

'Of course, Your Majesty.'

As soon as the older man departed the room Jag felt like a heel. It wasn't Tarik's fault that the woman was tying him up in knots.

And where the hell was his sister? If she was putting him through this for nothing he'd be furious.

'Okay.' A breathless Regan appeared in the doorway in record time. 'I hope I look all right. Since you're only wearing a suit and tie, I opted for something less formal than last night.' Her hands brushed over the waist of her sleeveless all-in-one trouser suit that faithfully followed the feminine curves of her body, accentuating her toned arms. Her face looked as if it was almost bare of make-up, and her hair fell around her shoulders in a silky russet cloud. 'I didn't have time to put my hair up,' she said, raising a hand to self-consciously pat it into place. 'If you think I should then I can—'

'It's fine.' He cut off her chatter, aware that this was something she did when she was really nervous. 'You look…' incredible. Stunning. *Beddable* '…very elegant.'

Sexual chemistry arced in the space between them, pulling him towards her as if by an invisible pulley system.

She fiddled with her engagement ring and Jag had to forcibly stop himself from reaching for her and wrapping those slender fingers around another part of his anatomy. A stranger to fighting desires as strong as this, Jag found himself growing increasingly frustrated. 'Let's go,' he growled, appalled at how she could arouse him without even trying.

'Okay. Oh, wait.' She stopped beside him at the door and smiled up at him. 'In all the rush before, I forgot to ask—how was your day?'

How was his day?

Shock made him go so still he could have been nailed to the spot. He couldn't remember the last time he'd been asked that question. Usually people were too busy reeling off a litany of complaints, or asking him to solve problems, to even consider asking him how his day had been.

A lengthy silence filled the room. How was it that this woman managed to uncover weaknesses in him he thought he'd long got over. 'My day was fine.'

'Sorry.' She gave him a faint smile. 'I've upset you again. I always seem to say the wrong thing around you.'

'I'm not upset,' he denied, 'I was just…' He took a deep breath. Let it out. 'Actually my day went very well.'

'Great, then we both had a good day, only…' Her brow scrunched and she paused to look up at him. 'Are you sure everything's okay? You've gone a little pale.'

No, everything was not okay. He was fighting with a very strong instinct to lock her up and throw away the key.

And not in the palace this time but some distant location he couldn't get to.

He thought about last night. The roundness of her bottom against his palms, her arms locked around his neck. The chemistry between them had been explosive but he'd possessed enough sanity at the time to know that doing anything about it would produce a list of regrets that would rival his inbox.

He felt his insides coil tight as the need to have her tried to edge out logic and reason.

As if she sensed the direction of his thoughts her throat bobbed as she swallowed, her eyes wary. As they should be. Because nothing good could come of constantly thinking about how much he wanted her and so he ruthlessly clamped down on emotions that he didn't want to feel, and needs he didn't want to have, and focused on his duties for the night. 'Everything's fine,' he finally said, directing her towards the door. 'Let's not keep my chef waiting any longer. His retribution isn't worth it.'

CHAPTER EIGHT

STANDING ON THE back steps of the palace balcony as the last of the summit delegates boarded a helicopter, Regan let out a long sigh. Presumably her duties as the king's escort would be over now that the four days were up, and she wondered why she didn't feel better about that.

For the past two days she had barely seen Jaeger. They had crossed paths only at social functions when he required her company, but always he seemed distantly polite and at the end of the evening he had done little more than bid her goodnight before heading to his office to do even more work.

She couldn't escape the feeling that he had been avoiding her a little, which had suited her fine. Spending time with him only gave her a false sense of connection with him that she didn't want to feel. Already all he had to do was look at her to make her burn, and she hated the fact that her senses had been awakened by a man who couldn't make it any plainer that he didn't want her. And why would he want her when she was merely a means to an end for him?

Wondering what would happen next given that their missing siblings had not yet returned she steeled her spine when he detached himself from the small party he was speaking with to approach her, his expression serious.

'I know the summit is officially over,' he began, 'and

that our deal only extended to today, however there is one more obligation that is required of you.'

'Obligation?' She forced herself to sound as composed as he did. 'Is this to do with Milena and Chad? Have you located them?'

Yesterday the security detail searching for Milena had reported that there might have been a sighting of her and Chad in a hiking store in Bhutan five days ago. It had eased Regan's mind because Chad was an avid hiker, but it still begged the question that if the two of them were merely hiking why hadn't they been more open about the whole thing?

'No I have no new information on our missing siblings,' Jag said grimly. 'This is a business obligation. The President of Spain is thinking about investing in our agricultural infrastructure. He wishes to see how he might utilise it in his own country and I have organised a short trip to the interior of Santara. As his wife is accompanying us, it would seem strange if you stayed behind. Particularly since she tells me that you have bonded over the past few days.'

'Yes, she's lovely.'

His head cocked to the side, his eyes curious. 'She also tells me that you speak fluent Spanish. Why didn't you tell me that you speak another language?'

'You didn't ask.'

Annoyance briefly pulled his brow together. 'I'm asking you now. How is it that you live on the East coast of America but have come to speak Spanish? It's not as if the language is prevalent there.'

'My mother was a Russian immigrant. She could speak five languages and spoke them often at home. I picked up my love of languages from her.'

'Does that mean you speak Russian too?'

Regan nodded. 'And French and German. Though my German is really basic. I wouldn't want to put it to the test.'

His eyes gleamed as he looked at her. 'A woman of hidden talents.'

Regan glanced at a pair of butterflies as they flitted over a row of flowers hedging the expansive lawn area, the admiration in Jaeger's eyes making her chest tight. The strain of hiding her physical reaction to him over the last few days was wearing her down.

'We will be gone most of the day. I suggest you wear something light and loose. The interior of my country gets very hot.'

Regan watched him stride away from her, immediately feeling a sense of deflation. She supposed it was to be expected since she felt as if she'd been on a roller-coaster ride since she'd arrived in Santara. It was as if she was living someone else's life. It didn't help that her feelings for the King were all over the place. One minute she didn't want to see him ever again, and the next she wanted to plaster herself all over him.

Back in her room she scanned the elaborate wardrobe Jag had provided for her, choosing camel-coloured trousers and a long-sleeved white linen shirt. Remembering the spider from the other night, and knowing they would be outdoors, she ignored the more delicate open-toed sandals and shook out a pair of her own white running shoes. Tying her hair into a low ponytail, she waited for Jag to return. When he did he looked ruggedly masculine in low-riding jeans, boots and a lightweight shirt similar to hers.

'Do you mind if I bring my camera?'

'Of course not. As long as you don't post any photos of me on social media.'

'No fear of that.' Regan grimaced self-consciously. 'I've learned the consequences of that particular lesson.'

His gaze turned thoughtful as he stopped beside her. 'Has it been so bad, *habiba*? Being here with me?'

Regan blinked. He could ask that after ignoring her for the last two days?

Fortunately she was saved from having to find an answer to his question when one of his bodyguards informed him that their helicopter was ready for boarding.

Never having taken a helicopter ride before, Regan was thrilled. Once they had left Aran her eyes were riveted to the vast expanse of sand dunes that stretched in peaks and valleys in an endless sea of gold and brown. In the distance she could see rocky mountain ranges with hints of green, and tiny villages dotted here and there. Jag sat opposite her and she felt his curious eyes on her. She listened as the two other occupants chatted about the sights but didn't join in, enjoying the sound of Jag's voice coming through the headset now and then as he pointed out some of the more interesting aspects of the countryside. At one point she nearly jumped out of her skin when he tapped her on the knee and said her name at the same time. Her eyes flew to his, her heart pounding even at that small contact, to find him pointing out of the window on her other side. 'Camel train,' he said and Regan couldn't contain a smile as she spotted the line of over twenty camels meandering across the top of a distant dune. He grinned back at her and for a moment the connection between them was so strong it was as if they were the only two people in the world. Then Isadora, the First Lady, fired off some questions in rapid-fire Spanish and Jag answered.

As they neared their destination Regan was amazed to see miles and miles of brilliant green fields. Jag explained how the ground was watered by both underground springs and the water that ran off the mountains. An engineering team had devised a revolutionary method for storing the water so that it didn't evaporate in the harsh sun that was a year-round issue for the desert nation.

Landing, they had lunch and took a tour of the various garden centres before the President asked if they could also stop at Jag's nearby thoroughbred stables. Climbing into a cavalcade of SUVs, they were once more whisked through an ever-changing landscape towards the stables.

Not being a horsewoman, Isadora was taken into the main house to rest from the harsh rays of the sun, while Regan headed to the stables, declining an invitation to join the men in the fertility clinic. She wandered from box to box, petting the muzzles of the horses she met and taking photos.

'Oh, you're a beauty,' she crooned as she came upon a giant white stallion, snapping off another photo. She grinned as the horse angled his head. 'And a real poser.' She laughed. The stallion snorted at her from the rear of the box, his black eyes studying her intently.

'You must be at least sixteen hands high,' she praised him. 'Come on. Come say hello.' The stallion stamped his foot a couple of times and then dropped his head, moving towards her and nuzzling her palm, inhaling her smell. 'I wish I had a carrot to give you,' she murmured, leaning in and breathing his horsey scent deep into her lungs.

'Actually he prefers sugar.'

At the sound of Jag's voice the horse whinnied and lifted his head. Man and horse eyed each other like long-time friends.

'I see you've become mesmerised by Miss James's soft touch,' he said, putting his hand in his pocket and pulling out a sugar cube. Instantly the horse nuzzled his palm, devouring the treat.

'He likes that,' Regan said, laughing when the stallion bumped her shoulder, urging her hand back up to his nose. 'You're a demanding thing,' she murmured, happily acquiescing and caressing beneath his mane where the hair grew as silky as duck down.

'Like his owner,' Jag said, his eyes following the movement of her fingers as she combed them through the horse's mane.

She wanted to ask him why he was suddenly paying her attention again, but the gleam in his bright blue eyes made the words die in her throat. Instead she asked, 'What's his name?'

'Bariq. It means lightning.'

The horse whinnied and Regan laughed. 'And I'm sure it suits you,' she assured him.

'He doesn't usually take to strangers so readily. You must know horses.'

'Yes.' Her throat thickened. Horse riding had been one of those things they had all done as a family when her parents had been alive. An activity that had stopped when her parents had become sick. She leaned into the stallion's neck and breathed him in. 'I love horses.'

'Why does that make you sad?' Jag asked softly.

Embarrassed at having given herself away, Regan shifted uncomfortably. 'It was my parents' favourite pastime. They used to take Chad and me riding as often as possible.'

He frowned, his finger lightly tapping the bridge of her nose. 'You have one or two new freckles.'

Regan rubbed at the place he had touched. 'Deft subject change, Your Majesty,' she said with a small smile. 'Unfortunately the freckles come with the hair colour.'

'Not unfortunately. Your colouring is as warm as your personality.' His voice had roughened and sent sparks careening through Regan's body. 'And I don't like to see you sad.'

Not knowing what to say to that, Regan focused on the

stallion. Why didn't he like to see her sad? She was only a means to an end for him, wasn't she?

'Good afternoon, Your Majesty.' A man in a groom's uniform strode down the blue stone aisle towards them. 'Would you like me to saddle Bariq for you to ride?'

Jag hesitated, his eyes on her. 'Care to take a ride with me, Regan?'

Regan immediately shook her head. 'I don't think so… I haven't ridden in a long time,' she admitted huskily.

'I guessed that, *habiba*,' he said, his eyes soft. 'But there is nothing to worry about. I'll be with you the whole time.'

'What about the President and his wife?'

'He is joining his wife for iced tea, after which they will be returning to the airport, where their plane is waiting to return them to Spain. I said goodbye on your behalf.'

Unable to think of another reason to not take this moment to enjoy herself, Regan smiled shyly. 'If you're sure?'

'I am.'

Twenty minutes later, having changed into jodhpurs and a fitted tunic, Regan waited with barely leashed excitement to mount her horse, a lovely palomino mare called Alsukar. Or sugar.

It had been more than a decade since she had ridden but she remembered it as if it were yesterday, bittersweet memories of shared family time filling her head.

'Okay?' Jaeger pulled up alongside her, his magnificent white stallion snorting and champing at the bit in his eagerness to gallop.

Jaeger barely tightened his hands on the reins, his deep voice alone enough to bring his prancing horse under his control.

'Yes, I feel like Bariq. I can't wait to get going.' A groom gave Regan a leg-up into the saddle. Regan took the reins and felt the energy of the horse beneath her.

She couldn't contain her smile. She was looking forward to testing her riding legs, and creating some new memories that were not entirely based on the loss of her parents. And then she wondered if Jaeger had suggested they ride for precisely that reason and told herself not to be fanciful. He had done this for no other reason than that his stallion needed a run, and she'd be a fool to entertain any other notion.

Before moving out Jag brought his horse close to hers. Leaning over, he shook out a piece of cloth and proceeded to fashion it on top of her head into what he told her was a *shemagh*. 'When we get outside you take this piece and tuck it into here so that it covers your mouth and nose.'

His fingers grazed along her jaw as he fixed the headdress into place, sending a cascade of shivers across her skin. Sensing her reaction, Sugar shifted sideways and Jag grabbed hold of her bridle to steady her.

'Thanks,' Regan said, not quite meeting his eyes.

He nodded and then proceeded to expertly fold his own royal blue *shemagh* that perfectly matched his eyes. He was a visual feast and she wondered what it would be like to be able to truly claim this man as her own.

They rode across oceans of sand dunes, taking the horses through their paces, and giving them their head from time to time. Jag tempered his horse to stay by her side and she felt sorry for the big stallion, who just wanted to gallop.

Finally they stopped to rest at a small watering hole on the outskirts of a village. Regan dismounted on jelly legs and immediately went to one of the guards who had trailed them to retrieve her camera from his pack. Completely enthralled by the humble beauty of the place, she snapped off a few photos of the contrasting colours and textures surrounding her.

A few locals came out of the low-lying buildings, bowing low when they saw who had arrived to greet them.

Jaeger was clearly a revered leader, greeting his people with kindness and respect.

Born to lead, he had said, or words to that effect, and, seeing him in action, as she had done over the past four days, she knew it was true.

A group of local men approached Jaeger and the two guards that had followed them dismounted and joined their King.

Regan snapped a photo of the impressive trio, raising her brow when he looked at her.

Is this okay? her look enquired.

Fine, his slight nod replied.

Feeling happy, she turned to find two young girls approaching her, carefully carrying a tray full of clay mugs. They curtseyed and offered one to her.

Taking the cup of cool water gratefully, Regan smiled. *'Shukran.'*

'Shukran, shukran,' the young girls tittered, dancing away as if they couldn't believe she had taken their offering.

She watched as they approached Jaeger, bemused at how beautifully he handled their shy attention, taking a mug and bowing to them in return.

Regan couldn't prevent the smile on her face, hot colour stinging her cheekbones as he looked across at her. Could he read her thoughts? Did he know how much she was enjoying herself with him? Did he know how hard it was for her to remember that she was only here with him like this because Chad and Milena were missing? That he believed Chad had committed a crime in running off with his sister?

Not wanting to dwell on any of that now, she turned back to the vast open space of the desert, the light breeze moving gently across the sand like a whisper. Enthralled by the deep quiet of the land, she raised her viewfinder again. When Jaeger came into view across the way she paused. He had unwound his blue *shemagh* and it framed his handsome face, giving his skin tone a golden-brown hue. Curious, she watched an old man approach, handing Jag an enormous bird of prey.

The bird made a noise in greeting and clung to Jag's gloved hand. As wild and untamed as its master, its proud profile perfectly mirroring Jag's.

Regan felt her breath catch. He really was the most magnificent creature, and before she could stop herself she depressed the shutter and snapped a round of photos.

A small crowd had gathered around him and he released the bird into full flight, watching as it soared into the air on ginormous wings. Jaeger gave a short, sharp whistle and the magnificent bird swooped and dived above them, putting on a magical display. Regan couldn't take her eyes off either man or bird as they worked together in perfect harmony, the bird circling high and waiting for Jaeger's commands before plummeting to earth like a bullet from a gun, completely trusting that the King would provide a safe landing for it. Which he did, without even flinching as those huge talons wrapped around his thick leather glove.

As if sensing the lens on him, Jaeger turned in her direction and stared at her, his features proud, his blue eyes piercing as if he were gazing directly into her soul. Regan depressed her finger on the shutter again, her lens capturing the moment before she lowered the camera. She swallowed as he continued to look at her, completely captivated by the heat and masculine energy that emanated from his riveting gaze. It was as if she had become the prey and he were the falcon, with her firmly trapped in his sights.

The memory of his fingers threading through her hair, cupping her face as he kissed her, thrusting his tongue into the moist heat of her mouth, made her breath catch in her throat. It was so easy to imagine him coming to her now, bending to her and kissing the breath from her body, tasting her with his tongue, and gripping her waist in his powerful hands, telling her everything he wanted to do to her. Then doing those things…

One of his men spoke in his ear, breaking the spell between them, and Regan realised it was time for them to ride back. The sun had already started to sink towards the horizon, the heat of the day also starting to ebb away.

Handing the falcon back to the old man, Jag made his way over to her. 'You look flushed, *habiba*,' he said softly. 'I should have given you a wide-brimmed hat as well.'

Regan felt flushed but she knew it had more to do with the scorching hot images of the two of them together than the sun. Safer, though, to have him believe that her heightened state was to do with mother nature than for him to realise that she couldn't look at him lately without wanting him.

'How did you find the ride?' he asked, adjusting the front of her *shemagh*.

'Wonderful.' She shaded her eyes from the sun as she looked up at him. 'It was truly wonderful.'

'No sad memories?'

'At the start but… I didn't realise how much I miss being around horses until now so…thank you.'

'It was my pleasure.'

'That bird—'

'Arrow?'

'Fitting name,' she said. 'He's magnificent.'

'*She's* magnificent. I found her as a chick at the base of a cliff when I was out riding years ago. She had fallen from her nest and wasn't ready to fly. The mother could do nothing for her and there was no way I could scale the side of the cliff to return her to her nest so I took her home with me. We've been firm friends ever since but I hardly get time to take her out any more. She wanted to hunt today but I didn't think you would want to see that.'

'What does she hunt?'

'Mice, hares, smaller birds.'

'Spiders?'

Jag laughed. 'Don't sound so hopeful, *habiba*.'

At the memory of the giant eight-legged monster in her wardrobe, Regan scoured the ground around them. 'You're safe. From creepy crawlies.'

His amused eyes grinned into hers and Regan felt the intimacy of the moment even though they hadn't even touched. For a split second she wondered if he was about to bend down and kiss her. And she wanted him to.

'We need to leave. It is getting late.'

'Of course. I can see the sun already dipping down towards the horizon and it gets cold in the desert at night. Or so I've heard.'

She was babbling, she knew it, and, by the way his lips tilted up at one side, he knew it too. 'It does. The desert is very unforgiving. It is not a place you want to get caught in during the day or the night.'

'Okay, well…'

'Sire, your horse.'

Thankful for the interruption, Regan turned blindly to the man who had brought their horses. Or, rather, Jag's stallion.

'What happened to my mare?'

'She grew tired from the ride out. She will be stabled here for the night and one of the men will return for her tomorrow.' Jaeger collected the reins from the man.

Placing a sure foot in the stirrup, he swung himself up onto the enormous horse, reaching his hand down to her, palm facing up. 'You will ride with me.'

Ride with him? No way. She was trying to lower her awareness of him, not elevate it into the stratosphere. 'That's okay.' She gave him a wan smile. 'I can…' She looked around, hoping to see some other mode of transport at her disposal.

'I'm afraid the A train uptown has left for the day.'

Regan laughed. 'Was that a New York joke, Your Majesty?'

'A pretty lame one,' he admitted unselfconsciously. 'Come. Give me your hand.'

Regan stared up at him. Everything inside of her said that she should not do this. That she should insist that he find another way for her to make it back to the stables. Maybe with one of his trusted guards, but she knew she'd be wasting her breath and really…just the thought of riding with him atop that massive horse gave her goosebumps.

She moistened her lips and placed her hand in his. Right now, out here in the desert, where it was wild and free, she felt very unlike her usually cautious self.

Jaeger's hand closed around hers and seconds later he had her seated on the horse behind him. He twisted around to face her, adjusting her *shemagh* once more so that it covered most of her face. Regan's heart beat fast as she stared back at him, so close she could smell the combined scent of horse and man. It was quite the aphrodisiac. She couldn't see his expression because his sunglasses were back in place, his own *shemagh* drawn across his face. He looked like the dangerous outlaw she had imagined him to be when they met and a thrill went through her. Back then her instincts had screamed at her to run. Now they were begging her to draw closer.

'You'll have to hang on tight, *habiba*. Bariq likes to have his head.'

Before she could respond Jag whirled the stallion on

his hind legs and raced them out of the small village and across the sand, giving Regan no choice but to comply with his suggestion or fly off the back of the horse and land on her rear end.

Determined to remain steadfastly immune to his proximity, she lasted about five seconds before she became aware of the lean, hard layer of muscle at his abdomen as her fingers flattened across his middle. Remembering what those muscles looked like without his shirt led to thoughts of sex, and the harder she tried to banish the word from her mind the more it stuck until it was all she could think about.

Between that and the smooth, powerful motion of the horse, she was decidedly rubber-legged when they arrived back at the stables.

Jag dismounted, his blue eyes hot and stormy as he looked up at her with his arms outstretched. Regan automatically swung her leg over the saddle, holding herself still in the circle of his arms as she waited for her legs to be firm enough to hold her upright.

Not wanting to meet his eyes in case he read every single hot thought she had ever had about him, she focused on the front of his shirt, glad when one of his bodyguards strode over and handed him a phone.

Thankful for the reprieve, she stroked the sweaty sides of the stallion's neck, telling him how big and strong he was.

'Careful, *habiba*, you don't want it to go to his head,' Jag mused as he turned back to her. 'This is supposed to be one of the fiercest horses in the land but he looks as if one word from you would send him to his knees.'

Regan smiled. 'He looks fierce because I suspect people have always been scared of him, but all he needs is to hear how amazing he is.'

Jaeger quirked a brow. 'Don't we all?'

Regan paused. Was that what Jaeger needed? To hear how amazing he was?

'That was Tarik. He has just informed me that the tribe of my ancestors has invited us to attend a congratulatory dinner tonight.'

Regan blinked at him. 'Because the summit is over?'

'No, because I have decided to take a bride.'

She stared at him blankly and he let out a rough laugh. 'You, *habiba*.'

'But we're not really going to be married!' she said, shock sending her voice high.

'To them we are.'

Regan shook her head, frowning. 'I'm not sure it's wise for me to meet even more of your people.' She shook her head, compelled to state the obvious. 'I mean, I'm not your fiancée. I'm a pawn. We both are because I'm using you to ensure Chad doesn't spend the rest of his life in some dungeon, and you're using me to get Milena back.'

A muscle flickered in his jaw, the one that worked every time he got angry. 'I don't have a dungeon,' he growled.

Before she had time to react he caught her face in his strong hands and raised her lips to his. Momentarily stunned, Regan stood there, her body flush against his. It wasn't a gentle kiss, or an exploratory kiss. It wasn't even a nice kiss. It was hot and demanding, skilfully divesting her of any willpower to resist. Not that she was trying to.

Instead her arms hooked around his neck and she rose up onto her toes, meeting the sensual onslaught of his attack with a hunger as deep as his own.

At her total acquiescence he groaned, shifting her so that she was pressed between him and the stable wall, her head tilted back so that she was his to command. And he did, softening the kiss, taking her lips one at a time before plundering her mouth with his tongue.

Her lips clung to his, a sob of pure need rising up inside of her. This was what she wanted, what she needed, what she had craved ever since he had kissed her and touched her that night in the garden suite. This thrilling throb of desire that she had only ever experienced in his arms. It was like a fever in her blood, a rush of sensation that couldn't be denied.

And then it was over just as quickly as it had begun. Once more he pulled back and she was left panting and unsteady, her body aching and empty.

She heard him curse as he turned his back on her. Then he spun towards her, breathing hard.

A groom exited a nearby stall carrying a tack box and Regan wondered if that was why he'd stopped.

She glanced up to see Jag watching her and for once he didn't seem completely immune to what had just happened between them.

'I think that should clear up any misconceptions you have that I didn't want a repeat of our kiss the other night.'

She blinked up at him, shocked at what he had just disclosed.

He looked shocked himself and shook his head. 'Wise or not, we have to attend the dinner tonight. It would be an insult not to, since we are already in the region. We will spend the night at my oasis and return to the palace first thing tomorrow morning.'

'Your oasis?'

'The place I come to when I want to unwind.'

CHAPTER NINE

WHEN WAS HE going to learn that kissing her was not the way to expunge her from his system?

He shook his head and strode inside his Bedouin tent. Set on the edge of a private rock pool and surrounded by palm trees, it was an upscale version of those his ancestors had used to live in. Usually he felt a sense of peace wash over him as he shed the suits and royal robes to reconnect with the man beneath, but not tonight.

He yanked his shirt over his head and made his way to the purpose-built shower at the back. He should not have let her words anger him, he thought savagely; that had been the problem.

He wasn't used to someone questioning the wisdom of his decisions and he didn't like the reminder of how they were using each other even though it was true. Riding Bariq back to the stables with her tucked against his back hadn't done his nerves any good either. If at any time she had shifted her hand an inch lower she would have realised that the only thing on his mind was sex.

Wondering how she was finding her own accommodation and whether she was wishing it was a five-star hotel, he donned a white *thawb* and royal headdress and went outside.

The sun was low on the horizon, his favourite time of day in the desert, the ambient light turning the sky a dusky mauve. Hearing a sound behind him, he turned to see Regan dressed in a brightly coloured *thawb* and flowing floor-length headdress. As soon as they had arrived at the village a group of local women had descended upon their future Queen to give her a traditional makeover. The results were stunning. She was completely covered from head to toe, and yet she managed to look like an exotic treat waiting to be unwrapped. Her chin tilted upwards in a tiny gesture he had first assumed was haughtiness, but now realised was one of self-consciousness. Despite her fair skin, she looked as if she was born to be here. Born to be his.

Perturbed by that last thought, Jag didn't realise he was frowning until Regan raised a brow. 'I did try to tell them to stop with the black kohl and henna. I look like I'm dressed for a Halloween party, don't I?'

Jag felt instantly chagrined at her pained expression. 'You look stunning. I just had something else on my mind.' Such as the fact that he might be slowly losing it.

'Well, whatever it was it obviously wasn't nice. Which is hard to believe when you're in a place like this.' Her gaze swept across the small cluster of tents and the deep blue lagoon. 'This is like something out of a fairy tale.'

'You don't wish for more modern accommodation?'

'Are you kidding?' Regan gaped at him. 'People pay a fortune to have experiences like this. I had no idea tents had carpets and real beds.'

'You're getting the upscale version. Come. It is a short drive to the village.'

'We're not going by camel?'

Jag couldn't prevent a grin at her teasing comment. 'I draw the line at some traditions.'

He held the door wide and her sheer veil caught on his arm as she made to step into the car. As he lifted his hand to disengage it his fingers caught around her silky hair and he nearly threw caution to the wind and buried his hands in the sexy mass and brought her mouth up to his again.

Moments later their car pulled up alongside a large purpose-built marquee. Inside low tables were set in a wide circle with cushions scattered throughout the tent for seating, soft music playing from the edge of the entertainment area.

He watched Regan as she greeted his local tribespeople, speaking softly and attempting a few words in his native tongue, her adept mind already picking up a few phrases. He remembered the way her face had lit up when they had ridden first in the helicopter, and then on horseback through the desert. He had half expected her to hate his homeland but to his surprise she had seemed enamoured by it.

As his people were fast becoming enamoured by her.

'Your Majesty, your table.'

The tribal chieftain guided them to the central spot in the marquee, where everyone would be able to watch him and Regan interact.

Seeing the smiles on his people's faces was like a punch in the stomach. He hadn't given much thought to how much they wanted this to be real and he conceded that Regan had been right to be hesitant in accepting the invitation. Probably he could have got out of it but once again he found himself making a decision to keep this woman close when it wasn't necessary.

He frowned. What was necessary was getting back to the palace and to what was important—work and finding Milena. But before that could happen he had tonight to get through.

'How are you feeling?' he asked Regan softly. 'Overwhelmed? Nervous? I should apologise because you're the centre of attention again.'

'I'm fine.' She gazed around the wide, brightly decorated space. 'Maybe you dragging me to your palace has been good for me. I think I've become a bit reclusive at home, keeping to my usual routine and never stepping outside of my comfort zone. My world is so small compared to yours. I don't know how you do it; having to be switched on all the time.'

'Sometimes it's tough,' he admitted, something he'd never said out loud before. 'Sometimes I'm presented with problems and challenges with no clear answers, and I find that the hardest of all.'

Especially now that Regan had started making him question his relationship with his siblings. Did Rafa stay away from Santara because Jag had not created a clear role for him at the palace? Had Milena run off with Chad James because she didn't want to go through with her royal marriage and couldn't tell him?

'We don't always get it right,' she said softly, as if reading his mind.

But he did. He had people depending on him. People who needed him to get it right. Especially when his father had been too caught up in his domestic dramas to lead the country as it deserved to be led.

Fortunately the tempo of the music increased, cutting off any further chance of conversation. A good thing, since he had a habit of revealing too much of himself around this woman.

Dancers poured into the tent, smiling and clapping, and, despite her misgivings about being here, Regan decided she was going to enjoy the evening. It wasn't as if she was likely to get a chance to experience something like this again any time soon. And yes, it would be better if she wasn't so aware of the man beside her, but there wasn't much she could do about that. Try as she had…

They might not have met in the most conventional of

circumstances, but the way her body responded to him was one hundred percent *conventionally* female.

And knowing that he was just as attracted to her was driving her crazy. It made her wonder what might have been if he had been an ordinary guy she had met at her local park. But he wasn't. He was a king, a man of supreme importance—and her brother had run off with his sister.

She gave an inward groan, wishing that Chad would return, wishing that this crazy situation was over so that she could go back to normal. If that was even possible after the way Jaeger had touched her, kissed her…

A kaleidoscope of butterflies took flight in her stomach as she absently watched his strong hands as he gestured with the person next to him. His wrists were thick, his forearms sinewy and dusted with dark hair. Everything about him was so potently male it made her feel breathless with need.

I'm falling for him, she realised with a jolt of dismay. *I'm really falling for him.*

She must have made a small sound of distress because he immediately turned towards her, his eyes scanning her face.

'*Habiba*, what is it?'

Regan shrugged helplessly. 'Nothing.'

His frown told her that he didn't believe her but he was prevented from asking more when she joined in the energetic clapping as a troop of new dancers took to the floor. This time the group was made up entirely of women in brightly coloured outfits and carrying sheer scarves.

You're not falling for him, she assured herself sternly. You're suffering from a serious case of lust for a man who knows how to kiss a woman into a stupor. You're not the first, and you certainly won't be the last, to imagine themselves in love with the sheikh. Princess Alexa was a good case in point. She'd met the King twice and fallen for him.

And maybe Jag was right in that the Princess only wanted to marry him for political reasons, but Regan had her doubts. She'd seen the woman's heartfelt misery in thinking she had lost him.

Blindly she turned back to concentrate on the dancers. The women were undulating their hips with practised ease, gracefully weaving silken scarves around their bodies in a coordinated display of confidence and femininity. Combined with the lyrical music, it was both provocative and sensual. But all Regan could really concentrate on was the man seated so closely beside her.

Glancing at him through her lashes, she noticed a fine line of tension bracketing his mouth. She wondered why he was having such a reaction to the beautiful display when the story behind the dance hit her on the head. This was no ordinary dance. The scarves, the hip bumps, the sensual spell that held the crowd captivated…this was a type of love dance.

One of the performers broke from the circle and Regan held her breath, only to release it again when she approached a young woman, encouraging her to join her on the floor.

The woman did, smiling shyly at the young man she had been seated next to.

The crowd cheered and clapped encouragingly.

'Please tell me they're not going to expect me to go up there?' she whispered raggedly.

Jag's blue eyes snagged with hers and she knew the answer before he even opened his mouth.

She shook her head. 'I'm a hopeless dancer. I have no coordination at all.'

'You forget I've seen you on horseback, so I know that's blatantly untrue.'

'Riding a horse is nothing like dancing. At least with

horseback riding if something goes wrong I can blame the horse.'

Jag laughed. '*Habiba*, I—'

Before he could finish one of the dancers undulated in front of her, beckoning to her. By this time three other women had joined the dance, mimicking the sensual movements in a joyful display of passion and love.

Oh, God, she was seriously going to die of embarrassment.

Jag's eyes were a deep blue as she slowly rose to her feet. His hand caught hers. 'Regan, you don't have to do this.'

It was kind of him to say so, but Regan knew she'd be disappointed in herself if she didn't do it. Not only because she would be disappointing the people watching, but also because it was another chance to step outside her comfort zone and own it.

'I'll be fine,' she murmured with more bravado than she felt, throwing him one last beseeching look, and she followed the dancer out onto the floor, accepting the rose-coloured scarf that was offered to her.

At first she felt rigid and clumsy, conscious of everyone watching her, but slowly, and by some miracle, the sensual music started to flow through her, luring her to lower her inhibitions.

Telling herself to stop being a coward, she raised her arms and twined her hands together above her head, undulating her hips slowly. The crowd clapped and the music throbbed in time with her heartbeat. Laughingly, she tried to emulate the movements of the other dancers. And then she just let go, closing her eyes and giving herself up to the moment.

Unbidden, Jag's tender kiss against the stable wall invaded her head. Her breasts rose and fell at the memory of his hard body pressed to hers, his mouth devouring her, tasting her, arousing her. A sweet lethargy spread through her limbs and she made the mistake of opening her eyes and staring directly into his.

It was like being torched by an open flame. The heat and hunger in his gaze was so intimate it took her breath away. His whole body transmitted unmistakable masculine desire and it seared her to her core.

The scarf floated teasingly in the air between them as she mimicked the earlier movements of the women, the delicate fabric wafting in front of him. With lightning-quick reflexes he grabbed hold of the end, bringing her to a standstill.

She couldn't do anything but stare at him, and then, as if in slow motion, he started to reel her in.

Regan was completely undone to see the delicate skein of silk wrapping around his big, tanned hand, the sight somehow enhancing his potent masculinity when it might have diminished it in a lesser man. But there was nothing lesser about Jaeger al-Hadrid and Regan knew that once she reached him there would be no turning back.

'Regan.'

His eyes were as hot as the sun, his rough tone pure sex.

Regan's breath hitched in her throat. There was only one thing she could say to that look.

'Yes.'

Understanding completely that the word hadn't been a question, he unfolded lithely to his feet. His height dwarfed her, the *thawb* making him seem even more powerful than usual. As soon as he stood the music stopped, but really Regan only vaguely registered the change.

He took her hand and not a single sound was uttered as he led her from the tent.

Once they were outside, the cool night air was a welcome relief against her heated cheeks but it did nothing to relieve the hot, pulsing desire that thrummed through her and turned her insides liquid with need.

When they reached his black SUV he dismissed his driver with a single nod.

Regan hesitated beside the open passenger door, forcing her eyes to meet his. 'I need to know one thing,' she said, her voice breathless with longing. 'Are you going to stop again and pull back from me?' Because if he did she didn't think she could bear it.

His large hand rose to cup her face, his thumb brushing along her cheekbone, his eyes as dark as the night sky above them. 'I've tried that. It doesn't work.'

A quiver went through her at his rough, gravelly tone. She gave him a tremulous smile and his fingers tightened against her scalp. 'Jump in.'

The big car flew across the desert road, eating up the distance between the marquee and his private tent in no time. Neither of them spoke, the air in the car so thick it made talking impossible. It made thinking impossible too and then he was beside her door, opening it, his warm hand pressing to the small of her back as he guided her towards the large tent she knew to be his. He raised the flap and she moved inside, suddenly nervous, the sound of it dropping back into place behind them like the crack of a whip in the stillness.

His hands framed her face and for a heartbeat he just looked at her. Then he lowered his head and took her mouth in a kiss of devastating expertise.

Regan could feel her heart racing, her body turning to liquid.

The kiss, slow and gentle at first, quickly turned urgent. He tasted of wine and coffee, and a deep male hunger that fed her own.

The only thing she managed to whisper was his name

but that must have been enough because suddenly she was being lifted and he was carrying her towards the rear of the tent. He placed her on the edge of the enormous mattress, taking a moment to reef his robe off over his head, leaving him in low riding cotton pants that left little to her imagination.

Her lips went dry as he stood before her, gloriously male, from the thick muscular arms and shoulders down to his lean hips and long legs.

'I won't stop this time, *habiba*, not unless you want me to.'

Regan's heart hammered inside her chest. Maybe she should stop, maybe she should say no, but she couldn't. Spending time with him these past few days, watching him command a room, seeing his quick mind in action, and then today, the way he handled Bariq and Arrow, seeing his gentleness with those less physically capable than himself, was… He was everything a woman could ever hope to find in a man and she loved him. Completely and utterly; as scary as that felt. 'I don't want to stop. I want this. I want you.'

She knew her words held a deeper meaning than he would attribute to them, and suddenly she was aware that this might not be the smartest decision she had ever made.

He lifted his hand to her, beckoning, and she no longer cared about being smart.

'Then come to me, Regan. Let me show you what you do to me.'

CHAPTER TEN

JAG COULDN'T CONTROL the shudder that went through him as Regan gracefully rose from the bed and came towards him. He wasn't sure how he had restrained himself thus far but he forced the aching need riding him hard to subside. He didn't want to impose himself on her or scare her with the strength of his desire. He wanted her to come to him as his equal. As a woman who wanted him regardless of how they had met, or why they were together. He needed her stripped bare because it was exactly how she made him feel.

She stopped a pace away from him, her eyes luminous in the soft light, the silky floor-length veil she still wore framing her beautiful face.

He lifted his hands and searched out the pins that held the veil in place until the fabric pooled at her feet, leaving her glorious hair unadorned.

'Turn around,' he instructed, his voice hoarse.

Silently she complied and he lowered the zipper in the back of her *thawb*. She wasn't wearing a bra and his blood surged at the sight of her pale, slender back. His fingers traced a line down her delicate vertebrae and back up, rejoicing in the tremor that went through her.

'Cold?' he asked, his hands sweeping her hair aside and lowering his head to the tender skin where her neck and shoulder joined.

'No.' She shook her head, resting it back against his

chest. He smoothed the gown over her narrow shoulders and held his breath as it too slithered to the floor.

'Then turn around, *ya amar*. Let me see you.'

Slowly she did as he instructed, her little chin lifted ever so slightly as she stood before him in only a tiny pair of black panties and delicate sandals.

He had been with many women in his life. Women he had admired and even liked, but he had never been with a woman who created in him this deep, gnawing hunger to possess, to brand, to claim as his own for ever and beyond.

Shaking off the sensation that he was in much deeper than he'd ever been before, Jag drew her closer. 'You're beautiful,' he said, his eyes memorising every sensual detail of her supple body; her straight shoulders and slender torso, the rise of her round breasts, high and firm, the narrowness of her waist, and the subtle flare of her hips and long legs. Hips designed to cradle a man's body, legs designed to wrap around him and hold him tight. 'Perfect.'

Unable to hold himself back, he gathered her close, groaning as the tips of her breasts nestled in the hair on his chest. She arched into him, her hands grasping his shoulders to pull him even closer. 'Kiss me, please.'

He did more than that, he devoured her, taking her mouth in a long, searing kiss that was a promise to how he intended to possess her with his body.

She made a soft keening sound, her hands kneading and caressing his naked shoulders. Jag dragged his hands down her ribcage, sweeping along her spine, before bringing his hands to her breasts. He cupped them gently, plucking at her tight nipples between his fingers.

She moaned deeply, arching against him, her body rising to his, climbing his until she was fully in his arms with her legs wrapped around his waist, her breasts inches from his mouth.

He gave a husky laugh. '*Habiba*, how very nice to meet you.' He leaned forward and cut off her answering chuckle by taking her nipple into his mouth. She clung to him, crying out in an agony of pleasure. He wanted to give her that pleasure. He wanted to give her everything.

He suckled her gently, flicking her nipple. Her thighs tightened around him as her arousal heightened and he rewarded her responsiveness with firmer and firmer pulls of his mouth. First on one breast then the other.

'Jaeger! Jag!' She writhed against him and he sensed she was close to climaxing. The knowledge sent his own arousal into the stratosphere.

'Regan, I—' He cursed as he laid her on his bed, his movements clumsy with his own imminent loss of control.

Shaking, he tried to steady himself, but she reached up to frame his face as he came down over the top of her, pulling his mouth back to hers.

'Wait,' he growled as her fingers trailed down over his muscled back and slipped beneath the waistband of his trousers. She was driving him to the edge of control and he needed to pull back for a moment, centre himself. But she didn't listen, her mouth opening wider under his, her tongue gliding into his mouth to mate with his, her clever fingers shattering his ability to keep a part of himself back.

'I don't want to wait,' she murmured against his neck. 'I need you. I need you inside me.'

'If you don't wait,' he growled, 'this is going to be over before it's begun.'

'I don't care. I need—'

He grabbed her hands and shackled them above her head with one hand. With the other he ruthlessly divested himself of his clothing. 'I know what you need.'

He came down over the top of her, pressing her into

the mattress. She parted her thighs and her hips rose to meet his.

'Dammit, Regan, I need to see if you're…' He'd been going to say *ready for me*, but he had already discovered the answer. 'Regan.' He positioned himself over her, his legs nudging her thighs wider.

'Yes. Please, Jag, do it.'

Her fingers dug into his hips and he surged into her, completely sheathing himself inside her.

She gasped and he instantly stilled. He smoothed her hair back from her forehead, putting his weight on his elbows. 'Okay?'

Breathing heavily through her mouth, she nodded. 'You're just so… Oh, that feels fantastic.'

He flexed again and felt her body go liquid around him. Then he stilled.

'Protection.' How in the world had he forgotten that?

She shook her head. 'We don't need it. I'm on the Pill and I've only been with one other man. Years ago.'

One other man?

'And I trust you.'

It was those last words that made his heart leap inside his chest and tipped him over the edge. Or perhaps it was the way her inner muscles rippled around him, drawing him further inside. Either way he no longer cared. All he cared about, all he could think about was taking them both higher, driving them deeper until time and space became irrelevant.

'Jag!' Her body gripped him tighter, growing taut as she moved more frantically beneath him.

'That's it, *habiba, ya amar*, like that… Yes, just…'

He felt the instant her body reached its peak, revelling in the way she screamed his name as she came apart in his arms. And then he couldn't think at all because her muscles were clenching around him like a silken fist. His body surged forward, driving into her with none of his usual finesse, until, with his own cry of release, he lost himself inside her.

Jag woke some time later to find Regan wrapped around him like ivy. One arm slung over his chest, her thigh positioned high over his. He couldn't remember the last time he'd slept all night with a woman. Sleep was a luxury he usually caught in snatches. Was that what had woken him so suddenly? The fact that he wasn't up? Or was it the warm, naked woman at his side who had given him more pleasure than he could ever remember having in bed?

His flesh stirred, definitely liking that second idea better than the first.

She must have registered the change in him because she made a small, sleepy noise, her body snuggling deeper against his.

Jag smiled, shifting a strand of her hair back from her forehead. He loved her hair. The colour, the texture… It felt like silk and fairly vibrated under the sunlight.

He told himself that he wouldn't wake her. She deserved to sleep and she would no doubt be a little tender from not having made love in such a long time.

She had only had one lover before him. He'd had no idea she was that inexperienced but he wasn't unhappy about it. Had he ever had a woman who had given herself to him so openly? So *wholeheartedly*? It was as if she'd held nothing back from him and he wasn't sure he entirely liked how that made him feel. Vulnerable. Open. A little raw, perhaps.

Slowly he became aware of his heart beating and knew it wasn't a sensation he registered very often.

Regan shifted again, her arm moving as if she was searching for something in her sleep.

Him?

Heat coiled through him.

On some elemental level Jag recognised that Regan had unlocked a deep-seated hunger inside him he wasn't altogether comfortable with. She made him think of things like loss and longing, like desire and need, and…

'The heart knows what the heart wants.'

Zumar's statement came to him from out of nowhere.

The heart?

This wasn't about his heart. It was about sex. Very good, very hot sex.

His hand tightened in her hair as she made another little sleepy sound. It was meant to reassure her that everything was okay but deep inside he wasn't all that sure that it was true. 'It's okay, *habiba*, you're only dreaming.'

'Jag?' Her brown eyes fluttered open, dark and confused in the pre-dawn light. She leaned up on one elbow, her lovely autumn hair sliding across one shoulder, the hint of jasmine and sunshine drifting between them.

'Is it morning?'

'No.'

They stared at each other. Common sense asserted itself, warning him to back away, to put some distance between them.

Obviously picking up on his thoughts she frowned. 'I should go back to my tent. You must want to sleep.' She swallowed, her eyes darting from his, presumably searching for the gown he had dumped on the floor.

Jag wanted to tell her that was a really good idea. The best idea. But he couldn't because it was neither of those things.

'That's a terrible idea, *habiba*,' he said, his voice husky.

Rolling her beneath him, he clasped her hands above her head. 'Especially when I have many more delicious plans for you.'

She gasped as their lower bodies connected, the uncertainty in her eyes replaced with a burning hunger that matched his own. She softened beneath him, her lips raised to his. He didn't hold back, sealing his lips over hers and swallowing her groan of pleasure with a deeper one of his own.

Nudging her thighs apart with his knees, he entered her in one smooth, deep thrust.

'Oh!'

Her eyes went wide, her lips parting.

'*Oh* is right.' He kissed her temple, her eyes and along the side of her jaw. She whimpered beneath him, her lips seeking his 'You're so beautiful, Regan. The sexiest woman I have ever met.'

'Jag.' His name was a sigh against his neck, her arms enfolding him, holding him to her as her hips moved under him.

Without warning he deftly rolled them both until he was on his back and she was held over him.

Her glorious hair fell around them. He moved it back, finding and cupping her breasts. She moaned, her head falling back on her neck. Using only his stomach muscles, he levered upwards and drew one of her nipples into his mouth. Her arms clasped around his back.

'Oh, I like this position.'

Revelling in her enjoyment of their bodies, he surged upwards, taking her hips in his hands and moving them both closer and closer to a place he knew he'd never been with any other woman.

Regan depressed the shutter button on her camera and hoped that she'd captured the moment the two hawks flew side by side in a perfect mirror of each other.

Hearing footsteps behind her, she glanced over her shoulder as Jag crested the small rise above the oasis.

A week ago if someone had told her that she could be so uninhibited with a man in bed, so relaxed, she would have laughed in their face. But there was something about this man that made her feel free and able to be herself. Maybe it was his inherent honesty and desire to do the right thing. It spoke to her and made her want to reciprocate in kind.

All morning she had refused to let herself overthink things as she was wont to do. What was the point? They had shared an incredible night of amazing sex and that was that. Yes, he had asked her to spend the day with him at his oasis, but again she wouldn't overthink it. The fact was, the man worked like a Trojan, he was entitled to a day off and this was his place to come and unwind. And if he wanted to spend time with her...well, that was nice, but he'd made his position about relationships and love clear from the start and, even though she could guess that those beliefs were driven by parents who hadn't loved each other or their kids enough, it didn't change anything.

It would be beyond arrogant for her to imagine that she could be the one to change him.

And what would that even mean anyway? That she would upend her life and move to Santara and really become his queen? She nearly snorted at the thought. Yes, those things happened to some people, but it was a one-in-a-billion chance, and it took both parties to want it. At the end of the day Jag didn't think love was important and she thought it was vital. And of course, there was still the issue of their siblings to sort out...

'Can I see?'

He gestured to her camera and she handed it to him. 'Go ahead.'

A lock of hair fell forward over his brow and she let out a sigh at the sudden urge she felt to push it back.

He paused on the photo she had taken of him with Arrow on his arm, his eyes staring at her.

'I wanted to know what you were thinking when I took that,' she said, her voice husky.

He looked up, his eyes intense, and for once she hoped he couldn't read what was on her mind. It would be beyond embarrassing if he realised she had fallen hopelessly in love with him.

'I don't remember.' He adjusted her *shemagh* and handed her camera back. 'You're very good.'

'You don't need to say that. You've already got me into bed.'

He gave a short burst of laughter at her deadpan comment, hauling her against him for a quick kiss. 'I never have any idea what you're going to say next. But I meant it.'

Regan shook her head. She knew her limitations as a photographer and it didn't bother her. 'Which goes to show that the almighty King of Santara doesn't know everything after all,' she said with a smile. 'I'm no Robert Doisneau.'

His eyebrows rose. 'Robert Dois—who? Is this someone I should be worried about?'

Regan laughed. 'No. He's a famous photographer from last century. When I was a teenager I became enthralled by a photograph of two lovers kissing on a Parisian sidewalk. It was one he had taken. There's a magic to it, a sincerity. The couple look so in love…it's as if they can't wait to get back home and had to kiss in the street or die.'

And suddenly Regan realised why she spent so much time photographing couples. They satisfied a deep longing to find the kind of love her parents had shared and which she feared she'd never experience. Unfortunately making love with the King of Santara had created the same longing inside of her.

She gave a little laugh at the improbability of it all. 'I've always wanted to take photos like that and go to Paris. Neither one has happened yet.'

'Both still could.'

'Paris, maybe. Some day. But photography, no. I'm a teacher now and I love my job. I love inspiring kids to learn, and one of my joys is taking a special photo of them during the year and presenting it to them on their birthday. They love it. And I'm not convinced that being a professional photographer would give me the same level of satisfaction. Oh, look, the hawks are back.' She shaded her eyes as she watched their majestic antics. 'Or are they falcons? I can't tell.'

'Hawks.' He watched them with her. 'Falcons are smaller but have a longer wingspan. And falcons grab their prey with their beaks, whereas the hawk uses its talons.'

'*Ouch.* Fortunately they don't seem hungry right now. Look, they're circling each other.'

She raised her camera and started clicking away right when their talons joined together.

'Oh, wow, did you see that? They're dancing.' She couldn't suppress the smile on her face.

'They're not dancing, *habiba*,' he said roughly, his eyes on her mouth. 'He wants to mate with her.'

Regan's breath caught at the raw, elemental hunger in his gaze as he looked at her.

'Falcons mate for life,' he continued. 'And once they've established a home they never stray from it.'

Regan's throat went thick. 'That's so lovely.'

They both watched the birds skim across the top of the blue lagoon. 'Now, that looks lovely.' His hands found her waist and he lowered his head to hers. 'Come swimming with me.'

* * *

Much later Regan lay with her head in his lap, shaded by the huge palm trees bordering the pool, the breeze gently rustling the fronds overhead.

Jag held a small piece of something or other to her lips. 'Try this—you'll like it.'

Regan opened her eyes to look up at him. 'You have to stop feeding me. I think my stomach is going to burst.'

'Just one more,' he said lazily, tempting her. 'You know I like feeding you.'

Regan felt herself flush with pleasure. Being with him that morning and afternoon had been wonderful and, despite her better judgment, she had let herself soak it up. Let herself soak him up.

They'd made love twice more, once in the lagoon and then again on the blanket. He'd done things to her that made her body instantly tighten with anticipation but she knew reality would set in again soon.

'What are you thinking about, *habiba*?'

'You,' she said honestly.

He gave a purr of appreciation, his thigh muscle tensing beneath her cheek as he shifted. He prowled over the top of her, his powerful arms and shoulders flexing as he moved. 'Anything specific about me?'

She ran her fingers through his hair, loving the way his eyes darkened to almost black as he looked at her.

'That you're not as scary as I first thought you were.'

'Not as scary, huh?'

'No.' Happiness surged inside her as he gazed at her with wicked playfulness. 'You're like a big domestic pussycat when it comes down to it.'

'Is that so?' She gave a squeal of delight as he flicked her sarong aside and lightly tickled her ribcage. 'Want me to show you how much of a pussycat I am?'

The sensual intent in his eyes was unmistakable.

'Are you sure no one can see us?' she asked, breathless with longing.

He nuzzled her breast, tugging her nipple into his mouth. 'I'm sure.' He licked her and tortured her until she was a mass of pure sensation. 'I told you this place is totally off-limits to anyone else.'

'Your own private paradise,' she husked, reaching to touch him anywhere she could.

His smile turned sexy as he kissed his way down her body. 'I think that's what I might start calling you,' he murmured, parting her legs so that he could press his tongue high along the inside of her thigh.

Regan cried out, gripping his shoulders, her insides pulsing with sensual anticipation of his wicked touch.

'My own private paradise,' he agreed, dipping his head to take her to her own private paradise, and leaving her wondering how she was ever going to get over him.

What must have been at least an hour later, given the placement of the sun, she woke to find Jag sitting on a nearby rock and staring out at the water. She took a moment to study him, drinking him in so that later, when he was no longer around, she could recall exactly how he looked. The feeling was at once bittersweet and utterly frightening.

As always, he sensed her eyes on him and turned to her. Their eyes met and for a moment they just stared at each other. Shockingly, the connection between them was almost more intimate than the sex. She blushed, wondering what thoughts were going through his mind, but she was too cowardly to ask. He wanted her; she knew that without a doubt, so she was determined just to enjoy it for what it was.

He held out his hand to her and a small smile tilted her lips. She loved the way he did that, offered her his hand as if it was the most natural thing in the world. As if she was the most important person in the world to him.

A rush of emotion made her fingers uncoordinated as she fixed the sarong over her breasts and tried to untangle the knots in her hair formed by his nimble fingers. When she reached him he slowly drew her to him and wedged her between his legs, her back to his front. She felt him bury his face against her hair and breathe deeply. Warmth suffused her and she turned, lifting her face for his kiss, when his phone rang.

Grimacing with annoyance, he reached around her and pressed the button. Regan heard an outpouring of Santarian and felt the immediate tensing of his body.

Slowly he disengaged them and strode across the sand. Watching him, Regan knew instantly what had happened even before he turned to her, a coolness in his eyes when before there had only been heat and need.

'They're back, aren't they?'

He nodded. 'Time to get dressed.'

CHAPTER ELEVEN

A HEAVY SILENCE permeated the helicopter ride on the trip back to the palace, making it seem interminable. Jag appeared to be as caught up in his thoughts as she was in hers, neither one of them making any overtures to the other. It was as if the lover she had spent the day with had vanished, to be replaced by the cold man she had met at the bar. Gone was the domesticated pussycat indulging her in endless pleasure by the side of the lagoon.

A sense of rising dread churned her stomach the further they flew, her feelings divided between wanting Chad to be okay, and concern over what had happened and how that would impact on the man beside her. She wondered if Jag remembered the deal they had struck. She knew that he would honour it. But then what?

With expert precision the pilot landed on the helipad and Jag jumped to the ground, only absently reaching back to assist her to duck beneath the whirring overhead blades.

He strode ahead of her up the path towards the rear of the palace, and Regan finally got to experience what it felt like to walk two paces behind him. Or maybe four. Quickening her pace, she barely noticed the decadent scent of the magnolia trees that lined the path, or the velvet dark sky above.

Jag pushed open a heavy set of doors at the end of a long corridor, his stride not faltering as he strode up to his sister and enfolded her in his arms.

He held her to him for a long moment. A lump rose in Regan's throat and then her eyes sought out the other occupant of the room.

'Chad.' His lanky frame looked as hale and hearty as always and she rushed over and hugged him tightly. 'I've been so worried.'

Chad hugged her back. 'Me too.'

The hairs on the nape of her neck prickled and she turned to see Jag staring at her brother.

Tension rocketed into the room like an incoming sandstorm. 'You have a lot to answer for.'

'No.' Milena placed her hand on Jag's arm. 'Don't blame Chad. It was all my idea.'

Jag's thunderous expression returned to Milena. 'What exactly was all your idea?'

'It's a long story.' Milena sighed. 'And I'm sorry I worried you. I know I did the wrong thing but I felt as if I had no choice. But first…you're engaged…' Her lovely eyes fastened on Regan. 'Is that right? Chad said it wasn't possible, but you're wearing the most important family heirloom in the collection, so it must be.'

Shocked, Regan stared down at the beautiful ring before lifting her eyes to Jag's, only to find his eyes completely devoid of emotion.

'Regan?' Chad stared at her hand. 'How is this possible?'

Regan shook her head, her brain struggling to keep up with the fact that Jag had trusted her not to lose something so precious.

'There are more important things to discuss,' Jag cut in coldly. 'Like, *where have you been*?'

Milena's face went pale as he bellowed at her, clearly unable to handle her brother's wrath.

'I think we need to calm down first,' Regan suggested

quietly. 'They're both safe and home. That's the most important thing.'

As well as her getting this ring off her finger and back in a vault.

'Stay out of this, Regan,' Jag rasped with icy precision. 'You will not influence how I deal with this.'

She felt Chad bristle beside her. 'I don't think you should speak to my sister that way.'

'I'm not interested in what you think.' Jag turned his lethally sharp gaze on Chad. 'And you're lucky she's here. If she wasn't you'd already be in jail.'

'Jag!' Milena cried.

'One of you had better start talking,' he grated. 'And if you have compromised my sister in any way, James, you'll be sorry you ever set foot on Santarian soil.'

'As you have compromised mine!' Chad burst out.

'Chad!' Regan stared at him. As he had grown up he had become as protective of her as she was of him, but she'd never experienced him coming to her defence so avidly before.... 'You have no idea what you're talking about.'

'Don't I?' Her brother puffed out his chest. 'There's obviously something going on between the two of you. I can tell by the way he looks at you.'

By the way he looked at her?

Right now he was looking at her as if she were chewing gum stuck to the bottom of his shoe.

'What has happened between myself and Regan is not your concern,' Jag advised with a killing softness. 'What has happened between you and Milena is.'

'That's your opinion, Your Majesty, but I can't believe my sister would be with you of her own free will.'

'Chad, stop,' Regan implored him. 'Don't make this about me. You've been gone for two weeks. Of course the King wants answers. So do I.'

'I feel terrible,' Milena mumbled. 'This is all my fault. Please, Jag; Chad isn't to blame.'

Regan watched him run a hand through his hair, clearly trying to rein himself in for his sister's sake. Her heart went out to him because she knew why he'd been so worried about her. 'Why don't you both sit down and tell us what happened?'

Chad threw Milena a quick glance but was wise enough not to approach her.

Milena cleared her throat. 'I'm sorry if I've caused a big mess, Jag, but I couldn't go into my marriage next month without having some time to myself.'

'You did this for time to yourself?' Jag thundered.

'No. Not just that.' Milena looked to Chad for reassurance. 'I just wanted to feel normal for once. No bodyguards, no photographers, no having to be polite all the time. I know you won't understand this because it all comes so easily to you, but sometimes I don't think I know who I am.'

'Milena—'

'No, let me finish,' she said, taking a deep breath. 'Chad and I have grown close over the last few months and…when I told him my plan to take a secret holiday he insisted that he come with me to make sure nothing happened to me.' She threw Chad a quick smile. 'I knew it would be a mistake, but I also thought that if you knew I was with a friend you would worry less. I was only hoping you'd find out it was a male friend after we returned.'

Jag's expression told her that it hadn't made an ounce of difference, but Regan heard the note in Milena's voice that said that she'd been hoping to return in triumph, presumably so that she could prove to her over-protective big brother that she had grown up. Unfortunately such a tactic was likely to have the opposite effect. Milena winced at Jag's continued silence. 'I guess not. But please, don't blame

Chad. If anything, you should be thanking him for being there for me. I didn't even know how to buy a train ticket!'

'I would be thanking Mr James if he had come to me with your hare-brained scheme instead of sneaking off and foiling my attempts to find you. Do you have any idea what would have happened if anyone had got wind of your disappearance? If the Prince of Toran had?' He paced away from her. 'It's only fortunate for us that he expects Santara to take care of all the wedding arrangements. If he'd once tried to call you—'

'I knew he wouldn't.'

'That's beside the point.' Jag turned to stare at Regan's brother. 'Tell me, just how close have you become?'

'Not as close as you and my sister,' Chad ground out.

'Chad, please,' Regan admonished. 'Don't make this worse.'

'How can my stating the obvious make things worse? I've been without internet access this past week, and when I reconnected I nearly died seeing photos of you and him together. You're everywhere in the news, do you realise that?'

She hadn't because she hadn't been given any access to the internet herself. 'I'm sure it's nothing.'

'Nothing? It's not nothing. Ask the King.'

Regan's eyes flew to Jag's. He stared back at her and she saw that he knew how big this had become and that he hadn't cared. The only thing he'd wanted was for Milena to come back and now she had. 'Chad, it's not important. I agreed to do it because we both wanted you to return to Santara.'

'You both agreed to what?' He looked from her to the King and back. 'To becoming engaged to him? My God. I can see it's true. Please tell me you didn't sleep with him for that as well.'

'Chad!'

Ignoring her, he glared at the King. 'How could you involve my sister? She had nothing to do with any of this.'

'I don't think you're in a position to question me,' Jag growled softly.

Before her brother could get any more aggravated and say something really stupid, Regan stepped in. 'I came to Santara to look for you, Chad. No one forced me to do that.'

'Why? I sent you an email explaining that I would be out of reach.'

Regan narrowed her eyes. 'The last time you told me not to worry I got a call from the police precinct to come and bail you out.'

'I was sixteen!' he exclaimed. 'And this is a completely different thing.'

'Yes,' Jag interjected coldly. 'It's far worse. And you should be thanking your sister, not haranguing her. If she wasn't here you'd be in a far worse position than you currently are.'

'I don't think—'

Jag turned on him then, using his formidable height and years of authority to silence her brother. 'No, for a smart man you didn't think.'

'Chad, please,' Milena pleaded. 'It will only make things worse and it's all my fault.'

'It's not your fault,' Chad corrected. 'It's that you live under the reign of your autocratic brother, who never takes anyone's needs into consideration except his own.'

'Okay, enough.' Regan stood up. 'Jag is not like that and you clearly have no real understanding of the worry you've both caused by sneaking off together.'

'Just tell me.' Jag pinned her brother with his icy gaze. 'Did you compromise my sister?'

Milena gave a shocked gasp. 'Jag—'

'Silence,' Jaeger snapped at his sister. 'You are betrothed

to be married to a very important man. If you've slept with Chad James I need to know.'

'She hasn't,' Chad bit out, facing the King with his shoulders back. 'Your sister is a beautiful person and I would never take advantage of her like that.'

Regan heard the protective way Chad spoke about the younger woman and stared at him. *Was he in love with Milena?*

'We didn't do anything like that, Jag,' Milena said crossly. 'Chad was a perfect gentleman. If you're going to be angry then be angry with me.'

'Don't worry,' Jaeger bit out. 'I'm furious with you.'

'I'm sorry,' Milena said, tears forming at the edges of her eyes. 'I was really desperate and I thought you'd say no if I asked.'

The stark truth of that flashed across the king's taut features. 'Who else knows about this?' he asked stiffly.

'Only Chad.'

Jag nodded curtly. 'You look exhausted. We will talk more about this in the morning. Mr James, you will not leave the palace until this situation has been officially resolved.'

'What are you going to do to him?' Milena asked.

'That is not your concern.'

Milena leapt to her feet, her small fists clenched. 'Dammit, Jag, sometimes I wonder if you're even human any more.'

'Milena!'

His harsh call stayed her exit, her slight body vibrating with tension. She didn't turn to look at him. 'Permission to leave your presence, Your Majesty.'

The muscle in Jag's jaw clenched tight. Regan's heart jumped into her throat because she could tell by the flash of emotion across his face that he had taken Milena's words to heart. No doubt he felt responsible for everything that had happened, and she knew he wouldn't welcome her attempts to make him feel better about that.

'Go. We'll talk more in the morning.'

'Don't expect me to go anywhere without my sister,' Chad said.

Jag gave him a faint smile. 'I would expect nothing less.'

Finally he turned to face Regan. 'I believe this is when you say "I told you so".'

A lump formed in her throat, her hands trembling. 'I don't want to say that.'

What she wanted to say was that she loved him, that she wanted to be with him, that she understood his anger, and wanted to be the one to soothe it, but knowing that he had never wanted anything like that from her held her silent.

'Gracious of you. But this is definitely the time I apologise for inconveniencing you. I was wrong.'

'I don't want your apology,' she whispered fiercely. What she wanted was for this formal stranger to disappear and bring back the lover she had known at the oasis.

His gaze seemed to take her all in at once, and then there was nothing. It was as if he had closed down every emotion he'd ever had. 'Mr James, please follow me.'

Regan felt shell-shocked by Jag's departure. Was he coming back after he'd talked to Chad? Or was that it?

But of course that was it. The reason she was even here had been resolved. His sister was safe and the summit was over. Did life just return to normal for him now?

A breath shuddered out of her body and she clamped her arms around her waist. Was it that easy for him? That simple? But then, what had she expected? It had always been going to end when Chad returned. She'd known that. All day she'd reminded herself of the same thing and had convinced herself that she was just taking it for what it was. Well, now was the time to prove that. He'd told her that practice helped him contain his emotions and, well… now would be the time for her to try that too.

Only she wasn't so sure she could move on from him that easily. She'd fallen in love with him. It was exactly the scenario she had feared. Falling for someone who didn't want her back. It was almost as if she'd willed into being the very experience she'd spent years avoiding. But then, fate had a way of making you face your worst fears. She should have known that. And what was the mantra after you faced your fears and survived? You'd be stronger for it?

A sob rose up in her throat and she stifled it. That might take a while.

An hour later someone knocked at the door of the garden suite and she immediately assumed it was Chad.

It wasn't, it was Tarik. He smiled at her soberly and handed her a document.

Regan scanned it. It was a press release stating that her engagement to the King was over. It completely exonerated her of any responsibility, merely stating that after careful consideration she had decided to return home.

'If you're happy with the wording, my lady, the King asks that you sign it.'

Regan nodded, her heart in her throat. 'That was fast.'

Tarik handed her a pen. 'His Majesty likes to work that way.'

'Yes, I know,' she said, moving to a table and scrawling her signature at the bottom. She took a deep breath and wondered if the buzzing noise she could hear was inside her head, or outside.

'His Majesty has also given you a settlement for inconveniencing you but said that if it wasn't enough to name your price.'

'His Majesty is very keen to see me go,' she said softly,

wondering if he would renew his engagement to the Princess Alexa now that he was free. It seemed unlikely but then this world wasn't her usual one. Royals made deals and arrangements in the blink of an eye. 'And Chad?' she asked.

'Chad is here,' a voice said from the doorway.

Regan glanced up at him blankly and then felt her resolve start to crumble. 'Oh, Chad!'

He stepped into the room and she raced into his arms.

'I'll leave you alone now, my lady,' Tarik said courteously. 'If there is anything you need, please let me know.'

'Wait, Tarik, there is.' She pulled away from Chad and tugged at the diamond on her finger. It resisted her initial attempt to remove it, but with enough force she worked it free. 'Please return this to His Majesty.'

'The King said that you were to keep it.'

The lump in her throat got bigger. 'No.' She shook her head to hold back tears that suddenly sprang up behind her eyes. 'It's not mine to keep.'

'As you wish, my lady.'

Regan nodded. 'And thank you.' She gave him a watery smile. 'It was nice to get to know you.'

Tarik nodded, bowing as he slowly turned to leave.

'Wow,' Chad said, releasing a long breath. 'This is really full-on.'

'What did you expect?' Regan asked. 'Did you really think you could go off with Milena and there would be no consequences?'

Chad sighed. 'I suppose I didn't really think about the consequences. Milena is a princess. If anything, I thought that once she returned everything would be fine and go back to normal.'

'Wrong.'

'Oh, Reggie, I can see you're upset. I'm sorry you got dragged into all of this.'

'It's okay.' She sniffed knowing that it was very far from okay. 'I'm fine.' It was the way it had always been in the past: her taking care of Chad, not the other way around.

'No, you're not. You look like you're about to cry.' He gave her a wan smile. 'I'm truly sorry. I had no idea that you would rush over to Santara to try and find me.'

'I probably should have stayed home in hindsight but… How did your meeting with the King go?'

Chad made a face. 'He pretty much bawled me out over what I'd done.'

'I don't doubt it. He was worried sick about his sister. It was pretty irresponsible.'

'It didn't seem like it at the time. But he didn't ball me out so much over Milena as over you.'

'Me?'

'Yeah, he dragged me over the coals for scaring you the way that I did. Told me I had to take better care of you.'

'Oh…that was…' She took a breath. It was typical of a man who took his familial responsibilities seriously is what it was. 'He's a decent person when you get to know him.' Funny. Sexy. Strong. Smart. 'And you? What happens for you next?'

'King Jaeger has ordained that I am allowed to continue to work for GeoTech if I want to, but I'm to have no contact with the Princess ever again.'

Regan heard the slight strain in his voice and groaned. 'You're in love with her, aren't you?'

'In love with her?' Chad looked at her, astonishment widening his eyes. 'Of course I'm not in love with her, we're just friends. I mean, she's incredibly beautiful inside and out but…honestly, she reminded me a bit of myself at the same age. When I felt unsure about my place in the world.' He grimaced at the memory. 'I felt bad that she didn't have anyone supportive in her life the way I had you and I wanted to be there for her. But right now I'm more worried about you.' He took her hands in his. 'Did the King hurt you in any way? Did he force himself on you? Because if he did I'll… I'll—'

'He didn't force me, Chad.' She gave his hands a reassuring squeeze before moving towards the windows overlooking the garden. 'Not in the way you mean. He was just incredibly worried about his sister. I might have done the same thing he did if our situations had been reversed.'

A sort of pained silence followed her statement and she glanced over to see Chad watching her. 'You're in love with him aren't you?'

Regan gave a shuddering smile. 'Is it that obvious?'

'Oh, Reggie. What are you going to do?'

'Nothing,' she said. 'There's nothing I can do. He's made it more than clear that he wants me gone, so I guess I'll go home.'

'Have you told him how you feel?'

'God, no.' Regan gave a resigned shake of her head. 'Believe me, Chad, if King Jaeger had wanted me to stay with him he would have said so. But the fact is he has everything he needs already.' And all she had to do was find a way to get over him.

'There's a car waiting to take me back to my apartment. Do you want to come with me?'

'Of course. It's not like I have anywhere else to go.'

'But the King… Are you going to at least say goodbye to him?'

Regan thought about it but she knew she couldn't do it. 'He knows where I am, Chad, and he knows I'll be going with you. Prolonging the inevitable isn't going to change anything.' In fact, it would only make her feel worse.

CHAPTER TWELVE

JAEGER LOOKED DOWN at the report in his hand that detailed just how phenomenally successful the summit had been. It was everything he could have hoped for and yet he had to force himself to feel enthusiastic about it. He'd had to force himself to feel enthusiastic about anything since Regan had walked out of his life a week ago.

It was as if every day was a test of his endurance. A test of his stamina.

He recalled the day the phone call had come through about his father's accident. At first the words coming out of Tarik's mouth had been surreal and then his brain had kicked into high gear. He'd made sure Milena was taken care of. Then he'd flown home to Santara and been met by a legion of cabinet ministers and officials, all awaiting direction on how to handle the death of the King and what to do next. It had been an immense learning curve, and Regan had been right when she'd said that he hadn't grieved properly. He'd been almost numb through those first difficult months and by the time he might have had some time to take a breath it had seemed indulgent to do so. He had a job to do and he'd done it to the best of his ability.

He'd thought *that* had been the greatest test of his stamina. Turned out it was nothing compared to watching Regan get into that car with her brother without a backward glance.

But what else had he expected? He'd scared her in the shisha bar and then again in her hotel room, he'd forced her to come to the palace, where he'd detained her, then he'd forced her to play hostess for him at an international summit, after which he'd forced her to go to his oasis and… His mind blanked out the events that had taken place in his bed after the celebratory dinner his tribesmen had put on. It had been the only way he hadn't jumped on a plane and immediately followed her to New York. But he hadn't forced himself on her that night. He knew she had come to his bed willingly, her ability to deny the chemistry between them about as strong as his had been.

Zero.

But what was the point in reliving it all? She was back in New York, back to her normal life, and so was he. Back to…back to…

A knock at the door prevented his brooding thoughts from continuing. Thank the heavens.

Tarik entered, looking harassed. The last time he'd looked this way a russet haired, cinnamon-eyed American had been the cause.

'I thought you'd finished for the day,' he told his aide.

'Almost, Your Majesty.'

'Did you see Milena?'

'I did. She is fine. The dress-fitting went very well.'

That surprised him. He still didn't know if his sister really want to marry the Prince of Toran. She hadn't said. In fact she hadn't said anything much to him these past few days, still angry with him for banning her from seeing Chad James. But what had she expected? That he would welcome their friendship with open arms? The man was lucky enough to still have a job. A concession he'd only made because of Regan.

'Good. So what's put that look on your face?'

'The PR department are querying the statement about the end of your engagement to Miss James…'

'What of it?'

'Well, sir, they'd like to know when you plan to release it to the media?'

Jag swivelled his chair to stare out at the dusky night sky. It was orange and mauve, almost a replica of the night he'd lain with Regan by the side of the lagoon. 'When I'm ready. I'm still not happy with the wording.'

'The wording, sir?'

'I don't want there to be any fallout for Miss James. I want the responsibility for what has happened to fall on my shoulders, not hers.'

'Admirable, Your Majesty, but it's a bit late for that.'

Jag's eyes narrowed as he studied his trusted aide. 'What are you talking about?' he asked, as fingers of unease whispered across the nape of his neck.

'The Press have been hounding Miss James ever since she returned to America, sir. I thought that, with the release of the statement ending your engagement, that might ease up for her.'

'What do you mean, the Press have been hounding her? I organised a full security detail to accompany Regan on the jet home. They were to keep the Press at bay for as long as necessary once she got there.'

'Miss James took a commercial flight home, sir.'

Jag surged to his feet, every muscle in his body tight. 'Why wasn't I told about this?' he asked with a deadly sense of calm.

'Because the staff are too afraid to mention her name around you, Your Majesty.'

'You're not.'

'Actually I…' His aide flushed. 'After I returned the ring to you I dared not saying anything again. But if you don't mind me asking, sir, why did you let her go? I thought she was wonderful for you. All the staff did.'

Why had he let her go?

Because he hadn't had any choice. He'd wronged her. A woman whose company he enjoyed. A woman he had come to respect above all others. A woman he had… A rush of emotion threatened to overtake him and he ruthlessly drove it back. This time, though, his formidable mind failed him. This time the emotions kept surging.

'The heart knows what the heart wants.'

Was it possible? Had he fallen in love with Regan? Logic told him that he hadn't spent enough time with her for that to happen but his heart wasn't listening.

He stared at his aide as all the pieces finally fell into place. 'Fear,' he enunciated succinctly, reefing his jacket from the hanger near his door and striding out of his office. 'Nothing but fear.'

'Are they still outside?'

'Still outside?' Penny turned from glancing out of the sitting-room window of Regan's apartment. 'They're outside, up the street, and in the trees. In fact I think there are more of them today than yesterday.'

Regan sighed. 'I was hoping they'd have started to lose interest by now.'

'This is ridiculous, Regan,' Penny snapped. 'You have to do something about it. They've been chasing after you like you're an animal. It's terrible.'

'I know. But what can I do? I told them I wasn't with the King any more but they don't believe me.'

Penny pulled a face. 'Once you become mistress to the King—voila, instant celebrity as far as the Press is concerned.'

'Who would want it?' Regan groaned into her hands. 'And I wasn't his mistress.'

'You did say you slept with him.'

'One night. That hardly makes me his mistress.'

'You know you blush every time you mention him, don't you? Was the sex that good?'

Regan blushed harder.

'Don't answer that.' Penny sighed. 'One day I want great sex like that. Even if it is just for one night.'

'You don't,' Regan returned. 'Believe me, I've been practising getting over him and…' Her voice choked up. 'I'm getting there.'

Regan knew from losing her parents that time healed all wounds. And when it didn't it at least dulled the pain to a manageable level. Unfortunately that didn't seem to be happening yet.

'I suppose in hindsight agreeing to pose as his fiancée was really naive,' Regan admitted. 'I thought there would be less fallout from that but there's been more.'

'That's because it's a romance story for the ages. Everyone wants it to be true.' She took a long sip of coffee. 'Whatever happened to the press release you said you signed?'

'I don't know.' Regan frowned; the lack of a press release had continued to perturb her. 'He must have only put it out locally.'

'It wouldn't matter if he'd put it out in the palace toilets… the world would still know about it by now.'

Regan gave Penny a faint smile. Having her by her side the past week had been a godsend. Penny had taken one look at her face the first day back at work and shuffled her into the staffroom and closed the door behind them, giving her a hug. Having been through heartache herself, she understood the signs.

The other teachers at the school hadn't been so understanding, some asking her intimate questions about what the King was like, obviously looking for some insider's scoop, and others upset because she had brought a cavalcade of media to the school gates and it just wasn't done.

'Have you had another look online?' Penny asked.

Regan didn't want to look online. When she did she was bombarded with photo after photo of herself and the King. It was too painful to look at.

'At least if you called the palace you could ask about it,' Penny persisted. 'Regan, you have a right to live your life without being harassed.' She slapped her mug on the counter. 'Give me the number. If you're not going to call, I will. It's not as if they'll put me through to the King or anything.'

'Penny, I love you for wanting to help but I don't think it will. I—'

A hard rap at the door brought both their heads around. 'How did they get up here? You have a security door downstairs.'

'Maybe one of the neighbours accidentally let them through,' Regan whispered.

Penny went to the window again and peered outside. 'Well, don't answer the door whatever you do—I can't see a single photographer outside, which means that they're all piled up against your front door.'

Regan groaned. 'What am I going to do?'

'Regan! I know you're in there. Open the door.'

Regan froze, her eyes flying to Penny's.

'Damn, but whoever that is they have a yummy voice,' Penny said. 'Pity they're probably scum as well.'

'It's him.'

Penny frowned. 'Who?'

Regan had to swallow before she could get the words out. 'The King,' she whispered.

'Are you sure?'

'Regan!'

Regan nodded. 'I'd know his voice anywhere.'

'Good lord…what do you think he wants?'

'I have no idea.'

'Regan, please open the door.'

Penny raised a brow. 'He said please that time. Do you want me to get it?'

Regan shook her head. 'I will.'

On legs that felt like overcooked spaghetti, Regan walked to the door and opened it. As soon as she did her heart stopped beating. When it started again it jumped into her mouth.

Jag stood on her doorstep with what looked like two paratroopers behind him, a dark scowl on his face. 'You're lucky you answered it when you did. I was just about to break it down.'

'Why?'

'I thought something had happened to you. You haven't answered a single call I've made in the last ten hours.'

'Oh.' Still trying to take in the fact that he was here, in New York, on her doorstep, she stared at him blankly. 'I've stopped carrying my phone around with me because it never stops ringing.'

'Do you know how dangerous that is?'

'At the minute I go from work to home and back again. Anything else is impossible.'

'That's because you didn't take the security detail I organised for you. That was not a good call.'

'You're not responsible for me.'

'The hell I'm not.' His blue eyes turned fierce. 'Didn't you think something like this would happen? That the paparazzi would want your story?'

'No. I told you my world is usually a lot smaller than

yours. I didn't know what to expect until I got here and then…'

'You should have called me to tell me!'

'I wasn't sure you'd take my call.' And she couldn't have lived with that. 'Listen, I'm fine. I appreciate your concern but… I can cope.'

He ran his eyes over her and she felt terribly exposed in her cut-off shorts and worn T-shirt.

'I know you can cope. You're the strongest woman I've ever met.' He dragged a hand through his hair and her pulse rocketed at the memory of how it had felt on her fingers.

The air between them seemed to throb as it usually did when he was this close, and she saw him swallow heavily.

'We're not having this conversation out here, Regan.' He strode past her into her flat and Regan felt helpless to stop him.

She nearly ran smack into the back of him when he stopped in the doorway to her living room.

'Who are you?'

'I'm ah… I'm ah… Penny, Regan's friend.'

'Well, Penny, Regan's friend, I'm King Jaeger of Santara, Regan's fiancée, and I'd really like to talk to her alone.'

'Oh, sure. Of course.' Penny seemed to visibly pull herself together at being confronted by royalty. 'Well, that is, if it's okay with Regan.'

Regan was still trying to process what he had just announced. 'You're not still my fiancée.'

He turned his piercing blue eyes on her. 'Actually I am. I haven't officially ended things between us yet.'

'You haven't…' She frowned. 'I gave you back the ring and Milena is home. The deal ended then.'

'I'm changing the terms of it.'

'You can't do that.'

He looked at her with patient exasperation. 'Will you

please give your friend permission to leave? Unless you want an audience for the rest of this conversation.'

'Oh, sorry. Yes, Penny, I'm fine. He won't hurt me.'

At least he wouldn't intentionally hurt her, but looking at him, being this close to him… Her chest felt tight with the strain of holding her emotions inside.

'I'll call you,' Penny promised before slipping out of the door. When it clicked closed behind her Regan had to place her hand over her chest to keep her emotions back. It was only then that she noticed how dishevelled and tired he looked.

'Look, I know you feel responsible about the paparazzi,' she began, 'but I don't know how you can fix it. I don't want to walk around town swamped by security guards. It will only make things worse. Did you release the press statement yet? Penny thinks that will make it easier.' She pulled a face. 'Even without the ring, they refuse to believe we're not still together. They think I'm trying to play coy.'

She plonked herself down on her favourite armchair and remembered the shelling of questions she'd received ever since landing back in New York.

'Where's the King? When is he planning to visit you?'

'Have you set a wedding date yet?'

'Give us a smile, Regan. Tell us how you met.'

She'd even been invited on a talk show.

'I didn't release the statement,' he said, pacing around her small flat and dwarfing it with his superior size.

'Why not? And what do you mean, you're changing the terms of our deal? Why would you want to do that?'

'Because I was wrong, and that's not easy for me to admit.' He came to stand in front of her. 'You were right when you said that Milena didn't want to marry the Prince of Toran. She doesn't. At least, she doesn't yet. You'll be happy to know that I spoke to her on my way over here and the wedding has been postponed for a year. I've also agreed that she can resume her job at GeoTech and keep working with your brother.'

'That's really nice of you. But you know you're not responsible for Milena's actions, don't you?'

'Not completely no, but after her health scare a few years back I stopped listening to what she wanted and thought I knew best. A mistake I don't want to make with you.'

'How could you make that mistake with me?'

'By presuming you want the same thing that I do.' He squatted down in front of her so they were at eye level.

Regan's heart leapt into her throat. 'What is it you want?'

'You.'

'Me?'

He gave her a small smile. 'When you left, *habiba*, you took a part of me with you. A part of me I wasn't even aware existed.'

The bleak look in his eyes made her feel suddenly hot and cold all over. 'What did I take?'

'My heart, *habiba*; you took my heart.'

A bubble of something that felt faintly like hope swelled inside her chest. 'What are you saying?'

He released a heavy sigh, his eyes full of emotion when they met hers. 'I'm saying that I love you.'

'But that's impossible.'

'You doubt it?' He gave a self-deprecating laugh. 'I detained you. I bound you to my side by making you my fiancée.'

'For your sister.'

'I told myself that too, but the truth is you got under my skin from the first moment I saw you in that shisha bar, and every decision I made from then on defied logic and reason. That should have been my first clue.'

Regan felt dazed. Dizzy. 'But you don't believe in love.'

'That's not strictly true, *ya amar.*' He gave her a small smile. 'I do believe in it. I just didn't think I needed it.' He took her trembling hands and drew her to her feet. 'The thing is, Regan, I'm hopeless when it comes to emotions. All my life it's been easier to shut down than to expose myself to pain. If you don't feel anything you don't hurt.' He gave a sharp laugh as if the concept was ludicrous to him now. 'It was that simple. I thought it made me stronger. I convinced myself a long time ago that I didn't need love in my life—I even thought I wasn't able to feel it—but I was wrong. I just didn't realise *how* wrong until I lost you.'

'You didn't lose me,' Regan said softly, stepping closer to him. 'I only left because I thought you didn't want me.'

He shook his head. 'Not want you? I can't stop wanting you.'

'Then why did you always find it so easy to turn away from me?'

'Practice. But I'm sick of practising walking away. It's what both my parents did my whole life and I didn't even know I'd taken on that part of them until you left. Now I want to practise staying put. I want to practise being open. I want to practise being in love. With you.'

Regan smiled so wide her cheeks hurt. 'You do?'

'I do.' A slow smile started on his face. 'Will you have me, *habiba*, flaws and all?'

'Only if you'll have me, flaws and all.'

'You have none.'

Regan laughed. 'Now I know you really do love me because I have loads.'

He swung her into his arms, his head coming down to hers for a desperate, heated kiss. 'I've missed you, *habiba.* Tell me you've missed me too.'

'Oh, Jag, I have.' Happiness swelled inside her chest. 'I really have.'

'Regan, *ya amar…*' He kissed her again. Harder. Deeper. 'I love you, so much.'

Regan stared at him dreamily. 'I can't really believe it.'

'Believe it, *habiba.* Do you remember that photo you took of me with Arrow? The one in the desert?'

'Yes.'

'You asked me what I was thinking when you took it and I told you that I didn't remember.' He smoothed her hair back from her face. 'Ask me again.'

'What were you thinking?' she asked dreamily.

'I was thinking how happy I was being in the desert with you. I was thinking that I couldn't remember ever being that happy before.'

Regan couldn't contain her joy and didn't try. 'I was thinking the exact same thing. You looked so magnificent I couldn't take my eyes off you.'

Jag dragged her mouth back to his, his hands skating over her back, holding her tightly. Finally he lifted his head, groaning with the effort. 'I want forever with you, *habiba.* Can you give me that, even though it means you'll be the centre of everyone's attention for ever and a day?'

'Jag, I could give you anything at all as long as I'm the centre of *your* attention.'

'*Habiba*, you already are. You're the centre of my world.'

EPILOGUE

MILENA STOOD BEHIND Regan and adjusted the train on her ivory wedding dress.

'You look so beautiful,' she murmured, misty-eyed.

Regan smiled, unable to believe that today was her wedding day. 'Thank you. I feel so nervous and I don't know why.'

'Bridal nerves,' Milena said, smoothing down her own rose-gold gown. 'But you don't have to worry about my brother. You've transformed him. I've never seen him so happy and it fills my heart with joy.'

'He makes me happy too. These past three months of being with him have given me more happiness than I could have ever hoped to feel.'

More than she had ever expected to feel. For so many years she had put her own needs aside and, although she would never regret any of those years, being with Jag had made her truly blossom. She gazed at the solid-gold bracelet on her wrist that he had given her as a pre-wedding present. The jeweller had inlaid a photo of her parents on their wedding day and she stroked a finger across their smiling faces. 'Thank you,' she murmured. 'For loving me and in the process showing me how to love in turn.'

Tears formed behind her eyes and she blinked them back. Jag had given it as a token of his love, asking that she be patient with him if he ever forgot how to express his feelings towards her, but she hadn't needed to be. He told her he loved her every time he looked at her, his eyes alight with emotion.

Milena stopped fussing with her veil. 'You already feel like the sister I never had, and I want you to know that I'm well aware that you're the reason my brother is allowing me to go and study in London later in the year.'

'You'll always be his little sister, and he'll always worry about you. But I think you're doing the right thing.'

'I do too. And I can't believe the Crown Prince is still willing to marry me even though I'm postponing things. But I want what you and my brother have and I'm determined not to settle for anything less.'

Regan smiled. 'Good for you. I can promise you that it's worth the wait.'

Brimming with happiness, Regan turned when Penny poked her head around the corner. 'You'd better get out here,' she said, stern-faced. 'Your King isn't going to wait for ever, Reggie. He looks like he's about to come tearing down the aisle and drag you to the altar himself.'

Regan grinned. She wouldn't put it past him and she wouldn't mind a bit. All her life she'd dreamed of finding a love that could rival her parents' and she had. Feeling her nerves finally settle, she took a deep breath. 'Where's Chad?'

'Waiting.'

Regan nodded and stepped onto the red carpet. The assembled crowd gave a collective gasp as they saw her. Chad stepped forward. 'You look beautiful, sis.' His eyes, the same shade of brown as her own, sparkled into hers.

'I love you, you know that, right?' she said softly.

He gave her a tiny smile. 'I love you too. Now, let's move before your possessive fiancé accuses me of holding up the wedding proceedings.'

Regan laughed, and placed her hand in the crook of his arm. 'Then let's go,' she said, turning to lock eyes with the man of her dreams waiting with barely leashed patience for her to join him at the end of the aisle.

* * * * *

2 BOOKS IN ONE
BILLION-DOLLAR TEMPTATIONS
Melanie Milburne
Kali Anthony

2 BOOKS IN ONE
GREEK Scandals
Abby Green
Caitlin Crews

2 BOOKS IN ONE
SEXY RICH BOSSES
MAYA BLAKE
TARA PAMMI

2 BOOKS IN ONE
One Night, Nine Months
Heidi Rice
Emmy Grayson

afterglow BOOKS

Afterglow Books is a trend-led, trope-filled list of books with diverse, authentic and relatable characters, a wide array of voices and representations, plus real world trials and tribulations. Featuring all the tropes you could possibly want (think small-town settings, fake relationships, grumpy vs sunshine, enemies to lovers) and all with a generous dose of spice in every story.

@millsandboonuk
@millsandboonuk
afterglowbooks.co.uk
#AfterglowBooks

For all the latest book news, exclusive content and giveaways scan the QR code below to sign up to the Afterglow newsletter:

SCAN ME